This sexy coming-of-age novel is whip smart, a fresh new voice in the language of the Glasgow streets with characters you know and believe. All the big themes, identity, loss, desire, handled with humour and honesty. I loved it.

— *Kit de Waal* (*My Name is Leon, The Trick to Time, Common People: An Anthology of Working-Class Writers*)

A self-proclaimed 'cheeky' rom-com mapping the queer scene of early '00s Glasgow, *Vicky Romeo Plus Joolz* is a wonderful wee book. Cheeky is one way to describe the swaggering protagonist Vicky and the mishaps she gets herself into. An essential read highlighting the journey to self-acceptance, it doesn't shy away from difficult topics (such as the protagonist's internalised bi-phobia). To say it redefines the rom-com would be an understatement – books like this remind you how heteronormative that narrative usually is, and it's refreshing to be given something different. Percy's tongue-in-cheek and whimsical writing will have you grinning from beginning to end. I find myself eagerly awaiting the next two instalments in Percy's trilogy.

— *Chiara Bullen, Commonspace* (*BookSpace*)

Ely is a fresh, unique, inspiring voice in rom-com. They are a fantastic writer who doesn't cut corners in this realistic, honest, up front romance. I loved it.

— *Zoe May* (*author of bestselling novel, Perfect Match*)

Ely Percy's novel is a vibrant window into 2001's queer Glasgow – a window that has been shut for far too many years. It would be fair to ask Scottish publishers why it's taken so long to get the laudable *Vicky Romeo Plus Joolz* its much deserved place on bookshelves. This has been the most captivating book I've read so far this year and I'm convinced it will be an iconic and stylish reference point for LGBTQ+ Scottish folk...

Percy's packed so much humour and sensitivity into these impressive pages – the characters, along with their quirks and their challenges, will truly stay with you and you'll keep rooting for them long after the final chapter. I haven't stopped talking about this book since I put it down and I can't wait to pick it up again, and take a step back into Sandra Dee's.

— *Ellen Desmond (Publisher at Monstrous Regiment Publishing)*

VICKY ROMEO PLUS JOOLZ

(a novel)

by Ely Percy

KNIGHT ERRANT PRESS

2019

For Shona, Sue and the L.I.P.S. crew

First published in the UK as a print and ebook in 2019
by Knight Errant Press.
Falkirk, Scotland

knighterrantpress.com

ISBN 978-1-9996713-3-4

Typeset by Knight Errant Press
Cover design by Louise Dolan
Editor: N. Kunitsky
Printed and bound in Great Britain by Clays Ltd, Elcograf
S.p.A

With special thanks to our patron Jamie Graham.

VICKY ROMEO PLUS JOOLZ

(a novel)

Author's note

I started writing *Vicky Romeo Plus Joolz* in the Spring of 2002 – nearly seventeen years ago. After securing a book deal for my memoir *Cracked* and seeing my short film *Outlaws* being showcased in the Glasgow Gallery of Modern Art as part of the 2001 Glasgay! Festival, I decided that I wanted to explore more social justice issues through my work. Back then, the Glasgow LGBTQIA scene was a haven for me as a young person coming out and getting to grips with my sexuality. I found queer solidarity and an adoptive family in places like West George Street's infamous (and now defunct) Sadie Frost's, and in some of the other backstreet gay bars in the Merchant City – as did many of my peers. Previous to this, I'd become completely enamoured by my first girlfriend whom I'd met in the Scotland_Room (one of gay.com's early internet chatrooms) – and being able to go someplace together, where we could be ourselves and not have to hide our relationship status, was a sweet release from the disapproving looks or cat calls we got anytime we dared to hold hands in the street. That romance fizzled after just a few short months, but I found strength and resilience from the support I was given by other members of the community – especially from the nearby Glasgow Women's Library that provided a safe space for the L.I.P.S. (Lesbians In Peer Support) group, a project for young lesbian and bisexual women aged twenty-five and under – and it wasn't long before I'd returned to pursuing and wooing new lady love interests as well as writing a fictitious book about them.

Of course it wasn't all rainbows and love hearts, because being queer doesn't necessarily mean you eschew other prejudices. Like many people, me and my pals were affected by the bigotry and bias that saturated the rest of our society. The Glasgow scene in the early noughties was very white, very able-bodied and very obsessed with the way folk looked; biphobia, bi-erasure and transphobia were the norm, as was fat-shaming and picking apart the identities of people who didn't fit neatly into a butch or femme or sporty-dyke stereotype.

I only ever saw one wheelchair user on the scene. And the only queer person of colour that I ever met in a gay bar was a girl I dated for a year. I constantly came into contact with young bi women who were pretending to be lesbians because they were worried about being stigmatized; visible trans women were sniggered at and labelled 'drag queens' on the rare occasions when they ventured out, trans men were completely invisible and non-binary people didn't exist (apparently).

I wanted to write about the infighting and the discrimination and the divisions of politics within the community back then as much as I wanted to write a funny, silly, romantic comedy where none of the lesbians died. It was important to me that my narrator and her friends were not portrayed as goody-goodies or victims, and that their world was seen from a queer perspective rather than through the mainstream heterocentric lens we've grown used to seeing in popular books and films. Authenticity was and is very important to me, which is why I made the decision to retain much of the biphobic and transphobic language that some of the characters use – it is also the reason I wanted to include references to real events like the twin towers disaster and Glasgay! (Although I've taken artistic license with the festival dates.)

Because it took sixteen years to find a suitable publisher for *Vicky Romeo Plus Joolz*, this book has technically become a historical novel. If I was to rewrite it today and set it in 2019, it would be a completely different book – the LGBTQIA community in September to November of 2001 (the time period in which this story is set) was still very much segregated, and this was largely thanks to the damage inflicted by the horrible Section 28 clause, which had only been repealed in Scotland the year before – fortunately, things have changed.

Lastly, I'd just like to reiterate that this is a work of fiction. None of the characters in this book is intended to represent real people – although I did pick up a few good phrases and lines of dialogue from barflies I met during the year I spent bouncing from Sadie Frost's to Delmonica's whilst I was writing the first draft. I hope you will enjoy reading about the adventures of Vicky Romeo and her cohorts; I enjoyed writing about them, and I am so excited that it's time for Vicky's story to finally come out.

Ely Percy
10 February 2019

For never was a story of more woe
Than this of Juliet and her Romeo

– William Shakespeare, Romeo and Juliet

One

I only ever cried over three people in my life:

First time I was six years old, and Ma had just told me that Dad had gone to live someplace else and that he wasn't ever coming back. Now I loved my daddy, I thought he was the best Dad in the world. He used to sing to me, he used to sing all the old jazz and blues classics by stars like Sinatra and Nat King Cole. He took all his records with him the day he moved out. And the note I left about the money for my school trip, he didn't even sign it.

The second time I cried was when my first girlfriend left me:

I was sweet sixteen and never been kissed until I met her. I was in love for the very first time; I thought I'd spend the rest of my life with her, then she broke my heart.

It was a long time later – felt like a lifetime – before I met another girl. I fell in love all over again. From the very first moment I ever set eyes on her I knew she was special. Her name was Joolz and she was the third.

☞ ♥ ☜

I cried again, today. I'd been dusting, keeping myself busy, trying to forget, when I found an old lipstick under my bed. French Kiss. "From the Miss Selfridge range" she'd said. I recognised the shiny silver heart imprinted on the bottom like a kiss mark.

I ran my fingers over the smooth lean body of the silver container. There was a small hairline fracture. I remembered now: that first day we'd met, she'd been walking towards the bar rummaging around in her handbag when she'd dropped it. I'd picked it up, gently fingered it, then gave it back. The first thing I noticed about her was her nails – small, slender, sculpted like her body and painted baby pink to match her pouting lips.

Joolz was the most beautiful girlfriend a girl could ever have.

As I lightly traced the crack with the tip of my finger, it widened into a small heart-shaped gap about a millimetre in girth.

Slowly, I removed the top.

All that was left was a trace of molten pink.

"Can I buy you a kiss?" I say. She laughs, as I stumble over my words. "I mean, can I buy you... a... a drink."

What is wrong with me tonight? She must think I'm a total pussy!

I've never had this problem before. I'm not normally this apprehensive with women, but there's something catlike, something predatory about her. I can tell at a glance that this kitten is a star-fucker of the highest order.

"You can try," she replies, jerking her head and running her fingers through her mane of burnt auburn hair. Her poison is Malibu: straight with plenty of ice and a slice of lemon. I'm impressed. Now *this* is a lady who knows exactly what she wants.

And as for me, well, it's Friday night and all I want is to have a few drinks and then get laid. The girls say I'm cute. I'm told I have a certain Leonardo DiCaprio-esque aura about me: short, bleached blonde hair that falls in soft titanic waves, a boyish grin and wide, deep blue come-to-bed eyes. Not that I've ever had any problems in that department. Not yet, that is.

I pick my jaw and my puppy-dog tongue up off the wooden floorboards, before they begin to gather sawdust. Swaggering back over towards the bar, I give her a sneaky sideways glance. She is leaning against a huge white pillar at the corner of the room. I watch her accept a light from a tall, effeminate twenty-something gay boy who looks like an eighties version of the Milky Bar Kid in his cowboy hat and gingham shirt.

His name is John-John or John-Joe or Joe-Joe or something equally camp and annoying. I recognise him as a regular who always hangs out with a posse of mini-skirted, high-heeled straight girls; the kind who totter about with their nail extensions and long, silky, Pantene hair – the kind of girls I like but know I can never have.

Shit, I hope she's not a fucking fag hag.

The scene is becoming so overpopulated with them: stupid, giggling hetty girls who come into our pubs to perv at us. I wouldn't mind being their little walk on the queer side – a little experimentation never hurt anyone. In fact, it should be compulsory – but they're all too scared to try it in case they chip their nail varnish.

"She's pretty hot stuff, eh?" A voice breaks in from behind the bar. It's my flatmate, Minty. A bottle-blonde butch with six-inch-high peroxide spikes and an infectious grin. I know Minty the same way I know most of my friends – from the scene. We came out at the same time and now, three years on, nothing much has changed; we're still haunting the same bars for a bit of skirt.

"Always get your hole, eh Minty?" was one of the first things I'd ever said to her.

She winked. "Fancy a Polo?"

We were both a couple of jokers, in fact we still are.

"That wee redhead burd you've been stalking– "

"Fuck you," I tell her, "I don't need to stalk anyone." I order the redhead's Malibu and a double Jack for myself.

"Straight with plenty of ice?"

"As always," I grin. "I like it raw." As always, Minty rings the drinks through as single mainline spirits. "Cheers."

"I'm surprised you can even drink straight," she teases.

"Cheeky bastard."

"Just be careful, mate." She nods in the direction of the red-head. "Her name's Julie – and get this – " her voice drops to a heavy sombre tone, "I've heard she's a swinger."

I shrug. "Still a fifty percent chance then."

Swingers don't bother me. A lot of gays don't like them, say they can't be trusted. Me? I don't believe in bisexuality. Eventually, they all go back to their men or come out the closet completely.

"Whatever you say, Romeo," smirks Minty, and she slides the drinks to me across the bar.

3

Grasping the glasses with one hand, I smooth down my hair with the other and wink at the little brunette that I pass on the way back. She comes into Sandra Dee's most Fridays, sits at the same table, and it's common knowledge that she's just waiting for me to jump her bones.

Sandra Dee's, or Sandy's as it's known, is the hippest place to be on the gay scene. Only a ten-minute walk from the town centre and right in the heart of queer-ville, it's a local institution that was established more than a decade ago. Inside there's three rooms that separate the joint: the Diner (which is where I am just now) – it serves food from ten till seven and allows kids in during the day; then upstairs you've got the Arcade where there's fun to be had in the form of pool and pinball; then tucked away down in the basement there's the Blue Room, which is my favourite, some guys call it the Aquarium or the Fish Bowl because it's for women only.

The brunette is still watching me. I look right at her and when I catch her eye her face turns the colour of her drink and she smiles, lowering her head and sucking up a cranberry alcopop through a candy-pink straw. I give her a seven out of ten for looks. Tonight might just be her lucky night – if it doesn't work out with the redhead I can always come back and do a number on her.

☞ ♥ ☜

"Hey babe," I frown. "What's up?"

Julie the redhead is rooting frantically through her bag while the Milky Bar clown is fucking about with a pansy pink cigarette lighter and waving it in the air as though he is at a Steps concert. "I've lost my purse!" she cries. So I ditch the drinks on the table beside her and stride over to the bar like a superhero, thinking about how good it will look if I single-handedly return this broad's purse. It has to be worth some kind of lip service, right?

And so she follows me, hanging on my every word, as I try to reassure her that everything will be fine. She reminds me of Dorothy from *The Wizard of Oz*, but the Milky Bar Kid is a poor substitute for Toto as he runs along panting at her heels.

"Sorry," replies Minty, stone faced and sober as a judge. "I'll take your phone number in case someone hands it in." The broad looks pissed off and unimpressed, but she hands over her number all the same, and I watch open mouthed as a small scrap of paper disappears into Minty's top pocket. I don't know what else to say. I want to keep her talking as long as I can, find out more about her.

"I can lend you money for a taxi home– "

Or you could always share my taxi home...

"No, it's fine." She adds, stiffly, "Thanks, anyway."

"You could get a lift with me and Paris," the Milky Bar Kid pipes up. "She's got the car." He's been making a chain out of the multicoloured, bendy plastic straws that come free with the bottles of alcopops, and is now wearing them around his head like some crazy party hat from a cheap Christmas cracker.

"I'm not going anywhere with that fucking maniac driving."

"Ooh touch-ee, just a suggestion," he bleats.

I want to slap the stupid fuck, kick his bitchy little ass, as he parades back towards the ladies' toilets – but I've been taught never to hit girls. I notice that his hair is dripping beads of sweat onto the DIY headband, and I wonder what combination of drugs he's been taking to get into such a state.

"I'd better phone my mum," says Julie. "Tell her what's happened and get a taxi, pay for it at the other end."

Shame.

The clock on my cellphone says it's just gone ten o'clock. I turn around, survey the room, and notice that the place is beginning to fill up with all the usual suspects. When you've been out as long as I have, you get to recognise the faces, and a lot of the couples are pretty much interchangeable. For example, these past four weeks, the new bouncer on the door – she goes online under the name *Fingers_of_God* – she's been screwing every one of the barmaids.

Most folk, though, come in packs of five or six and the age range varies from about sixteen to sixty. Whereas most hets hang up their dancing shoes when they hit thirty, we still got plenty of the old Moustache Petes that never seem to get tired of the game.

I notice a typed-up sheet of A4 paper on the wall beside the jukebox that says:

THEATRE GROUP SEEKS LESBIAN THESPIANS

Phone Tracy Broadbent on 0773 09002838 or email les_artistes@hotmail.com

Sounds pretty cool, I think. I did a show with Les Artistes a couple of years ago. Vagina Monologues it was called. The broad who used to run the group was Pippa Black but she retired. I thought the group had folded. I never heard of this dame, Tracy Broadbent, but I decide I'm definitely gonna give her a call.

I borrow a ballpoint pen off some old queen in a trashy cerise dress and scribble the details down on the back of a Bennet's 2-for-1 drinks flier. "Cheers babe," I say. He/she has a face like a dead donkey (and he's probably hung like one too) and that hardly qualifies you as a babe in my book. But I've noticed recently that I've had to watch my personal pronouns as some of these drag queens get really touchy over the whole gender thing.

I stretch over to return the pen, but the old queen just waves my hand away with a disconcerted look on his face. "I think you'll need that before I do, dear," he sneers, and he nods at it, drawing my attention to the embossed writing, which says 'London Lesbian Line', followed by a phone number.

☞ ♥ ☜

Ten minutes later, the redhead returns to the table with her face like burnt ciabatta, looking around for her 'friends', I assume.

"You gotta pen?" she asks.

"Sure."

"This is a fucking inconvenience," she says. "I'll have to phone this place early tomorrow morning because I don't believe that fat thing up at the bar is going to bother her arse phoning me." I pass her the pen the old queen gave me. "London Lesbian Line," she reads. "Hah, imagine having a lesbian pen." She writes the number for Sandra Dee's on the palm of her hand and keeps the pen, anyway.

I sit watching her for a minute before asking if everything is ok. "No, it fucking well isn't," she fumes. "Battery's gone on my mobile and the phone outside is fucked." She looks even sexier when she's angry and the trail of freckles across her cheeks stands out like golden glitter. She gives me this 'what-the-fuck-are-you-looking-at?' kinda stare and hisses: "What *is* your problem?" I shrug, throwing my hands in the air like an Italian mafia guy. "Why d'you keep following me then?"

I've been wondering the same thing myself. Why *am* I following her? I keep trying to tell myself that she's just another piece of ass. Sure, she's gorgeous, but quite possibly a straight girl who gets off on drinking you under the table, then going back home with someone of the opposite sex. I've been burnt that way before.

"I'm just trying to help."

"Well, don't. And cut the Chandleresque bullshit, alright."

Chandler? I don't even watch that frigging TV program. Jeezus.

"Listen," she says, her face momentarily softening, "I'm sorry if I've given you the wrong idea but..."

"You're not gay."

I should have known. I should have known that someone with such a perfect pout like hers would be a fucking cocksucker.

"No, I'm just not interested in *you*."

Ouch.

"Sorry, but you're just *not* my type."

"Fine."

This chick obviously doesn't know who I am.

And everyone who's anyone knows who I am: I'm Vicky Romeo the Italian stallion and I'm everyone's type. I can have my pick of the girls in here. I got plenty of other options and I ain't forgotten the chick who'd previously given me the eye.

I look away to check out the rest of the action. Almost as soon as I do, a slim, toned tomboyish dyke with a pony tail of black hair and smooth tanned skin walks past and winks at me. I know her as *Naughty_Nurse* from the chatrooms. She works in the dentist surgery nearby, and legend has it she's an amazing lay.

Even over the smoke and the sweat of the pub, I can smell a hint of coconut as she brushes past. I guess she is vaguely sexy in a second prize sort of way, and for a split second I'm tempted to follow her, but it would be a bit like settling for Britney Spears after being turned down by Sharon Stone. I know that I could go home with her tonight if I want, but I also know – despite the t-shirt she's wearing that says 'Super Pussy' – things that come easy never taste half as good.

Turning back to Julie, I tell her that I heard her friends say they were going to the Polo Lounge. Then I smile to myself, knowing that with her having no money to get in, my chances of taking her home have suddenly doubled.

She swears a couple more times, downs the rest of her Malibu in one go, then turns around and asks if I've got a mobile phone she can borrow.

"Look," I suggest, clasping my fingertips together like a priest, "why don't I walk you home?"

I've decided it's about time that I played the distinguished gentleman card.

She sighs, again.

"No strings attached. I just don't want to have it on my con-science that– "

"And how will you get back?"

"Taxi, of course... I could call it from your house."

Chivalry, Romeo, will get you absolutely everywhere.

We make small talk on the way home. Turns out she's a dancer, that's all she's ever wanted to do since she was a kid.

I have this image of her in one of those gorgeously designed West Hollywood night spots – she's standing under a blue spot-light in a sleek black dress and her hair covers part of her face just like Jessica Rabbit. There's live music going on and the DJ is spinning Latina and Salsa dance tunes, and later she'll be upstairs eating canapés and drinking cocktails in the VIP room.

I go to tell her about Les Artistes but then change my mind. Maybe she'll think it's a bit pussy, a lesbian theatre group. So, I don't say nothing about myself, I just let her talk, which is probably better, cause broads like it when you're a good listener.

As I wait outside on her porch for the taxi, I turn to kiss her and she offers me her cheek.

"When can I see you again?"

"Look," she begins, "it was really nice of you to walk me home and stuff, but I already told you– "

"Sure," I cut in. "Forget about it."

The next morning I'm back in Sandra Dee's. They serve an all-day vegetarian breakfast on the weekends. I sit up on a stool next to the bar, pushing fried tomatoes and cold baked beans around my plate, like all the escaped convicts do in the old road movies when they go on the run and end up in greasy spoons.

I ain't particularly hungover but then I ain't particularly hungry neither. It's just that I'm due to start work at Duffy's at twelve and I got nothing better to do until then.

Minty's cleaning glasses, one an hour, it seems. Every so often she gets up and takes a walk around the tables to empty a random ashtray.

"Nae luck, then?" She means the broad from last night.

I shrug. "What can you do?"

"I heard she shagged that twat Paris."

"No way," I tell her. Paris' got a face like a brick wall and the personality to match.

"That's what I heard." She sniffs. "And according to Paris, she was crap."

I ignore her. She's only saying this to get a reaction out of me, but I'm not biting.

I sit for another half an hour, flicking through a black and white brochure for films being shown in the Glasgow Film Theatre this month. *Casablanca... The Maltese Falcon... Little Caesar...* A whole weekend of classics and I got to miss them. Jeezus.

"I think I'm gonna head down to the net café, see who's online," I say, eventually. Then I stand up and down the last of my pint in one swallow.

"Look," sighs Minty, "if you're really *that* interested, I can give you her phone number." She slips me a torn piece of lined paper with the name Julie Turner, and a bunch of digits written in small, neat, feminine handwriting. I study it for a second, admiring the way she's added artful flicks to all her letters, and the way she's drawn a cute little kiss above the *i* in Julie, instead of dotting it. "I was just about to give her a bell."

She reaches behind the bar and pulls out a square purple purse that says 'Animal Girl' in tiny white lettering and has little beads sprinkled over it. "You might as well take this," she says. "Someone handed it in after you left."

"Cheers, mate."

"They've took the money out it, though." Minty drops her eyes and goes back to inspecting the glass tumbler she is holding. It's not unusual for her to skim from the lost and found.

"Well, cheers, anyway."

She shakes her head. "Your funeral."

☞ ♥ ☜

I plan to let the phone ring eight times and no more. And no way am I leaving a message. I take a deep breath and... It's ringing...

"Hello?" She picks up the phone on the eighth ring.

"Hiya Julie." I pause. "It's Vicky."

"Vicky who?" She sounds pissed off, plus I'm not used to ladies forgetting who I am. She's making me feel strangely unnerved, like a teenager phoning up a first crush for a date.

"I – I walked you home, last night?"

"Listen, I can't talk just now," she says. "I'm at an audition."

Shit, she did say something about that. That reminds me I should phone that broad from the theatre company.

"Hang on. I just wanted to tell you that I think I've found your purse."

Awkward silence.

"Oh right," she says, finally. "Thanks."

"What time does your audition finish?"

"Don't know, these things take ages. Could be hanging around here all day..."

She sounds tired, ratty, unimpressed that I had the brass neck to phone. She's gotta know that this is just a sorry excuse for me to see her again.

"Sure, just forget about it. Sorry to have bothered you."

"No wait," she says. "I should be finished by six o'clock. I could meet you– "

"I'm working. I don't finish till eight." Now it's me who's being deliberately awkward; I can feel a dryness in my mouth and I'm starting to wish I'd never called.

"Well, what if I met you at Sandra Dee's at about ten o'clock? I want to buy you a drink to say thanks for finding my purse."

"You don't even know if it is your purse."

"Is it lilac with silver diamantes?"

"Yeah, that's it," I reply, running my fingers over the little sewn-on jewels of the satin square pouch.

"OK. I'll see you later. Bye."

"Bye," I repeat, smiling to myself. I'm still holding onto the phone cord, still pivoting on my right foot about a minute later when she finally says: "Vicky, are you still there?"

My heart lurches in my throat and I mumble: "Yes."

"Well," she says, "could you please put down the phone?"

Two

Easy Net is the cyber café just around the corner from Sandy's. We call it Easy Wet or Easy Sleazy though, because of the number of creeps who go there just to download porn. It's not the prettiest of places, but it's basically the only option if you're queer and you can't or won't hook up your home computer to the best of the West's gay websites.

I choose a seat near the door that hasn't got any visible spunk stains on it, and I type in my unique ticket code and log onto gay.com's *Scotland_Room*.

There are seven other people online already, and I know all of them: there's Mikki Blue Eyes, and there's Kat, and there's Paris (who looks nothing like the real Ms Hilton), and there's Mel C and her girlfriend Sweet Cherie, and then there's little Princess Zest who's only just turned sixteen, and lastly there's that tramp Miss Scarlet (known as Scarface to me) whom I wish to god I didn't know so up close and fucking personally.

I'm about to pump Paris for information on how she knows a certain hot-headed redhead by the name of Julie, when my cellphone vibrates against my thigh, making me twitch in my seat. Cellphones – along with a list of other contraband – are banned in this establishment, so I have to squint towards the reception to see that no one's watching before I check the text message.

`Hiya look up!`

`SENDER: Kat`

Confused, I crane my neck left then right over the top of the monitor. My newest flatmate, Kat, full name Katrina Astrof (also known as 'Katastrophe' because of her clumsiness) – who is one of my all-time best friends – is hunched over the keyboard opposite me in her black PVC trench coat and purple crushed velvet pinafore. Next to her is an A5 notepad, a can of Irn Bru and her mobile phone.

"Another one?" I nod towards the handset, which is tarted up in a red and black Emily the Strange cover.

"Number five this year," she says, proudly. Kat's phones are prone to sudden dramatic deaths: her last one (the glitzy pink femme partner to my butch blue Nokia) met with a fatal accident inside our washing machine.

Kat and I are like family. She's like the sister I never had. Which is why she came to stay at my place last month after things went tits up with her ex.

"What you up to anyway, skiver?"

"Research," she grins.

"Yeah, whatever."

Kat works flexi-time as a supply R.E. teacher (but only because she can't find a better use for her philosophy degree); when it comes right down to it she's more Bloody Mary than Virgin, and her real dream is to write novels about lesbian vampires.

I smile then turn my attention back to the computer screen and realise that Paris has logged off gay.com, and that my mother has just logged on.

```
Sicilian_lesbian61>  Hey Vicky
```

"Aww, whaddafuck is SHE doing here?"

"Who?" says Kat, leaning towards me across the booth, and tapping her bottom lip with a rubber-ended pencil.

"Sicilian embarrassment sixty-one," I say. "I mean last week she didn't even know how to switch on a damn monitor."

"It's a good thing your mum's not single," she says, "cause imagine yous changed your usernames and then tried to chat each other up."

"You are one sick puppy."

Kat just laughs.

```
Sicilian_lesbian61>  Vicky are you there?
Vicky_Vegas>  Yeah
Mel_C>  ((Vicky))
Vicky_Vegas>  hi guys
Vicky_Vegas>  ((Mel))
Sicilian_lesbian61>  What do brackets mean?
```

```
Vicky_Vegas>   hugs
Sicilian_lesbian61>   ((Vicky)) are you coming
over for your tea tonight?
Vicky_Vegas>   no
Katastrophe>   I think my money is running out
I'll have to get a top up
```

"You can use this computer if you like," I tell her, "cause I gotta go to work in a minute."

Katastrophe has left the room

Juliet enters the room

```
Juliet> Hi Mikki, Mel, Cherie, Zest, Scarlet,
Vicky, Sicilian :o)
```

Vicky_Vegas has left the room

I quickly check my email, it's the usual junk mail shit: Hotmail Newsletter [delete] Gay.com Newsletter [delete] Friends Reunited crap [delete] Enlarge Your Penis Naturally [delete] [delete] [delete]

Shit, what's this? Les Artistes Drama Workshops?

From: <les_artistes@hotmail.com
To: <vicky_vegas@gay.com
Subject: Les Artistes Drama Workshops

Dear Friends,

Sorry for the group email. I hope you don't mind me contacting you. My aunt (Pippa Black) kindly passed on your details when I told her about my plans to reform the hugely successful Les Artistes theatre group.

I will be facilitating a series of free drama workshops commencing on Monday 24th September from 7 till 10pm. Each session will focus on a different aspect of drama, such as movement, script reading, voice, etc. The plan is to work towards a performance of Oscar Wilde's 'The Importance of Being Earnest' as part of this year's Glasgay festival.

Workshops will be held in the new extension of the Glasgow Gay And Lesbian Centre at 11 Dixon Street, just off St Enoch's Square.

I hope you are able to make it and bring along a friend if you like. If you have any questions please do send me an email or give me a ring on 0773 0900283

Regards

Tracy Broadbent, artistic director

I know I stand in line until you think you have the time to spend an evening with me...

That old Sinatra song I love keeps cropping up. All afternoon, some fool pretender has been crooning his regurgitated cover version on the radio. God, I can't stop thinking about her. Julie. Julie. Julie. Sweet thing.

I've been thinking about her all afternoon, all through my shift at Duffy's Muffins. During my afternoon break, I take her purse out of my coat pocket and give it an internal examination. You can tell a lot about a person by the things they keep in their purse. I keep everything in my pockets, just like I keep them close to my chest.

Slowly, I unravel the folds, undo the Velcro seal, and lay her purse out flat on the staffroom table. The first thing I notice is the see-through pouch with a picture inside that's been cut down to passport size – Julie and some other broad, cheek to cheek. I make a stab that it's been taken around two or three years ago. Julie's hair is almost as short as mine, with glittery pink butterfly clasps holding it back from her face. She looks cute. She has no make-up on, and she's wearing a brown school blazer and a brown and yellow stripy tie that I recognise but can't quite place.

The other broad has long, jet black curls and round, deep blue eyes. She's wearing the same uniform. She's cute, too. In fact, if I saw her in a bar, I'd probably try and buy her a drink. I wonder who she is? What she is to Julie? An old girlfriend? A friend? I turn the picture over. On the back, in Julie's tight, neat handwriting it says:

Siobhan and me the day before my grad ball.

I continue to rummage. This broad has way too many plastic cards: Switch, Solo, E-top up (her mobile phone uses BT Cellnet, same as me), Top Shop, Well-Women Gym and a membership for Destiny's nightclub. Her college ID tells me she's studying HNC community dance – not quite as glamorous as she made herself sound – and a proof of age card says she'll soon be twenty-one.

I slip the cards back into their pockets and dip into the middle section: a ten-pound gift voucher for HMV, folded in four places; some kind of receipt with yesterday's date; and an old payslip made out to Julie Turner by Greater Glasgow's Sport and Recreational Division.

In the last pouch, there is a folded blue ticket stub for a showing of *West Side Story* dated last August, and then more cards – United Casting Agency Ltd (I copy that number and address) and a heap of those things with little poems on them, the kind you get in high-street card shops that say 'Follow Your Dreams' and 'I'm Sending You a Hug Today'. It makes me think she's the type of broad who probably forwards all those emails that say: 'this is a friendship poem send it back to me if you are my friend, send it to at least ten other people or you will have no friends.'

I sit smiling and looking at the photograph of Julie for I don't know how long. And then my boss, fuck-face Maggie, who never does anything around here except eat and moan, comes in and tells me to get back to work.

☞ ♥ ☜

As soon as I finish my shift, I rush to catch the tube, almost knocking over a customer carrying a tray of espressos, on my way out. Then I get home, and I'm straight into the shower rubbing soap all over my skin and singing 'My Way' like I know I'm about to die and go to heaven. I've adopted this song as my own personal anthem and –

Tonight, baby, I'm gonna have *my way* with you.

I towel dry my hair then comb it into a middle shed and lightly spray it with a thin coat of gel before smoothing stray hairs into position. A mixture of musky deodorant and even muskier shower gel hang in the air, catching the back of my throat as I scrub my teeth. Then I slip on my new dark indigo pants with the button fly and the trendy crumpled hems, my white muscle top and my black retro sneakers that cost me seventy-five big ones from my Ma's catalogue.

Almost finished.

I wink at myself in the mirror then end my ritual by spraying cologne onto my palms and patting it onto my neck.

Looking mighty fine, Romeo.

I saunter through to the kitchen, making sure I've turned the cooker off and left the washing machine on. Then lastly, I open the fridge and press my hand against the cool body of the wine bottle that I bought on the way home.

I'm all set.

I like to make my ladies feel special: flowers, candles, moon-lit serenades, you name it. I hold doors open for them, light their cigarettes and cook five course dinners. I might be a player but when it comes to making women fall at my feet, you gotta admit, I got charisma.

☞ ♥ ☜

I arrive at Sandra Dee's at a quarter to ten. There's a new door-man out front and as I come close I realise there's some kinda argument going down.

"I'm sorry but that's the way it is," the doorman's saying to these two kids.

"You need to have some kind of identification."

These kids, a boy and a girl, they're maybe fifteen or sixteen at a push, and they look like Bart and Lisa Simpson.

"We don't want to buy any drink," says the boy. "I'm just look-ing for my sister."

"Do you think my head buttons up the back, son?"

"We just want to go in for a minute– "

"Well, you're not getting in and that's it," says the doorman. "So beat it before I call the police."

I feel kinda sorry for them, like maybe I should say something, help them out a little bit, cause I remember what it was like to be a sixteen-year-old gay with no place to go. And who knows, they might even be telling the truth.

"Ya big fucking gorilla," says the girl, and she spit right on him, and then the two of them leg it down the street.

"I don't fancy your line of work," I say to the doorman. He wipes his suit and I shake my head and go to walk through the door.

"I need to see some ID sonny," he says, putting one arm out in front of me.

"Hey, don't get fresh with me," I say, half-laughing, thinking this is some kind of early April Fool.

I continue to try and squeeze past, but he blocks my entrance.

"I'm sorry, I need to some ID."

"This is an outrage," I say, slamming my hand up against the door.

"I'm afraid I'm going to have to ask you to leave the premises, son."

I take two steps back from monkey boy and dig deep into my pockets, looking for my student card. "I'm a female, as you can see." I hold my card up to my cheek. It has a chronic passport picture of me with my old spiky haircut.

"Date of birth: eighth of the eighth, nineteen-eighty," he says out loud.

"Starsign: Leo," I add, "if you must know."

Read it and weep, sfigato.

"Oh, I beg your pardon," says the guy and he blushes and begins to back off.

"Hey, next time I see you," I say, unbuttoning my coat, "I'll remember to flash."

I can't believe what just happened with that bozo. That kind of thing happens to me all the time but never in gay bars. No wonder this place is almost empty tonight – dumb jerk-off probably chased away all the regulars.

I look around, but there ain't no sign of Julie. Yet. Of course, she'll be here. Who could resist a sweet, angelic face like this?

I hop up onto a bar stool and order myself a pint. "Hey!" I say to Minty. "Guess what?"

"You got a sex change overnight?" Minty's expression is deadpan. She can put on a brilliant poker face and you can never tell half the time if she's really being serious.

"No, you schmuck... I got a date with Julie."

"Who's Julie, again? I can't keep up wi you, man."

"The babe who lost her purse."

"Oh right, the hetty."

"She's no hetty – wassamaddawitchoo?"

"Gonnae stop that shit."

"Stop what?"

"All that fuckin Italian–American shite you keep spoutin."

"I *am* Italian."

"Yer fuckin maw might be Italian," slams Minty, "but you were born in Govan!"

Three

As far back as I can remember, I always wanted to be a gangster...
              - Henry Hill, *Goodfellas*

At home, I'm just plain Vicky. I'm just your average twenty-one-year-old dyke who rents an apartment with three other queers in one of the less-fashionable streets in Glasgow's Merchant City. I'm doing night classes in stand-up comedy and creative writing at Strathclyde Uni, whilst working in the world's worst coffee house and struggling to make ends meet.

The scene, however, provides me with an outlet to act out my fantasy.

I've always fancied myself as the godfather of the gay scene. When I'm out, everyone knows me as Romeo – a flashy, gregarious charmer, a chronic womaniser, a wise guy.

Ever since I watched *Goodfellas* on video when I was twelve, I wanted to slick back my hair, don a pinstripe suit and go out and kick some ass. (In the first year of high school, I even took up band practice – not because I was good at playing instruments – but just so I could carry around a violin case.) But I didn't want to be a psycho like Joe Pesci's character Tommy. I didn't wanna go round shooting people and shit. I just wanted to be like Jimmy, like Robert De Niro.

Jimmy was the type of guy who always rooted for the bad guys in the movies.

Jimmy was a mafia legend in *Goodfellas*. And I wanted people to think I was too. Pippa Black from Les Artistes, she always said I'd be a gay icon one day. Hey, I'm just biding my time. Today Glasgow, tomorrow the World!

I first realised there was something funny about me when I was watching *Bugsy Malone*. Then by the time I'd started watching real hardcore gangster movies, I kinda guessed that I was not your average hetero kid. It took me another three whole years, however, before I finally toppled outta the closet.

Appropriately, I was sitting in Sandra Dee's at the time, having lunch with Ma and her partner, Sam. Everyone always assumes that coming out for me was easy just cause my Ma's a dyke. But it was one of the hardest things I ever had to do in my life, and I spent more than a month rehearsing what I was going to say to her:

You talking to me? You talking to me? Cause there ain't nobody else here.

Now, my Ma is a very feminine, very straight-acting lady – she has long dark hair and an hourglass figure, and she looks like a curvier, bustier, forty-year-old Sophia Loren. Wherever she goes, Mamma always gets attention because of the way she looks and men are always asking her out. But they never believe her when she says she's a lesbian. A lot of lesbians don't believe she's a lesbian.

Of course, back then, Mamma wasn't out to anybody who wasn't queer – not the neighbours, not my teachers at school, she wasn't even out to her own parents because homosexuality wasn't something the Italians talked about.

I remember how I spent the entirety of that morning acting out lines from Hollywood classics in front of the bathroom mirror, pretending I was some big shot who didn't give a fuck what Mamma or anyone else thought:

You laughing at me? You laughing at me, you schmuck?

What's so funny about me?

You talking to me?

"Mamma... Sam..." I looked them both square in the eye, but the words wouldn't come.

On one hand, I was really excited because I had grown up surrounded by women who loved women, and men who loved men, and I wanted them all to know that I was one of them. But I was also scared that they'd think I was young and dumb and that I was just jumping on the same-sex bandwagon.

"What is it, bambina?"

Usually, Mamma says words like 'bambina' purely as a joke, because she's lived in Scotland her whole life, and her accent is about as Italian as a haggis supper. But this day she wasn't fooling. Her face blanched as she clasped my hand in hers, and I could tell that me being bothered about something was really bothering her.

I jumped to my feet. "I need to go to the bathroom," I said, and sprinted away from the table.

Taking great gulps of air, I dropped down onto the cold porcelain toilet bowl with my head between my knees. I thought of all the queers that I knew – all the funny, beautiful, loving queers that Mamma and Sam knew. Our house was always full of queer people: the lesbian mothers' group (and sometimes their kids), my two 'uncles' Philly and Paul who were a couple, and Sam's friend Lisa who used to be her girlfriend. There were also all the other waifs and strays who somehow ended up at ours, sometimes for a coffee and a half-hour chat, and sometimes for a whole weekend because they'd no place else to go.

I'd seen love and friendship blossom under our roof. But I'd also seen hatred and fear. I'd seen black eyes and bruises, and I'd seen grown women weep because their families had found out their secret, or because their ex-husbands had banned them from seeing their kids. I'd even seen my own Ma cry because someone she knew had hanged herself, because she'd rather die than tell her parents the truth about who she was.

I knew Mamma would never disown me or throw me out. But I wasn't so sure she'd throw me a coming out party.

Over the years, I'd listened to some of the other mothers from the group talking, and they'd say things like: 'My kids are just as happy and just as normal as kids who live with a mum and a dad' and 'Just because he's got two mums it doesn't mean he's going to grow up to be gay.'

And in a way, I felt a little bit sad too. Cause there was so much pressure on us kids to turn out good and 'normal' and straight. "Hey Vicky, are you alright in there?" I felt the hard knock of Sam's fist against the bathroom door. "C'mon, ye can talk to me."

"I – I – I..."

"Come on downstairs and I'll get you a beer."

Robert 'Robbie' Wilson the bar man winked at me, knowingly, as he poured the drinks. He was nineteen at the time, tall and skinny with a baby face, and he always wore silver sneakers and tight white pants. Later, when he became one of my flatmates, he progressed to silver high heels and tight white dresses.

Ma and Sam had been taking me to Sandy's every Saturday afternoon since I was twelve, so all the bar staff knew how old I was.

I climbed up on a tall wooden stool next to Sam and grimaced as I cupped both hands around the huge lumpy glass. When I took a gulp of my first ever pint – *eugh* – I gagged. I thought it tasted like tar.

Sam frowned. "Your mum thinks you might be pregnant or something."

"Whaa-at!?" I spat all over the arm of Sam's new lumberjack shirt.

"Thanks, pal."

"Sorry," I blushed, wiping my mouth with the back of my hand. Robbie grinned, handing me a napkin. Luckily, not many people witnessed my embarrassment.

Sam smiled at me. We'd always been close and I often asked her things about her coming out days. Maybe I had made it too obvious, or maybe I reminded Sam of herself when she was younger. Who knows? All I remember is the sudden rush of relief I felt, when she cocked her head to the side, looked at me conspiratorially and asked: "Vicky, are you gay?"

Sam was much more accepting about the whole situation than Ma.

"I knew it!" she said. "This is great news!"

Ma didn't think so. She was silent for a long time and refused to talk to either one of us for days. So Sam went to stay with her friend for a couple of weeks to give us space, but she phoned all the time to see how we were.

Every night for about a week, I would hear Ma crying in her bedroom. She never told me this, but I know she tried to phone around the lesbian mothers' group for support. They were all so obsessed with proving to the world that they were such wholesome role models that they didn't want to have anything to do with us.

When Mamma finally came around to talk to me all she could say was: "So Victoria, now you like girls AND boys then?"

Ma just couldn't understand how someone who liked the Backstreet Boys and put up posters of Sinatra could possibly be gay. She seemed to have forgotten her own obsession with Freddie Mercury. According to her I was 'confused' and one day I'd meet a nice boy and get married. I retaliated by telling her that I'd sooner become a nun, and that the only guy I'd ever consider marrying was Frank Sinatra and he was dead.

Eventually, after almost a year, Mamma calmed down. But that was only so she could have a different kind of hissy fit over my decision to quit studying.

At sixteen I ditched school as soon as I could. When my standard grade exams were over, I took up busking during the day and dish washing at the Hilton Hotel in the evenings.

Mamma accused me of being a waster.

"You're turning out to be just like him," she lamented.

She meant my father. She was always dragging my lame-ass dumbo of a father into everything she thought I did wrong. I rolled my eyes, having heard it all a zillion times before. He never worked, he never wanted, he was a lazy son-of-a-bitch. That was the way the mantra always started. I was going the same way. Apparently.

"Don't make faces at me, lady," she would say, waving a wet rag. "You're bone idle, just like he was. You should be helping me do some of these dishes."

"Yeah right, like I don't already do enough dishes at work."

"Work!? You don't know what work is. You sit on your backside all day, playing that stupid guitar. D'ye think someone's just gonna come along out of nowhere and say 'Hey Vicky, here's a record contract'? It doesn't work like that."

I shrugged. It was the same lecture, day in day out. She never let up.

"I can sing. I've got what it takes."

"Oh, you can sing," she nodded. "Well, that's OK then." But then she'd start on about my father again. "He thought he had what it took and look what happened to him. You want to end up like him?" Blah, blah, blah...

My father had been a singer. He was on the road a lot when I was small, and I used to love seeing him when he came home after a long trip. He'd make me shandy with lemonade and he was always full of stories about other famous bands he had supposedly met. All bullshit, probably, but my six-year-old ears believed every word he said. When he finally left home for good, after flaunting a string of floozies, he didn't even bother coming back to visit me, let alone pay Mamma child support.

I used to cry myself to sleep every night, wondering what I did to make my daddy stop loving me. I even blamed Ma for making him go away. This made her cry and left me feeling like a rat.

Eventually, I realised that I didn't need him, and that Ma was much happier when he wasn't around. She got a job working in a bar, and the lady across the road looked after me for a couple of hours a week. She even started to go out dancing once a month, which was something she used to love. After Dad left, we got to do all these things and go to all these places that we never had any money for before.

Now, normally, when Ma said things about my father I just let them wash over me, but on this day something inside me snapped. "Don't ever compare me to that useless fuck," I spat. "You never want to hear me play, you're never interested in anything I do."

Ma's lips opened into a wide 'o' then clamped shut again.

It was true though. She kept referring to my music as a 'hobby' and she'd say stuff like 'oh you'll never make any money from singing', and it always just felt like she was pissing all over my dream.

"Don't talk to your mother like that," said Sam. My eyes and face were burning and I wanted to smack something just for effect. I balled my fists so tightly that my nails left little red marks inside my palms.

"You can't tell me what to do," I screamed. "You're not my father." This last remark I regretted almost as soon as I'd said it. I knew it was shitty of me to bring Sam into this. She was only trying to help and, after all, our relationship had always been a good one. She'd never tried to emulate my father. She'd never tried to be anything other than a friend to me.

"Go to your room, now," ordered Ma. Her face was scarlet, but her words were slow and controlled.

"You can't just say, 'go to your room'," I mimicked. "You can't just treat me like some little kid." I must've sounded like one though, with my voice all high-pitched and whiny.

I always had big ambitions – I knew I could never be a real gangster, so instead I decided that I would become a singer or an actor or a stand-up comedian. Maybe I would do all three. I wanted to do something big like write or direct films, I didn't want to end up pushing paper around a desk in some drab, decrepit office where my creativity would be crapped on, and I told them as much.

"I think," hushed Sam, resting her arm, softly, on my shoulder, "that you should do what your mother says."

"Well, I never asked for your opinion." I shrugged her arm off and marched out of the room, slamming the door behind me.

Minutes later, with my ear pressed hard against my bedroom wall, I listened intently to Sam pleading my case. "It'll be fine," she kept repeating over and over, softly. "She'll take a year out, earn some money and then go to college just like I did."

I could hear Ma's deep sigh and maybe even a sob, I wasn't sure.

"It'll do her good, help her stand on her own two feet."

Yeah that's it. That's right. That's exactly right.

"I don't know, Sam. What if she doesn't go to college next year?"

"She will."

"She spends all her time playing music and chasing stupid fantasies..."

"Who says it's a fantasy? She's right, Maria. You never listen to what Vicky wants. She has a talent..."

"You think I don't recognise talent?" cried Ma, angrily. "I've seen hundreds of people with talent – Vicky's father was a prime example."

"But Vicky's different," Sam protested. "She's really fucking good."

"No. George thought he was different too. He wasted his life – he wasted years of MY life – on his stupid pipe dream. I'm not having my daughter going down the same road."

For some time afterwards there was an uneasy silence. I lay on my bed, staring up at the ceiling, my acoustic guitar rested on my belly. Slowly, I began plucking each individual string.

I could've had a more *respectable* job that Ma would've approved of, slightly. I could've been a silver service waitress if I'd wanted. But I couldn't quite see myself in a dumb skirt and one of those frilly little white apron things. It wasn't even worth arguing my case to wear the same outfit as the guys. Sinatra may have looked good in a tuxedo and bowtie, but I bet he never had to wear one of those crummy little red dickie bows. Make you look like a right dick.

Despite promising to look at prospectuses for courses starting in the next term, I had no real intention of ever going to any college. By next year, I'll have myself a proper band, I thought, and we'll be gigging all over the country, earning mega bucks and picking up lots of honeys.

Aside from making music, making a mess and washing dishes, I spent the next few months dreaming about all those honeys I was going to take backstage and seduce when I formed my band. The reality of it was though, I'd never even kissed a girl.

I felt like I was the only teenage dyke on earth. The only other dykes I knew were the ones that Ma and Sam invited over, and they were all in their thirties or even older. Ma hated the idea of me going to gay bars. She said they were full of wasters who wanted nothing but to take drugs and sleep around, and she tried, desperately, to keep me away from the scene.

"Vicky, if you meet a girl and she makes you happy, then I'll be happy for you," she said. "But you don't *need* the gay scene."

I was curious, though. And what I did need were friends my own age.

One of Sam's mob told me about a gay youth group in a place called the Gay and Lesbian Centre. But again, Ma dug her heels in. Why couldn't I just go along to a 'normal' youth group?

She'd been on a real downer about gay everything ever since the lesbian mothers' fiasco and had even stopped going to Sandra Dee's. I don't know, maybe she was still secretly hoping that I'd magically become hetero overnight. She never really explained what her deal was. And when I challenged her about how many straight friends she had left since she came out to them, she wouldn't answer me. "That's because you don't talk to any straight people," I said, "apart from the ones that serve you in the supermarket."

Where we stayed – Paisley – was hardly the queer capital of Scotland. And it was only after I told her I might go crazy and leap off a bridge like that Bobby Griffith kid in America that she finally gave in. I went about half a dozen times to the GLC Youth Group and each week I'd get my hopes up, but then I'd see the same crowd of junior hairdressers and fifteen- to sixteen-year-old high-school sissy boys. In short: it sucked. There wasn't one other girl. I couldn't tell Mamma though, because I couldn't stand the thought of hearing all her I-told-you-sos. So I never said nothing. And she never asked.

It was a huge relief when they started the women's drama group in the centre. Finally, I'd found something that wasn't dominated by guys. The downside was that almost everyone else who went there was at least ten years older than me. Honest to god, it was like dykes under thirty just did not exist.

Kids can be really cruel. By then I had no friends left from high-school because I'd come out to a girl in my fourth-year class and she'd told everyone. I got called names like 'Victor-Victoria' and it didn't really help that by some cruel and ironic twist of fate my second name just happened to be Mann. 'Wants to be a man' was what the kids used to say about me. I got into fights all the time and the teachers wrote me off as a waste of space; they didn't want to have to deal with the homophobia, so it was easier for everybody if I just left after I did my standard grades.

"Maybe when you go to college," said Ma, "things will be different."

I didn't want to wait till college, though. I wanted a girlfriend, now.

And then finally, I did meet a girl. Her name was Shazia. And she soon became the apple of my eye. But I didn't meet her in any gay bar. In fact, she wasn't even gay. She had a boyfriend when I first met her.

☞ ♥ ☜

It was November ninety-six. Three months after my sixteenth birthday. The hotel had begun recruiting new staff over the festive period. Shazia had started working nights and weekends, waiting on tables in the function suites. She was fifteen, still at school, studying for her Highers: English, French, Spanish, Geography and Home Economics. I can still remember her exact timetable. I can still remember how we used to synchronise our breaks. I'd sneak ice cream and Elizabeth Shaw mints out of the kitchen and we'd sit together, munching, in a corner for fifteen glorious minutes each night whilst she recited her French and Spanish lessons for me.

Languages were second nature to Shazia. Her Ma was Filipino and her father was from Saudi Arabia. She'd lived in Scotland since she was four. So at home they conversed in a mix of all their languages. This supposedly gave us a common ground point and I experimented, badly, trying to impress her with the few dodgy Italian phrases I had learnt.

"*Troppo buono per essere vero.*"

"That means: too good to be true," I told her. I always said she was too good to be true. And it turned out I was right.

"Yeah, well I'm sure that'll come in really handy if I ever go to Italy," she said. She had some mouth on her, that girl. She was always taking the piss.

I never really thought I stood a chance with her. Every night since we met, I'd lie in bed thinking about her, about how I was gonna tell her... But what if she freaks out? What if she never speaks to me again? Why do all the cute girls have to be straight? Why do I have to be a fucking bent shot?

All the hotel staff had been invited to Julian the chef's twenty-first birthday do. We went to a place called Bennet's. I was excited at the prospect of my first work night out and even more excited when I heard the venue he'd chosen was a gay club.

"Oh my god, I haven't got anything to wear," I panicked. My parents laughed and poked fun at me. "You're worse than a gay man," said Sam.

"Anyone would think you were going out on a date," teased Ma. "Where is this big night out, anyway?"

She'd become easier to live with and we'd been fighting less since I stopped reminding her that I wanted a girlfriend.

"Oh, I dunno," I shrugged, casually, trying not to be too obviously evasive. "It's just some club in Glasgow." She was uncomfortable with me going to any nightclub but I knew she'd never let me outta the house if she knew where I was going.

I confided in Sam that I had met a girl I liked. "But," I sighed, "I think she's straight."

"And what makes you think that?"

"She wears nail varnish and skirts and..."

"So does your mother!"

"I know, but..."

"Lots of dykes wear feminine clothes, that's why we call them 'femmes'."

"I know that, it's just..." I sighed, again, "She has a boyfriend."

"Ah, I see," Sam nodded, sympathetically. "That could be a bit of a problem." Yeah, like a major problem.

"Then again, your mother was still married when I met her."

I smiled, enthusiastically. "You really think she might be gay?"

"Who knows," shrugged Sam. "Everyone has the potential to be bisexual."

I screwed up my nose. Even back then, I didn't believe in all that 'fall-for-the-person-not-the-gender' crap. As far as I was concerned, you were either gay or straight and anything in between just didn't exist for me.

"Well, why don't you just try being her friend first and see what happens?"

I nodded, slowly, but in my mind's eye all I could see was me and Shazia holding hands like two real-life sweethearts.

☞ ♥ ☜

The day after that was Sam's day off. While Ma was working, she took me clothes shopping for the first time, and helped me pick out what I was going to wear.

I chose a pair of sleek, black over-dyed pants and a white, long-sleeved Oxford shirt with a button-down collar. I also spotted a pair of round sunglasses with antique gold frames that I just *had* to have. Got myself a shirt-style coat no problem, too: black leather with patch pockets on both sides.

Next, I had to do something about my hair.

"We don't cut girls' hair," grunted the guy in the barbershop. He was in his late fifties, old school, looked a bit like Don Vito Corleone.

"That's ok. I don't want a girls' haircut," I told him. He stared at me open-mouthed as I flung myself onto the high-backed red leather chair. "I'd like a number one, please."

"You want me to cut ALL your hair off?"

My hair was chin length then. The longest it had ever been.

"*All* of it."

☞ ♥ ☜

"Very slick," admired Sam.

I was ready now for my big gay night out. I pushed my new shades onto the crown of my newly shaved head.

"Victoria!" Ma screamed when she saw me. "What have you done to your hair?"

"Do you like it?" I grinned, running my fingers across my fuzzy blonde stubble. "Here, feel how short it is."

"I can see how short it is." She turned to Sam, accusingly, "How could you let her do this?"

Sam shrugged. "Maria, she's old enough now to choose how she wants to look. And I think she looks great." I smiled at Sam appreciatively and she winked back at me.

"But she looks so... so..."

"Gay?" Ma stared at me. She opened her mouth like the words might fly out. Nothing came though, and she clamped it shut again. "Ma, I *am* gay."

"It's just so different."

"You mean butch."

Butch. Soft butch. Baby butch. I rolled the word 'butch' around in my mouth for a bit, as though I was trying to decide whether I liked the taste. At school, we had only ever used it in a derogatory way to describe our French teacher, Mrs Batchelor. She was overweight, with a moustache, and pretty damn ugly in universal terms, and to my knowledge lived happily ever after with Mr Batchelor and their four, equally ugly children.

I'd learnt from Sam though, that being a 'butch' was more to do with the person on the inside, and less to do with how much you resembled the bulldog from the Tom and Jerry cartoons. Still, even today, I'm careful as to how I throw the term around, for even some of those whom I'd consider the most hardcore sensible-shoe-wearing dykes take offence at being called by that name.

Me, I like my label. I'm proud of who I am.

Ma's face flushed scarlet and I noticed Sam's mouth twitch as we stood side by side with our matching hairdos.

"Ma." I paused. "There's one other change I want to make."

"Vicky, the answer is no... You are not getting a tattoo." I saw Sam flinch and rub her left arm through her shirt. A reminder, obviously, of the snake she'd had carved with a needle when she was my age.

"No. I want to change my name."

"Your name?" Both Ma and Sam looked at me, equally confused.

"From now on, I want to take your family's name, Mamma." And still my parents stared at me, utterly confused. "I want to be known as Romeo," I stated.

Victoria Angelina Romeo.

Four

It's quarter past ten and Julie still hasn't arrived. Minty makes a few smart comments as she passes then begins serving a crowd who've just come through the door.

Maybe Julie has car trouble or maybe she's the kind of girl who likes to make an entrance. Yeah, that's probably it.

Rachel Hunt alias Doc Martin Boi, owner of Sandra Dee's, and apart from Sam the closest person I have to a godparent, swaggers over to the bar. She's the same age as Sam but looks nearer forty and has a hairline scar up one side of her face. She's run a lot of rackets in her time and someone once told me that she'd even been in the can for GBH. But her bar, it has to be said, is the smoothest run operation in the pink triangle, which is probably why she drinks there herself on her nights off.

Rachel claps me on the back and signals to Minty to bring us some drinks.

"Pint of heavy, Min, and whatever Vick's having."

"Cheers," I say, trying to resist the temptation to watch the door.

"How's yer maw and Sam? They've not been in for a while," she says.

"Sam's got a new job managing a gym that's just opened in Paisley," I reply.

"So," says Rachel, "how long's that now they've been together?"

The time is getting on, Julie's late, and much as I like Rachel, I can't be bothered getting into a conversation about Ma and Sam's love life. You'd think after more than a decade, people would get sick of asking that question.

I've always seen Sam as a friend, rather than just a step-parent. Although sometimes I call her 'Daddy' to mess with her head. Anyway, she did a better job of helping Ma bring me up than my real Dad ever did.

There are only ten years between Sam and me, and almost ten years between Sam and Mamma. They met at a gym class when Ma went there to get in shape, but their relationship was never really talked about when I was a kid. They never kissed or hugged in front of me or did anything that would allow me to acknowledge them as a couple. As far as I was told – she was just Ma's friend who sometimes stayed overnight.

I liked Sam right from the start – she was never too busy for a game of dominoes, and she taught me how to play gin rummy and poker for matchsticks. I always thought it was funny how she dressed like a boy and had a boy's name, but then I knew Sam was short for Samantha so that was ok.

Sam also took me to ball games and ice hockey, which is something Dad had never done. It almost felt like we were a real family. I'd never seen Ma so happy before and sometimes I even wished Sam *was* a boy cause then they could get married and live together.

I was twelve when I found out that Ma and Sam were gay. Looking back, I suppose I should have guessed because there were only two beds in our house.

It was a Monday night, I remember cause I had band practice. Sam picked me up outside the school gate and told me she was taking me for a burger, her treat. I don't know where Ma was – probably working – her being a chef meant doing a lot of crazy hours. Anyway, I was thrilled, and I didn't mind trailing my books plus my violin all the way to Glasgow, because a) I loved spending time with Sam, and b) going out for fast food was a no go ever since Ma declared a zero-tolerance policy on meat.

So there I was all psyched up to go to Burger King, mentally ordering my regular coke, regular fries, regular hamburger 'hold the mustard, please', when Sam walked straight past it and crossed the traffic lights at George Square, leading me through the Merchant City area, down John Street and past the 'posh' Italian Centre. There, on the corner of fifty-eight to sixty-eight Virginia Street, just outside the vestibule of what had looked to me like an ordinary red sandstone building (except for perhaps the two-tone split love-heart on the handle of the shiny wooden double doors), she explained to me how this was the place she called her second home – she had taken me to Sandra Dee's Diner.

For the first time in my life, I felt as though I'd just landed on my own planet. Inside, there were people I could identify with – there were dames with short hair who dressed in guys' clothes, and one of them was even wearing a shirt and tie.

"Hey, Sam!" A big guy with a slicked back pseudo-mullet clapped Sam on the back. He looked so tough he could have played a part in *Goodfellas*.

Sam's face broke into a huge grin. "Hiya Rach! How you doing, girl?"

I blinked and had to do a double take.

"Hey, who's the baby dyke?" Rachel meant me, of course: grass stained pants, baseball cap and a baggy football top that barely masked the recent eruption of my small but noticeable breasts.

"It's about time we got you fitted for a bra," Ma had stated, only days before.

Not likely, I had thought, Joe McPherson in my class has bigger tits than me and he doesn't have to wear a girly bra.

"Vicky, this is a good friend of mine, Miss Rachel Hunt." Rachel took my hand in her huge fist, shaking it, lightly.

"Rachel, this is Vicky," she said, pausing, before adding, "Maria's daughter."

"Who, the hetty?"

I'd never heard the word 'hetty' before, and I assumed it was another name for someone who's Italian.

"Shut it," said Sam. Then she glanced between me and Rachel with a conspiratorial look in her eye and said, "I think it's about time me and you had a little chat, pal."

That evening, I heard the whole story of Sam and Maria's forbidden love – how Mamma was young and naïve when she met my father, how she did her best by me, how Sam and Mamma had tried to hide their relationship...

"Ye see, me and yer mum... We're... We're..."

Spontaneously, I interrupted: "Dykes?"

Sam laughed, nervously. "Dae ye know what a dyke is?"

Slowly, I nodded; then I paused, chewing my bottom lip, and I said: "But I thought only guys could be poofs?"

I sit studying my watch. It's a quarter to eleven now. Half an hour is fashionably late but any more than that is bordering on disrespect.

She's playing me. She's playing me like I played all those other girls before her. I've never had to try very hard to win any woman's affections. I've always had more than my fair share of honeys falling at my feet. And if at first I don't succeed... Candlelight, soft music and a bottle of red wine usually does the trick.

I sit examining my fingernails.

"Hey see that wee burd over there– " Minty's on form tonight, chatting up everything with a pair of tits. She nudges the third pint of the evening into my hand.

"Her up at the bar," she points.

"Mmm."

"She was asking about you, wanted to know if you were single." I shrug. It's the same little alcopop-drinking brunette that I seen last night, but suddenly I ain't interested. "C'mon man, what's the matter with you? You're not still hung up on that hetty burd, man, are you?"

No comment.

"She's fucking stood ye up, man." That's three times in fewer than ten seconds she's said 'man'. I tell her that. "Fucksake. Who the fuck cares, man? What is it wi you lot, anyway? Yous are all acting like a bunch of pansies. Mel and Cherie are playin happy families wi their new flat, rings on their fingers. All they need is the two point four cats. And Paris, she had an argument wi her maw and now she's moved in wi Scarface."

I roll my eyes and shake my head. I always said Paris was a loser.

I find it hard to believe that someone like Julie Turner would give her the time of day, but there are plenty of folks who are backing up the rumour.

"You let a burd into your life and all of a sudden, the walls are all poof pink..."

"...there's pot pourri all over the bog and knickers in your cornflakes," I finish Minty's sentence. It's a line from one of her favourite films, *Gangster No. 1*. She used to insist on watching it every time she came over to stay at Ma's house. Sam was pretty into it as well, but I think it's a bit of a sucky film.

"D'ye think they're shagging?" she says.

"Who?"

"Paris and Scarface."

"I don't know and I don't care," I tell her.

"Imagine leaving a fucking posh house in Kelvinside where she'd been staying rent free wi her parents," continued Minty, "to go live in a bedsit wi that skanky weirdo."

"Yeah," I agree. "Pretty fucked up." I'm getting bored of this conversation. And the idea of Scarface and Paris getting it on is making my insides crawl.

"But not as fucked up as you mate," smirks Minty. "You're chasing some stuck-up rich bitch who's not even a real dyke." I tell her to shut the fuck up, but I'm beginning to think she might be right. "Awright, but tell me one thing, first."

I sigh and take another swig of flat beer. "What's that then?"

Minty grins at me. "Has she gave you yer Nat King, yet?"

"Hey, gimme a lil bit of respect," I say. "Why does it always have to come down to that?"

"Obviously that's a no then." I scrape back my bar stool and push away my pint. It tastes like cat piss, anyway. "Where are you going?"

"I don't have to listen to this shit. I'm getting the fuck outta here."

Minty sits there looking all smug like she was judge, jury and executioner and she's just proved that Julie was a bonafide heterosexual.

I'm just about to put my coat on when Julie minces in. "Hi, sorry I'm late," she says like it's no big deal, like I should be pleased she's even shown up at all.

"I got your purse," I say.

She holds out a hand – two tones of pink nail varnish and a tonne of silver rings on her fingers – but I pretend I ain't seen the gesture and lay her purse down on the bar. She knows I'm sore because she immediately launches into some lame excuse for why she's late.

"...and then I had problems with my car... I'm sorry..."

Yeah right, pull the other one. I'm not even listening to what she's gotta say. I'm tired of being made to look like an ass by this broad. I should just leave now. Yeah, I should just leave. If I were wise I would leave.

"What do you want to drink?"

My stomach turns over. I fold my arms tight across my chest and shift my weight from one foot to the other. I have to stop all this crap. She's just a broad. My brain is telling me to just get the hell out of here, to leave her standing, but somehow I can't take my eyes off her.

"Jack D. On the rocks."

I surprise myself by accepting a drink. But then I'm finding it hard to stay angry with her. She's far too beautiful to make me feel pissed off. I suggest we go next door into the blue room (as far away as possible from Minty). "It's women only," I tell her. "And the music ain't so loud."

"Sure," she says. "Whatever. I'm easy."

We go next door and Julie leaves her handbag on the seat beside me while she goes over to the bar. Her handbag is black and square with a white kitten wearing a red bowtie on it. She's pinned some small metal badges onto it and I squint to read what they say:

Bitch, moi?

Innocent

Girl Guide

If you can read this then you are too close

I don't get to see what the rest of the badges say because Julie comes back with drinks. She sits down and lights up a cigarette before offering the pack to me. I tell her no thanks, I don't smoke, and she goes to put the cigarette out, but I tell her it's ok I don't mind if she does.

This situation is the reverse of the usual – I'm so nervous I have to get myself drunk instead of the broad. Not that they usually need much alcoholic persuasion. This broad, though, she makes me so jumpy I can hardly hold a conversation.

Shazia was the only steady girlfriend I ever had. Normally, I'll just sleep with a chick for one night only. Then I'll maybe take her out to dinner a few times, make her feel special and then get rid of her in the nicest possible way. That way, you minimise the risk of hurting their feelings and they get to say that they once had a thing with Vicky Romeo. I make it a rule to never kiss and tell and I expect the same in return, but if she's really good looking and you know that she genuinely does like you then you can't exactly hold it against her for mouthing off to all her friends.

The ones I hate are the hard-ass bitchy ones who set out to screw you just so that they can tell everyone and gain status on the scene. The kind of broads you do the job on and then they don't even spend the whole night.

I wonder what kind of girl Julie is?

We talk a bit about her audition, about how she's hoping to get into musical theatre when she leaves college. Then she asks what I do, and I tell her I'm in the acting business.

Her eyes widen, and she smiles at me, and I know then I've got her hooked. We both start to relax more, and the conversation flows as we talk about the plays and movies and performers that we like. She seems surprised to be having such a good time with me, and I'm surprised too, because normally the women I pick up are only good for talking about favourite lesbian kiss scenes, and whether they'd prefer to fuck Gina Gershon or Jennifer Tilly.

I really like her. I really really like her. But there's just one thing bothering me...

"So tell me something, Julie..."

She asks me to call her Joolz. "That's what all my friends call me."

I smile and lean in a little closer.

"So tell me something, Joolz..."

Joolz, Joolz, Joolz. I have to be careful not to overuse that word.

"Yeah?"

"Are you and Paris..."

I tilt my head.

"Are we what?"

"Is she your..."

"God, NO!"

Silence.

Relief.

Her face is beetroot.

Mine feels hot.

"Ugh. I mean we did... Once... And it was... Oh god... But we're not..."

Gutted.

She tells me that it was a one-off. A mistake.

"Hey," I say, putting up my hands, "it's none of my business."

She continues to talk though, telling me about how it was her first night out on the scene and how she only went because she didn't have any other lesbian friends.

"...And I got pretty drunk... And my head was all over the place... And I'd never actually been with a girl... And I just needed someone to..."

I nod and make sympathetic noises, even though I'm not sure I want to hear all this.

"You must think I'm a total slut."

"Not at all."

I'm about to reach over and squeeze her hand when she reaches for her cigarette pack.

She sighs. Lights up. Inhales.

"How did you meet?"

"Gay dot com."

I nod.

"I know how dodgy this must sound," she says. "Going out on a date with someone I'd never even met, someone I'd only spoken to through a computer screen..."

"I understand."

"She seemed really nice though, and she said on her profile that she liked sports and dancing. Obviously, she meant watching Sky Sports and going to 'the dancing'."

"Obviously."

"And I was pure all dressed up, really excited about coming out for the first time, and then she turned up wearing a Kappa tracksuit."

"Typical."

"And do you know what the worst thing was?" she says.

I brace myself.

"She stank of fucking foundation."

She grins at me. I grin back.

"Oh god," she says again, "I can't believe I slept with someone who looks like an Oompa Loompa."

We both laugh.

"These things happen," I tell her. Then I ask her if she wants another drink.

"I probably should go," she says, looking at her watch. It's stainless steel with a pink mother of pearl dial, and it matches her nails.

It's just gone half past eleven. Last orders in about fifteen minutes. I don't want her to leave. I don't think she wants to leave either.

"Go on, have another drink."

"Ok." she says, she'll have a diet coke. I hope she's not one of those girls who likes to starve herself just so she can wear pretty clothes.

I buy more drinks, sit down, and then watch her light another cigarette. She's one helluva nice broad but she smokes way too much.

"Stress," she says. Her family don't know she's gay, that's why. And she's got a sister who's a rat who's always snooping around and looking for ways to cause trouble. She asks me if my family know and I say that they do, but Mamma took it real hard in the beginning. "My mum would die if she knew. And Siobhan would love to be the one to tell her."

I tell her about the time my flatmate, Robbie, took his whole family out to dinner before he told them. In the middle of the starter his Dad began telling fag jokes. "It worked out ok in the end, though," I say. "It usually does."

☞ ♥ ☜

Joolz gives me a lift home and I invite her in for coffee. The others are all out clubbing and I don't expect anyone home for hours. When I say 'coffee' though, I seriously mean coffee. I have a very nice, very expensive, Italian blend that I only use on special occasions, and I'm not sure why but this feels like one of those times.

It's stupid, maybe, but now that she's come back with me I'm starting to feel all dumb and nervous again. And although part of me is dying to get into her pants, there's another part of me nagging at the back of my head, telling me that I should play things slow, cause I feel sorta protective towards her because of what she just told me about Paris.

So I tell her to make herself at home and have a look around. She's eyeballing my CD collection, and I tell her to go ahead and put some tunes on while I go through to the kitchen to boil the kettle.

"Hey, you want an ashtray?"

She doesn't answer me but I guess that's because of the music. Through the open door I can hear Jelly Roll Morton's 'Hesitation Blues' playing in the background, and I'm smiling and thinking to myself, this girl has taste.

I find an ashtray under the sink and lay it on top of the work-top while I go to get the milk for the coffee. Then I open the fridge door and I see the wine... On second thoughts...

"Would you like some Chianti instead of coffee?"

Again she doesn't answer me.

So I ask her again, "Hey you want some Chianti?"

"Yes please," she says finally.

I carry the wine plus two of our best glasses through to the living room. Joolz's busy fixing out her bag on top of my coffee table: car keys, hankies, purse – the works.

"I brought the bottle," I tell her, "saves walking back to the kitchen."

She looks perplexed.

I ask if she's ok.

"Emm... I need to drive home."

I tell her that's fine – she can crash here if she wants. It would be nice to spend some time with her and get to know her better. We can watch a movie if she likes. I got tonnes of good movies. I even got popcorn and Doritos. Would she like some? I know it doesn't really go with the wine but still...

She goes cold on me after that, scoops her things back into her bag and says she's leaving. I try to figure out what I've done wrong, but she won't even speak to me.

"Hey, I'm sorry if I said something to– "

She slams the door in my face.

Fucking bitch. Fucking cunt tease. Fucking Jelly Roll Morton is still singing *"Can I get you now or do I have to hesitate..."*

About five minutes later, she raps on the door.

"You change your mind, sweetheart?"

"Don't flatter yourself."

I follow her as she marches back into my living room. "Hey, I could sleep on the sofa if that's what's– "

"I just came back to get my purse."

"Oh."

She snatches it up from the arm of the sofa. Pockets it.

"I'd started to actually like you a little bit," she goes on. "When you dropped the olive oil smooth talk I thought you might even be more than just a glorified man."

"Oh."

"But this whole fucking seduction scene you've obviously set up – for all I know you probably stole my purse and had that idiot hide it behind the bar."

"Hey, I– "

"Save it, *sweetheart*," she says, and then she pushes past me and gives that block of wood another almighty slam.

Five

"What is your problem, baby? You're good looking, you got a beautiful body, beautiful legs, beautiful face... Only you got a look in your eye like you ain't been fucked in about a year."

"You said that to her?"

I grin, and Kat puts her hand over her mouth to pretend that she doesn't find this funny. It's Sunday afternoon, and I'm enjoying myself, performing for my friends the things I should have told that dumb broad last night.

"You walking out on me?" I said, "Nobody, but nobody walks out on Vicky Romeo, you hear that sweetheart?"

"Aye, then ye woke up!" says Minty. "You're full of shit, Romeo."

I say nothing, except to order another round of drinks. I don't really care what they think. It's not like they'll ever find out the real story, and besides – I got artistic licence.

"Anyway," says Minty, "that's what you get for being a *hetty* lover!"

Everyone laughs and I tell Min to piss off. She goes back to her glass cleaning ritual and the rest continue to talk while I sit, quietly, sipping a pint. Then a couple of minutes later, I go into my inside coat pocket and take out the battered paperback copy of *The Importance of Being Earnest* that I got from Oxfam in Royal Exchange Square that morning. I crack open the book jacket and run my finger down the cast list.

☞ ♥ ☜

If there's one thing I love more than anything in my life, one thing I love more than being gay, it's being on stage. Comedies, tragedies, musicals... I love 'em all, and I don't care who knows it. Doesn't matter if it's an amateur performance or a who-dunnit-style dinner theatre thing, or whether it's strictly for family and friends or in front of the frigging Pope. I just love acting and entertaining. And I love getting right under the skin of a good character.

A lot of people find this hard to believe when I tell them, but before I went along to Les Artistes I was really very shy. Back in high-school I hung around the music department at break times, and so by default, my friends were other shy and geeky kids who played geeky instruments like violin and clarinet. And sure, I went in for all the school shows – *Mary Poppins*, *Kiss Me Kate*, *West Side Story* and *Grease* – we all did. But I was too pussy to try out for the principal parts, and that's something I've always regretted.

There I was, this tiny skinny loser kid with a big voice that nobody got to hear.

I was walking round with all these big dreams inside me, and I was bigging myself up to Mamma – telling her that I was gonna be famous one day – but none of it mattered one iota because I wasn't putting myself out there. And I'm not saying I'd have my name up in lights if I'd just bit that bullet, but maybe I woulda been further along the road to success by now.

I always sounded great in my own bedroom, or on the corner of Sauchiehall Street where nobody stopped to listen longer than the drop of a ten p coin. But as soon as I had the chance at a proper audience I went to pieces. It was the same with the songs I wrote. I never showed them to anyone, because what if that person told me they were crap? Underneath it all, it came down to this: I was terrified of being a failure.

And then something quite amazing happened to me. I took a wrong turn inside the GLC one night and accidentally ended up in a room full of dykes who were putting on a play.

"Les Artistes is not like any other drama group you will ever have encountered," preached the artistic director. Her name was Pippa Black and she was in her mid-fifties with bushy black hair and sallow skin, she dressed like a bag lady on her way to a funeral. "First of all, I'd like to take this opportunity to say thanks to you all for coming."

"Most of you," she continued, "will have heard of *The Vagina Monologues*..." There were sounds of 'hooray' and stifled laughter from the back of the room. "... And I'd just like to say one more thing before we all get started... *VA-GIIIII-NAAA!*"

Eh?

More laughter.

Pippa Black smiled at me as I sat, shyly, in the corner, chewing on the edge of my coat sleeve. And as she smiled, her eyes lit up like glow-in-the-dark marbles. She had one blue eye and one green, and together with her wide, high cheekbones they made her face look sleek and elegant and clever as a cat's.

"Come on," she said, "let's all stand up and say it: *VA-GIIIIIIII-NAAA!*" She stamped her foot and climbed up onto a chair and from there she stepped onto the desk in front of her. I looked at the broad sitting next to me and she shrugged and we looked around at the others, some of whom were already getting to their feet.

"CUNT!" Pippa shouted.

"CUNT!" came the reply from all four corners of the room. The broads on either side of me had also begun to join in and were clapping their hands.

"I can't heeeeear you..."

"Cunt," I said, not really getting the point of this exercise. My face and ears were burning as Ms Black danced around the room waving her hands like a frenzied orchestra conductor.

Now I was young and green and I hadn't yet popped my cherry, and part of me wanted to run outta there and never come back. But then another amazing thing happened. While all the other crazy cats were jumping and whooping and shouting out names that described a personal part of the anatomy, Pippa Black took me aside and she asked me how I was doing.

"You sure you're OK kid?" she said. "I've noticed that you haven't said very much."

I shrugged.

"Do you find it embarrassing to say the word 'vagina'?"

"Uhh, it's just not a word I've ever really used."

"Oh, and what word do you use then?" she asked me, her eyes crinkling up at the corners as she smiled.

I thought about it and then I glowed red before replying: "Pussy. I like pussy."

Someone behind me sniggered.

"Hey, don't we all," said a cheeky-faced young butch. Then she grinned at me and asked my name. I told her I was called

Romeo and waited for the punch line. "Nice to meet you, Shake-speare," she smirked. "My name's Minty."

Right then and there, I knew that I had just met my best friend in the whole universe; I also knew that everything else was gonna be OK.

☞ ♥ ☜

"What's that you're reading?" Zest asks, leaning over my shoulder. "Morning room in Algernon's flat..."

Zest aka Zesty aka Princess Zest is the youngest in our crew and she's still in school. Her real name's Kirsten Best, but she got her name because she's always hyper. It's not her fault though. Poor kid had some shit gone wrong with her thyroid and it made her go bald. Still, she's sweet and cute as a fairy cake, even if she does have Lego hair. (Not that I've ever, or would ever, dabble with a high-school kid.)

"It's a book," I tell her, "as you can see."

She giggles. "No, but what's the book about?"

"Yeah Romeo," says Sweet Cherie, curling a loose strand of platinum blonde hair around her pinkie. "What's the book about?"

I look at Cherie with her huge, glazed-over, baby doll eyes that rarely blink, her glossy smile and her Pamela Anderson figure. She's not exactly the brightest penny in the bank. But then neither is her girlfriend Mel, who used to think cottaging was something you did in a game of monopoly.

Cherie is chewing ferociously on one side of her mouth and then stops to blow a huge pink bubble. I grimace as it makes a loud popping noise and she drags the entrails of the gum back into her mouth.

" 's probably some more poofy poetry," says Minty, hanging over the bar.

I tell her to go fuck herself and call her a goon.

"I'm a goon?" she says. "I'm not the one that was getting all gooey over *Shakespeare in Love* last night!"

I turn the page, pretending to ignore her.

"I've seen that," says Cherie.

"Yeah, don't knock it," says Kat. "That's a brilliant film."

"Yeah," adds Zest. "*And* it's got a drag king in it."

I smile to myself, knowing that one of my main reasons for watching was cause it's got Gwyneth Paltrow in it.

"Ooh," says Minty. "A plague on *all* your houses," she grins and flicks her wrist, limply.

"Hey, did I miss something?" Mel sits down beside Cherie, puts two drinks down in front of them and gives Cherie's back a rub. She is wearing baggy black combats and a tight black t-shirt that says – MY FANTASY: TWO MEN: ONE COOKING, ONE CLEANING. "Is that the play you're going in for?" she asks.

I nod and clap the book shut to avoid any further questions.

"Oh, what play is it?" asks Zest.

"The Importance of Being Earnest."

Silence. Cherie pops another gumball. "What's it about," she says, stretching the gum with the edge of her thumb.

"Umm... I don't think you'd be interested."

What I really mean is: you've got shit for brains and you'll never be able to follow it. But I wouldn't say a thing like that. They're still two of my best friends, even if they are schmucks.

"Awww go on..."

"Ummm... Well... It's about these two broads who– "

"Broads?"

"Chicks," I say. "It's about these two chicks– "

"I object to the use of the word 'chick'!" says Cherie, throwing back her shoulders and sticking out her tits. She recently discovered feminism and made a bonfire of all her underwear in the back garden. "Not all women are bimbos, you know."

I put up my hands in mock defence. "Settle down, baby," I tell her. "It's just gangsta talk."

"Huh, I don't care what kind of talk it is." She continues, "I'm sick of hearing, 'Yo brutha, dis here's my bitch', and all that crap."

"Umm, honey..." says Mel, "that's gangsta *rap*."

"Ha," says Cherie, "I know dat yo herb!" I scratch my head and bite my lip with amusement. "You want some grill, ma brutha? Ah git aw-ul da hoes." I clear my throat. I got no idea what she just said. I don't think anyone has.

"Yo da Fresh Prince of Bel-Air over der, gonna shut yo mutha fuckin trap before I wup yo ass." Everyone turns around and looks at Minty. She flashes us her dentures then slaps her glass-cleaning cloth down on the bar like she really might slap someone with it next time.

"Now, she's good," points Mel. "She should really audition for your play."

"Yo nigga, what you sayin, boy? You ben smokin da Buddha?"

"Emmm," says Kat, "perhaps not."

☞ ♥ ☜

I was stunned when I got a part in *The Vagina Monologues*. And not just any part. I had to recite the 'My Angry Vagina' monologue, which involved cussing and swearing at the audience and screaming about how crap it is that women have to menstruate.

"I can't do this," I said to Shazia, one night when she was helping me rehearse.

"You can't do what?"

"This part, these words."

It was three days before the show.

"Of course you can," she said. "Anyway, you'll have cue cards to help you."

"No, I can't even read it," I insisted. "It's too embarrassing."

Shazia held the cue cards out towards me whilst she picked up the script.

"Read."

"No."

"Read."

"Fine, but I'm not saying the F word cause your Ma's in the next room."

"Why the *FUCK* not?"

"Shut up." I punched her playfully and she grinned at me.

"And I'm not saying the P word either."

"What's the P word? D'you mean 'pissed'? Why can't you say 'pissed'?"

"Keep your voice down!"

"You're the one that's shouting."

"Anyway, I don't mean that word, I mean the P-U-S word."

"PUSSY! You can't say 'pussy'? Oh for fuck's sake, Vicky."

"SHUT UP! Your Ma will hear you."

Shazia just laughed. "I don't give a fuck," she said. "She probably wouldn't understand what we were talking about anyway."

"I think she would somehow."

I folded my arms and looked out the window. I used to do that a lot when Shazia teased me. I was always so scared to lose my temper or have an argument with her in case she walked out and didn't come back. So whenever I felt angry with her, I'd just take a deep breath and imagine that I was sucking all the bad thoughts inside my belly. When I breathed out again, whatever window I was looking through, well, I tried to make myself believe that that's where all the bad feelings would go. Back then I couldn't imagine life without that girl.

"Come on," Shazia said, softly, and she put her hand on my shoulder. "Read."

"OK." I said, finally.

Any doubts I had about her leaving would melt as soon as she touched me.

"But, I'm not saying the T word, either."

"Oh, come on, Vicky."

"Uh-uh, I'm too shy."

"Well, what do you say when you go to the shops for them?"

I don't answer.

"You can't do a monologue about fucking periods if you can't say the word 'tampon'."

"As I was saying – the play is about two *women* who both think they are marrying a guy called Ernest but, in fact, neither of them are."

"So it's about infidelity?" says Zest.

"Nah, it's two different guys who both use the name Ernest because the chicks – sorry – the women that they are in love with have this idea that they will only marry someone by the name of Ernest."

"Why Ernest?"

"They believe they are destined to marry someone with that name."

"Awww," sighs Cherie, who is now chipping away the excess varnish around the edges of her fingernails. "Sounds really ro-man-tic."

"Sounds complicated," says Mel.

"It's a good play," I tell them. "It's all about secret identity and taking the piss out of heterosexual relationships. You should read it sometime."

"I have, and it's shite," says Minty. "*The Importance of Being Earnest* is almost the equivalent of putting your fingers in a vice and crushing them."

"Ouch," grimaces Mel.

I drink up and begin putting on my coat, not wanting to get into a big debate because I know if I take the bait I'll be here all night.

"And the characters are fuckin stupit... They all talk shite the whole time and pretend to be somebody else... This lassie gets engaged to someone she's not even met just cause she likes his name..."

"Where are you going?" Zest asks.

"Home," I tell her, "I'm working at eight tomorrow morning."

"I better go too," says Kat.

Zest pulls a face. "Aw but it's still early," she whines.

"Those two need their beauty sleep," chimes Minty.

I call her a cunt.

"Hey, at least I'm a happy cunt."

"True," I concede, and I give her my empty glass to take back to the bar.

I'm half-way to the door when Zest shouts:

"If you need someone to help with your lines..."

I wave. "No guarantees I'll get a part."

"I love Oscar Wilde," says Kat, catching me up.

"He's shi-ite," sings Minty. "You only like him cause he was a poof."

I smile at Kat. She is a brilliant actress. She once told me that she had roles in *Taggart* and *Dr Finlay* when she was younger. "You should try out for it," I tell her.

"Oi, when's the audition?" shouts Zest.

"Tomorrow night."

"Whereabouts?"

"The GLC."

As I'm heading into the street with Kat, I can hear the beginning of the big debate: "Am telling ye," says Minty, "he was bent as a brush that Oscar Wilde…"

Then Kat turns and says to me in a ridiculously over-the-top English accent: "Victoria, old bean, the way you flirt with Kirsten is perfectly disgraceful. It's almost as bad as the way Kirsten flirts with you."

"Whaddya mean?"

"C'mon Vicky, Zest fancies the pants off you and you know it."

"No she don't."

"Well, any money she turns up at that drama thing tomorrow."

Six

It's nine AM and I'm in Duffy's trying to clean the espresso machine, whilst taking a call from fuck face Maggie who's saying that she can't come in today because she has another one of her headaches. The place is a pigsty and there are a million bags of rubbish to go outside, because whoever was on late shift wasn't doing their job and I need to get rid of them and take the first two trays of muffins out of the oven before the customers start to pile in.

Already I'm wishing I stayed in bed and pulled a sickie. If it wasn't for the fact I need to pay my rent I woulda stuck this douchebag job in years ago. So many times I've thought about quitting, but then I imagine myself doing something worse like shovelling Big Macs for a living.

Maggie asks if Brian the new start has shown up this morning. I tell her that he hasn't yet. She says she doesn't think he will and that she's gonna fire him next time she sees him. Then she asks me if I can work past my scheduled ten-hour shift? I expected this. None of the underlings in this place are on a full-time contract (and you can't get the hours when you want them) but Maggie expects you to be available around the clock in case she thinks she might have diarrhoea. I tell her I have plans to go see my dying aunt in hospital tonight and that it may be my last chance to do so. She moans and groans a little bit about staff shortages but even she isn't evil enough to insist I stay.

"Well hen, you'll just have to phone round and find someone else to cover," she says, and then she makes a long, loud sighing noise into the receiver, right before she hangs up on me.

I spend the next few hours making dead-end phone calls, pouring coffee, and cleaning up after a bunch of morons who've thrown their straw wrappers all over the floor. (If this were Maggie running the place on her own, she'd have shut up shop and gone home long ago.)

Still it's not as bad as some days. Most of my regulars are pretty cool people, and I enjoy shooting the shit with Chocolate Frappuccino boy and Caramel Macchiato girl. I've even got a deal going with Laptop Bob (our gay writer in residence), if he edits my piss-poor attempts at poetry he can have all the free refills he wants whenever Maggie's not here.

By two o'clock I'm stressed out, wiped out and caffeinated up to my eyeballs. I haven't had a proper break, but still I'm expected to smile politely at the jerk-off customers who bitch and whine about the temperature of their steamed milk and how much whipped cream I've put in their mochas.

And then, when I'm apologising, profusely, to the woman who didn't get all twelve of her venti, non-fat, sugar-free, vanilla lattes with the extra sugar-free vanilla syrup all at the same time, my worst nightmare happens – Julie 'call-me-Joolz' Turner appears in the queue.

"Oh my god," she says, in a syrupy, over the top voice. "Fancy meeting you here, Vicky."

I want to die. I want to stick my head in an oven or bury myself in a vat of burning cookie dough – *anything* to get away from her. Right at this moment, I would be eternally grateful to a proactive, hot-beverage-hating suicide bomber, who believes that his mission in life is to rid the world of independent coffee houses.

Joolz is standing about a metre away from me at the hand-cooked crisps basket with an armful of shopping bags, and she's with this flame-haired, muscle-bound, balls-on-his-ass himbo of a guy who looks like he's just walked off the cover of Scotsgay.

"So do you work here often?" she smirks. "Because I wouldn't have thought you'd have time for an ordinary job. Not with all your big acting roles coming up."

The himbo says he's gonna find them a table. "You stay and talk to your friend."

I watch him walking away, hating him for leaving me with this bitch, and hoping that some time soon he'll get a dose of pubic lice or a nasty hairline fissure up his rectum.

Joolz gives me a saccharine smile that makes me want to pour sour milk over her. "So Duffy's Muffins…" she says, "that's quite an ironic place name for a lesbian to work in."

Fuck you, I almost say. I don't though, because knowing my luck she's probably one of those mystery shoppers and she'll have me fired. Besides, I've already heard all those jokes about cherry pies and eating cake and there's nothing she can say that can hurt me.

I give her a tight smile. "What can I get for you, Julie?"

"Well, an apology for the other night would be nice..."

Again, fuck you.

"But in failing that, I'd like two medium... No, actually, make that two large caramel lattes with skimmed milk."

"Two venti non-fat caramel lattes coming right up."

"Oh, and could I have two shots of coffee in one of them?"

"No problem."

I ring up the till and tell her the damage. She leans forward and our hands touch briefly as she transfers the cold coins into my palm.

I make her coffee, and when it's ready I leave it on the counter.

She takes it away without another word.

☞ ♥ ☜

Two hours later I'm still serving coffee and she's still sitting there. I watch her from behind the machine, tossing her hair, laughing and arching her neck. I would love to kiss that neck. I would love to run my fingers through that hair.

The guy she's with isn't as faggy as I first thought. I begin to wonder if he's her boyfriend and if he knows she's half a dyke. Maybe that's what he likes about her.

I make a point of walking past her table several times, pretending that it's the most important thing in the world that I collect all the empty dirty mugs that are lying around. She doesn't even look at me though. I don't think she even notices I'm there. I was expecting a dirty look or a snide comment, but the fact that I'm completely invisible to her is somehow worse than all the other knockbacks I've ever had rolled into one.

And I've had plenty knockbacks in my time. For every woman I've ever taken home, I've had six others telling me to take a hike – I just don't advertise this fact.

I watch Julie open up one of her shopping bags and take out a skimpy cotton ringer t-shirt. She holds it up to show it off and I see that it's one of those black and white, vintage retro ones with a picture of a simpering housewife holding out a steaming pastry; underneath, there's a slogan that says: 'Here's Your Pie, Asshole!'

I'm not really into all that male-versus-female humour – mostly I think it's a crock of shit – but this t-shirt makes me smile. It reminds me of the old 1950s lesbian pulp books I read when I was a teenager, and how they all had buxom models on the covers, alongside taglines that said things like: 'The immoral story of a love-starved temptress and her insatiable desires' and 'A confession of love as shocking and honest as spring fire.' My favourites were the stories about the swashbuckling butch Beebo Brinker and her straight acting, on/off lover Laura Landon. They'd duck and dive in the shadows of the Greenwich Village bars, trying to keep their 'forbidden love' a secret. Unfortunately, at the end of every instalment there would always be someone nursing a broken heart.

And the thing about the old pulp books is, nothing much has really changed. Sure, we got Ellen DeGeneres and the cast of *Queer as Folk* (which typically is full of bum sex) waving the pink flag on TV – and of course there's Helen and Nikki snogging till the credits come home at the end of *Bad Girls* season three – but the path to true lesbian love is not paved with dental dams. It's not as simple as girl meets girl, it's more like: girl meets girl then girl's boyfriend catches them in bed before they even get to do anything, and then one of them ends up married and the other becomes a rebound queen, or a raging alcoholic, or she tops herself a la Vega Purvis.

Or maybe that's just the kinda girls I meet.

Truth be told, I'm getting tired of the one-night stands, and the having to dodge angry husbands. It's fun at first, but after the initial buzz of having totted up another notch on the bedpost, it feels pretty shitty lying there next to someone you don't really care about. And I've lain awake plenty of nights thinking about that kiss in the rain ending with the make-believe Miss Right who gives me that fireworks-going-off-my-head sensation. Of course, I'd never tell people this, because they'd laugh at me.

Julie's may-or-may-not-be boyfriend doesn't look too impressed with the pie shirt. In fact, on closer inspection, he doesn't look too happy, period. I begin to wonder if maybe she's brought him here to break up with him, or come out to him, or maybe it's a double whammy! Or maybe it's him who's finally realised that he's been a sucker all along. I start to feel sorry for him because I know what it's like to put your whole heart into a relationship only to discover that your sweetheart's betting on a whole other ball game. You love someone so much and you think they love you too but just because you've got the wrong combination of chromosomes, they put their money on some schmuck who's got a different type of tackle. My sympathy, of course, only lasts for about three seconds, because then I remember that he's probably a straight white man, and jilted straight white men can easily pick up another chick just as easily as they can a bar of candy or a ticket to the movies.

Joolz is getting up. She's putting on her coat and her pink nylon scarf and she's slipping her handbag over her shoulder. She puts her empty muffin wrapper and her coffee cup in a neat pile on her tray. She catches my eye as she walks past the counter but her face is expressionless.

She lets the door swing behind her when she leaves, and she doesn't look back.

☞ ♥ ☜

At the end of my shift I switch on my phone and I have about a million text messages and missed calls from Mamma:

Where are you?
What are you doing today?
Are you working?
Why haven't you called me back?

And the usual:

Are you coming over for dinner tonight?

And every one of these texts has a smiley face at the end, including the one she sent at seven-thirty AM to tell me that my old babysitter had just died of a heart attack.

"Hi Mamma," I say. "How are you?"

"Where are you?"

"I'm just on my way home from work."

"Why haven't you called me back?"

"I've been in work all day."

"Are you coming over for dinner?"

"No, I can't tonight because I have a thing on."

"So you are not coming for dinner?"

"That's what I said."

"Why do you not want to come for dinner?"

"I've just told you, Mamma. I have a thing on."

"What thing?"

"Just a thing."

I don't wanna tell her about Les Artistes because I know she'll just start on at me again about how I'm wasting my time.

"What about tomorrow night?" she says.

"I can't tomorrow. I have my class."

"What class?"

This was a mistake, I should have told her zilch.

"You know the night classes I do at Strathclyde Uni?"

"Oh," she sniffs. "Those leisure classes."

"They're not leisure classes. They're continuing education classes. I get Scotcat points and everything."

"And what's all that going to get you in the real world, Vicky?"

She launches into her old routine about how I should get a proper education and stop living in cloud cuckoo land.

"Ma, I don't have time to listen to this."

"You've never got time," she bleats. "And you've got very serious problems if you can't take five minutes to have a conversation with your mother."

"You're the one who's got the problem," I tell her.

And then I kill the call.

Seven

It's a quarter to seven and I have to run all the way from the flat to the GLC because I'm late, because Mamma called me three more times (firstly to moan at me again, then to tell me we got another letter from my dead beat Dad, then basically to reiterate everything she'd already told me earlier).

When I get to the centre I'm sweating cause it's one minute past seven and I don't know where I'm s'posed to go, and I'm thinking this could be a big opportunity blown cause this Tracy Broadbent might just decide my tardy ass belongs out on the kerb.

I find the room a few seconds later. It's not started yet and only Kat and Zest have turned up. I'm glad in a way cause it means I get to fix my hair in the washroom, but on the other hand I'm unimpressed with the sloppiness of the so-called artistic director.

"Vicky, chill out," says Kat, as she sits sharing a huge vinegar-stinking bag of chips with Zest, who has come straight from school and is still wearing her uniform.

"You just don't get it!" I tell her.

"I do. I totally get it. You think if you get onstage at Glasgay then a talent scout or someone might– "

"No. Nobody fucking gets it!" I shove the chair nearest me and it tips back and spins on one plastic leg before landing on all fours again. "My tutor at uni says I need to get more involved in the arts scene... I need all the experience I can get... I need to make contacts... I need to..."

"Chill. The. Fuck. Out. That's what you need to do."

I thump myself down onto the seat, arms folded. This sucks.

Two minutes later I say: "So where the fuck is everyone?"

"Maybe we're it," says Kat.

"Do you want a chip?" says Zest.

Another two minutes pass and Mel and Cherie poke their heads around the door, followed by Mikki Blue Eyes and a hippy chick called Salsa who I haven't seen since *The Vagina Monologues*. The lot of them sit chatting away about who's broken up and who's sleeping with who, like it's some kind of les-be-friends reunion.

Ten minutes later:

"OK. Where the fuck's this Tracy Broadbent character?"

"Maybe she's been held up in traffic," says Kat.

"Maybe she's got the time wrong," says Zest.

"Or maybe she's getting fucked in the mouth somewhere," I say. "I don't care."

"Is she a lesbian?" asks Zest.

"She better be," I tell her.

"What difference does it make?" says Kat passing her chips to Mel who finishes them, rolls the bag into a ball and volleys it towards the waste paper bin. It hits the rim and bounces back and Cherie runs over and picks it up. "Being gay won't make her a better drama teacher."

"This is a *lesbian* group for *lesbian* women," I tell her, "and we don't want any straights trying to muscle in."

"Can they do that?" says Mikki, her brow furrowed. She looks genuinely worried and I know it's cause a) she, like me, got shit all through high school for not looking like a Barbie doll, and b) because she's doing an Acting and Performance HNC at college and we've obviously been given the same advice.

"Nobody's trying to muscle in," says Kat.

"Pippa Black started this group because there was no platform for queer female artists in Scotland," I say. "And I don't want to be led by some trying-to-be-politically-correct hetero twat who doesn't know anything about our issues."

"That's like saying a Protestant or a Sikh teacher can't teach in a Catholic school."

"Well, they can't can they?"

Kat shakes her head. "Don't get me started."

"Yeah," says Zest, "don't get her started."

Sigh.

"Anyway, I don't know what issues you're talking about, Vicky.

I came here to have a laugh and maybe get a part in an Oscar Wilde play."

There's a chorus of 'me too' and 'me three' from Mel and Cherie, and even Mikki fails to get my back. I'm about to tell them all to piss off when the door swings open.

No prizes for guessing who the femme wearing the turtleneck sweater and the matching black beret is.

"Hi," she says, in a fake London accent, with a fancy French fag in her hand and a stack of scripts in the other. "I'm Tracy Broadbent," inhale, "and we're a little bit behind schedule tonight," inhale again, "so let's get started." She waves her script hand at Kat. "You– " she points, "gothic girl, yes, you– " she waves again, "give these out, please."

Kat's chin almost touches her toes.

"Well, c'mon, chop-chop," says Broadbent. "We haven't got all night."

I expect Kat to come out with an assertive yet witty one-liner but she doesn't. She just takes the scripts and distributes them with a frown.

Broadbent takes a seat, surveys the room, sucking on her cancer stick.

"Oh," she says, finally, "I hope no one in here minds if I smoke?"

Les Artistes Introductory Training

PLEASE REMEMBER TO BRING THIS WITH YOU TO EVERY SESSION

1. Trainees should arrive promptly at 19:00 PM

2. No cruising

"What's *cruising*?" says Zest.

"Think George Michael in the Los Angeles public toilets," I say. Everyone else laughs except Broadbent and Zest whose faces are blank.

"It just means no chatting up, no dating other cast members," says Broadbent.

Already I can tell that the second rule is gonna pose problems, as Salsa is making baby-doll eyes across the room at Mikki Blue.

"You're asking dykes not to chat each other up?" I grin. "That's like asking Bill Clinton not to wank."

"What's your name?" Broadbent says.

I tell her.

"You see that door over there, Vicky?"

"Sure," I say. "There's nothing wrong with my eyesight."

"Well, feel free to walk out of it at any time."

"Huh?"

"If you want to participate in *my* drama group," she says, "you will obey *my* rules. Is that clear?"

"Crystal," I say, biting down on my back teeth.

"What if you're already in a relationship with someone in the cast?" asks Cherie, as she snakes both arms around Mel's waist.

"Well, obviously, I'm not going to insist that you break up," says Broadbent, "but it can create problems if two people have been involved..."

3. Appropriate clothing recommended e.g. no skirts or kilts

I don't get to read any further because Kat nudges my arm.

"Look up," she whispers. "Bunny boiler at twelve o'clock."

Zest mouths the words 'oh my god' and pretends to hang herself.

"Hello, you must be Penelope," Broadbent smiles. "Come in and take a seat. You haven't missed much."

"Unbelievable," Kat mumbles.

I make a fingers down the throat gesture and almost get caught in the process by Broadbent, but I manage to disguise it as a cough.

Now, I know this 'Penelope' broad from old, and where I come from she goes by a different identity. I know her as *Miss_Scarlet* as in Scarface as in my once-upon-a-time and biggest-mistake-of-all-time one-night stand.

Not many people realise this, but Scarface is the real reason why so many people know me on the scene. She is also the reason why I became such good friends with Kat. And not only does she have more holes in her face than Rab C's string vest, but she's also a world-class stalker.

So I'm really not surprised to see her here with her new blue mohawk, fifteen additional lip piercings and her tits popping out of a nasty looking black PVC corset. Cause no matter where I go – she's there. If I go to the pub, she's propping up the bar; if I go to the supermarket, she's practically riding in my trolley; if I went to take a shit she'd probably be there ready and waiting to wipe my ass.

But let's get a few things straight right from the start:

1) Her stalking me is not my 'own fault'.
2) I was drunk (practically paralytic, in fact) when we did the business.
3) Otherwise I wouldn't have touched her with someone else's
4) And I only slept with her once (despite anything she says).

"Don't say hello then Ro-me-o," Scarface crows.

A cold shiver runs down my neck.

"Do I have a choice?" I mumble to Kat, whose body is shuddering with silent laughter. To the Bride of Medusa I say, "Hello then."

Frankly, I blame Minty for my unfortunate liaison with Scarface.

It was a long time ago, and I had gone along as a fresh-faced eighteen-year-old to L.I.P.S., a new lesbian youth group, which had formed inside a place called The Women's Archive Trust for Scotland. Minty popped up there too, and I was glad to see her because we'd lost contact since she quit Les Artistes.

I liked L.I.P.S. right away. I liked the people and I liked taking part in all the art, drama, writing and the other workshops they had going down. Minty, however, did not share my appreciation of the group and after a while she became 'too busy' – these days she only makes an appearance on high days and holidays.

I still saw her all the time though, and we became bar buddies.

Minty had been doing her own 'research' into Glasgow's dyke life and she uncovered a Sapphic hotbed during her visits to Easy Wet.

This is how she met Scarface:

```
Scotland_Room
5 people
Mel_C
Sweet_Cherie
singleandlookingforashag
Fingersofgod
UR_SEXY
```

Miss_Scarlet has just entered the room.

```
Miss_Scarlet>  Hi ur sexy!
UR_SEXY>   thanx so they tell me
```

"See her, Miss Scarlet, she's fae Shawlands and she pure loves me," said Minty.

"Is that you there?" I pointed at the screen. "You're sexy?"

"Oi, stop trying to poke me," she said. "Who gave you the big head?"

Minty asked if I'd like to see her profile. I said sure and she opened up another window.

```
Profile for ''UR_SEXY''
Dom Butch Looking For Fun Times (18 Years Old)
Area: Scotland
City: Glasgow, United Kingdom
Mail me: ur_sexy@gay.com
```

About me

I'm looking for an older submissive femme

General

I am a Single Gay Woman

Interested in meeting a Single Gay Woman, a Couple, a Group

For Friendship or Email/Chat/Relationship/1-1 Sex/ Other activities

Between the ages of 25 and 45

"What does 'other activities' mean?"

"Dunno," she said, "use your imagination... Bit of bondage or something."

Personal

Occupation: Wannabe Porn Star

Height: 5'10

Body type: Defined

"Defined? You're a fat fuck!"

"It's mostly all muscle," scowled Minty. She closed down the window after that so I never saw what other shit she wrote. Then she went back to tapping messages into the keyboard, while I sat bored outta my brain.

"Hey, lemme write something."

"Nope."

"Aw c'mon – two seconds."

She grumbled before finally passing over the keyboard.

```
UR_SEXY>   hey miss u wanna phuck me n da ass
UR_SEXY>   (_|_)
```

"Oi whit ye daein..."

A week later, Minty arranged to meet Miss Scarlet inside Sandy's. Trouble was, she'd never seen her picture. I got dragged along as chaperone, the idea was that we'd go early to sneak a look at her and if she were a dog we'd get the hell out.

When we arrived, there was someone already sitting inside the booth where Minty's Scarlet woman said she'd be. She had long, black hair with purple streaks and a stud in her nose, and she was reading *Wuthering Heights*. And, boy, was she a looker!

Minty nudged me.

"Here, that's her," she grinned.

I had my doubts.

"I thought you said she had pink hair?"

"Pink, purple, fuck's it matter? That's her, man."

I still wasn't sure. For a start, she looked several years short of twenty-eight and, from what Minty had told me, the closest she'd likely gotten to reading 'gothic literature' was Bizarre magazine.

I tried to point this out but Min wasn't listening. "Good book, eh," she shouted, her voice rumbling across room. Purple hair looked up and smiled right at me, sweeping a loose lock behind her ear. My face and neck began to burn.

"That Emily Bronte," continued Minty, "was she no a muff diver?"

Oh god.

Why did she have to say that? Why did she always have to make everything about *that*?

The broad grinned. "Precisely what I've been saying for years."

Before long, the two of them were discussing some famous eighteenth century dyke novelist who ran off with a fourteen-year-old girl. I hadn't a clue what they were talking about, but it turned out Minty (who always gave the impression that she had shit for brains) had an A in higher English.

A little later, Minty slipped me a tenner and sent me to the bar. I knew she really meant for me to take a hike cause this had never happened, her lending me money – it was usually me subbing her for everything, from cigarettes to paying her share of the rent.

I spent the next half hour talking to Robbie who was still working behind the bar. He was looking for a flat and we needed another roommate.

Rob told me that he knew the purple-haired broad.

"Very well, in fact," he said.

I squinted at him. "How well?"

He laughed and shook his head. "She used to go out with my cousin..." dramatic pause, "who is also female."

Her name was Kat. She was twenty-one, a philosophy student and he was pretty sure she did not go on chat rooms. Besides, she had a long-term girlfriend.

I was about to go back and relay this information when the real *Miss_Scarlet* showed up. She came crashing through the door with her arm locked around the waist of a seven-foot something, pin-thin, ponytailed fag hag in a trench coat, who was being dragged to the bar against his will. I understood his reluctance entirely – this guy got enough abuse for just looking the way he did, without people thinking he was bent as well.

"Please," she whined, "I don't want to go by myself. She might be a freak."

I almost snorted out loud. This chick looked like a cross between Chucky from *Child's Play* and Marilyn Manson, only stockier and with cleavage and flamingo pink hair. Plus she had a semicircle of black studs below her bottom lip that I initially thought were raisins.

She caught my eye and smiled. I nodded, turned away, and paid for the drinks.

This should have been the end of it, but no, she followed me to the table.

"Hey Kat!"

No. Fucking. Way. I couldn't believe it. How could those two be friends?

And after that, "Is this seat taken?"

I opened my mouth to reply, but didn't get the option as she was already squeezing her enormous ass in beside me. The guy followed but sat down at the end of the table on a stool, and began staring into a cigarette pack that he dropped on the table.

"Excuse me," I said, getting back up, "I have to go to the bathroom." My hand accidentally brushed against the fabric of her skirt then, and I stammered an apology.

"Don't be sorry, honey," she smirked. "You can touch my leg anytime you like."

When I came back, it had been established that *Miss_Scarlet* (or Scarface, as I'd decided to name her) was the older sister of someone Kat had gone to school with.

I tried to swap seats with Minty but she was having none of it, not even when I whispered to her that I was not the one Scarface was here to meet. The raisin-faced moron, by this time of course, had taken to licking her lips, smiling at me and running her foot along the inside of my leg.

The fag hag escaped to catch his bus at quarter to eleven and I followed a half hour later, using the excuse that I was on an early shift, but not before they had gotten me stinking drunk. I had just started working at Duffy's the week before. Sick of washing dishes and trying to erase the ghost of Shazia – that girl had been my entire world for nearly two years – when I saw the vacancy for coffee baristas I went in and asked for an application.

I had been going round with Minty more too. We'd just moved into the flat together and I was hitting the scene really hard, drinking to forget the break up. Mamma hadn't wanted me to move out. She didn't think I was ready. But she knew that there was nothing she could say that would make me change my mind. Besides, she really liked Min – she'd invite her over for dinner and to the cinema with us all the time. What she didn't like were the new places and people that Minty introduced me to. But Ma also knew that she had to let me make my own mistakes. "You're eighteen now, an adult," she said. "But I'll always be your mother and there will always be a bed for you here."

Halfway home I realised that I'd lost my keys. I went back to the bar and searched every inch of the place, scrambling about on my hands and knees, but no luck.

It was Scarface who picked me up off the floor.

"Hey sweet cheeks, is this what you looking for?"

After a few drinks she didn't actually seem so bad. Next thing I remember, I was in a taxi, whizzing past strange houses with a warm hand on my knee.

So that was it, I went home with her. And even though I didn't fancy her one iota, I fucked her brains out. When I woke up she gave me her phone number and I promised to call, but I tore it to smithereens as soon as I left.

I saw her a couple of times after that, on the scene. I never spoke much to her though, apart from one night when she cornered me in the toilets of the Polo Lounge – she asked me why I told all her friends she was a crap lay. I told her I never said that. I never did. People asked me if I'd slept with her and I said it was my business. At least, that's what I said most of the time.

"Even if it was true," I said to her, "I wouldn't say that about anyone."

"Well, I told everyone about you," she said. "Now they all want a multiple orgasm."

We play zip-zap, traffic lights and some other icebreaker games that are supposed to help us get to know each other better. I wish Broadbent would just hurry up, because the clock is ticking and so far she's not even mentioned an audition. Although, there really wouldn't be much point considering there are more parts than there are recruits.

Broadbent asks us to think up three statements about ourselves. "Two of them should be true and one of them a lie," she says.

"Can they be about anything?" says Scarface.

"Anything," replies Broadbent.

Scarface is the first to make her statements. "My name is Penelope. I am thirty-one years old. I am straight." Kat and I look at each other and shake our heads, and then we look back at Scarface who is grinning, like an escapee from Carstairs. "The third one is the lie," she says to Broadbent, who in turn nods and frowns.

I can tell this is going to be a looong warm-up exercise.

Eight

I'm in Easy Wet with Kat, trying to convince her to come to Ma's house with me for dinner tonight, but she's ignoring me and trying to palm me off with the profile of some random that she and Robbie met at the gay hillwalking club.

"You'll like her," she says, "she's really nice."

"If she's so nice then why don't *you* go out with her?"

"Because unlike some, I don't feel the urge to sleep with every female I meet."

Ouch.

"Ok. But she'd better not be another one of those weirdo pagan vegans," I tell her.

"Moon-river is NOT a weirdo."

"Whatever," I say. "Her name sounds like a frigging ballad."

"Would've thought that was right up your street," she smirks.

Hmph.

"Anyway," she says, "your mum's a vegan."

"Yeah, have you seen some of her friends?"

I have a sudden fleeting vision of Mamma's hippy-dippy, tree-hugging cronies in their hemp smocks and rubber sandals.

"Ok. Point taken."

Kat stamps 'Juliet' and 'Glasgow' in the search box and then presses return. "I promise," she says, "you will *really* like her."

Profile for ''Juliet''
Disco Diva (20 years old)
Area: Scotland — Glasgow
City: Glasgow, United Kingdom
Mail me: juliet@gay.com

About me
Why don't you just ask...

General

I am an Open Minded Woman
Interested in meeting a Single Gay Woman, a Single
Bi Woman
For Friendship or Email/Chat/Relationship/1-1 Sex
Between the ages of 18 and 25

Personal

Occupation: Got one
Height: Rather not say
Body Type: Rather not say
Ethnic Origins: Rather not say
Hair Colour: Rather not say
Eye Colour: Rather not say
Attire: Rather not say
Out: Not applicable
Bust Size: Rather not say
Smoke: No
Drink: No
Drugs: Never

My Hobbies

Have lots

Her profile doesn't interest me. It has no picture.

"Awww, that's a shame," says Kat. "She must have taken the photo off."

Huh, I'm thinking that she must be a dog or she'd show her face.

"She's totally your type, though."

"What do you mean my 'type'?"

I hate it when my friends tell me someone is my type, even if they are correct. I can do my own matchmaking thank you very much, and I can't stand chicks that do the whole 'my friend fancies you' routine.

"She's really femme," continues Kat, "and she's into sports and outdoor– "

"Well, I think I could've figured that out for myself."

"And she does cheerleading."

"Cheerleading?" I say, raising one eyebrow. "Well, that's... Different."

"I thought you'd like that. Perv."

I grin then take a second look.


```
GMT: 17:27:15
Scotland_Room
8 people
```

```
Mel_C
Sweet_Cherie
Zesty
Mikki_Blue_Eyes
Paris
Katastrophe
Vicky_Vegas
Juliet
```

Vicky_Vegas has left the room

"Vic-ky!"

"OK, OK." I hold my hands up in defeat. "I'll say hello to her." I smile to myself, thinking that maybe Kat has a point. Maybe she really is a babe. Besides, how cool would it be if Romeo were dating Juliet?

"I'm just making a new profile," I tell her.

"Why? What's wrong with the old one?"

Profile for ''Romeo''

```
I settle down with a nice girl every night… then
I'm free the next morning
```

"You can't write that!" says Kat, nudging the keyboard away from me.

"Why?"

"Because – because you just can't..."

She types:


```
Last Of The True Romantics (21 years old)
```

Area: Scotland — Glasgow
City: Glasgow, United Kingdom
Mail me: Romeo@gay.com

About me

I am Romeo's flatmate Kat and I am writing this profile because she is pretending to be shy. She's very cute and sensitive and romantic (she writes her own love songs and I've heard her singing them in the shower). She's honest, trustworthy, a good friend and the type of girl you could take home to your mum (if you're out).

"Hey gimme dat keyboard."

"No," says Kat. "It's for your own good."

"Bitch."

General

I am a Single Gay Woman
Interested in meeting a Single Gay Woman, a Single Bi Woman
For Friendship or Email/Chat/Relationship

"Relationship?!" I pretend to shoot myself in the head with my finger.

"Do you want to meet girls who aren't psychopaths?" says Kat, giving me one of her raised-eyebrow looks.

I shrugged and sighed.

"Well, shut it."

Between the ages of 18 and 25

Personal

"Can I write something now?"

"I suppose."

Occupation: Actor/Writer/Stand-up comedian

"Vicky, you work in a coffeeshop!"

"Soooo... I moonlight."

"Why don't we just put 'student'?"

Hmmph.

```
Height: 5'5
Body Type: Defined
Ethnic Origins: White
Hair Colour: Blonde
Eye Colour: Blue
Attire: Trendy
Out: Yes, it runs in the family
Bust Size: Small
Smoke: No
Drink: No
```

"I drink."

"Well, now's the time to start eliminating bad habits."

I sigh and she changes it to:

```
Drink: Occasionally
Drugs: Just caffeine
```

My Hobbies

"You can do this bit if you want."

"Oh, you're so kind!"

I can't be bothered typing anymore though, so I just leave it blank.

```
Romeo has entered the room
Zesty>   hey romeo sexy n original name hehehe
Katastrophe> Leonard-a DiCaprio meet Kate Winslet
Zesty>   zit not Claire Danes??
Katastrophe> you know what i mean
Juliet> hi
Romeo>   hey

Private_Chat
Romeo+Juliet
```

```
Romeo>  so what art thou up 2 2night sweet maid-
en?
Juliet> haha
Juliet> having a few drinks with my straight
friends
Romeo>  str8 nights yuck h8 them
Romeo>  u ever go out on the scene?
Juliet> been to Sandy's couple of times
Romeo>  Love Sandy's! What did u think?
Juliet> full of arseholes
Romeo>  ?
```

"Ok. So what am I supposed to say now?"

"Use your imagination," says Kat.

"She's *your* friend!"

```
Juliet> anyway moving swiftly on…
```

"This isn't gonna work," I say. "I don't like set-ups."

"Wimp."

```
Romeo>  I should probably go
Juliet> awww
Romeo>  my mothers cookin dinner for me tonight
Juliet> oh yeah whats it like having an ital-
ian-vegan-lesbian for a parent?
```

How the fuck does she know that? I turn around to ask Kat what she's been saying about me but she's off talking to some pink-haired punk in a Lesbian Avenger's t-shirt.

```
Juliet> are there groups for italian-vegan-lesbi-
ans? is it quite common?
```

How should I know? Why does she have to say it like that, like it's all one word? What's with the fucking film star hyphen?

```
Romeo>  I really better go
```

☞ ♥ ☜

The air is thick with the smell of olives and sweet basil when I arrive, and Mamma is in the kitchen chopping chillies and onions and throwing them into the pan. If there's one thing I miss about living at home it's Ma's cooking. She makes *the* best penne al'arrabiata.

"Come in and sit down," she shouts over her shoulder.

I do this and immediately she pours me an orange juice and launches into a story about how she came out to the new head chef in her work today.

"You should have seen her face when I told her that Sam was a 'she'."

"And then what happened?" I ask. I'm pleased that Mamma is finally getting herself a life instead of playing the pronoun game all the time.

"She said your mother was the best looking vagitarian she'd ever seen," comes a voice from outside. Ma's face twists and I hear the crunch of Dr Martens being taken off at the door.

"Samantha Haggarty! She did NOT say that!"

Sam says hi to me and gives Ma a quick hug and a kiss, and then Ma goes back to chopping and stirring while I snigger into my juice.

"Have you thought anymore about getting in touch with your father?" He's been sending me letters to Ma's address for the past six months, and she thinks I should open one and see what he's got to say.

Like hell! Why would I want to waste my eyesight reading his baloney? Anyway, I know Mamma doesn't *really* want me to get in touch with him, cause all the time I was a kid she kept ragging on about how he was nothing but trouble. She said she was glad he was out of our lives. And besides, I've turned out pretty much all right despite not having him around.

"I don't have a father," I say. "He's dead as grunge music."

We sit down for dinner and Mamma asks me what I've been doing these last few weeks that I've been so busy. I tell her about the university, about how the guy who's teaching the writing class thinks I've got real talent, and when she asks me: "And where will all this get you?" I tell her about how my tutor has asked me to read some of my poems out at an open mic.

Sam pats me on the back and says she's proud of me. I tell her it's nothing major and that I'm only on for five minutes and it's not gonna happen till the end of term. "Doesnae matter," says Sam, "you should stick in there." She says she always knew I had a talent, but then Mamma frowns at her and Sam goes quiet so I switch to talking about the Earnest play instead.

Ma says she's never heard of it. "Well, it starts off with this guy called Jack who everyone thinks is called Ernest," I say. "He's come to town to propose to this broad who's the cousin of his friend Algy– "

"I can't believe I told Shirley I was gay!" says Mamma.

I sigh and slam my napkin down. I don't know why I bother talking cause she's never interested in *anything* I say.

"It's not such a big deal," I tell her. "I come out to people all the time."

"Well, maybe it is a big deal for your mother," says Sam, frowning.

Ma ignores us both and begins telling us her lame-o story again like it's the most exciting thing that's happened in her life.

☞ ♥ ☜

Mamma had never heard of *The Vagina Monologues* either, until the night that I came home raving about the play. And I can remember clearly how, four years ago, I sat in this kitchen and took great pleasure in educating her.

"And I thought you knew everything Mamma," I teased. "How can you not have heard about the *vagina* monologues?"

OK. So I'd never read it, myself, until the day after that first rehearsal, and I hadn't really known what it was about. But I had heard of it and I'd wanted to read it for a long time (purely because of the title), so I pretended to be outraged.

"See that *Vagina Monologues* play you did," says Sam, "that was on the telly the other night." Spooky how two people can often be thinking about exactly the same thing at the same time. I tell Sam that I watched it but I didn't think it was as good as our performance. Mamma says she somehow managed to miss it again.

"Remember how you thought it was a porno, Mamma?" Sam and I laugh but Ma doesn't. She's never exactly said that she thought it was a porno but I could tell from the expression on her face that that's what she was thinking when I first said the name.

"No Mamma, an American named Eve Ensler went round interviewing over two-hundred women about their private parts and then turned the interviews into different stories."

I kept trying to tell her that it was nothing to do with sex but she didn't want to listen. Mamma never listens.

Over coffee and tofu tiramisu, the conversation turns to talking about my primary schools and sex education, because Ma's new pal, Shirley – whoever she is – has ten-year-old twins who've recently started asking questions about the birds and the bees.

"Remember that first time when Mamma tried to tell me about the facts of life?"

It was in primary six, in between watching the period video and finding out about her and Sam. "I remember coming home in a rage one day because she'd let me believe that all you had to do to get pregnant was sleep in the same bed as a boy." Even Mamma eventually smiles at this one. "I was disgusted when I found out what really went on and I ran straight from school to confront her about it."

After that it was easy to work out what men and men did together in bed, but what did two women-fags do? The night that Sam took me to Sandra Dee's for the first time I asked her that question, but she said I should talk to Ma. Later on, when they thought I was asleep, I overheard them having a whole big discussion about what I should be told.

Ma came to me the next morning and, slowly and carefully, she said:

"Lesbians use... fingers."

That was it – they used fingers! That was all she said, end of story. But I still felt I needed clarification, so I asked:

"Do you mean... They poke each other?"

Mamma says she still doesn't know what was the point of putting on a play about vaginas.

"What sort of name is 'The Vagina Chronicles'?"

"*The Vagina Monologues*, Mamma."

What was it all about? Why had I even wanted to take part in something like that? And if the woman who wrote it ain't a dyke then why would she want to interview people about something like that?

"She wanted to know why broads felt shy to talk about down there." I point down into my lap with my fork. "So she asked them," I say. "She asked them things like: what would your vagina wear if it got dressed to go out to dinner?"

"What do you mean 'what would it wear'?'"

"A tie and a smart black suit," grins Sam. "Wi a fat wallet in the pocket." Sam winks. It's Mamma's fortieth birthday next week and I know that Sam's taking her out somewhere special for a surprise.

"My vagina would wear a white tuxedo and a blue velvet bow-tie," I say, "and put gel in its hair."

Mamma's still not playing the game. She thinks we're being stupid now, and that I'm making it up. I tell her that I'm deadly serious, and that this play is made up of both humorous and sad parts, and that maybe if she had come to see it she would have identified with it.

Ma's face flushes red. We eat on in silence for the next few minutes and all I can hear are knives scraping across plates. I wasn't brought up to use 'rude' words like 'vagina', certainly not at the dinner table. (That's probably the real reason why other dykes always think she's straight, cause anytime she's out in the pub and someone makes a sex joke she excuses herself and runs off to the bathroom.)

Finally it's Sam who speaks first and she says that the meal is delicious. I nod in agreement. Then Sam asks me where she might get tickets to see this new play. I tell her that the cast hasn't even been chosen yet, and with the way things are going it could end up being a one-man show.

Last time, all the money we raised from the performance went to help Say Women, and this time Broadbent's talking of giving it to Rape Crisis. This last piece of news seems to cheer up Ma and she asks how can she become involved.

"Mam-ma! What you trying to do to me? I got a reputation to protect. You can't audition for *my* play!"

That's the last thing I need – Mamma dragging her prissy ass round after me.

"It's no your play, Vicky," laughs Sam. "You've said yourself that anyone can go in for it."

"Yeah, but not Mamma! That's a total embarrassment..."

Silence. Ma ducks her head and lets her fork fall onto her plate with a clink. Sam clears her throat.

"Have you finished?" Ma says, finally.

Not sure if she means with the dessert or the conversation, but I don't dare ask. I just nod and put my cutlery down and she starts to swiftly clear away the plates.

I feel bad, and when Mamma goes to the kitchen I follow her and try to apologise, but then she gets all melodramatic as usual.

"Victoria, why d'ye always have to cut me to the bone?" She says it like I've really tried to stab her through the heart or something. But I know better than to argue.

"It was just – well – you coming to do the play is a bit... I dunno..."

"And who said anything about auditioning? I was going to try and sell tickets for you and put up posters in the café."

"Oh."

"You know your problem, Vicky?"

"What's that?" I say and wait with baited breath to be told the usual 'you're selfish' and 'your head is full of wheels' yadda yadda yadda.

"See you, Vicky," she says, "you never listen..."

It's quarter past eleven and I'm lying in bed, too wide awake to sleep. The conversation I had earlier with Ma is still stuck in my head. All throughout dinner, I'd been painfully aware of how much I could not stop myself from saying the word 'vagina', over and over again, and how much this seemed to irritate Ma. And now that I'm home, I can't stop thinking about how alien the word still sounds to me: Vagina. Vagina. Vagina.

Following the performance of *The Vagina Monologues*, I was totally obsessed with saying that word. And I couldn't stop telling people about it, I told everyone I met that they had to read it.

I had not been able to put the book down. I read it on the bus and on the tube. I even carried it in my coat pocket to the supermarket with me one day and I didn't even realise that I had dropped it until a greasy palmed checkout boy ran after me and handed it to me with a grin on his face.

I have an idea.

I throw off my duvet and rush out of bed and into the bathroom. Lifting the A4 mirror down from the hook on the wall, my hands quiver and a ripple of excitement rushes down my spine; I can feel my face hot and puffy, just as it felt on the night of that first rehearsal. For I have just realised that although I've seen plenty of other girls', I've never actually inspected my own genitalia.

Not sure what is the best way to do this, I step out of my black Bart Simpson boxer shorts and lie down on my back with my knees bent, my t-shirt is riding up and the hooks of my bra are scoring along the carpet. I sit up again, nervous. Who knows why? Maybe I should relax more first, go for a bath or something, and put on some music?

So I lie steeping in hot water filled with Radox blue muscle soak. The hair around the nape of my neck is getting warm and wet as I sink down further, growing sleepier. Steam is rising up to my nostrils and then it hits me – I've still gotta do what I've gotta do tonight.

I push myself up, quickly, onto my palms; when I do this I slide and my skin against the acrylic surface sounds like a loud farting noise. I snigger. It reminds me of the first year of high school. There was this girl in my gym class who could do what she called 'fanny farts' just by pressing her pelvic floor muscles together. I always wondered how she did it and she explained it to people one day when we were in the changing rooms. I never quite got the hang of it myself and I was always too embarrassed to ask for a repeat demonstration.

'I was one of those women who'd looked at it and from that moment on wished I hadn't... I pitied anyone who had to go down there...'

Pippa made us, one by one, read aloud that whole monologue at the first workshop. It was called 'Because He Liked to Look at It' and was about a broad who'd had a good experience with a guy. I was one of three people in the room who hadn't read the play and I was glad. I read without really comprehending the words, saving my blushes till I was alone.

I dry myself and trail back through to the bedroom with another white bathroom towel wrapped around me. I spread the towel out on the carpet and fasten the bedroom door. There are noises coming from Kat's room, footsteps and the sound of drunken laughter.

I shiver and turn up the radiator, I then put on a Frank Sinatra CD at a low volume.

Lying on my back, knees bent and wide apart, I begin to, reluctantly, stroke the whiskers around my pussy.

After about five seconds, I have to stop and turn the music off because it feels like Frank is watching. I've never allowed anyone to touch me down there. I've never seen the point. With all my past girlfriends, I've been the one to make all the moves – I've always preferred to make love rather than take it. Nobody has ever made me come before. God, I can't even do it to myself. I tried it once and nothing happened. I'd never really thought about it again. Not until recently. Until tonight, the only time I ever touched myself there is when I'm washing.

I have to turn the mirror around, change position until I finally see it. I stare at it in silence for some time. My pussy. My vagina. I had expected it to look soft and gentle, to be baby pink. Like rose petals. But instead it looks to me, not like a flower, but like the mouth of a wild animal. It's red and angry like it's yelling its head off, but no sound is coming out; I half expect to see little teeth popping out any minute, come to chew on my fingers.

I look at it again from another angle and it looks to me like it's a baby's mouth, a hungry baby waiting to be fed. I can see the little wrinkles on its brow, its tiny nose.

I've been down here for about twenty minutes when I catch sight of my own face in the mirror, and when I see my red puffed up cheeks and how dumb I would look if anyone were to walk in right now, I begin to laugh. I laugh so hard I hit my head on the floor. I drop the mirror then, roll over onto my hands and knees; I'm covered in goosebumps, the light brown hairs on my arms and legs are all standing on end and my toes and butt are freezing.

I fold the damp towel into quarters and leave it by my bed with the mirror. I'm too tired now to make another trip to the bathroom. I reach over and switch off the light, and then I crawl into bed and pull the duvet up around my ears.

Nine

The next night, I write about the whole vagina inspection at my writing class. I write about it as though I am some intrepid adventurer who has found a deep, ancient, unexplored cave, which turns out to be the mouth of some weird, enormous, Loch Ness monster...

I get so lost in the story that my tutor (who is a guy) has to ask me three times to put my pencil down. I find it hard to concentrate while the rest of the class goes around in a circle reading their work aloud, and when it comes to my turn I grow so red, and the paper quivers in my hand, and I stumble over the words so much that he has to ask me to read it all over again.

The tutor stops me after class and I am sure that I've been rumbled. Then he tells me that he *loved* my story.

"You have got to be kidding," I say.

"No," he says, he thinks it is the best story he's heard from any of his classes this semester. "I wish you had told me before," he says, "that you were interested in writing sci-fi."

```
Scotland_Room
4 people


Mel_C
Sweet_Cherie
Romeo
Naughty_Nurse


Juliet enters the room
Mel_C walks over to Cherie
Sweet_Cherie walks backwards
Mel_C walks towards her

Juliet>  hi you guys
Mel_C puts her hand on Cherie's hip
```

Sweet_Cherie leans in and shows some cleavage
Juliet> What's going on in here?!
Sweet_Cherie> Mels teaching me to salsa dance
Mel steps on Cherie's toes
Sweet_Cherie> OUCH!
Mel_C> Concentrate!
Mel_C> When I put my hand on ur hip, u put ur
arm on my shoulder
Sweet_Cherie> OK
Juliet> salsa dancing is great!
Mel_C> wev started teaching salsa classes at my
gym
Romeo> did u ever notice that in gay bars
Romeo> the poofs r al disco bunnies and the
dykes cant dance
Juliet> speak for yourself!

I'm having a hot and heavy, one-on-one, cyber session with *Naughty_Nurse* when another private chat box pops up:

Juliet> hey hows you this evening?
Romeo> peachy

I've just convinced her to get naked on the webcam.

Juliet> so did you have a nice dinner at your
mum's the other night?
Romeo> yup
Juliet> what did she cook for you?

She's taking off her t-shirt.

Romeo> pasta

She's unhooking her bra.

Juliet> what kind of pasta?

Baby, keep going. It's been almost a month since I got laid and I'm practically drooling outta the corner of my mouth. Then–

PING!   **PING!**   **PING!**

My screen starts to vibrate. Whaddafuck?!

Juliet has sent you a nudge

The webcam has disappeared. I try to bring it back but all I get are a series of popping, flashing windows:

```
Juliet> Romeo
Juliet> Romeo
Juliet> where for art thou Romeo
Juliet> ????
Naughty_Nurse has left the webcam conversation
Naughty_Nurse> did u like that hot lips?
Naughty_Nurse> well that's all ur getting 4 now
haha
```

Damn.

☞ ♥ ☜

It's a quarter past eight, I'm sitting on top of my bed reading aloud the first scene from the play, trying out all the parts for size. My cat, Sinatra, is my only audience and she's making herself a nest in my duvet whilst occasionally looking up at me as if to say waddafuckareyoudoin?

"...I have introduced you to everyone as Ernest. You answer to the name of Ernest. You look as if your name is Ernest. You are the most earnest-looking..."

DA-DA-DA-DA-DAH   **DA-DA-DAH**

Somewhere in this room my phone is ringing.

DA-DA-DA-DA-DAH   **DA-DA-DAH**

Shit. Where is the damn thing?

"Where's the phone?" I look at Sinatra and she begins burying herself further under my bedcovers. "Come on, where's the phone? Are you hiding it? Are you, huh?"

DA-DA-DA-DA-DAH   **DA-DA-DAH**

I pull back the duvet to find that the rubber cover of my mobile phone has been scratched to ribbons. "Bad pussy," I say, shaking my finger at Sinatra. She just gives me one of her fuck-you looks and crawls deeper inside the duvet.

"Hello?"

"Hi, is that Romeo?" The voice is smooth, like dripping honey, and it sounds familiar but I can't quite place it.

"Yeah, who wants to know?"

"Hey Romeo... it's Juliet."

Giggle.

"Hey."

More giggles.

"You're probably wondering how I got this number?"

Damn right.

"Kat gave it to me."

Shit, that bitch does not give up.

"So... Ummm... How's your night going?" I say, feeling kinda awkward. I'm not really in the mood for small talk but I know if I blow her off I'll just have Kat ragging on at me about how I never made any effort.

"My straight friends are soo-o fucking annoying me right now," she says. I make concerned noises. "I'm at Nikki's, and we're supposed to be having a girlie night in, and all they can do is sit around and bitch about their stupid men."

"Oh right."

"I haven't seen Nikki for weeks, not since she's been back shagging that prick Allan fuck face Rogers."

"Mmhmm."

"And tonight, she's spent half the time bubbling down the phone to him and defending her reasons for coming out with us when he thinks that we are just a bunch of whores that are trying to lead her astray. News flash, buddy: you were the one that got caught dipping your dick elsewhere."

She makes a big sigh. "Sorry, I'm a bit drunk. And I had to get that off my chest. How are you, anyway?"

"Hey, I'm just fine."

She giggles again.

Okaaaay.

"Soo-o..." I say, taking another stab at conversation. "What yous up to right now?"

"Well, Mylene and Liane are too engrossed in painting each other's toenails and discussing the finer points of heterosexual sex to notice me..." I can hear voices in the background saying 'Who's that?' and 'Who is it?' "And Nikki is rifling through her mother's toxic CD collection..."

Music is gradually getting louder in the background. Not sure what it is.

"OH FOR FUCK'S SAKE." I have to hold the phone away from my ear. "She'd better not be fucking– " I can hear laughter and I think a dog is howling. "Oh my god, listen to this," says Juliet.

"DON WANNA BE ALL BY-EE MY-EE-SELLLF..."

The dog turns out to be her friend Nikki singing.

"She's a fanny. She does this all the time," says Juliet. "I'm sorry, I'm gonna have to go. Nice talking to ya. Mwah." She makes a kissing noise down the phone and then she clicks off, leaving me with a million questions and a what-da-fuck-was-dat-about feeling.

Body Awareness and Movement

Begin with the students lying on the floor. Ask them to create the following visualisations:

Bacon frying

Porridge bubbling

Popcorn popping

Chewing gum being stretched

Broadbent sure likes her A4 handouts. She keeps them all in polypockets inside a shiny, black ring binder and gives them to us as soon as we arrive.

There are eight of us tonight, including Broadbent, and Salsa who isn't actually acting because she's organising the PR side of things. Although she did say she would stand in as Lane the butler if need be.

Kat is not here. She left the flat early, said she had to go meet a friend. I think it may have been a date but she's denying it.

So here I am with Broadbent, Salsa, Zesty, Mikki, Mel and Cherie and Scarface.

We start off in neutral position. Standing in a circle with our backs straight, legs apart, arms by our sides. Let's pretend we are all marionettes and that we have a wire attached to the tops of our heads. My name is Pinocchio and this is a real drag. Later, we might even pretend to be trees. Body awareness, phooey. I've seen more action at a Punch and Judy show.

"Vicky, pay attention!" Broadbent sticks her neck out like a cartoon roadrunner to indicate that I may have missed something of life-and-death importance. One of these days, someone might do her a favour by dropping an anvil on her head. Everyone else begins rolling their heads on their shoulders, so I make like one of those nodding dogs you see on the dashboards of trucks. "OK," she continues, "working your way down the body..."

I know whose body I'd like to work my way down. That naughty nurse texts me a picture message of herself during the break wearing nothing but a pair of black stockings and a suspender belt. Oh yeah.

Just when I'm thinking about what to reply, I get another text message from Minty:

```
Just served that wee hetty burd u fancy. Shes in
wi two hetty pals. U shud cum down+join them 4 a
4some
```

Then she adds:

```
Ther playin giant pub jenga ha ha
```

☞ ♥ ☜

For the past forty minutes, I have been put through the humiliation of being a piece of bacon, a coffeepot, a toaster and a boiled egg. What's next, a cucumber sandwich?

"OK," says Broadbent. "Before we take a break, I'd like you to get into pairs with someone you haven't worked with yet..." I look from left to right, the lovebirds Mel and Cherie have half-heartedly paired up with Mikki and Zest, and Salsa looks miserable next to Scarface.

"It's ok. I'll sit this one out," I say.

"Just join another group," says Broadbent.

"Yeah," says Scarface, leering at me. "Why don't we make a threesome?"

Sigh.

Broadbent snaps her fingers at me and says 'chop-chop'. I hate people who say that. Even more than I hate people who snap their fingers at me. "OK, working in your twos and threes," she says, "I'd like you to create a tableau – a frozen statue – of a household appliance."

"You mean like a vacuum or something?" I say.

"Yes," she says. "When I clap my hands, the appliance will begin to work. Everyone must be involved in the appliance – no operators!"

Scarface smirks, "I know – we could be a vibrator."

☞ ♥ ☜

At the end of the workshop, Broadbent asks if there is anyone who doesn't have a copy of Earnest yet. I smile smugly as everyone apart from me and Mikki raises their hand. Broadbent passes out some dog-eared books. Finally, I'm thinking, we might get this show on the road.

"I would like you all to read this play," she continues, "and then choose one of these assignments to finish for next week."

Silence and blank looks all round as she hands out more sheets of A4 paper.

```
After reading 'The Importance of Being Ear-
nest', students will be divided into groups
to discuss and then perform an oral presen-
tation of no less than four minutes on:


    The playwright and the play.


                  OR


The social and historical environment of
       the play and its central issue.
```

"What does it mean by 'oral'?" whispers Cherie.

"Don't bother about the discussion part," says Broadbent. "I'd prefer you all to do this on your own."

"How perfectly delightful," I say, under my breath.

Zest giggles and Broadbent shoots me a look that would freeze Africa. "Did you have something to add, Vicky?"

Only that I am not wise sitting here listening to this shit.

"No," I smile sweetly back at her, "I didn't say nothing."

"Well, I just hope we will be able to make this project work," she says, her steely gaze still fixed on me. "Because you will be onstage at the Tron Theatre in six weeks' time."

"THE TRON THEATRE?!"

"Yes, Glasgay are commissioning this project..."

All at once there is a flurry of voices.

"GLASGAY!!!"

"Ohmygod!"

"Everyone I know will be at the Glasgay festival!"

"There'll be newspapers and shit and I might get on TV!"

"I don't want to be on telly."

"What if my mum sees it?"

"This is like a really big deal!"

"Have you been to the festival before?"

Then all at once everyone shouts:

"WHAT ARE WE GONNA WEAR?"

OK, so I'm lying – that was just me who shouted the last bit. I knew we were going to Glasgay – it said so in the email – but somehow I'd forgotten.

Two minutes ago my ass was about to walk out the front door of this building without ever looking back. Now, with the prospect of fame hanging over me like a golden fleece, my breath's baited and my buns are squeezed tighter against this seat than a bullet inside the cradle of a semi-automatic firearm.

☞ ♥ ☜

Kat and I are in the net café doing research for the paper Broadbent has given us. Mikki, Mel and Cherie are here too, but they're holed up in a corner dishing the dirt on some ex-girlfriend they've all got in common.

"By the way," says Kat, "what is the relevance behind Merriman and his cucumber sandwiches?"

"It's Lane."

"Well, whoever it is," she tuts, clicking the mouse vigorously. "C'mon. Move. These computers are crap, Vicky. It's a bit phallic, don't you think?"

"The mouse?"

"No, fucking Oscar Wilde and his obsession with cucumbers."

"Who are you, Sigmund Freud?" I ask her. "I think it's just

basically there to show you that everything they talk about is so trivial."

"Do you know what Bunburying means?"

"He's the offstage character..."

"Nope."

"Well, not offstage. He's the excuse. Bunbury is the imaginary character that Algy says he's going to visit when he doesn't want to have dinner with Lady Bracknell."

"Nope."

"Well, what is it then?"

My lame-o computer keeps crashing and I'm starting to get pissed off because it's not letting me into gay.com.

"Bunburying is Victorian slang for anal sex between gay men."

"Honestly?"

"'Being Earnest' used to be the slang term for being gay."

"Are you making this up?"

Kat points to the screen. "It says so on this website. And do you know what else Bunburying could also mean?"

"No, but I'm sure you're gonna tell me something even more gross."

"The secret life that gay people have when they are in the closet."

I shrug.

"I guess all my life I've been earnest."

"OK! Is everyone ready?" says Broadbent, looking around the room. Zest has just come in out of the rain and is trying to dry her wig on the radiator; Cherie is applying her lip gloss, Mikki and Mel are playing trumps, and Scarface is staring out of the window and picking at her earwax with what looks like a lolly-pop stick.

"Ready as we'll ever be," I say, cracking my back and taking my stance in neutral position.

"No warm-ups today," says Broadbent. "I have a surprise for you..."

Sounds ominous.

"We're going to do a read-through of the whole play."

"So is this like a proper audition?" says Cherie.

What!? She can't audition us today. I've not had time to rehearse this morning. I've not even decided which part I'm going for!

"Think of it," says Broadbent, "as an informal audition. Everyone is guaranteed a part."

She makes us stand with our scripts in a line, with microphones in front of us, while she puts on a pair of large, black and white headphones.

"I feel like one of the Jackson Five," whispers Kat.

"OK Michele," nods Broadbent, "could you read Algernon for me? Mel could you read Jack? Vicky could you read Chasuble... No, actually, could you be La– "

Lane. The butler. What a shitty part. I get to carry the cucumber sandwiches onstage.

"Kat, could you read Miss Prism? I'll read Lane and Merriman."

"Hey, I thought you said I was to read Lane?"

Broadbent eyeballs me for a second then says slowly: "Vicky, pay attention, you are Lady Bracknell."

☞ ♥ ☜

Broadbent reads out the stage directions as well as the two butler parts. I hope she's not planning to cast herself.

JACK> *Worthing is a place in Sussex. It is a seaside resort.*

LADY BRACKNELL> *Where did this charitable gentleman who had a first-class ticket for this seaside resort find you?*

JACK> *In a handbag*

Zest sniggers and elbows me in the ribs unexpectedly. This makes me cough, so the words come out sounding more pretentious than I'd intended.

"A ha-haaand bag."

"Yes, Lady Bracknell," says Mikki, "I was in a... Emm... Handbag."

Giggles.

Broadbent looks up. My face is scarlet and everyone, apart from me and Broadbent, is splitting their sides laughing. She gives me a look that suggests that if she had a gun she would shoot me. I can forget about Glasgay. I think I might have just blown my chances.

I hang around to speak to Broadbent at the end, try to see if she'll let me try out for another part. "Vicky," she says, slipping her arms into her jacket, "you only get one chance at an audition."

"Oh." She does up her buttons and strides towards the door. I scramble after her. "But... hey... I don't think I'd be suitable as Lady Bracknell..."

"Well, that much was obvious," says Broadbent.

"Oh."

I didn't think I was *that* bad.

"I'll email you with the cast list over the next couple of days."

"Fine, thanks for nothing," I mumble.

"I'm going this way," she says, and points to the bus stop across the road.

"Bye," I say.

She gives me a wave over her shoulder and says: "See you next week... *Jack*."

☞ ♥ ☜

Scotland_Room

9 people

Mel_C
Sweet_Cherie
Sicilian_lesbian61
UR_SEXY
Mikki_Blue_Eyes
Zest
Katastrophe
Miss_Scarlet
Juliet

Jack enters the room
Katastrophe leaves the room
Cecily enters the room
Mikki_Blue_Eyes leaves the room
Algernon enters the room

Jack> Why hello Algy old bean

Zest> Whos an ugly old bean

Zest leaves the room

Algernon> Evening John

Gwendolen enters the room
Jack leaves the room
Ernest enters the room

Gwendolen> My own sweet Ernest!

Gwendolen embraces Ernest
Algernon leaves the room
The_Real_Slim_Ernest enters the room

Cecily> Ernest my own Ernest

Ernest> We can't both be called Ernest

The_Real_Slim_Ernest> I'm ERNEST

Mel> I'm confused

Sicilian_lesbian61> i thought this was meant to
be a womens chat room

Sweet_Cherie> THIS IS A WOMAN'S CHAT ROOM

UR_SEXY> can I have some of that crack cocaine

yous have been taking?

Miss_Scarlet> Is this an online rehearsal???
The_Real_Slim_Ernest is eating muffins
Ernest hits the really ugly Ernest with a handbag
The_Real_Slim_Ernest> A HANDBAG!!!

Gwendolen> A HAAAND BAAG
Juliet leaves the room
Mel_C> I got hit wi a stiletto heel once
Bunbury enters the room
Gwendolen> haha

Cecily> hahahahahaaaaaaaa

The_Real_Slim_Ernest> Ok Romeo I think you are kicking the arse out of it now

Ernest> Eh? Im here

The_Real_Slim_Ernest> then who's Bunbury?

Ernest> I bet it's Minty

UR_SEXY> is it fuck
Mel_C is still confused
Bunbury> :oP
Bunbury leaves the room
Juliet-just-been-doing-a-spot-of-bunburying enters the room

Ernest> u?

Juliet-just-been-doing-a-spot-of-bunburying> I studied Oscar Wilde in 6th year

The_Real_Slim_Ernest> spiffing performance old bean
Juliet-just-been-doing-a-spot-of-bunburying takes a bow

☞ ♥ ☜

After the Bunbury thing I start chatting to Juliet on a regular basis. Initially, it's just small talk like 'how art thou' and 'tis a fine morrow', and she always ends things by saying 'parting is such sweet sorrow'.

Gradually, though, she mentions her family: her brother who hates gays and her sister who hates *her*, and her mother who she claims is her best friend but she won't come out to because she's scared she'll be disowned. I ask her if she knows many people on the scene and she says she doesn't. She's just come out to a couple of her straight friends and her best friend Mylene has been a bit weird. I tell her that she'll come around eventually and if she doesn't then she ain't worth bothering about. She says she knows this.

I can't really relate to most of the problems she's going through, but I've heard them all before. Living in Ma's house for so long has made me wired, so I can't walk away from a dyke in distress. So I listen. Even when it means I have to turn down an invite for some saucy online action.

And Juliet always tells me how nice I am and how sweet I am and how she hopes we'll meet in person one day.

☞ ♥ ☜

```
Private_Chat
Romeo+Juliet


Juliet> hey I just read your email
Juliet> lips group sounds cool
Juliet> will thou definitely be there on thursday?
Romeo> thy should b but I'll tx thou f I cant make
it
Juliet> great I'll give it a go
Romeo>  u never no thou might meet someone spe-
cial
Juliet> I'll look to like if looking liking move
Romeo>  eh?

Juliet> never thou mind ☺
```

☞ ♥ ☜

The night before the L.I.P.S. group, Juliet gets cold feet and she calls to say she ain't coming.

"I just don't think it's my cup of tea," she says.

"Ok so... Hot, single lesbians under twenty-five aren't your cup of tea?"

I laugh. She doesn't.

"Come on, I thought we were supposed to be friends. Tell me what's wrong."

"Nothing's wrong," she says. "I just don't think I'll fit in."

"How so?"

"I just don't."

"Is this because you don't wanna meet *me*?"

"No!"

"So does that mean you do or you don't wanna meet me?"

"Yes. I mean, no. I mean, of course I want to meet you. You're the most normal gay person I've spoken to."

"Thanks... I think."

She laughs this time.

"So what's the problem?"

She sighs again and I can tell this is gonna be a long drawn out process. I ask her if she wants to go on the webcam and mime it to me.

"Haha. I told you before – I don't have a webcam."

"So tell me."

"I don't know where to start."

"Try the beginning."

Silence.

Then finally she says: "I'm different from other lesbians."

Juliet says she just doesn't get 'the whole butch thing'. She says that most of the lesbians she's seen are fat and ugly with shaved heads and they wear rugby shirts, and that she doesn't have anything in common with them.

"I mean, why do they act all manly?" she says.

"Manly?"

"Yeah, why do they dress and act like men? Is it so guys don't chat them up?"

I'm disappointed in her and I tell her this.

"Well I'm sorry if that sounds a bit harsh," she says. "But I'm just being honest."

"I think it's really offensive saying all butch women are fat and ugly."

"Well they are!"

"I disagree."

She sighs.

"Look," she says. "I'm a girly girl and I want to meet other girly girls..."

I hate it when femmes (or people who think they're femme) hit out with the whole 'if I wanted a man I'd get a real one' speech, and I can tell that this is exactly where the conversation is headed.

"The first time I went to Sandra Dee's, this big manly girl with spiky hair said I shouldn't be there because there were far too many 'hetties' on the scene."

"Well there are," I tell her. "But that's not the point. She was obviously a dick."

"I told her I was gay and she didn't believe me. And I ended up leaving because she was just really rude."

"Honey, that is *one* idiot."

"No, all her friends were laughing at me and saying things as well because I was wearing a skirt."

"Ok then, one group of idiots. There are loads of them in this world and they're not all gay."

"I know that."

"The point is," I say, "you're never gonna meet anyone if you shut yourself away."

"I know."

"So come to L.I.P.S."

She giggles.

"I bet you use that line a lot."

"Occasionally."

"Ok I'll come."

"But do me one favour."

"Yeah?"

"Lay off calling people 'manly'."

Juliet emails me to tell me that she's had to change her number because some girl she met online has been stalking her. She says she'll text me as soon as her new SIM card arrives. I tell her I'm looking forward to meeting her tonight. She says she is too.

It's weird – because the closer it comes to meeting her for real, the more nervous I'm feeling. I get the shakes just thinking about it and I don't know why.

"I think you like her," says Kat.

"Sure, she's a nice chick," I say.

"I think you fancy her."

"Nuh-uh. No way."

She's right though, or half right. I have been thinking recently that maybe, maybe we could be a match after all. Behind that computer screen she could be anyone.

She could be my dream girl come to life. It could happen. But the chances are it won't. The chances are she's a buck-toothed donkey with a ratty perm and a personality disorder.

There's something about meeting people in cyberspace, something about typing things into a faceless computer that makes you feel less inhibited and more intimate with the person that you're talking to. I tried to be vague with Juliet, keep the conversation solely on her. But she never gave up asking questions. Did my Dad know I was a lesbian? And did he know Mamma was a lesbian? And did I think that he thought it was Mamma's fault that I was a lesbian? Did I think I was a lesbian cause I'd been brought up by lesbians? And so on.

At first I thought these things were pretty intrusive, but then little by little I began to open up. Did I ever sleep with a guy? No. Kiss a guy? Nope. Want to kiss a guy? Not for a million bucks.

I told her things about me, personal things I never even discussed with my closest friends. And because I couldn't see her face it made it easier. I told her everything about Shazia, and Scarface, and Julie Turner (although I changed the names); I even told her about how everyone knew me as a flirt and a player, but really all I wanted was to meet a nice girl and fall in love.

So, yeah, I'm nervous as hell about meeting her.

Then Juliet just stops coming online.

Two weeks go past and she doesn't text or call, she doesn't reply to my emails and she doesn't come to the L.I.P.S. group either.

☞ ♥ ☜

```
Private_Chat
Romeo+Juliet


Romeo>  Hey stranger
Juliet> hey sexy wot u up2
Romeo>  ben worried about u
Juliet> :o(
Romeo>  has ur sistr been givin u a hard time
again
Juliet> hey I ment 2 say
Juliet> im juliets sis
Romeo>  o
Juliet> juliet wil b bak soon
Romeo>  does she no ur on this
Juliet> she said I cud use the comp
Romeo>  how is she?
Juliet> :o)
Juliet> di she tell u about her huj colection of
dildos
Juliet> only kidn ;o)
Juliet> im gonna get her to take me 2 a gay club
:O)
Romeo>  realy
Romeo>  so ur cool with ur sis been gay
Juliet> shes stil my sis
Juliet> even if she is a big mad dike
Juliet> :op
Romeo>  :o)
Romeo>  u still ther?
```

```
Romeo>    ?
```

She doesn't reply to my messages although the chat box says
she's still hooked up. I wait for almost fifteen minutes and I'm
just about to go when another box pops up at the side of the
screen:

```
Private_Chat
Romeo+Juliet


Juliet> oh my god my sister knows I am gay
Romeo>   Juliet?
Romeo is confused
Juliet> yes its me I can't believe my sister was
on gay.com
Romeo>   yeah I jus talk 2 her
Juliet> shit what was she saying to you?
Juliet> whatever she's said is probably all lies.
Romeo>   u should talk 2 her
Juliet> TELL ME
Romeo>   TALK 2 HER
Juliet> can I call you tomorrow? she's bugging me
and trying to read what I'm saying
Romeo>   hey do you still wanna cum 2 lips
Juliet> sure
Romeo>   2mro nite 7pm @the archive
Juliet> its a date
```

The computer times out before I get a chance to say goodbye.

Ten

L.I.P.S.

Lesbians In Peer Support

Every first and third Thursday of the month, from seven till nine, is a L.I.P.S. night. And every second and fourth Saturday afternoon, from two till four, is a L.I.P.S. day. It all gets a bit confusing when there is a fifth week in the month or when there's a public holiday, and that's why I keep all the dates on a slip of paper pinned on the back of my door.

The nerve centre of the L.I.P.S. girls' multifarious activities is The Women's Archive Trust for Scotland, on the fifth floor of an old office block building in 109 Trongate. Cash was given to us recently by Comic Relief to keep the project afloat for another three years, and so far we've had almost two hundred members come through the doors since our first week.

Dykes come from all over – not just Glasgow – Clydebank, Renfrewshire, Ayrshire and beyond. They come to meet other dykes because there are none living in their area or because they don't know of any living in their area; they come because they're fresh out of the closet or because they need a helping hand out of that closet; they come because of all different reasons, and sometimes they come, like little Zesty, because they're not too sure if they're queer at all.

☞ ♥ ☜

First thing I do when I arrive at the archive is go upstairs to the fourth floor to fix my hair. There's a washroom on the fourth floor that has wheelchair access and the door is light and swings shut behind you and sometimes the lock don't work. I've seen people being caught short and this is why I always take my bag in with me or push the sanitary bin tight up against the door.

There are posters with snippets of speech from women writers pasted up all around the walls and ban-the-bomb stickers on the cistern. My favourite is the monologue by Janet Paisley about the little girl who needs to pee.

I decide to empty my bladder too. My nerves are giving me gyp again and my stomach is up and down.

Juliet has been texting me all day long. Some of those texts have been borderline horny and their content came as a very – interesting – surprise. I mean, it's not like we've never flirted before. Once, when I said I'd been playing my guitar, she asked if I was practising my 'finger work'. And that time I asked her if she was a real redhead she replied by saying 'are you asking if my curtains match my carpet?' We exchanged a few winks and the odd kiss message too, but nothing major. We never had cyber sex. She never even so much as hinted that she might want me to fuck her.

I wash my hands and check my watch. It's a quarter to seven. I wet my hair then run a comb through it again and inspect my side-on profile in the mirror.

Another text from her comes through:

`Just comiiiing. I'll be meeting your LIPS any minute ;)`

I grin to myself.

Look no further, Juliet, baby – your Romeo is here.

I unwrap a piece of minty chewing gum, pop it into my mouth and climb the stairs, slowly, one by one, taking in the sign that says 'wet paint' and being careful not to get any on my new 'I Declare a Thumb War' t-shirt.

I can hear voices and laughter. Harry, with her short, fuzzy brown hair and denim dungarees, is sitting smoking on the outside landing. She is rolling a cigarette for a girl whose name I can't recall. Kat is there too, sucking a menthol and flicking through a copy of this month's Diva magazine with Mikki, not Mikki Blue Eyes – Mikki The Hat. We call her 'The Hat' because she keeps her headwear on even when she's inside nightclubs.

Harry asks if I've had a good day.

"So-so," I shrug. "I've been looking forward to tonight."

"Oh yeah, hot date?"

She asks if I'm meeting my internet girl. I say nothing, just smile. Word travels fast around here.

Harry rolls another cigarette and puts it behind her ear. She says she's going downstairs because there's a new girl coming who doesn't want to use the lift or come upstairs on her own because she doesn't know anyone. I wonder if she means Juliet but decide not to ask. I guess I'll know soon enough.

There are a lot of new broads here tonight. Laurie, the femme half of Harry's youth leading job share, stands like a sentry outside the iron grille elevator, waiting for everyone to arrive. The brunette from Sandra Dee's who has a crush on me is here too, sitting pretty on a wooden chair beside the fire. Her name badge says she is Rosie and when I hear her speaking to the girl sitting next to her, I notice that she has a gorgeous Irish accent. I smile at her and she goes pink and hides behind her hair. I sit down facing her, on the arm of the couch because Zest and two new broads have taken up the space.

My back is to the door as I turn around to talk to Zest. She asks me if I think Juliet will definitely come, and I say of course she will because she's crazy about me.

Kat walks past and I tell her she'll need to point out which one Juliet is.

"Oh Ernest, the suspense is terrrrrible," says Zest, giggling. "I hope it will last."

Kat looks over her shoulder, grins. "Don't look now," she says, "but she's right behind you."

I take a deep breath. My palms are sweating and my heart is like a samba drum. This is the moment I've been waiting for, and first impressions are all-important in this game. I turn, I smile, and then I see her – slim, gorgeous and wearing a pretty pink t-shirt to match her pink pouting lips.

Then she's looking straight at me and all I can say is:

"*You*?"

She jerks her head, haughtily, and runs her fingers through that sexy mane of flaming hair.

I can't fucking believe it. For the first time in my life I am one-hundred percent speechless and so, it seems, is she.

"You must be Julie," Laurie cuts in. "Come and sit down. We're all glad you could make it."

Juliet smiles. Or should I say Julie T-for-Turner.

"What can I get you to drink, Julie?"

"A Malibu. Straight. With plenty of ice."

Laurie's eyebrows shoot up. One of the rules of the group is that there's no narcotics or alcohol and it says so clearly on the A3 sign that's pinned to the door.

"Only kidding... Do you have any diet coke?"

☞ ♥ ☜

Well, what do you do when the girl of your dreams turns out to be the girl of your nightmares?

I do nothing, at first, except sit and watch Julie as she takes a seat across from me. She picks up a pink velvet love heart cushion and hugs it to her chest. She tries to pretend that my presence doesn't bother her, but when I catch her eye her mouth twitches slightly and she colours and quickly looks away.

She picks up a copy of the archive newsletter, which is lying open on the table. The page she starts to read is an article that I wrote about the residential trip that some of the L.I.P.S. girls took in the summer to a place called Camas. It was one of the best trips in my life. There's a photograph of Kat and Zest in a canoe and one of me abseiling down a cliff, but you can't really see my face because it's side on and I'm wearing a helmet.

I don't think she's guessed yet that I am Romeo. She's probably still waiting for some tomboyish femme with Nikki Wade hair and a heart-shaped face to walk through the door. Yeah, I bet she thinks that Romeo is some baby doll that doesn't use make-up and likes wearing men's Levis from time to time.

She closes the magazine but keeps her head bent down like she's acting shy or something. A long amber ribbon of hair falls forward masking the side of her face and she folds her arms tight into her chest, drumming her fingers on her elbows. Her hands are nail polish free for the first time since I've met her and I see she's not wearing any rings. After a few minutes, she drops her hands to her sides, allowing the cushion to sit limply on her lap. I watch her chest rise and fall as she begins tapping out the same boring rhythm on the sides of her thighs.

I continue to stare at her legs and then let my eyes drop to below her knees. She is wearing white retro sneakers with a baby blue stripe on them, her laces tucked into the sides unevenly and the hem of her pants has fallen down so that it catches on her heel and is splashed lightly with mud. I look down at my own feet. Our shoes are the same except mine have a red stripe.

☞ ♥ ☜

The lift opens and closes again with a shudder.

"Ok. Shall we make a start?" says Laurie. "There are lots of new faces tonight."

A roll of sticky labels with lipstick stamp marks is circulating the room. Mikki The Hat passes the labels to Zest who takes a London Lesbian Line pen from the jar on the tabletop and writes her name – Kirsten. She giggles and adds 'aka Princess Zest' then sticks it on the shoulder of her t-shirt, smiles at Joolz and passes the roll over to her.

Harry asks what Zest's name means and they begin talking about the internet. Harry says she doesn't use gay.com, she says it's too fast for her. She prefers the message boards on the Diva Blue Rooms. Zest giggles. We call that site the 'Blue Rinse Rooms'.

Joolz takes a pen from the jar. She looks at it for a moment then smirks to herself. "My mum found one of these lesbian pens in my living room," she says. "I told her it must be my sister's."

Here's looking at you, Miss Maturity.

She laughs to herself then begins writing her name.

"What language is that?" Zest screws up her face. "It looks upside down."

Joolz smiles. "It's backwards."

"Mirror writing," I say. "Seen it done before."

Joolz doesn't look over at me, she smiles to herself and slaps the badge on her tit. Then she puts the pen in her handbag and zips it shut. Her writing is larger and looser than I remember but still maintains its neatness.

"Leonardo Da Vinci used to do that," says Kat.

"Well impressive," nods Harry.

Laurie asks what it says.

"Julie aka Juliet aka Bunbury."

"Oh right," says Laurie. "Are you another internet addict?"

She says she is a bit and I snort, thinking about the number of times that I've come online and she is already in the room, and how she is still there when I leave.

"And what about you, Vicky, is this the same chatroom that you go into?"

"Yeah it is," I reply. "Scotland room on gay.com." I pick up the roll of stickers and take another green pen from the jar and I write, slowly: Vicky (Romeo).

☞ ♥ ☜

Laurie starts off the group by reading the announcements.

"Ok. First of all, just a reminder about the Have Your Say needs assessment on Saturday. For those that don't know, there is a seminar in the Lighthouse between ten AM and two. It's to discuss the health needs of young LGBT people and it would be really good if a few of you were to come along."

Joolz has picked up a copy of the Have Your Say newsletter, which has my mug shot on the front page along with Kat and Mikki The Hat. She asks how much it costs and what do we have to do when we get there. I switch off at this point because I've already heard about this and know that I gotta work. Thank Jeezus. Those seminars are so boring.

The announcements that follow are general stuff that are of no interest to me – the new Diva is on sale (I already read it); new courses on the life-long learning thing at the library; stuff about the Sappho clinic for sexual health (I know where it is if I ever need it). To me, safe sex is all about keeping my nails short.

"And lastly, we have free tickets to the annual butch/femme party for any L.I.P.S. members who wish to go. This year's theme is Guys and Dolls."

Hey, I wish to go. In fact, my name is top of the list followed by Kat, Zest and four or five others.

Joolz raises her hand. "Where is it?"

"Sandra Dee's," says Harry.

"Oh, I love it in there!"

I roll my eyes. "I thought you said it was full of arseholes?"

She ignores me.

"So is that like a fancy dress party?" she says.

"It's a butch/femme party," I say.

"You have to dress as a gangster or a gangster's moll," says Zest.

"Sounds fun," she smiles, but not in my direction.

"The dress code is open to interpretation," replies Laurie, as she passes around the pink cardboard passes with the L.I.P.S. logo on the right-hand corner. "As long as you don't turn up in your normal jeans and trainers."

Joolz nods and then she asks for a piece of paper to write down the date. "Can you bring guests?" she asks.

"Yes, there's two free tickets for every L.I.P.S. member," says Laurie.

"Yeah," I add, "but we don't want you bringing no hetero-sexuals."

"I was thinking about bringing a date."

"As long as it's a woman, sweetheart."

"Well, you won't have to worry, *sweetheart*."

☞ ♥ ☜

Next, we play the name game. We do it every week. Everyone has to sit around in a big circle and rhyme off who we all are, and there's always a different question that you have to answer. This week it is: what's the first thing you'd do if you won the National Lottery?

"Ok. I'm Harry and if I won the National Lottery I would... Take my kids to Disney World."

"I'm Kirsten and I'd buy Disney World!"

"I'm Vicky and I would buy a casino in Las Vegas."

When it comes around to Joolz, I expect her to opt out of playing or at least just say her name and then 'I can't think of anything' (that's what most newbies do). But no, not her.

"I'm Julie and I'd buy a whole street in Beverley Hills so that all my friends could stay beside me and we'd have pool parties, and I'd offer Louise Redknapp an indecent proposal and then..." And she goes off into a huge fantasy story, which has everyone, except me, rolling around laughing, and Harry and Laurie just let her keep talking because she's new and the last person.

Tonight's workshop is on Bisexuality Awareness. These two broads have come to give a talk on what it's like to swing both ways. According to them, sometimes being bi makes it harder to come out because they say they don't fit into the straight or the gay community.

"Surely," I say, "bisexuals have the best of both worlds? I mean, they can choose to say they are straight if they want." There is silence and Joolz throws me a dirty look.

Then one of the bisexuals, a forty-something Chinese broad kicks off with her story. "I was seventeen when I came out as a lesbian. I previously had boyfriends and I liked sex with them, but I was more attracted to women..."

I snicker behind my hand. Pull the other one, sister, you just want your cake and eat it. Laurie looks at me with furrowed eyebrows and then puts one finger up to her mouth. Yeah, yeah, yeah. I hear you.

For the next fifteen minutes I have to sit and listen to both of these two switch-hitters going on about their 'negative experiences' of coming out. The room is quiet while all this is happening and everyone, especially Joolz, seems to be hanging on their every word.

"So for the next seven years," says swinger number two, "my sexual identity was lesbian, that's what I told people... I was scared to come out because of my own internalised bi-phobia..."

Bi-phobia. Is that even a real word?

I find myself drifting, wondering, how many people in this room are really one-hundred percent gay? I know I am. But maybe they have a point. Maybe. I mean, take a look at Zest, she's never kissed a girl and she says until she does she can't be sure. Then again, I've never kissed a guy so how do I really know? I guess sometimes you just do. A lot of people come out to their families at first as bisexual, just to soften the blow, but

I've never heard of anyone doing it the other way around.

"And when I finally told people, it was other lesbians, other gay people who had a problem with it. Even now, I still get people asking me when I am 'coming back out of the closet'."

She's right about that though. How many of the dykes I know – if I came out tonight and said that I wasn't gay anymore – how many of them would still want to know me? I think I could probably count them on one hand.

"So would you say that you had an equal attraction to both men and women?"

This is a Joolz question and is directed at the Chinese broad whose name is Sylvia Plath. This isn't her real name but the one she's chosen to be known as ever since she ditched her heterosexual identity.

"I would say that I'm more attracted to women and I prefer having relationships with women," says Sylvia.

"Why don't you just say you're a lesbian then?" Zest chips in.

Because she's a greedy bitch who can't make up her mind that's why! And it's kinda fashionable to do the Anne Heche thing. What a bore this is.

Finally, Sylvia stands up and goes over to the flip chart and then she asks us all to shout out all the things we've ever heard said about swingers:

Greedy	Like a bit of both
Want their cake and eat it	Pan-sexual
Batting for both teams	Omni-sexual
Swingers	Swing both ways
Sleep with anything that moves	
Best of both worlds	Threesomes
Bi-curious	Non-monogamous
Straight	Kinky
Gay	High sex drive
Confused	Nymphomaniac
Sitting on the fence	Indecisive
Sexual tourist	Polyamorous
AIDS	Orgies
Promiscuous	Not fussy

Not fussy. I like that one. That's my favourite one. I smile to myself, wishing I had thought that up.

"What's pole-im-or-us?" Zest shouts.

"Poly-amorous," smiles Sylvia Plath. "Whose word was that?"

Of course, it would have to be Joolz.

"It means 'loving many'," she says, looking smug as she is asked to explain it. "It means that you can have more than one partner at the same time and they can have more than one partner and sometimes they all sort of interact and swap– "

"What, like swinging parties?" I say. I've got the urge to start singing that song from *Jungle Book*.

Oo oo oo, I wanna be like you oo oo...

"It's not exactly swinging," she says, avoiding my eye.

"What is it then?" I say. "How can you say that you ain't a swinger if you swap– "

Joolz's face is flushed and her eyes are blazing. If looks could kill and all that... I continue to watch her out of the corner of my eye, picking at her watchstrap as she tries to explain what her word really means. "Polyamory means... It means... It's like..."

Ha! Go suck an egg, bitch. You do not know what you are talking about.

I pull my top up over my mouth to hide my smile. If I start laughing, I think I might piss myself.

"Polyamory means a relationship which has more than two adults," jumps in Kat. "The word comes from the Greek root 'poly' which means 'many' and the Latin 'amor' which means 'love'."

I turn around and stare at Kat. "Who's been feeding you the Dyke-tionary?"

She ignores me and continues. "So Julie is right in the sense that it does mean loving many or many loves but it isn't necessarily swinging because swinging is about recreational sex." Joolz's face has returned to its original smugness. Her mouth is a light pink curving slit that looks like someone has drawn it on with a magic marker and it won't come off. "Someone who is polyamorous," says Kat, "believes in an open relationship and can have several long-term romantic relationships at the same time. Isn't that right?" She turns to Sylvia who nods and says, "I couldn't have said it better myself, Kat."

☞ ♥ ☜

At break time, I plan to go over and talk to Kat to find out why she deliberately made me look like an asshole in there, but she walks right past me in a mood, disappearing outside with Joolz for a smoke.

I don't want it to seem like I'm stalking either of them, so I go down the stairs as if I'm going to the toilet. I get caught up in a conversation with The Hat about how wasted she was at the weekend and how she lost her favourite grey tweed trilby, and when I come back upstairs everyone has already gone back inside as the workshop is resuming. I think Kat is pissed off with me for something, probably something Joolz has said, because every time I catch her eye she turns her head so that her hair covers her face.

I wonder if Joolz is really bisexual, or thinks she might be, because when the workshop starts up again she looks as though she's deeply engrossed in what this Plath woman is saying, while I can't concentrate on anything apart from the back of Joolz's neck.

☞ ♥ ☜

"So do you have like a type or anything?" I hear Joolz ask as everyone is leaving.

Oh my god, she doesn't fancy Plath does she? How could she possibly like that shaven egg-head and those big wooden Oxfam earrings? Anyway, what do I care?

I do care.

I love the sound of her voice. I love the way her mouth moves when she speaks. I love the way her ass moves in those tight jeans.

I should really go talk to her. After all, I did invite her. Besides, I really couldn't give a shit what persuasion she is anymore, if only she would fancy me. Even if she was straight like my very first girlfriend was – and I said I was never going down that road again – it wouldn't matter as long as she didn't want a threesome. I mean, I guess there ain't anything wrong with a threesome if everyone concerned is happy, but I'd be too worried to have one in case I was the one sitting there reading the newspaper.

"I like feminine men and feminine women," smiles Sylvia. "But I don't sit down and think 'oh, today I'm going out to look for a guy and tomorrow I'll look for a woman.'"

"Fall for the person not the gender," I quip. Joolz turns around and draws me another dirty look as I throw her a smile. She is one hot bitch.

"Hey Vick," shouts The Hat. "You coming to the pub?"

Thursday nights after the group, us L.I.P.S. girls always go to Sandra Dee's. There are about fourteen of us going to Sandy's tonight but we lose a couple of bodies on the way in because of some big gay.com reunion. I say I'll catch everyone up later. I'm more interested in keeping an eye on Joolz.

I saw the way they all crowded around her earlier in the archive. She seemed to fit in really well. And even though all she was doing was writing her name, it felt, somehow, as though she was stealing my crown. I had kinda hoped she'd be all shy and submissive and maybe even threaten not to come back to the group because of me, and then I would have to go over and say to her: "Hey, stick with me. I know it's hard being the new kid, and I know we ain't exactly got off on the right foot but..." And then I'd sweep her of her feet.

"Hey Romeo! What you having?" Shouts Minty as she lumbers over towards me wearing her new Puddle of Mudd t-shirt.

"Black and jack," I tell her, "same-same."

"You want ice?"

"Yeah," I nod, as I watch Joolz and Kat disappear downstairs to the toilets together. I want to know what they've been saying about me.

I switch on my cellphone. I've three new messages: one from Mikki Blue saying that she would see me in the pub after L.I.P.S., one from Zest quoting a line from the play, and one from Joolz, telling me that she would meet me inside the archive.

Sitting down, I begin to finger the buttons.

~~Hey Juliet hope u enjoyd LIPS?~~

~~Hey glad u cam 2 LIPS?~~

~~U gonna com 2 LIPS again?~~

Sigh.

I start again. But this time I press **SEND** instead of **CANCEL** and my cheesiest chat-up line of all time is whisked off towards Joolz's phone.

`Hi, can I buy you a kiss … I mean … a drink ;o)`

Approximately eight seconds later my phone beeps in response.

"Bing-ba-da-boom! It worked! She replied to my text message!"

Minty shakes her head at me. "Sad bastard," she says. "You're pure fucked-up in head." I ignore her. I'm too happy, too busy staring into my phone to listen. "Catch," she says, and slides a pint across the table.

"Hey, I asked for Jack Daniels."

"Well it's fucking happy hour and I'm skint. So you can take it or leave it, man," she says. "See you later, man, I'm going to find myself a burd."

The place is pandemonium tonight because of the reunion. I see Mikki Blue Eyes with her ex-girlfriend and her new girlfriend and her ex's new girlfriend, who I've just realised is actually Kat's ex-girlfriend. They are lining up shot glasses on a table, and Mel and Cherie are there too, except it doesn't look like they are drinking anything other than bottled water. Cherie has apparently got them both on the Atkins diet.

Joolz and Kat come back upstairs and Joolz says she would like a Malibu. Well, her text message says she would like a Malibu because she still hasn't actually spoken to me in person. She looks at me, and smiles a bit, and then she sits in the seat across from me, next to Kat, but still she doesn't say a word.

I go up to the bar and I'm third in line, but even though I'm standing right up at the front, the guy that's serving looks straight past and serves the gay boy behind me. This goes on for about ten minutes until I elbow the next guy in the ribs who tries to step forward into my place and say: "Hey, am I invisible or something?"

The guy behind the bar just stares at me and then someone says, "It's OK, I'll get this one – what can I get you, Romeo?" It's Scarface. I almost don't recognise her because of her new purple punk spikes. They clash with the red shirt that all the bar staff wear.

"When did you start working here?"

She says one night last week, although she can't remember exactly which night. Fuck's sake, I'll never see the back of her now.

Kat comes up from behind me at the bar. "You want a Smirnoff Ice?"

"No," she groans. "I'm off the drink. I'll get a bottle of water later."

Kat's trying to lose some weight. She's another one who's on some newfangled diet plan that she got from a hetty health magazine. The Carol Vordemam diet or something. Mostly vegan. I think she's crazy but at least someone's eating all those tofu pizzas that Ma keeps sending over.

"So," I say to Kat, as Scarface seeks assistance to find the ice cubes. "What was all that about in the archive?"

"All what?" she says, "I don't know what you're talking about. You'll have to be a bit more specific."

"All that poly-walrus shit," I say. "Why the fuck did you get on my case about that? And how did Sylvia Wannabe-a-Dead-Poet know your name?" Scarface pushes two dribbling tumblers towards me. "Bottle of mineral water as well," I tell her and turn back to Kat, "you made me look like an ass in front of Juliet."

"Vicky," she replies, "you were acting like a total arsehole."

Scarface is leaning a little too heavily into our conversation. I flash her a smile and hand over a ten-pound note. "Whaddya mean I was acting like an asshole? Who are you calling an asshole?"

"I'm calling YOU an arsehole, Vicky, and I'm not the only person that thinks you were out of order."

"Oh, so now you're on a crusade to save the bisexuals?"

"Vicky, I don't know what your problem is but you'd better change your attitude or you'll be minus a few friends."

Scarface gives me a handful of dripping wet pound coins. I pocket them and don't bother thanking her, slipping the glasses off the edge of the table.

"Hey what's it to you, anyway?" I say as we are walking over to our table. She shrugs. "And you never said how you know that Sylvia freak."

"She's not a freak. And she happens to be a good friend."

"Well," I say, half-laughing, "you better watch or everyone will think you're one of them."

"One of what?" she says, irritably.

"Bisexuals."

"I AM 'one of them'."

"What did you just say?"

"I AM BISEXUAL."

Eleven

I can't believe that Kat is a swinger. How could I not know this? We've been friends for three years, jeezus. I can't believe she never told me. As I walk, slowly, towards the table, my legs feel hollow and it hurts deep in my chest thinking about all the other secrets she might have. It just goes to show that you can never trust anyone.

To take my mind off the situation, I start to bitch about Scarface:

"Last time at rehearsal she comes in and shows me this application form for Wetherspoons, and she says she don't know what to do with it. I want to tell her to shove it right up her ass, that's what I think she should do with it."

Kat and Joolz laugh and they both light a cigarette in tandem.

"Instead, I tell her that it's hardly rocket scientists they are looking for. And then she laughs. I don't think she catches my meaning. So I have a look at the form, there's nothing much to do except fill in your name, address, date of birth and previous place of employment. You know, the sort of thing a monkey could understand."

"That reminds me," says Joolz. I hate being interrupted, but because it's her, I don't say nothing. "I got a part in *Starlight Express*!"

Kat asks her if that's the show where they all wear roller skates, and Joolz says it is and starts talking about how her college class are doing it this year and how it's gonna be really cool.

"Is it a lesbian play?" I ask this cause I want to wind her up, not because I actually expect a 'yes' answer.

"No," says Joolz, coldly.

"Well, I won't be going then."

She ignores me. Then she turns to Kat and says: "You should come some night."

"Yeah, I think I just might."

Yeah, go find yourself a boyfriend. Turncoat.

"I'll ask Robbie."

I'm not really listening to what they're saying anymore. I'm getting impatient, I want to finish my story; I want to get Joolz's attention again, I want to make her listen to me.

"So anyway, Scarface says she knows the answers to all those questions. I say that's good, no problem. Then she says: 'But, I don't know what to put down for why I left my last job'."

"Aw how can you not know why you left your last job?" says Joolz. She says it without looking at me. "Is this girl a fucking retard or what?"

I hate the word 'retard' but again I let it slide.

"Have you met her?" Kat says to Joolz.

"No, but Ro– " She pauses then fixes her eyes on me. "Vicky," she continues, still staring, "told me a lot about her."

I'm determined to stare this chick out, to make her look away first, to make her eyelashes flutter.

"So I ask her," I say, coolly, "why did she leave her last job."

Joolz still never takes her eyes off me, but I've had years of experience in this game and I *will* crack her.

"And you know what she said?"

"No, tell me," says Kat, "before I go up to get another drink."

Joolz finally looks away, showing me the side of her defiant cheek. There is no victory in making her look away because she does it without blinking. She does it because she wants to; without moving her eyes she makes a quick ninety-degree turn of her head and neck, she does this to let me know that she's the one who's in control.

"What did she say then?" says Kat.

I resurrect the story, go back into spitting image mode, pushing my chin and my cheeks and my lips out as far as they can possibly stretch and dropping my voice to a Scarface-esque monotone: "Cause the staff were a bunch of fan-nies."

They both laugh, although Joolz tries hard not to.

"I advised her not to write that on her application form."

"Oh my god," says Kat, "you sounded just like her. You should write a script about how you met her."

"Or," says Joolz , "she could always write a script about how she met me."

☞ ♥ ☜

The atmosphere is charged now that Kat has gone. One by one, our friends have slowly dwindled, leaving us to sit by ourselves. And this is no accident. I can see Mikki Blue Eyes, Mel and Sweet Cherie all giving us sneaky sideways glances, none of them wanting to come over to our table in case they get caught in the crossfire.

So far, Joolz and I have managed to ignore or talk around one another, but the sexual tension surrounding us is growing. It's just like when we met for the first time, I feel weakened in her company.

Why does she have to look so god damn amazing?

I watch her as she lights another cigarette, blows smoke in her own eye and then waves her hand in front of her face. I pick up her lighter and begin to play with it, flicking it on and off and changing the size of the flame. It's the silver torso-shaped one that JJ gave her.

"Nice tits," I mumble. I can feel her eyes on me, undressing me, looking me up and down. This continues for about five minutes before she takes another cigarette from her packet, and seeing as I'm still holding my new toy, allows me the honour of lighting it for her.

"Don't say hello then, Ro-me-o." She smiles, sarcastically, rolling her tongue around the 'R' in 'Romeo' as she exhales, emphasizing my name as if she were hinting that I'd double-crossed her. As if I'd taken part in some subterfuge and known all along that she, Joolz, Julie Turner, was the same Juliet that I'd been intimate with in cyber space.

"Hello then," I reply, shortly. "Miss *non*-smoker." She doesn't blink, she doesn't smile or move her mouth; she has absolutely no reaction to this comment. "So... You're a cheerleader these days," I say.

"I *am* a cheerleader."

"Show us your pom-poms then."

"Show *me* your feckin equity card."

I am not used to playing games. I like to get straight to the point and I like women who tell me what they want, right away. The conversation grows stale again, with Joolz alternating between looking at her fingernails and her cigarette packet. I wish Kat would hurry up, she still hasn't come back from the bar and it's been more than ten minutes. I look over at the drinks queue but I can't see her, and then my eye falls on the gay.com table. Kat gives me a wink and a wave as she turns to whisper something in Minty's ear.

My phone begins to ring, crying loudly to the theme of *The Godfather*.

"Hel-lo?"

I just can't get you outta my head...

"Hang on two seconds–" I go outside because I can't make out a word the guy is saying as the DJ has chosen this precise moment to turn up the background sound of Kylie Minogue. It turns out it's only the BT operator who's been hassling me for weeks with new offers to update my phone. "No, I'm sorry, it ain't convenient to talk," I say, clicking off the handset. "And it never will be. Schmuck."

☞ ♥ ☜

I go back inside and Joolz is still sitting on her own, pouring something orange from a cocktail jug.

"What's your poison?" I say.

"Fuck knows," she shrugs, twirling a cherry that is speared on the end of a cocktail stick. "Polo fruit or whatever her name is," she nods her head in the direction of the gay.com table, "she gave us it."

"Minty," I say, "her name's Minty."

"What's her real name?"

I grin. "I can't say. That's classified information."

Joolz says something I don't hear. She looks well on her way to getting wasted. I'm a bit light-headed myself. I smile at her and she shrugs again. "She better not have put anything in it."

"Nah, she ain't like that." Joolz holds a glass out to me and I take a swig. "Come fuck me," I say to her.

"I beg your pardon?"

"It's called 'Come Fuck Me' punch." I tell her. "Southern Comfort, grenadine, amaretto and orange juice."

She picks up the cocktail menu.

"Have you ever had a quick fuck?" she asks, stroking the cherry with the tip of her tongue.

"Yeah," I reply, leaning forward in my seat, "but I much prefer a long, slow, comfortable screw against the wall."

Our eyes are locked now, staring at each other across the table.

"But what I really want," she says, "is a screaming orgasm."

"Anytime, baby."

She ignores my comment and pours herself a drink, and then asks who was on the phone. "BT Cellnet."

"Oh, exciting stuff," she says and begins to snicker, hiccuping into her glass.

"Told him to fuck off, I was busy. I hate those guys. They keep calling me."

"Ooooooh, a wanted woman! Must be because you are soooo sexy!"

I ignore her and go off into a little sideways rant: "And I hate the ones that phone you up about double-glazing and fitted kitchens. Ma always lets them talk for ages, running up their phone bill, then tells them she doesn't need new windows, she lives in an igloo. I hate door-to-door salespeople. I hate surveys. I hate the frigging charity muggers who hi-jack you in the street – not the ones who stand outside Safeway rattling cans because I always give them spare change – the ones that have a different green or orange bib on every day of the week. Monday is Barnardos, Tuesday is Shelter, Wednesday is Animal Aid and so on. They come at you with their clipboards, chasing you along the road..."

"Well," says Joolz, "I'll give you an even fucking better one than that– " Her hand twitches as she lifts the jug to fill our glasses again; I reach over and steady it for her. "Cheers," she says. "Yeah, this guy, this fucking hippy Christian guy stops me four times today in fucking Ar-gyll street..."

I love the way she says *Arrrrr-gyll*, her mouth opening out into a huge, wide cavernous shape; her tongue dipping and falling as she rolls it around the *r*, same as she did before when she said my name. I pick her lighter up from the table and begin rolling my thumb over it again. R. R. Rrrrr.

"Romeo," she says, "are you listening?"

I love the way she says it: *R-rrrrom-ee-o.*

She takes the last cigarette from the carton, puts it in her mouth and stares at me.

"Wha?" I say. "Wassamaddawitchoo now?"

Joolz reaches over and prises the lighter from between my fingers. Her own hand is icy cold, probably because of the ice in her drink, but I want her to go on touching my hand. I want to take her hand in mine. I want to press the back of her hand against my lips.

She lights the cigarette, takes a drag, exhales, and then leans in towards me. My heart thuds and I can feel my bottom lip tremble slightly. I think she's going to kiss me, I'm sure she's going to kiss me and I'm not used to broads making the first move. Instead, all she does is hold out her hand to me and press the cigarette to my lips.

I take a quick puff and then another. I don't even know why I do it cause I never liked smoking. I tried it once as a kid and threw up straight afterwards. But tonight, I do it, and you know what, it feels liberating. It feels sexy.

"Whit ye daein Romeo, ya fucking fanny," shouts Minty as she swaggers over towards our table. Leaning right into my face, I catch a whiff of beer on her breath as she says: "You don't smoke." She takes the cigarette from my mouth and puts it in her own and walks off.

"Cunt," mutters Joolz, then she adds, "what does her t-shirt say?"

"Pud of muddle... I mean puddle of muddle... Sorry, Puddle of Mudd..."

"Fucking puddle of shite," she laughs then hiccups. "Big mad fucking mud monster." I ain't sure why but I begin laughing as well. "That's what I'm going to call her from now on," says Joolz. "The mud monster."

Joolz says that she has to go to the cigarette machine and asks me if I want another drink. I notice that the cocktail jug is completely empty and I can't believe we've finished it already, it's only half past ten.

It's only when Joolz goes back over to the bar and Minty leaves with some broad she's pulled that I realise I have no house keys. Kat has disappeared too, but I'm not worried because, if worst comes to worst, I can find a friend's house to crash in or go down to Café Insomnia and drink coffee till dawn.

There's no point in asking Joolz if I can stay at her place. Even if she didn't slap my face for asking, I know there's no way her Ma would let me in the house.

I think tonight is finally picking up, though. I mean, if she weren't at least a tiny bit interested, surely she would've left by now?

I can't take my eyes off her. She's standing at the bar talking to Mikki Blue Eyes who is just in front of her in the queue. They're laughing at something. I hope it ain't me. They'd better not be laughing at me.

Mikki settles her bill then comes over to my table. "Alright Romeo?" she says. "You having a good time?" I tell her I am. She says she hopes I'm behaving myself and I say what's that supposed to mean. She winks at me. Then Joolz returns with our drinks and Mikki starts telling her to have a good night too, and not to do anything she wouldn't do.

☞ ♥ ☜

We drink some more and flirt some more and then two random gay guys ask if it's ok to share our table. It's a quarter to eleven and I notice Sandy's is getting crowded, so I suggest we go upstairs for a game of pool.

I can't believe it when she tells me she's never played before.

"Is this how you do it?" she says, holding the cue in a vice-like grip.

"You need to relax your right hand a bit more," I tell her. "You wanna hold it firm enough so that it doesn't slide around in your fingers, but you don't wanna make it too tight or you'll stiffen up all your muscles."

I put my arm around her waist to try and help her, but she wriggles away saying, "Ha. That's just an excuse so you can touch me. Rrrrrr-o-me-o."

She clips a few balls and pots the white.

"Ok my turn," I say. "Here, I'll show you."

She gives me the cue, notices that I'm left handed.

"Ambidextrous in certain situations," I grin.

She gives me a salacious smile. "Isn't everyone?"

I lean over the table. Take aim. Sink one. I can feel her hot breath on my neck and I'm pretty sure that she blew deliberately in my ear to try and make me miss.

I'm starting to get sober now and I want to kiss her but there never seems to be a right moment. There is always someone hovering round about us, or a shitty song is playing. I want the mood to be right. How are you supposed to kiss when someone's singing – *a friend with weed is a friend indeed*?

Finally, Atomic Kitten comes on singing 'Whole Again'. That's more like it. Music's a bit loud, and it's not exactly seduction material, but it's way better than the previous shit. Here I go. Perfect. I am standing right next to her. I go to lean in, and she leans in, and then she shouts right in my ear:

"DO YOU NOT JUST FAA-ACKING HATE THIS SONG?"

She asks me if I was going to say something there. I just tell her that she should aim for the orange ball nearest the corner pocket. I'm not sure she even likes me after all. I feel like such a jerk. And I can't help but get the feeling that she's deliberately sending me out mixed messages, playing a cat and mouse game.

I let her win at pool – well, she pots the black ball but I tell her that she's won. I get ready for another slagging match about my pool-playing prowess but she seems to have run out of cheeky comments. I am about to give her a kiss to say congratulations but then I pussy out and just shake her hand instead.

She looks disappointed. Maybe I should've given her a peck on the cheek or something. But, maybe she wouldn't want our first kiss to be in a bar? Maybe she wants to make it really special?

It's twenty to twelve, she sends me to the bar again and when I come back I decide I'm gonna ask her out on a proper date.

There are still three balls on the table and I'm about to roll them down into the pockets when Joolz stops me. She leans over the table in front of me then – pop – pop – pop – she sinks all three. She takes both glasses from my hand, downs the shot of Sambuca she asked for and chases it with *my* glass of water.

"Ready," she says. "Get me my coat."

I'm standing there open-mouthed, thinking waddafuck just happened, and she gives me a grin and goes, "Oh, I forgot to say... I'm left-handed too."

☞ ♥ ☜

Outside the rain is pounding off the sidewalk. We run around the corner and join the conga line outside Bennet's.

"You got an umbrella or something?" Joolz shakes her head. She is only wearing this skinny little white throw-over thing, which is already beginning to suck up all the rain. "Here," I say, "take my coat."

I curl the warm thick leather up over her head like a shelter. Dad used to always do that to me when I was younger. He used to take me to the park and Ma would go daft cause I'd be out 'half-naked'. That was when he was sober. Once in a blue moon like.

I look at Joolz and then back at the snaking queue. Wish I could just whisk you away from here, babe.

I can see Minty, Kat and Mikki who are half-way up and they signal for us to jump in.

"Fuck it, I can't be arsed with this," says Joolz. "Just take me home."

I am totally taken aback by this because I really thought she was up for staying out all night. So, I guess she's not interested in me after all?

"Wait, we can skip in with them– "

I really don't want her to leave tonight and I figure I should try one last time to get her to stay. If she goes home now I might never see her again.

"Just take me HOME!" She grabs my hand, pulling backwards

and out onto the middle of the road where she manages to flag a black hackney.

"Listen babe, I've got no house keys," I begin. "I need to see if I can borrow some from– "

"For fuck's sake," she hisses, then adds softly, "come home with *me*."

My heart lurches in my chest. I open my mouth to speak – I'm not sure if I'm reading this right – but I hope to god I am, I just don't want to fuck it all up like the last time.

"Are you getting in or not, mate?" The taxi driver grunts. "We're not even supposed to stop here."

With one hand on the taxi door, Joolz grabs my waist with her free hand and pulls me towards her, breathing into my ear: "Spend the night with me." We both topple into the taxi and the guy puts his foot down. Our bodies knock together like skittles, and then Joolz pulls my face towards her and we kiss.

"Shhhh," giggles Joolz as we tumble out onto her front porch. "Everyone's in bed." I catch my breath leaning against the red brick wall as she fumbles around in her handbag looking for her keys. "Got them," she says, and she wiggles something sharp and shiny under my nose.

The main door creaks open and she whispers at me to remove my shoes and *quietly* come inside, except it's her who's making all the noise. I slip my sneakers off and carry them in my right hand, she squeezes my left and leads me along a hall that has a squeaky floor. It's so dark I can hardly see where I'm going.

As we come to a second door, which is slightly ajar, Joolz pauses with her fingers on the handle, and I can see over her shoulder a television screen, a sofa and a coffee table. Jeezus, this ain't even her bedroom. I guess I'll be sleeping alone then. I expected too much. What a schmuck. What a dumb-ass. Dream on, Romeo.

Joolz pulls me closer towards her, kissing me, dragging me inside.

"What if someone..."

"Sssshhh," she says, "it's through here." She points to yet

another door leading off from the living room. I hadn't noticed that, I guess it must have been a sort of dining area at one point and they've converted it into an extra bedroom. I stumble after her, trying to walk on my tiptoes.

Joolz closes her bedroom door behind us and I pull her hand to my mouth and kiss each finger slowly, in turn, and then I kiss the back of her hand, just like a gent would do. "Are you sure you wanna do this?" I want her so much but I'm giving her a get out. I'm trying to let her know that I'm a good guy and I don't mind. I'm trying to tell her that I respect her and that I wouldn't do anything to disrespect her, that I would be happy just to talk all night, I would be happy just to kiss her hand, just to hold her like this.

I can't believe I'm here, in Joolz's house, in her bedroom. Waking up with her would be like waking up and finding out the Easter bunny was real. Any minute now, she's going to sober up and tell me to take a hike.

"Kiss me," she mumbles and pulls me towards her. Hey, what can I do? Her hands are all over me. I keep asking her if she's sure she really wants this, if she wants to stop at any time. She rubs herself up against me, making my heart speed up inside my chest, and I can hardly breathe, her kisses are like dynamite and I feel like I'm about to ignite.

She runs her hands over my ass cheeks and then the zip of my pants. "Take these off," she whispers.

"Uh-uh," I say, "I can't do that." She takes hold of my t-shirt with one hand, wrinkling the logo, except now I don't even care. I'm sure it would look much nicer on her bedroom carpet anyway.

Joolz pushes me backwards, down onto the bed with her hands on my breasts pinning me down and tickling. I'm used to being the one on top, so it's kinda weird, but kinda nice. I fold my arms behind my head and let her play. I let her ruffle my hair and run her hands under my t-shirt and I even let her kiss my belly button. But when she tries to unzip my pants again, I push her hands back and lean in to kiss her. She sighs as I work my hand up under her top and search for the hook of her bra – but then I realise she's not wearing any bra – I cup her breasts and slowly push her t-shirt up over her head, letting it drop down onto the floor.

She tells me that she never wears a bra and this surprises me. I thought all femmes wore bras. She says only on special occasions. "Like weddings and funerals."

I laugh and take my t-shirt off, she wants to play with my nipples. It amuses me, for no girl has ever given them this much attention.

She has such an amazing body. "You have the world's most perfect breasts," I tell her.

"They're fucking lopsided," she says. "One's bigger than the other." I shake my head and smile at her, but I guess she can't see me cause it's so dark. I tell her that her breasts are beautiful, that she's beautiful.

Joolz takes my hand and guides it down towards her pussy. I slip two fingers inside her, slowly, gently, scared of tearing her. Her insides are so soft, so warm, it's like they've been upholstered in silk.

"Deeper," she gasps. "Harder." The fact that she knows exactly what she wants turns me on so much. I put one more finger inside her. I can feel her skin tight around my fingers like a mouth, sucking, trying to swallow me.

"Does this hurt?" I ask. "I don't want to hurt you."

She gyrates against my hand. "Fuck. Me. Har-der."

I can't believe she just used the F word to me. I've never used the F word to a broad. Not in a sexual situation. I always say I'm 'making love'.

"I'm gonna fuck you so hard, Romeo," Joolz says to me. "I'm gonna fuck you so hard." She puts her hand down the inside of my thigh but I pull my body away from her. "Take these jeans off," she says. I tell her no. I tell her it's her night. It's her night and I want to make her orgasm.

I kiss her again and I imagine my entire hand, my entire self, inside Julie Turner. I imagine my hand is a revolver and I'm sliding it in and out of a leather holster. My hand is a cold, hard steel cylinder, and it cannot bend or break. I'm holding it up to someone's mouth and I'm about to pull the trigger, this gun is gonna make someone explode.

"Are you OK?" This is about the tenth time I've asked her this question. She must think I'm such a jerk. I can't help it, as soon as I got into bed with her the whole Godfather act just fell apart and I became a pussycat.

"Uh-huh," she murmurs. "Are *you* ok?"

She reaches over and presses on her bedside lamp.

"Yup," I smile at her, my eyes dewy with tears. Her head is rested on the pillow, her hair splayed out like a giant red-gold halo.

"Then why do you look like you're about to cry?"

"Because, Joolz," I whisper, "I think I'm falling in love with you."

The words come flying out of my mouth before I can stop them. I know I've said the wrong thing because she can't even make eye contact with me now. We kiss some more and talk some more and touch some more and then she says we should probably get some sleep. I can't help how I feel. I had to tell her. Well, if she says anything about it tomorrow, I can always just say it was the alcohol talking.

I slip between her thighs and she wraps her legs around my waist, drawing me closer towards her chest. I kiss her breasts again, slowly sucking her stiff, beige nipples.

"Where," she gasps, "do you think you're going?"

Down, down, I trace the line of her breastbone with my lips, surrounding the coil of her perfect tummy button that has been pierced with a blue gemstone shaped like a firefly. She squeezes my hand as my cheeks brush against the insides of her thighs and I can feel the warmth of her, slick and wet, as I nuzzle the copper curls of her pubic mound, before making love to her once more, with my tongue.

Afterwards, we lie with our legs entwined – her naked, me just in my boxer shorts. She sleeps face down between my breasts while I look up at the ceiling, stroking her long glossy mane of hair and thinking about how this has been the most amazing, most passionate night of my life.

Twelve

It's Friday morning, seven-ish, and Joolz and I are kissing as though we're trying to suck the life outta each other. We've been awake for ages and we've bypassed all the 'oh-my-god-last-night-was-wow' and 'I-can't-believe-it-was-you-online-how-did-I-not-guess' and now we've come full circle.

This feels so good. She feels so good. I want her so badly all over again. I'm running my hands through her hair, down her neck, her back, her tits, her hips – oh my god she's so fucking sexy. I'm on top of her and I'm parting her thighs with my knee and–

"Vicky, we can't."

"Aw baby, just please let me..."

I move to kiss her again but she ducks away.

"Believe me," she says, tugging a stray curl behind her ear. "It is *not* that I don't want you to."

"So let me."

I push her down onto her back again and trap her there with my pelvis.

"You're terrible," she giggles.

"You love it."

"I do," she says. And our mouths meet again, tongues touching, hips grinding, and my hand is moving south... "But we can't."

She pushes me over.

"Aww."

"You have to go, Vicky."

I make a sad face.

"I'm sorry. I don't want you to go... It's just..."

"I know."

"Anyway, I thought you had work?"

"I do."

Footsteps padding down the hall.

"Ju-lie?" says a female voice. "Are you awake?"

Joolz holds a finger to my mouth.

"Yep, I'm just up. Don't come in, I'm getting changed."

"What time did you get in at last night?" says the voice behind the door. It's stern and disapproving, but then it is her Ma's house and she's entitled to make the rules.

"Emm, just after eleven."

"Pants on fire," I whisper.

"Shh."

Silence. Footsteps retreat.

I grin. "That was close."

"You really, really have to go..."

"Uh-huh."

I lean over to kiss her one last time.

"Now," she says, firmly.

"You're the boss," I say, getting up. My clothes are in a crumpled heap on her floor, and when I bend to pick them up she slaps my ass and says: "And don't you forget it."

"Ju-lie here's your..."

Joolz's bedroom door yawns open and her mother shuffles forward with a pile of clothes.

"I SAID DON'T COME IN!"

"Ironing."

Joolz scrambles under the bedcovers, pulling them up to her chin. And I clamp my arms across my chest, but its too late cause Joolz's Ma has already seen everything.

We stand staring at each other: me with my hair all mussed up, wearing nothing but my boy boxer shorts, and her in a pencil skirt and a white cashmere cardigan. She looks like an older, skinnier version of her daughter, but with shorter hair and crow's feet, and obviously she's not as gorgeous.

A thought runs through my mind that it would be polite to say hello and introduce myself. But my throat has gone dry all of a sudden and I am frozen to the spot.

Finally Joolz speaks: "Mum, this is my friend, Vicky."

Joolz's room looks different in the morning light. Before it was all just bumps and shadows, now it's an explosion of colour with pop posters lining the walls and clothes and shoes strewn across the floor. Not that I had time to look around last night. But now all I got is time. I'm sitting on the edge of her bed with my arms folded, wearing yesterday's stinky crinkled slacks and t-shirt, and wondering what her Ma is saying to her and when she's coming back.

Normally, in a situation like this, I woulda flown the coop. I woulda been long gone out the bedroom window, shinning down the drainpipe as soon as she turned her back. But I don't want it to be like that with her. I don't wanna leave Joolz in the lurch. Besides, how bad could things really get with her family?

I look around, sucking in every tiny detail. I wanna know all there is to know about this girl. And I can't believe how untidy her room is: paperback novels with broken spines, soft toys thrown everyplace, several pairs of high-heeled shoes upended, and a pair of dirt encrusted army-style boots that I cannot imagine her wearing.

Her make-up table is the worst though (I don't know how she finds anything): nail polish bottles with no lids, a jewellery box with necklaces spilling from the lid, photo frames, used tissues, cotton buds, eye pencils, loose change, hair brushes, an egg cup that's been used as an ash tray, and that torso-shaped cigarette lighter.

I stand up to look at her bookcase. She's got everything from Byron's poetry and Charles Dickens, to Elizabeth Wurtzel's *Prozac Nation* and *The Little Book of Stupid Men*. There are also a few raunchy titles in the corner of the bottom shelf: *Macho Sluts*, *Eating Mango* and *The Mammoth Book of Lesbian Short Stories*. On the floor, next to the bookcase, she has a life-size, semi-naked cardboard cut-out of a pouting Britney Spears. How the hell could her Ma not know?

Through the wall, I can hear raised voices:

"What do you mean 'why'?" shouts Joolz. "Why am I gay? Why do I fancy girls? Why what?"

There is a sound of crashing pots and pans and 'shit' and 'now look what you've made me do.'

Joolz's Ma is saying over and over that she can't believe it – she can't believe that Joolz has done this to her, has done this to her family. She's guilt-tripping her, telling her that she's being stupid and selfish and not thinking about anyone else's feelings. How is this gonna affect all the other important people in her life? What is she gonna tell Joolz's father about all this? What is she gonna tell her gran? Her gran's not fit for a shock like this. It could give her another heart attack. And what are the neighbours gonna think?

"Who gives a fuck about the stupid neighbours?"

"Julie, don't speak to me like that."

Silence.

Then:

"It's all those queer folk you've been hanging around with."

"Aww for God's sake!"

"I've said it time and time again – you're very easily led."

"Did you never wonder, mum, just why I'm hanging around with 'all those queer folk'?"

The voices grow quiet. I have to strain to hear what they're saying and I keep missing bits of the conversation.

"Mum, don't say that," says Joolz. "Mum, please, she'll hear you." There's a tremor in her voice and the threat of a sob. My own throat tightens and I clench my jaw. I want to run to her, and hug her, and protect her.

"Mum, I don't know why you're being like this."

I press my ear up against the wall.

Joolz's mother is telling her how disgusted she is. How could she bring someone like that – like me – into the home? And with her younger sister in the next room!

"She's seventeen," says Joolz. "Somehow I think she knows what a lesbian is."

"*Lesbian*!" shrieks her mother. "So you're a *lesbian* now?"

"That's what I've been trying to tell you."

"I want that *person*," she spits, "out of my house."

"Mu-um!"

"I mean it Julie," she says, "by the time I get back."

Silence again. Then footsteps. I jump aside and pretend I'm studying her book collection. Joolz comes in and shuts the door behind her.

"Did you hear that?" she says.

"Yeah," I nod. "Pretty much." My face is burning.

"I'm sorry," she says. Her eyes are red and puffy from crying.

"Hey, it's ok."

"No, it's really not." She sniffs.

I want to give her a hug but I'm not sure if it's what she wants.

"My mum's a cunt," she says.

"I thought she was your best friend?"

"Still a cunt."

The front door slams shut.

"Hold me?" she whispers.

I wrap my arms around her, fiercely.

She cries.

I squeeze her tight.

"It'll be ok, baby," I tell her. "The worst is over. I promise. There is nothing anyone can do to hurt us."

She looks at me, uncertainly, and then she smiles, and I kiss away her tears.

And in this moment, I really believe that what I'm saying is true.

Joolz drives me to the taxi rank just outside Central Station. She says she'd take me all the way to Paisley but she has to get back and face the music. I tell her it's fine. "I don't know if Mamma's home anyway," I say, "and if she is, well, I think we've had enough meet-the-parents scenarios for one day."

She gives me a long, slow kiss as I'm getting outta the car.

"I'll text you this afternoon," she says.

"Promise?"

She mimes a cross on her heart.

"You're beautiful," I tell her.

"No, you are."

This makes me laugh, and it comes out in a kind of high-pitched giggle cause 'beautiful' is not a word that has ever been used to describe me.

"Till we meet again, sweet Romeo."

She shuts the door and drives off.

I'm so happy right now I feel I could leap tall buildings. I even attempt to do that jumping in the air and clicking my heels together thing that you see people doing in movies, but I give up when I start getting odd looks. I'm so so fucking crazy about this girl. I wanna shout it from the rooftops. I wanna post it on billboards. It's been a helluva long time since anyone made me feel like this.

It's a pain in the ass having to go all the way to Paisley though. And Ma had better be in or else left the spare key under the plant pot. Cause if not, I'm fucked. Cause Kat and Robbie are both at work and Minty is no doubt hooked up in some chick's flat cause she's not replied to my text messages. And Maggie would have a triple canary if I called in sick today.

As I walk through the station towards platform twelve, I pass a young broad of around sixteen or seventeen selling flowers from a white trailer. I stop to buy a bunch of giant daisies, chrysanthemums I think they're called. "That's right, chrysanthemums," she nods, and she smiles at me, she has a pretty smile.

It helps to be familiar with these little details, for most femmes are easily impressed. I must remember to send out that email questionnaire to Joolz, the one that asks 'what kind of flowers do you like best?' and 'what's your favourite gem stone?'

I pay for the chrysanthemums and the broad wraps them twice, first in white paper and then in a sheet of cellophane. "Are they for your girlfriend?" she asks.

"My mother," I say.

"That's nice," she says. "I wish someone would buy me flowers." With a smile and a 'have a nice day' I take one of the 'daisies' from the bouquet and I give it to her.

I call Ma when I'm on the train. No answer. Shit.

The journey takes ten minutes longer than usual because the train stops for ages at Hillington East and West and Cardonald, where a whole load of students come aboard with backpacks. A few of them give me stares because I am grinning like a goon, but I don't care.

I get off at Paisley Gilmour Street and pass the taxi rank with the new plastic shelter and the fountain that has just been built in honour of Prince Charles coming to visit. Then I cross the road and go by the Hippy Chippie, where a group of school kids are loitering outside throwing fish suppers at each other.

One kid shouts: "Hey, are you a boy or a lassie?"

I keep walking.

"Hey," he shouts again, "have you got a hot dog or a hamburger?"

There's an explosion of laughter behind me, followed by a few catcalls. Normally this kinda thing pisses me off but I just ignore them and keep on smiling, cause no way am I gonna let these idiots spoil my mood today.

A battered sausage whizzes past my head. More laughter. Then something warm and sticky hits the back of my neck. I jerk my arm up, a reflex, and get tomato ketchup all over my fingers. A half-eaten pie falls to the ground.

"Ho! Ya little shit! C'mere."

"Sorry big man, I mean big wummin, sorry." Footsteps slap against the pavement and this time I do look round because the voice I hear is Sam's.

"Fucking better run, ya wee bastard."

This is not the first time that Sam has stopped me from getting my head bashed in.

The first time was when I was fifteen. I was coming home from school one day when a group of kids, mostly all boys from the year below me, decided to use me as target practice for their rotten eggs.

At first I thought it was a random joke, that I was an easy hit because I was quiet and walking down the road on my own, until they began shouting things like 'dyke' and 'queer' and 'lesbo'. Now, I use these words all the time to describe myself, and my friends, but it doesn't feel so great when straight people do it (especially when you know they're not being friendly).

When I didn't turn around, one of the guys ran after me and shoved me hard in the back, the rest of them laughed as I landed on my hands and knees on the sidewalk. I didn't fight back. There were too many of them and things would just have gotten worse for me. But I didn't cry either or beg for mercy. I just lay there with my head down, while they pelted me with more eggs and more names.

"Get up, ya ugly fucking fanny basher!"

One of them, a guy called Psycho, grabbed me by the hair and yanked me backwards. Yolk got into my ears and up my nostrils, and the stench of it – oh boy.

"Fucking state of you," he said. "You're disgusting." He hit me three times in the face while the others watched; an old couple that were passing made some quiet comments about how terrible fighting was but they never made a move to stop him. He hit me a fourth time and blood exploded from my nose, spraying all over his hand and the cuffs of his white school shirt. He let go of my hair and I dropped to the ground. "Fucking dyke bitch," he said, and then he hawked up a huge ball of mucus and spit it square on my mouth.

"Ho!" A twenty-five-year-old Sam Haggarty sprinted across the turf towards where I lay surrounded by Psycho and his morons. She was one-hundred and sixty-five pounds of solid muscle, an amateur boxing coach for under-eighteens, and God help any bastard who got on the wrong side of her.

"Fuck!" someone shouted, and all those cowards took off in different directions.

"C'mon pal, up you get." Sam grabbed me under the armpits and hoisted me to my feet. Blood and yolk covered my white shirt and Sam did her best to wipe my face clean with a handkerchief.

I said I didn't know their names. I didn't recognise them. Sam nodded, she knew I was lying. She said she'd come to pick me up, take me out to see a movie as a surprise because Ma was going to an opera with her friend. Lucky for me that she did.

When we got home, Sam combed back my blood-stained hair, careful not to jab the gash above my left eyebrow, and then put me in a lukewarm bath of salts.

We made an agreement not to tell Mamma what happened.

"She would just get upset."

"Yeah," said Sam.

"And she would want to go up to the school and it would just make things worse."

Sam agreed. She had a far better idea on how to tackle the bullies.

☞ ♥ ☜

A week later, when my bruises had started to go down (we told Ma that I fell over on my roller blades), Sam took me to the YMCA boxing club where she coached twice a week after school.

She paired me up with a short, tubby, ginger kid. His name was Michael Goodie and I recognised him as being one of Psycho's goons. He'd been one of the first to split when Sam appeared, and now I understood why.

"Aww what's this?" whined Michael. "I'm not fighting a lassie."

"You're not fighting anyone," said Sam, and she threw two beaten-up leather hand pads to me.

"This is so gay," he muttered.

"Ok Vicky, I want you to call the shots," she said. "Just like we practiced."

Then she turned to Michael, whose face was purple as a plum. "Mikey, when Vicky shouts, I want you to aim for the centre of the pads."

Hook, jab, cross, uppercut, uppercut, straight... I called all the punches I could think of. Sweating, I held my arms up and stood my ground whilst Michael Goodie rained blow upon blow, grinning at me and trying his best to knock me off my feet.

Then we swapped over.

Michael smirked as I slipped on the sweaty, red pigskin gloves. They were miles too big and I lost my thumbs someplace inside.

"Is it true that you're a lezzie?"

Jab.

"Why do you want to know?"

Hook.

"I heard you like to munch the rug."

Miss.

He laughed and wiggled his tongue at me.

Miss again.

"Fuck off."

"C'mon Maaaann," he gloated. "Catch the fly, catch the fly." That was Sam's mantra and Michael was taking the piss. "You punch like a poof," he said to me, and I bit down on my bottom lip and swung hard at him.

"Jab, jab, upper, hook, jab – oops – forgot to say duck," he sniggered as he caught me on the side of the head. I rubbed my ear and clenched my other fingers tighter, ready to take a pop at his ugly, flat nose.

"You OK Vicky?" Sam asked. I told her I was, that it was just a dumb accident. She nodded and turned her back to speak to some other kid.

"Aye, away tae fuck ya big man," said Michael. I glared at him. "D'ye not find it weird living wi somebody like that?"

"Someone like what?" I said through gritted teeth as I hammered out four more straight punches.

"Yer maw's *pal*."

I ignored him, breathing heavy, stopping to readjust the straps on the boxing gloves. "I bet she straps one on at night," he said, pointing at Sam. "I bet your maw likes it when– "

SMACK.

I socked him right in the kisser and he went reeling back into a pile of skipping ropes. "Hey, calm down you guys," said Sam.

"That's it," said Michael, wiping a stripe of saliva away from his cheek. "Where's the headgear? I want to spar."

"I thought you didn't want to fight with girls?" said Sam.

"That's no a lassie, that's a pit bull."

I squared up to him with my eyes, my fists clenched into tight balls by my side. "Anytime, anyplace, anywhere..."

"I don't think it's a very good idea..." But Michael and I were already rummaging through the sports cupboard, pulling on the protective head guards. "OK, come over here then," Sam sighed. She drew out a six-by-six box with white masking tape on the floor. All the other guys stopped what they were doing and crowded around.

"This is the ring," she commanded. "And you *must* stay inside these lines." We both nodded and waited for Sam to blow the whistle.

HWEEE.

WHACK.

I wasn't ready. Michael caught me square on the chin. I could taste the iron on my lower lip. "Take it easy," said Sam, "you're not supposed to be killing each other."

I breathed hard then stood up tall. Michael swung his arm at me again. I weighed just under a hundred pounds while Michael was easily a hundred and twenty. He could pack a fair punch but he was slow. I ducked and he missed me and someone shouted 'hooray' from the sidelines. I smiled to myself as I continued to dance a jig around the back of Slow Poke, giving him a simultaneous slap to both ears as I did this. His face grew red and his freckles redder; sweat trickled down his cheeks and his lip trembled as he began breathing like an asthmatic. He had no stamina. I knew I could take him.

"C'mon fatboy," I grinned. His chest and shoulders plunged up and down whilst I skipped from foot to foot. "Wassamattawichoo? You ain't gonna let a dyke beat you are you?" He came swinging at me again like an orangutan having a fit.

"VICTORIA!"

I paused for a second, hearing Ma's voice, before realising my error – Michael Goodie clipped me on the side of the right temple and sent me flying backwards. But it wasn't his punch that finished me – no, it was the way I spun around and stumbled into the huge black punch bag. That was what knocked me out cold on the floor.

☞ ♥ ☜

Ma ranted and raved that night when we got home. I was not to go back to that club again. I said it was my choice and Sam stood by me, saying that it was important for me to learn how to defend myself. Ma said Sam was irresponsible and that I was grounded until further notice.

A week later, Sam erected a punch ball at the back of the door in our garden shed and she gave me her old bench set of weights. Mamma watched with pursed lips, saying nothing more on the subject.

I was still not allowed back to the YMCA, not even for a visit. But the next time Michael Goodie saw me in the playground, he turned on his heel without a word.

☞ ♥ ☜

Sam falls into step with me, holding her chest. I slow my walk. "Nice to see you," she wheezes. "What you doing here?"

"Hey, do I need a reason to come visit my family?" We cross the road together and walk down Causeyside Street and Sam spots the flowers.

"Your mum's not in," she says.

"Ah shit."

"That new chef chucked it last night and they've got no one else to cover."

"They should give Mamma a pay rise," I say, "she's the glue that holds that place together."

"Too right," grins Sam.

I grin back.

In a way I'm secretly pleased that Ma is not gonna be home. I don't get to spend a lot of time with Sam on my own these days, and it's always fun when it's just us butches.

We turn into George Street, go up the front path and Sam unlocks the front door. "You'll be wanting a shower and something to eat then," she says.

"You read my mind."

"No, I smelt you coming."

"Hey!" I try not to laugh, act like she's hurt my feelings.

"Get in there and get scrubbed," says Sam. She takes the flowers from me. "I'll put these in some water and then you can tell me all about her."

"I don't know what you mean," I say with a wink. "And I want to know every detail."

Thirteen

It's Saturday, nine forty-five in the morning, and Maggie has just stomped into work a full hour and three-quarters late. She has bags under her eyes and windmill hair, and I think if she smiled her entire face would obliterate.

I wish her a cheery good morning and she gives me the evil eye before pouring herself a venti cappuccino with a triple whammy of cream. Being late and guzzling coffee is part of her daily regime, a regime that includes talking excessively about the diet she's on and moaning about how nothing ever gets done around here without her. In about an hour, she will vamoose across the street to the café that sells the five-star breakfasts and she will buy sausage, egg, bacon, black pudding and mushrooms. All fried, of course. But she will not take the complimentary buttered toast. "Too many carbs." In fact, the only contribution Maggie ever makes to the running of Duffy's before noon, is to break four or five miscellaneous muffins into pieces and lay them out in a basket on the counter for the customers to sample.

"What are you grinning at?" she snaps.

I just shake my head and smile. I wanna tell her that I'm in love love love love but I don't think an old bag like her would understand the concept, because even if she has a heart it's gotta be all shrivelled up like a dried mushroom.

The customers have noticed my cheerfulness too. Chocolate Frappuccino Boy gives me a fifty pence tip and Laptop Bob says whatever it is he hopes I'm writing about it. I also get chatted up by a teenage Jennifer Tilly clone who looks like she just stepped off the set of *Bella Mafia* with her oversized cat eye sunglasses, but I don't so much as flirt back. And even when Maggie disappears at ten thirty for 'lunch' (leaving me with a dumbass office junior who comes in looking for thirty hot drinks to go, and then complains that she can't carry them all), there is absolutely nothing that can break my shiny happy mood.

By four in the afternoon, I still haven't heard from Joolz and my happiness is starting to wean. I've had my phone on silent all day but I've been sneaking cursory glances at it whenever Maggie's not looking, and now I'm beginning to imagine all kinds of scenarios with Joolz telling me that last night was a mistake, or an experiment, or just something that she never wants to repeat.

Maggie is sitting on a stool behind the counter eating a giant fairy cake smothered in the fattiest, sugariest fondant icing ever imaginable. I'm in the store cupboard getting extra cardboard cups when I hear a customer come in and ask for me by name.

"What do you want her for?" says Maggie, in her usual abrupt manner.

"It's personal," says the guy.

I snigger to myself, knowing that this will annoy her infinitely because she likes to know everyone's business, and also because she's not used to someone standing up to her. Maggie isn't having any of it though, and she begins to tell him that I'm busy and he'll have to either buy something while he waits or come back in another four hours when I'm finished my shift.

A few more words are exchanged. Then the shouting starts. "Where is she? Where the FUCK is she?! Tell her to come out!"

I'm trying to think whose coffee order I could have gotten so badly wrong that it would merit a reaction like this. When I finally come through he's got Maggie by the neck-string of her apron and he's practically hauling her over the counter.

"Hey," I shout. "What the fuck?"

Maggie's face is turning purple and even though she's an utter cunt, I wouldn't see her come to any harm.

The guy lets her drop. He looks up at me. And only then do I recognise the muscles and the red hair.

Joolz's gay boyfriend/ex-boyfriend/wannabe love interest is staring at me. I'm staring back. His eyes are blazing and they look like they're about to pop right out of his head.

"You," he says, "I want to talk to you."

He raises his hand and at first I think he's gonna throw a punch, but instead he just points at me.

"You," he repeats, "stay the fuck away from Julie."

I knew this was coming. And I wonder how he found out about us. Did she tell him? She must have. Or maybe her sister did. I don't suppose it would have been her mother.

I shrug. I'm trembling inside but I don't want him to know that.

"So what if I don't?"

"I'm warning you," he says, teeth clenched, finger wagging.

"We love each other," I say, matter-of-factly. I don't even know if this is remotely true on her part, but it sounds good.

"You're sick."

Yeah, lovesick.

"You're warped in the head."

"Great," I say, "anything else to add? Keep the insults coming, buddy, I'll tell you to stop if you say one I haven't heard before."

He inhales, puffing out his huge himbo chest.

"Just stay away from my sister."

OK. His *what*?

I study the hair, the blue eyes, the trail of freckles across the nose... Damn it, of course she's his sister!

He swipes his hand across the counter, scattering the basket of Maggie's muffin samples everywhere.

"Or else."

Then he walks out.

After he is gone, I stand open-mouthed. I'm wondering if we should call the cops but I don't want to do anything that'll get anyone connected to Joolz in trouble, in case it ruins my chances with her.

Maggie looks close to tears. She's shaking and stroking her neck. I ask her if she wants a cup of coffee or something but she just rolls her eyes at me.

Then she points down at the scattered muffins and croaks: "They're coming out of your wages, hen."

Five minutes later I'm sweeping up muffin crumbs while Maggie has gone outside to smoke. There are hardly any customers left because most of them legged it the moment they saw Maggie being garrotted.

The *Bella Mafia* girl who tried to chat me up earlier brings her empty coffee cup over to the counter and sets it down in front of me. She's tall and curvy with short, black, kiss-curled hair that kicks up at the back, just like Tilly's does in my favourite lesbian-noir movie (just like a million other teenage femmes). I wait for her to speak but she doesn't. Instead she stands with her hand on her chin, head poised in my direction. It kinda creeps me out a bit cause I can't see her eyes.

"Umm... Can I help you?" I say.

She grins. And I have this sudden vision of me and the remaining customers being taken hostage and held at gunpoint by a team of feisty female robbers wearing spiked heels and carrying submachine guns.

Finally, she laughs and says: "You don't look like a Romeo to me!"

I frown.

Earlier she asked my name and whether I went on gay.com, but I didn't give it. And I'm not even wearing a name badge today (something Maggie complained about earlier) because I had to get my spare anonymous apron from Mamma's closet.

"I was getting so bored waiting," she says. "And your boss is one mean bi-atch by the way. Does she ever stop moaning? Is she married? Is she a lezzy? By the way I don't think she's getting any."

She's talking a million miles a minute now about gay.com, and how we met online that time, and my head is buzzing; I keep thinking that any minute now Maggie will come bursting through the door and sack me.

"Oh and I'm sorry about my brother," she says.

"Who?"

"I would've tried to stop him but then he'd have known I was here and he'd have wanted to know why and then it would've all gotten pure complicated and you have to admit it was quite funny– "

"I'm sorry, who are you and why are you here?"

She sighs. "Well, du-uh! I'm Siobhan!"

She takes off the glasses and I recognise her (minus the long hair) from the picture in Joolz's wallet.

"Oh!"

I'm still confused but I think I'm catching up.

"Joolz said you were a bit daft."

"Hey!"

"Just kidding." She smiles at me. She's a very attractive girl but she couldn't be more unlike Joolz in looks. "Anyway, she sent me to give you this."

She takes a crinkled letter out of her pocket.

The pink envelope has the name 'Romeo' written in silver ink. She hands it over and then waits.

I put it in my apron pocket.

"Oh, you have to read it just now."

"Eh?"

"I've to wait for your answer."

"My answer?"

She shrugs. "I didn't read it."

Somehow I find that hard to believe.

"Thank you... I think."

"I would have read it," she continued, "but then Joolz threatened to remove my fingernails with pliers if I did, and I think she would too." She gives me a sly smile. "Your girlfriend is evil by the way, I hope you know that."

I grin. I like the use of the word 'girlfriend'.

Then I tease the envelope open, careful not to tear the page inside.

"Just rip it!"

I don't.

The paper inside is a paler pink with tiny purple roses at the margins. It says:

Dear Romeo,

Sorry I haven't texted. My mum confiscated my phone. She pays the bill. She's watching my every move now, so it's too dodgy to meet you at Sandy's tonight.

Do you know the twenty-four-hour laundrette on Aikenhead Road? Can you meet me there @ 9? I know it's all a bit Monica and Chandler but she won't follow me there cause I told her I'm washing my bed sheets.

Please say you'll come. Give your answer to Siobhan.

Love always

Juliet

"Yes," I say. "Tell her yes."

I'm grinning again.

"You owe me a tenner."

"Eh?"

"Joolz said she'd give me a tenner for delivering her message," she says, flashing me a butter-wouldn't-melt smile. "But if you want me to give her your reply it'll cost you too."

"Umm."

"The longer you thi-ink the more the price goes up," she says in a sing-song voice.

"Well..."

"That's ten-fifty now."

"OK-OK!"

I root around in my pocket and take out the fifty pence tip plus a crumpled tenner that I was keeping for the lunch break I've still not had.

"Thanks," she grins, snatching it from me. "Suck-er!"

Maggie comes back from her multiple fag break. The phone rings and she answers it, telling the person on the other end not to call again because nobody by that name works here.

"Bloody prank calls," she mumbles. "That's the third time this week I've had someone asking for a Vicky Mann."

"Hey, that's me!"

Maggie shrugs. "Well, I've told you before about personal calls at work."

Jeezo.

"I wish you'd taken a number from them," I say.

She gives me the evil eye once more then looks at Siobhan then back at me and I know she's about to tell me off for chatting.

"That was *theee* best cuppa coffee I've ever had," says Siobhan, totally over the top.

"Thanks," I grin. "Glad you enjoyed it."

"She should be employee of the month," she tells Maggie.

I stifle a snigger. Siobhan gives us both a cheeky wave before disappearing out the door.

It's almost closing-up time. Maggie has long gone home and there's only two other customers left: Laptop Bob and a skinny kid with a saxophone case and Bart Simpson hair who comes in and buys a strawberry shake and then pays for it all in small change.

I'm cleaning tables and turning chairs upside down onto tables, and thinking about my unorthodox date with Joolz and what I'm gonna wear.

Eventually, Laptop Bob says "Good luck for tonight!" packs up his computer and leaves. Bart Simpson finishes the rest of his shake, sucking loudly on his straw, and then he straps the saxophone case onto his back and heads for the exit too.

Then he stops, turns around and looks at me, nervously:

"Is there... umm... Someone who works here called Vicky?"

"Who wants to know?"

I'm sure I recognise him from someplace but I can't think where. Joolz doesn't have any more brothers but maybe he's a cousin or something. He doesn't look like any kind of threat but I'm not taking chances, especially when there are no witnesses around.

"I'm... umm... I'm her brother."

Ha. That's a good one. We get all kinds of idiots with tall stories coming into Duffy's, but this has to be the best in a long time. I decide to humour the kid.

"If she's your sister," I say. "How come you dunno where she works?"

"Umm, it's complicated," he says. "We've kind of... well... not actually met... We have different mothers."

I bet you do.

He's staring down at his shoes. I dunno what his deal is but I'm sure he has nothing to do with Joolz.

"Who told you Vicky worked here?"

"It was listed on her Friends Reunited profile."

I dunno whether to slap this kid or commend him on his investigative abilities.

"Well, she don't work here anymore."

"Oh."

"She split about a month ago," I add.

"Do you know where she works now?"

"Nah. I dunno where she went."

He looks doubtful.

"So you don't know how I can get in touch with her?"

"It's like I told you."

He nods.

"Anyway, I have to close up now," I say. "I'm sorry I can't help you."

He takes a pad of paper out of his pocket and a pen and rips a page out and scribbles something down in a spidery hand.

"If she comes back, give her my contact details?"

"Sure," I say. "Have a nice day."

"You too," he frowns.

☞ ♥ ☜

I'm almost ready to leave. The piece of paper the little twerp left behind is still staring up at me. I grab it, ball it up in my hand and I'm about to put it in the bin when a nagging curiosity stops me. I unscrew the crumpled page.

There's a phone number on it and beside it a name I know all too well.

Something jerks inside me when I read it. It's like someone's put a fishhook through my belly button and is pulling me ashore.

He couldn't be my brother. I don't have a brother.

I read the name again – George Mann.

Fourteen

I walk home in the rain in a daze. Water runs down my face, my ears, my chin and my neck. The wind is icy and it stings, but soon I can't feel anything.

Ma says when I was small I used to always wet myself whenever I went out in the rain. She says I had green Wellington boots with frog faces and I liked to play in the puddles, but I always ended up with a chill. I can't remember this at all, but maybe it's because I don't wanna think of myself as a pissy child.

I'm so spaced out that I walk two blocks past the flat before I even realise where I am. I can't get George Mann Junior outta my head.

I used to wonder what it was like to have a brother or sister. And sometimes I'd get jealous of other kids with big families who always had someone to talk to and play with. Though friends at school would tell me that I was lucky because I didn't have to share a room or wear hand-me-downs. I once dated a girl with seven sisters who invited me to family gatherings (with all the cousins and nieces and nephews), and I found it both fascinating and terrifying to watch the sibling drama unfold. I guess you could say that I was kind of a stereotypical loner child: quiet, thin-skinned, a little bit sheltered and a little bit odd. I liked my books and my movies, especially ones with fantasy stories that had imagined worlds and colourful characters. But then I wasn't spoilt or pampered and I was pretty independent.

I also had an imaginary friend called Peter. Ma says I used to blame him for all the naughty things I ever did. Again, I don't remember this, but Ma says that whenever toys got broken or one of her ornaments got knocked over, I'd point the finger at him.   Apparently he came to dinner with us and Ma would have to lay out an extra plate and a glass of milk, and one time on the bus I told an old lady she couldn't sit down in front of me because that was Peter's seat. Then shortly after I'd just started infant school I told Ma that Peter had gone to live with new parents and I stopped talking about him. He made a guest appearance for a few weeks after Dad left, but then he disappeared just as quickly.

I think about all the times I wished that Dad would come back and spend time with me. There were other kids at school whose parents didn't live together, but they moved between two houses and their dads took them to the movies or the funfair at weekends. I wonder if Dad ever married George's mum? Did he take George on day trips and buy him popcorn and candyfloss? Did they ride together on the dodgems laughing? Did he like George better because he was a boy?

I have a burning pain in my chest and my heart feels like it's trying to melt its way through my rib cage. I push the feeling down into my gut with every step I take.

My father is dead. And I never had a brother. The George Manns of this world are nothing to me.

By the time I get back to the flat my shoes and socks are soaked through and I only have thirty-five minutes left to get ready and go meet Joolz.

I jump in the shower, wash my hair and scrub myself down then I change in and out of three shirts before deciding on my most expensive made-to-measure white one that I've only worn twice.

Minty is waiting for me in the living room (reeking of cologne) when I come out. She tells me that we're going on a double date tonight.

"I can't," I say. "I'm busy."

I try to escape into my room, but I'm too slow and she follows me out into the hall wanting to know where I'm going and what I'm doing and who I'm doing it with.

I give her an edited version of the truth because I don't wanna hear anymore of her bull crap about Joolz not being a real lesbian.

"Fucking laundry!" she snorts. "What's more important?"

"Hey, we all gotta wash our pants!"

She doesn't laugh.

"This is all set up," she says. "I might have known you'd let us down."

She goes off into a big spiel about how she really likes this girl but the girl won't go out with her unless someone else comes along as a date for her friend.

"Can't you get Kat or someone to be your wingman?"

"Hey, I'm no one's wingman," comes Kat's voice over the babble of *Buffy the Vampire Slayer*.

"Just shove yer gear in the machine and go," says Minty.

"I can't."

"How? It's no as if ye have to sit and watch the spin cycle."

"Cause I have to... umm... I have to..."

"I'd do it for you," she wheedles. "C'mon, just come out..."

I'm running out of time and I can't think of an excuse for why I'm going all the way to the Southside when we got a washer in the flat.

"Vicky," says Kat, in a really arsey tone, "you'd better not be planning to use the washing machine tonight. Cause tonight's my night for laundry." (She's referring to the rota we made up when she moved in that nobody actually pays attention to.)

I shrug.

"See," I tell Min, "I have to haul my cookies all the way into town just so I can get clean underwear."

Minty wrinkles up her face.

"Can you not just swap nights?"

"NO!" shouts Kat.

"Sorry," I say.

"I never get to see you these days," moans Minty.

"Waddya mean you never get to see me? You see me every morning!"

"Aye but we never do stuff like we used to cause you're always busy."

I feel bad about this. It's true. I have been taken up with classes and Les Artistes and now Joolz. But I don't feel bad enough to make myself late for a date just so we can stand here chatting about my social calendar.

"I have to go," I tell her. "I'm in a hurry."

"For the laundrette?"

"The queues are huge after nine."

She scowls and stomps off in a bad mood. I shout after her, telling her that she can come along if she wants.

"I've got better things to do than watch you wash your manky knickers!" she shouts back.

I knew she wouldn't wanna come. I peer into the living room where Kat is still watching the TV. "Thanks for the decoy," I say. She doesn't look my way, her eyes glued firmly to the screen. This is the longest conversation we've had since the bisexual revelation, and I've a feeling she's still pissed at me, or maybe she just really likes watching kick-ass chicks drive wooden stakes through hearts.

"Anytime," she replies. "Where are you going really?"

"To meet Joolz."

"Thought so."

"How did you know?"

"No one wears a hundred-pound shirt to do laundry."

I nod. She has a good point. I wouldn't wanna look like a schmuck.

A demon punches and swings, Buffy ducks, and he hits a high-voltage electricity box and explodes into a ball of fire.

I say goodbye then go into my room to find something else to wear.

☞ ♥ ☜

It's ten to nine and I'm in a cab that's crawling its way up Aiken-head Road when I decide to cut my losses and walk the rest of the way. I tell the cabbie to stop, pay him and get out even though it's pissing it down and my hair will probably go wild. I spy a woman selling flowers and glow sticks across the street. I pause thinking 'Hey, I might get some roses for Joolz' and almost get run over by a First Bus that decides to reverse as I am crossing. I watch the woman disappear up an alley. Damn it. Then again, flowers and dirty laundry don't really go together.

Now I'm stuck on a traffic island and there's a million cars snaking their way up and around my ass. This is gonna make me late, I just know it.

My phone rings. It's Minty. Before she even speaks I wish I never answered it. "Hi, where are you?" I finally cross the road and keep walking.

"On my way to the laundrette like I told you."

"What laundrette? I need to talk to you. It's important." Someone shouts my name.

"Hang on," I tell Minty, and I turn around and it's Joolz – she's by my side, her arm on my shoulder, her face streaked with rain and her hair all wet and tangled in ringlets.

"I got stuck in traffic," she says. "I got off the bus way back there."

I want to ask her how she is, and where her car is, and where her frigging laundry is (because all she has is her handbag), but I'm too busy staring at her gorgeous mouth and wondering how she continues to rock pink lipstick when her hair is as bright as a fire truck.

Instead, I nod. She smiles at me and my stomach does a kind of flip thing, and then it does it again when I remember that I've left Min hanging.

"Scuse me for just one second," I say as I put the phone to my ear, straining to hear, but the pips have gone and the line is silent. Oh well.

☞ ♥ ☜

Joolz and I are laughing as we make our way to the laundrette through the driving rain.

I ask her if she's ok, can she cope without an umbrella? She's prodding my arm, telling me to fuck off and poking fun at my bedraggled hairdo. I'm so glad to see her. I'm so glad to be walking out with her, taking her out like a regular beau, even if it isn't the sexiest of dates. I can't wait to go inside, have her sit beside me, just the two of us. I'm thinking maybe we could buy sodas and chips from the shop next door, and then we could–

"Fancy meeting you here Ro-me-o!"

What the fuck?

Scarface is standing right in front of me on the sidewalk, just outside the laundrette. She has a goofy grin stuck to her face and she's with her white-haired, orange-faced, half-baked sidekick who's looking me up and down and snarling like a rabid dog.

"Oh hi, Paris," says Joolz, weakly.

I don't say nothing. My plan was to walk on in, ignore them, but they're blocking the entrance.

"You haven't returned my phone calls, Julie," Paris whines.

"Sorry, my phone's broken."

"Or my emails."

"My account got shut down."

She stares at Joolz and then at our linked arms and then back at me. Her lips are pursed, her fist clenched tight – and for a moment I think I might get smacked around the head with the horrible gold lamè handbag she's got perched on her shoulder.

My tongue has gone dry and my jaw is tense. And even though I know that Joolz doesn't wanna be with Paris, that she doesn't even remotely like the girl, all I can think about are Paris's hands and Paris' lips and Paris' skinny hips pressing against Joolz's body...

"We're still friends though, aren't we?"

"Of course," says Joolz.

I feel like I'm gonna boak.

I can't believe that Joolz's still talking to her. She ought to make her excuses and go. Paris is asking if we wanna have a drink with them and Scarface is bouncing about in a puddle and clapping her hands saying 'yes' over and over.

"Why don't you," Paris says, trying to act like some goddamn consigliore, "put your laundry in for a service wash and come to the pub with us."

Like hell.

"We're kind of on a DATE," Joolz tells her, finally.

Yeah, and you're not fucking coming.

"Haha," sniggers Scarface. "Is this your idea of a dirty week-end?"

My head is really starting to ache now.

"Right," I say, "what's happening?" I'm pissed off and now I just feel like going home. Joolz squeezes my hand. Then she smiles at me, at my chin, but doesn't look me in the eye. "Why don't we stand inside?" she says.

We finally manage to ditch Dumb and Dumber, but not until we've agreed to go around to Scarface's house for a drink one night. As if. Turns out she stays a couple of blocks over. Which basically means that I can never set foot in this part of town again.

I open up my rucksack and start emptying garments into one of the washers. Joolz thinks this is hilarious. She says she didn't think we were actually gonna be washing our clothes together for real.

☞ ♥ ☜

Joolz has never used a washing machine before. She says that her mother does all the chores in her house. Except for the cooking, sometimes. "I can make French toast," she says, "and fried eggs and obviously sandwiches and anything that comes out of a tin."

I'm shook by this. I tell her I've been doing my own washing and ironing since I was nine-years-old, and I can make a five-course dinner if the need arises. She teases me and calls me a 'closet femme'. I tease her back by calling her 'princess' and 'lady muck', and asking her how she feels about losing her laundry virginity with me.

I show her how to set the machine to different temperatures and she pours in the detergent. After a while it doesn't really matter that we're in this stinking, sweaty place full of students and bums and single men, because us just being together makes everything else fade to soft focus.

I am on my best behaviour. It wouldn't do for her mother or some other random member of the Turner clan to come waltzing in here and find us smooching in among the piles of unwashed underwear.

"It would be funny though," she says.

"Would it?"

"Yeah," she grins. "At least my mum would know what you looked like with clothes on."

"True."

Joolz grins at me and I hold the drier door open. She lifts out the warm fluffy clothes and her hand brushes against mine, sending little jolts of electricity right through me.

"I can't believe Mum's totally refusing to wash my bed sheets because of last night," she says. "I think she thinks we contaminated them with our gayness or something."

"So what are you gonna do?"

"Oh, that's already sorted. I took them round to Mylene's earlier. She's got so many brothers and sisters – her mum won't notice the extra load. Mum thinks I'm doing them myself, hence why I said I'd meet you here."

"Will she not wonder why you've come home without them?"

"Probably. But then it's not my fault if there's an electrical fault and I have to leave my clothes to dry overnight and come back tomorrow to pick them up."

I give her a raised eyebrow.

"And if you just happen to be here again," she says, "washing some of your very interesting pants..."

She lifts a pair of my Homer Simpson doughnut boxer shorts up in the air with one finger.

"Hey, gimme those," I say, blushing.

"Make me."

I stretch up to grab them back but Joolz goes way up onto her tiptoes, ballerina-style, so that I can't reach.

"People are looking at us," I whisper.

"So," she says, "let them look."

It's only a junkie couple eating McDonald's Happy Meals and a drunken student who keeps dropping his socks on the floor. It still makes me nervous though. Cause most times when straight people see lesbians together they act like you've thrown a stink bomb at their feet.

All of a sudden I feel weird and vulnerable but I'm not sure why. I tug on her arm.

"Give them back, Joolz."

"Give me a kiss, Vicky."

"Eh?"

"You heard me," she says, licking her lips.

"What, here?"

I've managed to narrowly avoid getting my head beaten to a pulp so far today, I'm not sure my luck will hold out. I try to tell her this but I don't get a chance cause she moves in close to me and pulls my mouth to hers. I melt. Our arms find each other. And as we kiss, it feels like the whole room, no, the whole world is spinning.

We're still kissing a half hour later in the backseat of another cab on the way to the Candle Bar. It was Joolz's idea that we should go somewhere gay. And when I come around, she is grinning at me and stroking my thigh and the driver is saying impatiently, "THAT'LL BE THREE POUNDS PLEASE."

Fifteen

"**F**uck sake you two, get a room!"

The Candle Bar is almost empty and Joolz and I are in a corner with our arms and lips wrapped tight around each other when Minty comes marching in with two flannel-shirted semi-femmes in tow. One is Rosie from the L.I.P.S. group (clearly this was a set-up) and the other is a busty blonde I slept with months ago and then never called back.

"Long time no see, Vicky," says the blonde. She has one hand around her drink and the other on her hip and she ain't smiling one iota.

"Hey," I nod, bracing myself for a double vodka and coke shower.

"Didnae know yous knew each other," grins Min, pushing my rucksack onto the floor and crashing down into the seat beside me. "Small world, eh? We were just talking about going to Bennet's if yous two lovebirds want to come."

I'm about to politely decline when the blonde gets in first. She says she has a headache suddenly and she'll be leaving as soon as she finishes her drink. "It's Sharon, by the way," she adds, looking me dead in the eye and curling her lip, "just in case you've forgotten."

My face grows hot. I can feel Joolz's fingers warm against the skin of my wrist. I search for her hand and give it a squeeze.

"Of course I remember," I lie. "You sing rhythm and blues and you got a Shih-tzu called Harry."

That night was a blur amongst many, many blurry nights, but one thing that did stick in my mind is waking up and seeing her shit of a dog chewing the heels out of my best baseball boots.

"It's bluegrass jazz actually," she says. "And his name's Henry."

"That's what I meant."

"Well," she says, throwing her head back and emptying her glass, "I'll see you around. Or not."

Minty jumps to her feet and starts trying to convince Sharon to stay out and go clubbing "Aww just come out... Just come out... That's pure baws... We all want you to stay out..."

She's practically down on her knees begging and it's embarrassing to watch because the girl clearly doesn't want to be here – and I'm sure I'm one-hundred percent of the reason.

She turns to me and says: "Romeo, tell her she should just come."

I tell Sharon she should do whatever she feels is best.

"Aw just come out."

Sharon says she's going home and that's that. She pulls her jacket on, tosses her hair like some L'Oréal hair model and stomps away towards the door.

"Pure. Actual. Baws." moans Minty. Then she shoves past us and says: "I better go and make sure she's alright."

"I think I'm going to head too," says Rosie, quietly. "It was nice to see you again, Julie." She smiles. "You too, Vicky."

"Awww man, whit is this? You should think about changing your washing powder, Romeo, cause as soon's you arrive every cunt wants to leave."

I say nothing. My face is growing hotter by the second and my insides feel like they're being used as a punch bag.

"Right, don't move," says Minty. "I'll be back in five."

She disappears after Rosie.

Joolz's fingers wriggle free from mine.

"Our hands were getting a bit sweaty," she says.

"Sorry," I wipe my palms dry on the legs of my pants.

Joolz tilts her head and grins. "So... What was all that about then?"

I sigh and shake my head. "Trust me, you don't wanna know."

"I think I get the picture."

We don't go to Bennet's. Instead, we end up staying for the queer pub quiz and I impress Joolz by answering the first six questions right away.

"How do you even know all that stuff about gay people from the fifties?"

I smile and she starts saying something else but I don't hear her because Minty is nudging me and saying that she has just seen *Naughty_Nurse* up at the bar and apparently she was asking after me. I'm pretty sure she's only telling me this to wind up Joolz but I can't be certain. Joolz doesn't say anything, she just picks the pen up off the table and writes down the number seven with a question mark beside it.

☞ ♥ ☜

"Which famous tennis player came out as a lesbian in 1981 shortly after being granted US citizenship?"

"Martina Navratilova!"

Joolz is really excited now that she has finally answered a question. She jumps up and down in her seat and claps her hands together. This makes me want to kiss her even more.

"Well done, gorgeous," I say, and I pull her towards me, pressing my body against hers.

"Aw fuck sake, gonna stop that!" says Minty. "Yous two are putting me off ma pint."

I tell her to fuck off. I really wish she would too. For years we've had this unspoken rule that if one of us gets lucky whilst we're out drinking then the other will disappear.

Joolz is grinning at me and biting her lip and I really want to get out of this place so that I can take her home and show her just how much she means to me.

"Anyway," says Minty, "my granny could have got that one, and she's seventy-six and in a home for homophobes with dementia."

"Ok lovelies," continues our camp compère, "on what date does the very fabulous National Coming Out Day take place in the USA?"

I don't know this one but really I should.

"October the eleventh," Joolz says, confidently.

"Are you sure?"

"Positive," she replies and writes it down on the piece of paper. I make a joke about her coming out to her Ma a little too late and she sticks her tongue out and pinches me on the under-arm. We both giggle.

Minty rolls her eyes. "Well, I think you're full of pish," she says. I ask her why she thinks that. "Well, I'm pretty sure that if something as big as that took place this month then we'd have known about it."

"Not necessarily," I say.

"Somehow," she says, "I don't think folk are going to miss a chance to have a big bent booze-up."

"Actually," says Joolz, "this is the first year since nineteen eighty-eight that they haven't celebrated it."

I tilt my head, "Zat so?"

She grins and shakes her almost empty alcopop bottle at me. "We can talk about it when you get back from the bar."

As I queue for the drinks I spy *Naughty_Nurse* standing there sure enough. She walks right up to me, puts her arm over my shoulder and practically pins me against the bar with her bosom. Tonight's the first night I've seen her in weeks, and I have to admit I like what I see. But no way I'm going to bollocks things up with Joolz though, not this time, and I make this clear. The medicinal minx throws her shoulders back, pushes her tits out and tells me that I don't know what I'm missing.

A couple of weeks ago I would have taken her straight home and shown her a really good time. I would have stripped her as soon as we hit my place and shown her my best bedside manner. I can still remember clearly all those pictures she sent me of herself, especially the shaved pussy ones that left absolutely nothing to the imagination. I would have ridden her like a Cadillac. But that's the old Vicky Romeo talking, and I'm done with all that tomfoolery.

Minty is gone again and Joolz is smoking Marlboro Lights and peeling the label off of an empty bottle with her thumbnail when I come back with the drinks.

"So is there anyone in this pub," she says, "that *isn't* in the Vicky Romeo Fanny Club?"

I tense up and ask her what she means.

"Is there anyone here tonight that you haven't slept with?"

I stop for a minute, have a think, cause there's Rosie for a start and Minty, obviously, but I don't think that's the answer she's looking for.

"I'm sorry," is all I have to say.

"You don't have to apologise," she says. "I'm not pissed off that there's been other women. I don't give a shit about who or what you've done in the past."

"But you are pissed off?"

"No, I'm just disappointed that you asked me out on a date and I thought it was going to be one on one but instead..."

"I can't control who turns up in the pub."

"Yeah, but you don't have to invite them into our company."

"I didn't!"

Joolz sighs and I begin to feel all weird, I start shifting my weight from foot to foot.

"Vicky," she says, "are you going to sit down or not?"

"I don't know what you want from me."

"What do you mean?"

"I can't not speak to people when we're out... I can't just ignore..."

"I never asked you to."

"You don't understand what it's like... God, the scene is so frigging small..."

"And incestuous," says Joolz. "Does your friend Minty know that she just took out one of your sloppy seconds?"

We both start to laugh, even if it is a nervous laugh that catches in the back of my throat.

She beckons me to sit down. I sit and she throws her arms around my neck. It's comforting and I feel like burying my head under her chin.

"I didn't plan for things to happen this way," I say. "I brought you here because I thought Min and the others would be at Sandy's."

Joolz screws up her face. She looks cute when she does that. Her lips go all pouty and her nose is all wrinkled up. "Why are we still talking about this?" she says. "Why are you wasting time when you could be kissing me?"

"So," I say to Joolz. "What were you saying about National Coming Out Day..."

She shrugs. "Martha was talking about it at the L.I.P.S. group. She said it was cancelled because it fell on the one-month anniversary of the September eleventh attacks."

I nod. "That makes sense."

"Ironically, I was actually *in* The Women's Archive the day that the twin towers collapsed."

I cough and my beer goes down the wrong way.

"What? You mean you'd been there before?"

She sighs. "Yeah. It was kind of all a bit embarrassing which is why I never told you..."

☞ ♥ ☜

The first time Joolz ever went to the Women's Archive was the first time she properly came out to herself. It was also the same day that Al-Qaeda hijackers deliberately crashed two airliners into the World Trade Centre, killing everyone on board.

"I remember seeing the news later on that night," she says. "Hundreds of people had lost their lives but all I could think about was how terrible it was that I fancied girls."

I smile at her and stroke her hair. I'll never identify with all that 'oh my god I'm gay I'm destined to burn in hell' crap but I don't tell her that cause I don't wanna put her off or make her feel bad.

Joolz's neighbour, Christine, was a volunteer in the archive and she'd helped Joolz with her Suffragette project for her Standard Grade History class when she was still at school. "That was five years beforehand and I didn't know anything about the place other than the fact that it was a feminist organisation," she said. "I'd always wanted to go there though, but I didn't know why, and this day I just got up and did it."

I nodded. That was like me wanting to go every week to Sandy's even before I knew what being a homo meant.

Joolz said she didn't wanna ask Christine where the archive was, so instead she went on the college library computer and googled the address.

It was only a fifteen-minute drive from where she stayed and she told her mother that she was going to do some research in the library.

"Well, it *is* kind of a library, because they have books and videos and stuff..."

"Hey, you don't have to explain yourself," I say. "You were just scared your Ma would want to tag on after you."

"Precisely."

"And then you wouldn't have been able to look for all that hot lesbo porn.""Very funny."

I snicker into my beer.

"She thought I was doing my history of dance essay and I just didn't bother to correct her."

"So did you manage to find the 'Chick-licking for Cheerleaders' book?"

I laugh and she gives me a playful punch.

"Or what about 'The Choreography of Cunnilingus'."

Joolz folds her arms in mock indignation. "Vicky, do you want to hear this story or not?"

"Uh-huh."

She begins again in a serious tone.

"It wasn't easy," she says. "I had to be really sneaky. And I was shitting myself the whole time I was driving, worrying about what would happen if Christine turned up unexpectedly cause she'd swapped a shift or something."

"But you went anyway," I say, "and you obviously found out what you needed to know or we wouldn't be sitting here and you'd still be in the closet half-way to Narnia."

"Probably," she mumbles.

She says she met Martha and she was given a tour of the place, and it was all going really well until someone handed her a leaflet and asked if she'd like to join a youth group. "I got as far as 'Are you a young lesbian or bisexual woman under the age of twenty-five?'..."

She shakes her head.

"And then what happened?"

Joolz says she threw the leaflet back in the woman's face and walked out. "I was absolutely mortified," she went on, "and I just said to her 'do I look like a fucking dyke to you?'"

"Harsh."

"Yeah, and then I went home and bawled my eyes out."

The quiz is over and the scores are being counted. I'm enjoying the alone time with Joolz, while Minty is up at the bar hitting on Mikki Blue's extremely straight cousin.

"So you really didn't have a clue that you were gay when you were growing up?"

Joolz shrugs.

"What – no secret crushes on TV stars or school teachers?"

"Well..." she begins, smiling and looking down into her drink, "I suppose I did have a bit of an obsession with She-Ra."

"Who?"

"*She-Ra: Princess of Power*! How can you not remember? She was He-Man's twin sister and a total feminist!"

"You fancied a cartoon?"

"She was hot."

"She was a cartoon."

"Still hot."

I make a big deal of pulling faces and pretending to be out-raged, but really I think it's cute as hell.

"I suppose you fancied Miss Piggy as well," I say, leaning close and teasing her with an almost kiss. "I mean why stop at car-toon characters when there's sexy muppets in high heels..."

"Actually," she says, "my ex-boyfriend used to have a thing for her. She always kind of annoyed me though. I preferred Kermit the frog."

We come in second place with nineteen and a half out of twenty and I'm amazed that a team that didn't have me in it managed to win. Joolz says she is amazed we managed to score so high especially when we only answered eighteen questions. "Bonus points," I tell her, knowingly. She just gives me a raised eyebrow.

Two tables along from us there are shouts and cheers and a row of tattooed arms go up in a Mexican wave. I stretch out my neck to see who they are but Joolz mistakenly thinks I'm going in for another kiss and she takes precedence.

When we come up for air the music's tempo has escalated and lights have gone really low. Bodies with luminous pink drinks are bopping and bouncing past.

Minty is back sniffing round us again too and being a major ass-pain. "Hey," she shouts, "did you hear that prat JJ got barred from Sandy's cause he was caught taking ecky?" And then, "Somebody says wee Zesty tried to get in here earlier wi a fake ID and she got a knock back." She goes from being ridiculously animated to putting her head down on the table and complaining that she's been overworked in fewer than sixty seconds. And when those things fail to make her the centre of attention, she announces: "I thought I just seen your step-maw there."

"C'mon," I say, "let's go get drinks."

I take Joolz's hand and we zig-zag our way towards the bar. I buy two alcopops – a blue one for me and a pink one for her – and then we slip into a private alcove away from everyone else.

But like a bloodhound giving chase, Minty finds us again. She *has* to come over and point out every chick I've ever been remotely linked with. She spots one, two, three, four of my old one-night stands plus a broad I only got to second base with. I can see a tiny frown appearing on Joolz's face, but she doesn't let on that she's pissed or anything. Then I see Naughty Nurse with her arms around Mikki The Hat, she grins at me over Mikki's shoulder and waves.

It's Sam who nearly gives me a heart attack though, cause I don't even know she's here until she throws a hot and heavy arm around my neck. "Hey Vicky," she bellows. Her eyes are glassy and her face is a shiny pink. "I see we kicked your butt in the quiz. You need to do better than that, pal." I grimace. She asks if I'd like a drink and I tell her, thanks, but I've already got one. Oh, would my girlfriend like a drink then? No, she wouldn't.

"Is Ma here too?" I ask.

Sam shakes her head. "Nope. Just me on my todd."

Thank fuck.

I relax and quickly do the introductions. Joolz says she is pleased to meet Sam, but there's a shake in her voice. I curl my arm around her waist and hug her closer to me.

"And it's lovely to meet you, Julie." Sam takes Joolz's hand and she gives it a squeeze before adding with a wink: "I'll give yous two yer space cause I know what it's like..." Then she pats me on the back and says: "Catcha later, Vicky."

Minty bounces over.

"It's like swinger city tonight!" she moans. "And you'll never guess who's here?"

I brace myself.

Joolz's rib cage rises and falls in a quiet exasperated sigh.

"My ex," she says, wrinkling up her nose. "The bisexual one."

I give her a sympathetic nod then move to rearrange my attention.

"And have you seen that mad cow Kat? I mean, talk about fucking flaunting it, man..."

Joolz is waving at someone now. I look round and see Robbie waving back. He's wearing a silver dress and a long black wig and has his arm around Kat's waist. And then he bends down and kisses her full on the mouth.

My feet are weighted to the ground and gravity is pulling my jaw open. I can't stop staring at them.

Joolz is leaning into me, whispering in my ear about how she knew all along those two were an item and how great it was that they'd finally decided to come out; and Minty is going on about how straights and trannies should have separate pubs and how her ex-girlfriend (who's from Falkirk and has a boyfriend now) only shows her face on the Glasgow scene to wind her up.

"You know what I hate about gay clubs," Joolz muses. "If I was dating a guy and then we split up, I'd probably never see him again because there's a million other clubs I could go to."

I nod. "I know what you mean."

I don't though. Not really. At least I never really thought about it till now. Part of what I always loved about going to gay bars is that everyone knows everyone, and even if it does blow up in your face from time to time, surely it's better the devil you know.

I'm still watching Kat and Robbie who are now writhing rhythmically on the dance floor. He's supposed to like boys and she's supposed to like girls and they've known each other for years... I just don't understand...

"I just think they look so cute together," says Joolz.

"I'm away to the bogs to throw up," Minty growls and storms off.

"Good riddance," Joolz sighs and goes to light a cigarette.

"Come on, let's go," I say to her, and I pull on her arm.

"What? Vicky, where are we going? I want to say hi to Kat."

"I just wanna get outta here..."

We walk fast then, towards the exit and past everyone I know, past shouts of 'Hey, how's it going, Romeo?' and 'How's yer maw?' and 'Are you going to Bennet's later?' and as soon as we hit the pavement we start sprinting.

☞ ♥ ☜

Joolz and I have slowed to a walking pace. I didn't think I was particularly wasted but I must be cause my flat's in the other direction and I've no clue where I'm going. I ask her if she's ok cause she's holding her chest and breathing hard. "I need a fag," she says and pulls the packet from her coat pocket, but the lid is open and neither of us notices till her last smoke does a nose dive into a muddy puddle.

"I think that's my sign to give up," she says.

"You want me to buy you some more?"

She shakes her head.

"It's been some day," I say.

"Tell me about it."

So I do.

☞ ♥ ☜

I tell her everything that's happened to me today, and when I get to the part about my long lost teenage brother, Joolz stops right in the middle of the street, drops my hand and looks me directly in the eye. "Shit, that's pretty fucking intense."

I nod. "Tell me about it."

She puts her arm around my waist. I don't even care that there's a group of drunken hetty boys walking past and staring at us.

"So what you going to do?" she says.

"Nothing I guess."

She stops again. "OK, hang on, you've just found out you've got a brother you didn't even know existed – and possibly a whole other family out there – and you're going to do nothing to find out about them?"

My shoulders stiffen. "I got all the family I need, baby," I tell her, "and they're right back there in that club."

She pauses for the longest moment in history. And I'm left wondering what wheels are turning inside that femme brain of hers.

Finally, she speaks. "That's actually quite sad, Vicky."

"Waddya mean?"

"Nothing. Never mind. I shouldn't have said anything."

"No, I wanna know what you think."

"It's just that I'm really close with my family. I know you've not exactly seen the good side of them. But they're not bad people. And if I found out that I had another sister or brother, another person that shared my blood – I'd want to know about them. But I guess that's just me."

☞ ♥ ☜

We're walking down my road in silence – having eventually gotten back onto the right route – and I'm thinking about how good it's gonna be to just get into bed and wrap myself up in her, when I spot a skinny, bent over figure with a saxophone case sitting on my front steps.

No. Fucking. Way.

"What's up?" says Joolz.

"It's him. It's that fucking kid– "

I look around as if there are cameras watching, cause this feels like the biggest set-up of the century.

He stands up when he sees me coming, even gives me a sort of smile.

"What the fu– What the hell are you doing here, kid? I mean, how did you even get this address?"

He takes a deep breath. "I followed you." He says. "All due respect, but I think you're talking bullshit. I think you know where my sister is."

I raise my fist and I shake it at him. It's just a ruse but he doesn't know that.

"Why I oughta pound your– "

Joolz reaches up and puts her hand over my fist.

"Why don't you just talk to him, Vicky?"

The kid stops. He stares at me like he's looking at me, really looking at me for the first time.

"Vicky?" he says. "*You're* my sister?"

"Yeah," I say, quietly. "I guess so."

Sixteen

I went through a phase of being obsessed by the possibility of alternate realities when I was younger. It started after I watched a TV show about a scientist who fell through a wormhole into another dimension where he met a carbon copy of himself. I used to ride the bus to school and imagine all these parallel worlds where I was femme or straight or sometimes even male. Mostly I was just like myself though, except that sometimes I had a different haircut and I was living in Sicily.

It's dumb, I know, but it just made me think about how things shoulda, coulda or woulda happened if one tiny thing in my history was different. For instance, what if my Ma and Dad had stayed together? What if Ma had some kind of sneaky, clandestine affair with Sam that stayed secret for over a decade, only to be dramatically uncovered on the eve of my twenty-first birthday? And what if Dad had managed to resist being a lying cheating scumbag? Then there might have been another George Junior who would have cancelled out the existing one.

And what if Joolz and I had never met? What if, instead of picking up her lipstick in Sandy's that night, I was somewhere in southern Europe picking up another similar accessory (a hair brush or an eyeliner perhaps) that belonged to a dark haired, busty, opera-loving Italian with an una bella figure?

What if we'd gone to Bennet's tonight just like everyone else? Or even made a detour at Santino's chippy? Would the kid still be waiting outside on my doorstep like a shit-smeared sneaker? Or would he have gone home by now and given up the ghost?

Silence.

It's almost midnight and Joolz is in the kitchen making coffee, while I'm sitting staring across at this skinny teenage fool who should be at home tucked up in bed.

I take a deep breath. Clear my throat. Lean towards him.

"So..." I start.

"Umm..." he says.

His hands are clasped tightly around his saxophone case and he's rocking back and forth ever so slightly and tapping his heel to an inaudible beat.

I've decided that he's either a nut or very nervous. I guess it really doesn't matter which. It's not like half of my friends aren't nuts.

Thing is, I'm not even angry anymore. All that outrage I was holding against him for stalking me has evaporated like powdered garlic, and now it's just plain awkward having him here.

"I won't be a minute," Joolz told me a quarter of an hour ago. Sure, she was only trying to help – probably she thought it would be better to give us some time alone – but she was the one who invited him in and now I've been left to play babysitter.

"So..." I repeat.

I drum the arm of the sofa with my fingertips and Junior picks at a loose thread on the strap of his case. After that, we just sit staring and saying fuck all for the longest minute in history.

I simply don't know what in the hell I'm supposed to say to this kid. I mean, what does he expect me to say? It's not like I know a single shitting thing about him.

Eventually, Joolz sticks her head around the door.

"George," she says, "how do you take yours?"

I snigger and she frowns.

I'm thinking about the old Cadbury's creme egg advert ('Hi, I'm Aries and I like to give it a good battering!'), normally this would prompt a flurry of gay entendres but there's no Minty here to crack the follow-up jokes. It's probably just as well.

I'm starting to realise how horribly drunk I am. I'm so drunk I'm starting to fall asleep.

Joolz smiles at the kid and his face softens. "Milk and two sugars, please," he replies.

She disappears again and we lapse back into silence.

"So do you live near here?" says Joolz.

Junior shrugs. "I guess so... Sort of."

Joolz tilts her head, leans her chin against her hand. The coffee is helping to bring me back to life and so is the fact that I can practically see right down her top.

I grin to myself.

The kid blushes.

Then I realise that if I can see then he probably can too. Well, I think, taking another swig, he'd better not be looking at my girlfriend's tits.

"I just can't believe how alike you two look," says Joolz suddenly.

I swallow too quickly and the coffee burns the back of my throat. I cough and my eyes water, and Joolz asks me if I'm ok to which I can only nod and mouth the word 'hot'.

"I just can't believe the similarities," she continues, looking from me to Junior and back to me again.

I want to protest against this comment, to shout 'it ain't true!'; I want to be able to say with conviction that he looks nothing like me. But by doing so it would make me exactly like all the other brothers and sisters in denial all over the world who wail and shriek whenever someone highlights a ginger gene or a Tefal forehead or some other incriminating hereditary howler. Because the proof is right in front of me. This kid has my Dad's blue eyes, and my Dad's smile and he even has the same dimple in his chin as Dad. His nose belongs to someone else and his skin tone's a bit lighter than mine but there's no denying that we're blood relatives.

So now all those shaky arguments I was planning to throw at him – like 'How do I know you are really who you say you are?' and 'This could be a scam and you could have found all this out over the net!' – have wilted completely.

I think my brain might be wilting.

I find myself grasping at questions like: does Ma know? Did she hide it from me too? Was she trying to protect me? Who else knows?

This is like watching a car crash: you know you shouldn't look but you can't tear your eyes from the road and all at once it's both horrible and spectacular.

Joolz is asking George if he's still at school. Yes, he is. Which one does he go to? What subjects does he take? Is he planning on staying on after his exams?

Fuck. How old even is this kid? Fourteen? Fifteen? Was he conceived before Ma and Dad broke up? Was he an accident or deliberate? Are there any more of him?

And then he hits me with the juggernaut: "Our Dad told me so-oo much about you, Vicky."

Kablooey. My mind has officially been blown.

George says something else, but I don't hear him. I'm thinking about another time, another place, when I was a different me. I'm thinking about being six-years-old. I'm thinking about the day I came home from school and saw my Daddy's record player gone and a vase on top of the sideboard where our family portrait used to be.

"I've been dying to meet you for *such* a long time."

I'm thinking about all those nights I spent lying awake, praying that Dad would come back for me.

"It's so-oo amazing to finally... Well, you know..."

No. No, I don't.

I don't have any idea what it was like for George, and I don't know what our father could possibly have to say about me or my life because he was never fucking there.

But I don't say any of that.

How can I when George is sitting there all wide-eyed, grinning at me?

I think he's waiting for me to respond. Only I don't. I can't.

My brain hurts. This is too much. Not just the 'our Dad' thing or the idea that the old man would be sober enough to string together a sentence about me, but also the whole scenario with Gonzo over there practically pissing himself with excitement.

It's not amazing I want to say.

I want to tell him about how our Dad was a selfish, fucked-up loser who didn't care enough about me to even pick up a phone.

"Dad talked about you all the time... He said he wished things had been different with you two... And he kept wanting to get in touch..."

A rock is lodged in my throat. I swallow and blink back the tears.

"He said that?"

Joolz squeezes my arm.

"Of course he did," says George.

So we sit chewing the fat, filling in the blanks about our dead Dad. That's why George is here. It's what he came to tell me, what the letters were about.

"I tried to get in contact sooner but…"

I nod, not sure how I'm supposed to react. Turns out the old man died a fortnight ago and I missed the funeral.

Is it really bad that I don't so much as get watery-eyed over this? Am I the biggest asshole on the planet for thinking 'thank fuck' because I don't have to face him or smell his beery breath or worry about being rejected by him ever again?

The kid explains how it was him who wrote the letters, how Dad had talked so many times about calling me but kept putting it off until finally the cancer made it so that he couldn't do nothing.

Throat cancer. Not liver like you'd think. Ma always said the drink would be the death of him, but she was wrong.

"He'd been completely sober for almost four years," said George. "He even started a band with a couple of the guys from the drug and alcohol support group where we live, and they were actually pretty good."

"He tried to help Mum give up the bottle too… but… well… That didn't really work. And now she's worse than ever."

I grimace. "That must be hard for you."

He waves his hand dismissively.

"It's fine, I'm fine."

"Is there anyone that can… I mean anyone else there to help?"

"Only Georgia." He pauses then smiles sheepishly. "I forgot to tell you that you have a sister."

My heart thuds against my rib cage. I had been bracing myself for this sort of revelation but second-guessing didn't make it any easier to take.

George pulls a crumpled photo out of the small side pocket of his saxophone case and stabs at it with his index finger.

"That was taken about a year ago, just after Dad started the chemo."

I goggle at the picture. It's Dad sure enough, just older, fatter and balder than I remember. He looks ok though, not like he's dying or anything. On either side of him sit a girl and boy who could be taken for twins.

"Georgia's seven minutes older than me," he grins, "and way bossier."

I grin back.

"Have you got any brothers or sisters?" he asks.

I shake my head. "No." Then I add, "Just you guys, I guess."

We talk about likes and dislikes after that. About how George plays the alto saxophone and listens to punk pop and has never heard of *The Godfather trilogy*. The time flies so quickly I don't even realise it's gone four AM till Joolz points towards the clock.

"Maybe we should get you a taxi," she says. "It's really late."

The kid shrugs.

"Yeah," I say, "this is true." I pick up my cellphone and start scrolling through my contacts for a cab number. "Where do you live anyhow?"

He shrugs again.

"What does that mean?" I say, joking with him. "You don't know? You don't care? Hey, if you stay here any longer, kid, I'm gonna have to start charging you rent!"

His face twitches.

Then something inside my belly twists and my eyes swivel towards his saxophone case.

"Kid, what the ef is going on here?"

I have a pain in my gut and I don't know where it's coming from.

He says nothing.

"Tell me you haven't done a bunk, huh?"

Still no answer.

"So what now?" I say. "You're gonna busk for your breakfast?"

The reason I know that's exactly what he's planning is cause I cut class one day and ran away to Edinburgh with nothing but my guitar and my train fare when I was around his age. After earning fifty-six pence in seven hours, I used my 'wages' to call Ma to beg her to come and get me.

He shrugs again.

I think about telling him that story but I'm too tired and wasted and it was so long ago I can't even remember why I split.

"I'm never going back to that dump," he mumbles.

"Well," I snap, "you're gonna have to– "

Joolz shushes me with her fingertips and crosses the room to sit beside him. Quietly, she says: "Do you want to talk about whatever's happened?"

Shrug. Shrug. Shrug.

I sigh.

He sighs.

Joolz sighs.

I surprise myself by saying: "Ok, you can sleep here just for tonight."

Once upon a time, somewhere in another dimension, there might be a me who was helped by an older and wiser relative. Maybe that other me ran away from home too, but instead of crawling back to Mamma they lucked out and hitched a lift all the way to Italy. Maybe then they decided to look up Nonno and Nonna and all the uncles and aunties and cousins in the Romeo family. And, maybe, just maybe, they found them and were welcomed into the fold.

Joolz gives me a look of reproach.

I throw one straight back at her that says 'what?'

I know what she's thinking though – she thinks I should make the boy give up his home address and his telephone number, that I should call his mother and tell her where he is or at the very least send him home in a cab. But I'm not gonna do that. And I'm not gonna make a big fuss by calling the cops to find out if he's been listed as a missing person either. Cause let's face it, from what he's told me about his Ma, she is probably lying in a puddle of her own puke someplace.

"This is so unbelievably awesome," says George, his eyes lighting up as I pass him the spare duvet from the hall cupboard.

"It's just for tonight," I repeat.

"Sure," he grins, "that's cool."

"I know it ain't much..." I say to him, as I pull out some extra pillows.

"That's cool," he says, patting the sofa as he slumps down onto it wearing one of my old tracksuits. "I've slept in worse places."

I nod my head. Sounds like the kid has had a really bad life – well, maybe not a 'bad' life per se but he's obviously had it rough.

I ask him again if he's sure there's nothing else I can get him.

"No thanks, this is great."

His eyes are heavy now and he looks like such a little boy wearing my clothes. It's still hard to believe that I have a tiny teenage brother.

☞ ♥ ☜

I'm ready to put the light out when the front door cracks open.

Kat, Robbie and Minty, followed by a low, husky voice I don't recognise, are talking about the rising cost of cab fares and some miscellaneous catfight.

"Hey," Kat nods. "Wasn't sure if you would be here or not."

"Yeah, where the fuck did yous swan off tae?" says Minty.

She doesn't give me a chance to answer, just launches full-force into a story about Mel and Sweet Cherie and Mikki Blue Eyes in the Polo Lounge toilets.

"I thought Cherie was going to have an aneurysm or some-thing," says Kat. "You should have seen them, Vicky– "

"Aye," says Minty, "Mel's like that to her 'it was just one time I swear just one time...' and Cherie goes 'shut it just wait till we get home'..."

"I can't believe she's taking her back after that," says the dude with the raspy voice.

Heads shake all round.

"This is Al, by the way," says Robbie.

"Hey," I nod.

Al nods back.

I feel a little bit on edge. This person's hair, clothes and gestures are all uniformly androgynous; they've got no facial hair, no visible Adam's apple or tits, so I can't tell if they're a he or a she or something in between. Not that I really care which category they fall into, I just pride myself on using the proper pronoun.

I don't ask whether Al is a man or a woman though.

a) Because it's rude and b) because the kid is listening, and I haven't quite worked out how and when to tell him about my own gayness, never mind serving him up with the genderfuck soup that is Robbie and his cronies.

"Anyway," says Kat, "it was some night."

"Sounds like it."

"But I don't know what'll happen with the play now that Mel..." She stops, looks down at the half-asleep kid. "Oh my god, is that– "

"Hi, Miss Astrof!"

"Ok... Why is one of my third-year pupils bunking on the settee?"

"Kat," I say, throwing my arm around her, "meet my baby brother, George."

"I know who he is but... What? Brother?"

"We only just kind of found out we were related."

"I always said your maw was a dark horse," Minty smirks.

I ignore that remark and she wanders off back down the hall followed by Robbie and the mysterious Al.

"So, ok, I'm going to bed too," says Kat. "When I wake up I'll realise this is all a dream and a punishment for overdosing on the blue Wickeds."

"We can talk about it tomorrow," I tell her.

"Good night," she says and wobbles out of the room.

I switch the light off and tramp back to my room where Joolz is waiting in my bed.

"Boy, what a night," I say, pulling off my t-shirt.

"Mmm."

I climb under the duvet and snake my arm around her.

"You think I did the right thing with George?"

She mumbles something that sounds like 'don't know' followed by 'your feet are cold'.

"Maybe I should go check on him... I mean it's his first time here... It's a strange house..."

Joolz hauls herself up on her elbows, looks me straight in the eye and, with her voice full of sleep, says: "Vicky... You are so, unbelievably, gay."

"Whaaaa?"

She throws her head back and laughs and I do too.

"You love it," I tell her.

"Mmhmm."

She squeezes my waist and we kiss. And part of me feels incredibly horny even though I'm incredibly tired. I'm thinking about this when Joolz shuts her eyes and murmurs: "Good night, Vicky."

Seventeen

"Tell me you did not meet him in the Polo Lounge," whispers Kat, cocking her head towards my dead to the world little brother. She's sitting on the edge of a breakfast stool at our kitchen table drinking water with Alka-Seltzer, this is the closest we've had to a normal conversation since the other night at L.I.P.S.

"Jeezus, no!" I say. "He was here waiting on the doorstep when I got home..."

She frowns and I tell her it's complicated.

"It usually is with you... Just wait till you meet the sister."

"Is she a student of yours too?"

"She was." Kat stops and takes another slug of water. "Up until last week when she got excluded."

"Great," I reply, shaking my head. "What did she do?"

"Apparently she took a bottle of vodka into Home Economics and thought it would be funny to add it to the cake mixture of one of her other classmates. I say apparently because it didn't happen on my watch and there was a group of the little shits involved."

I say nothing. It stands to reason that Georgia would have easy access to booze, what with her Ma being a chronic alkie and all.

"The girl they spiked was diabetic and she ended up being seriously ill."

"Shit."

"Shit indeed. It was very nearly a police matter."

"Probably she never knew that the kid had a health condition and would get so sick."

"Maybe so, Vicky, but she shouldn't have been bringing alcohol into school in the first place, and she certainly shouldn't have been adding it to someone else's food."

"That's true," I say. And I hope that that's the conversation about Georgia ended because I feel strangely protective towards her even though we haven't met.

I'm about to change the subject, ask her what she thinks about the whole Mel fucking Mikki Blue Eyes caper when the door whizzes open and Minty crows: "Right, who's for a roll and fried egg and tattie scone?" Kat groans. "No thanks, I couldn't even look at a fried egg."

"Well," Min grins, patting her belly, "all the more nosh for me then."

☞ ♥ ☜

I want to ask Kat about the thing with her and Robbie but I don't know where to start. I know if we don't sort it out – if I don't accept this whole bisexual situation – then I'll lose them both as friends. I tell her this, and I also tell her how sorry I am that I reacted the way I did, and how I've been having sleepless nights thinking about it ever since.

"It's just that, after all that stuff with my first girlfriend, I promised myself I'd never trust another swinger – I mean bisexual – plus it kinda felt like I'd been lied to... Even though you never actually told me any lies. You know what I mean?"

Kat nods sympathetically. She doesn't correct me for using the word 'swinger'.

"But then I realised that this is how the hets must feel when they find out that their friend or their daughter or their sister or whoever is gay. They don't see how hard it is to come out, or how scared some people are of being rejected or called names – they just see you as a two-faced scheming cunt who's been keeping secrets from them."

I'm getting so worked up and talking so fast I end up panting like I've run a race. Then I realise that I've not let Kat get a word in, which is particularly bad form considering she was the victim in all of this.

"Sorry," I blush. "I got carried away. Sorry, I didn't mean to– "
"Don't be," she says. "Please, go on, I'm really interested in what you've got to say."

"Uh, well..."

She gives me a small encouraging smile.

"I was thinking that sometimes even the best parents, or the best friends, they can't cope with what they're hearing, and they turn it on its head and focus on how it's going to affect them and how they might take some backlash because of it."

"You know, when the lesbian mothers fell out with Mamma because of me, I felt so shit for her, but I got over it by labelling them all a bunch of hypocritical pricks." Pause. "The way I treated you though was just as bad."

Kat reaches out across the table and squeezes my hand.

"Do you think you can forgive me?"

She grins. "I'll let you owe me a drink."

"Deal."

We both sigh.

"Now all I gotta do," I tell her, "is fix the problem that's currently residing on my sofa."

"Well, if you need any help..."

"Thanks. I definitely do."

It feels so good to be on talking terms again. I tell her this. Kat says she's glad too.

"There's one other thing though, Vicky."

"Wassat then?"

"I don't want you to take this the wrong way or anything..."

Here it comes. I know exactly what she's gonna say. I been expecting her to give me grief about the kid, have her tell me that I did everything wrong and could get into trouble with the authorities.

"Hey, whatever it is..."

"Well..." Pause. "It's just that I've found someplace else to live."

"Oh."

"And it has nothing to do with the stuff that's been happening over the last few days."

"Uh ok." I am dumbfounded. I've gotten used to Kat and her ways and I just assumed that we'd carry on being flatmates even though it was only ever meant to be short term. "Well, I guess that's great you found someplace."

"Thanks."

"Is Rob going with you?"

"Hell no," she laughs and I give a little nervous chuckle.

A phone beeps, interrupting the awkward silence that has lodged itself between us, and Kat fishes it out of her pocket, reads the text message, tuts and puts the phone down on the table.

"Bad news?" I ask.

She slides the phone across to me and I read the message. "Fuck," I say. Then louder: "Fucking cunting fucking bastarding cunts!"

The door swings open and in strolls Minty brandishing a bottle of brown sauce and a bag of morning rolls.

"Did somebody call?"

Then George sticks his head around the door and says 'morning' in a tentative voice.

Robbie traipses in behind them wearing one of Kat's dressing gowns, followed by Al who is still in last night's crumpled clothes and Joolz who is dressed to kill after spending the last half-hour in the bathroom.

"Mel and Cherie have dropped out of the play," I tell them, soberly.

"Nae luck," says Minty, turning on the cooker.

Another text comes through. Kat reads it out. "Cherie says she's really sorry but her relationship with Mel comes first."

I thump my fist on the table. "Fuck fuck fuck."

"I'm sure you'll be able to find someone else to fill in," Joolz pipes up.

"Yeah, right," I moan, "like who?"

"What about Minty?" says Kat.

"Fuck off!" scowls Min.

"I'll do it," says Robbie.

"I knew those two lousy fucks couldn't be trusted... I said it all along that– "

"Vicky, I have to go," says Joolz, silencing me with a kiss on the forehead.

I am fizzing mad because I know that with only two weeks left and two men down it's obvious that Broadbent is gonna cancel the whole thing, which basically means I'm gonna end up with egg on my face. Because I told everyone I knew about this play. I told every person I met in every gay bar. I even got Joolz to tell all her friends about it and

Joolz.

Ohmygod.

Of course.

I am so fucking stupid sometimes.

And I'm so overcome with relief and excitement I can hardly speak.

"What is it?" Joolz asks. "Why are you looking at me funny? You scare me sometimes when you pull that kind of face."

"You," I say to her, jumping up and grabbing her by the shoulders. "You could do it!"

I can see it now: me and Joolz sharing the limelight, me and Joolz debating over costume choices and the most dramatic way to make our entrances. We won't get to have an onstage kiss, and most likely our time together will be spent studying our scripts instead of each other, but sometimes you have to suffer for your art.

"Och, no, Vicky, you know I can't. I'm stressed out my nut with college stuff and I seriously need to find some form of job and– "

"I said *I'll* do it." Robbie has his hand in the air and is manically bouncing up and down.

"Come on, baby, it won't take you long to brush up on the play..."

I tilt my head and give her my best come to bed eyes.

"I would if I could," she replies, "but– "

"I SAID I'LL DO IT," squeals the boy wonder. "I've seen the film and I've been helping Kat with her lines, and with the right wig and a close shave I could totally pull off a middle-aged virginal governess."

I look from Joolz to Robbie then back to Joolz again. This has got to be the dumbest suggestion I've ever heard. I want to say 'hey, this isn't *Priscilla Queen of the Desert* we're performing' but I'm scared things will blow up with Kat again, so I decide to keep a lid on my opinions. Besides, I know that Attila the artistic director will never allow a guy in the show.

"Actually, that's not a bad idea," says Kat, finally. "Robbie would make a great Miss Prism and Minty could be Chasuble."

"My answer's still FUCK OFF." Minty roars from behind the frying pan. She is alternately flipping potato scones and scooping over-easy eggs into a succession of buttered rolls.

"I'm sure he would," I say, picking my words carefully. "And if it was up to me I wouldn't have a problem with it. But there is no way that Broadbent is gonna go for it."

"Are you sure about that?" chimes in Al.

The room goes quiet. All I can hear is the sound of sizzling oil. This is the first time Al has said anything directly to me, and I can't help noticing that he or she seems to be talking a whole octave higher than they were last night.

Oh here we go, I think. Now we're going to get the 'it's not the penis that makes the man' spiel.

Al turns to Robbie and says: "Do you identify as a man or a woman?"

"Both," comes the reply.

I roll my eyes. This is the first I've heard about it.

"Look, it's up to you if you want to go and ask Broadbent," I press on, "but all I'm saying is there's no way she's going to let a– a– "

"Tranny," Robbie interjects.

"I was going to say 'cross-dresser'," pause, "take part."

"You might be surprised," says Al.

I raise an eyebrow as if to say 'who the fuck are you and what do you know?'

"I'll talk to her," they say. Then they look from Robbie to me and add with a smirk, "she's my girlfriend."

My jaw drops open.

"There," says Joolz. "You don't need me." Pause. "But I need *you* to phone me a taxi."

I don't go into work. Instead I call in sick right after breakfast, and I ask the kid to take a walk with me. He does this without a word, although his shoulders hang low and he drags his feet all the way to Merchant City. I don't speak either, although I have plenty to say. There are things I need to tell him about life, about the world, about me – and I don't know where to begin.

Sandra Dee's is graveyard quiet. I'm glad because this means that there won't be any interruptions or exchanges where I have to explain who he is.

"What soft drink would you like?" I say, emphasising the word 'soft'.

I'm under no illusions that this kid is and always has been teetotal, but I'm also not in favour of buying booze for minors.

"Irn Bru, please."

I order two and we sit down at a table at the back, far away from the TV screens and a lonely lesbian football fan who is helping her hangover by knocking back the Guinness.

I start by telling him about Sam, about how her and Mamma met, and how she fought the school bullies for me, and about how she helped make me become the person I am today. And all the while I'm very careful not to say 'she' or reveal Sam's gender.

"So you see, Sam was like a parent and an older brother rolled into one, even though we weren't blood relations."

The boy takes a swig of his soda. "*She* sounds like a really amazing person."

I nod. I don't ask how he knew Sam was female. Maybe I slipped up. Or maybe he overheard me saying something to Kat when he was meant to be asleep. I know if I was bedding down in a strange house I'd have one eye open under the duvet and one ear pointing to the door.

It's not important though. What is important is that he doesn't care that my parents are gay. Cause I been really worried about coming out to the kid. Cause even though I come out to people on a regular basis this just isn't the same. George has been through so much shit and I don't wanna hurt him in any way, or provoke any prejudices, but I really need him to know the truth. If I'm gonna help him at all and have any kind of relationship with him – I need him to love me the way I am or not love me at all.

We talk some more about me and where I grew up, and what it was like not having any brothers or sisters. He tells me about Georgia and how they used to be close but since Dad got sick she's been running with a bad crowd. He doesn't mention the vodka incident or her exclusion and I don't let on that I know.

I ask if he has a girlfriend. He doesn't.

"Or a boyfriend?"

"Definitely not."

"Hey, I was just being PC," I tell him, "you never can tell."

He laughs at this.

Then.

"I really like Julie," he says. "She's a really nice person."

"Yeah," I nod, "she is."

Our conversation comes to a natural lull. I'm starting to understand how awkward it must have been for Sam that day she first brought me here ten years ago. She was twenty years old, and not only had she just committed to being step-daddy to someone else's almost adolescent kid, but she stepped up and explained the rainbow-coloured birds and bees to me too.

"The thing is..." I start, "it's just that Joolz is my... well... She's not just my friend..."

George grins.

"I already got that," he says. "And I think you two make a really-ly cool couple."

"Thanks," I say, breathing a sigh of relief. "That means a lot to me."

We drain our drinks and put our coats back on. George is wearing one of my old windbreakers because it's been raining all afternoon.

"You know that you have to go home now, don't you?"

"Yeah," he says, quietly.

"Georgia really needs her brother right now."

He nods.

"And I promise you, kid, I'll be there whenever you need me."

He throws his arms around me suddenly and we stand hugging in the middle of the doorway, much to the annoyance of two teenage super-femmes who are shaking off their matching pink umbrellas.

"Anytime, anyplace, anywhere," I add.

☞ ♥ ☜

When I get home, Minty is in her room playing Sonic the Hedgehog on the PlayStation.

"We need to talk," I say, pulling the plug.

"Aw c'mon man, fuck sake, yev just ruined ma game!"

She stands up and throws the controller down onto the bed.

"What is it, well?"

"I'll give you ten bucks," I say, "if you'll take over Cherie's part in the play."

"Get tae fuck."

"OK twenty."

She sniffs and says "Forty."

I take out my wallet and wave it at her: "Thirty bucks, and that's my final offer."

"Thirty-five."

"OK, done."

☞ ♥ ☜

"The curtain rises on Algernon's apartment. The piano is playing backstage whilst Lane enters with afternoon tea– " Broadbent stops, she waits for a couple of seconds and then repeats, "Lane enters." The imaginary stage that we have drawn on the floor with white masking tape is empty. Lane is neither here nor there. "Where is Lane?" she snarls.

No one knows. Up until now, Salsa (who didn't even want to do any actual acting in the show but ended up with two bit parts) has never been late or missed a rehearsal, but it's worrying all the same.

Mikki looks up for a second before going back to highlighting her lines with a yellow marker, Scarface is sitting daydreaming as usual, and Zest is popping a bright yellow lollypop in and out of her mouth and swinging her legs back and forth under her chair.

"Kirsten," Broadbent snaps, "lunchtime is over. Bin that." She sounds stressed-out – maybe even close to breaking point. I'm not surprised though, because we're scarily close to the deadline yet half the scenes are a shambles.

Then she sighs and gestures to Zest with her script. "Could you be Lane for just now."

LANE> Mr Ernest Worthing

That's my cue. I take a quick, last swig of my Coke then push the bottle under my chair. I am about to enter from stage left when the door swings open from behind me and Minty bursts into the room with a white polystyrene cup in one hand and a plastic bag from Finelines' Books and Music in the other.

"I didnae miss much, did I?"

"We started ten minutes ago," replies Broadbent, gritting her teeth. She points at a chair by the side of the stage and tells Minty to sit. "Take it from: 'Mr Ernest Worthing'," she says, turning back to face the stage.

LANE> Mr Ernest Worthing

The door opens again and Robbie creeps in. "Sorry," he says, clicking the door shut behind him. "Call of nature."

Eighteen

I'm late to meet Joolz and it's all because of Minty. Because of her pussying around this morning and bugging me to agree to go clubbing with her while I was trying to get ready for work. I was late for my shift. And because of that, Maggie made me stay an extra hour to shovel shit. And because of that, I was late for rehearsal and missed the first two scenes of act one, which resulted in Broadbent keeping everyone there till a quarter to ten.

Who goes clubbing on a Tuesday night anyway? I said this to Minty right before I left but she just started sulking and saying that I was busy every other night of the week. It's not like it's my fault, though. I hardly got time to eat, sleep or take a piss, and I'm missing my classes for the next two weeks because Broadbent wants us in every night to rehearse – every night apart from Wednesdays of course, because Broadbent can't do Wednesdays. I told Minty this, but she didn't seem to care; she just shrugged and screwed her face up and said that I could always quit the show. I felt like saying to her 'yeah you'd like that', I really did, 'cause then you'd have a pal to sit drinking with you in Loser-Ville.' In the end though, I kept quiet and I told her she could come out for a pint with Joolz and me tonight.

It's ten o'clock and I've left Minty dawdling at the door of the Rainbow Centre with Mikki Blue and her harem of ex-lovers. I'm supposed to get Joolz and two of her friends out front – their names are Mylene and Liane and they both have boyfriends – but there's no one else around, and a quick text check on my mobile says that they've gone on over to Sandy's without me.

Originally Joolz's friends wanted to go to their local, but I put my foot down. Joolz tried her best to talk me round but I said, uh-uh, no way. She totally doesn't get why straight bars and me don't mix, even though I've explained it to her about a million times. But then, that's because she's never suffered the embarrassment of being asked to leave the ladies' room ('Sir'), or had to listen to pigs with small pricks asking her why she's 'trying to look like a man'.

Inside Sandy's, Joolz sees me before I see her and she jumps up from a table in a back alcove and bounces towards me with her arms outstretched. She's drunk and when she leans in to kiss me she squeezes my ass and I feel mildly irritated, although I'm not sure why.

On the way back to her friends, she holds my hand and this pleases me but again the irritation rises its head inside as she gives me the rundown of her day: she hates her mother because she's giving her such a hard time, one of her college lecturers was grilling her about why she doesn't have a boyfriend, she hurt her wrist at cheerleading practice...

"And I'm thoroughly skint," she says finally. "Which is why I'm seriously thinking of dropping out of college and getting a full-time job."

"That's a bit of a rash decision, is it not?"

She shrugs.

We sit down then, and she introduces me to Liane, her friend from college who is also a dancer, and Liane's boyfriend (Chas) and his friend (Dave) who look so clean cut and who are sitting so close together that they could easily be misconstrued as a couple in their own right.

"And Mylene isn't fucking coming out tonight."

"How come?" I ask.

"She's refusing to set foot in a 'poof pub'."

"Oh."

I'd been looking forward to meeting this girl Mylene. Not because I actually thought I'd hit it off with her – because she sounds like a homophobic, up her own ass creep to me – but because Joolz told me all about her, about how they'd been best friends since they were about five and how she had a crush on her all the way through high school (although I've been sworn to secrecy because no one else, especially not Mylene, knows this), and I was dying to see what she looked like.

Joolz's new pay-as-you-go cellphone starts to ring.

"Hello?" She looks pissed off. "For you," she says, passing it over.

It's Minty.

"Hey."

"Where are you?"

"In the pub."

"Which pub?"

"Sandy's." I reply. "Where did you think I was?" It's not like I never told her what the plans were. Joolz rolls her eyes and says something to Liane.

"Sound. I'll not be long," says Min and cuts me off.

Joolz sighs, folds her arms and slams both elbows down on the table.

"Why the fuck has she got my number?"

"Oh, I called you from her cellphone earlier and she musta recorded it." I shrug.

"Well, tell her to fucking unrecord it cause I don't want prank phone calls from that cow." I tell her I'll make sure she doesn't call again, although I know that if I say to Minty not to call she'll go out of her way to do the exact opposite. "What did she want, anyway?" I sink deep into my chair. "What did she say? Fuck sake, she's not coming here is she?"

I don't answer. The two metrosexual boys exchange glances. "Anyway..." says Chas, "would anyone like a drink?"

Joolz has gone from being mildly intoxicated to becoming seriously slaughtered, and I notice she is not the most amicable of drunkards. I point out that she's had rather a lot and that maybe she should give it up for the night but she just sort of sneers and tells me that I'm being boring and then goes on to tell Liane about how Minty crashed our date the other night.

"I swear to god," she says, "she's a fat fucking– "

"Hey," I say, "don't be mean."

Min might be a pain in the ass half the time but she's still my best bud, and I'm not gonna sit round and listen to her name being trailed through the mud.

"Yeah, you're such a sad bitch, Joolz," says Liane. "She's probably just lonely. Does she not have a girlfriend?"

I watch Joolz take another shot of Sambuca from the row on the table, throw back her head and gulp it down. "You kidding?" she coughs. "Nobody'd have her."

"Al-right!" Joolz's mouth snaps shut. Minty saunters over with a dripping pint of Guinness in her hand. She thumps it down on the table almost spilling some on Joolz's packet of cigarettes – the cigarettes she's meant to have given up smoking.

"Drink, Julie?"

"Well, if you're buying, I'll have a large white wine."

She looks at me and grins. I glare back at her.

"Vick?"

"I'm fine."

"Yer pals want drinks?"

Minty looks around the table at Liane, Chas and Dave. They shake their heads, point to their glasses and say: "Thanks, anyway."

"Cheap round then," grins Minty. "Hey yous watch ma pint?" she adds, taking two steps towards the ladies room. "Come to the bogs wi us, Vicky. I got something to tell you."

"Is that it?" I say, when Minty says that she saw Sam going into the Polo Lounge a few minutes ago.

"She looked pure fucked oot her heid, man."

"Well, she's a big girl," I tell her. "She's allowed to cut loose once in a while."

"I was just saying."

Sigh.

"Anyway, I wanted to ask how things were going wi yer burd?"

"Fine," I snap.

"Aw... Well, that's good." Pause. "Yous actually look really good thegether."

"Thanks."

Joolz and Liane are rolling around in their seats laughing, and I am thoroughly bored now because their entire conversation so far has been a mix of personal remarks about people they know and hate, and strangers in the bar who've had the misfortune of blundering into their line of vision.

"Oh my god, look, that's just so-ooo wrong." Liane nudges Joolz and points to a sweet old butch with brylcremed hair and a blazer who is sitting beside the jukebox.

"Yeah, somebody should tell her it's not Halloween yet."

"That's cruel," I say.

"It's so true though," sniggers Joolz.

"Does anybody want another drink?" asks Minty.

Everybody does apart from Chas and Dave, who stand up and put on their identical black sports coats and announce that they're off to play pool at the Scotia.

Yeah, sure you are. More like off to pot the brown.

There is a chorus of 'see you' and then Minty chimes in "Aye, nice to meet yous."

Joolz picks up a cigarette and tries to light it backwards.

"AHAAA ya fanny!" Liane roars as little red flames burst out of the filter. "AHAHAHAAAH!"

I don't like this girl at all. She's loud and coarse and she reminds me of those broads who laughed at me all through high school. The majority of them smoked and drank their way through secondary and then left at fifteen to have a kid or to go do travel and tourism at the local shitty college.

"Ugh fuck off ya mad hetty!" says Joolz.

"Hetty? What's a hetty?"

"A fucking hetero-hetero-fucking-straight person, daft boot!"

"I'm bisexual actually."

Joolz rolls her eyes. "You are NOT bisexual."

"Am so."

"She's kissed one woman," says Joolz, "and all of a sudden she's decided she's bent."

This revelation of part-time lady loving doesn't surprise me in the slightest, since Liane looks like the type who'd dabble at parties just to try and turn her boyfriend on or engage the attention of some other dickhead.

"I've always been attracted to women," she rambles.

"Would you ever sleep with one?" asks Minty.

"Eugh, no."

"Well," says Joolz, "you're not fucking bisexual then are you?"

The conversation goes along this vein for a few more minutes with Liane admitting that, yes, she definitely does prefer the penis and, besides, she doesn't really understand what lesbians do in bed anyway.

"They sleep," I reply.

"And sometimes they paint each other's toenails," adds Joolz with a smirk.

"Wouldn't the nail varnish go everywhere?"

"No, because it's special lesbian nail varnish."

"I see," says Liane, furrowing her brow.

"I don't," says Minty.

I know what I'm seeing: I'm seeing a different side to Julie Turner – a side that's superficial and bitchy and immature – and I don't particularly dig it. And I think she knows that I'm pissed off with her because now she's starting to make eyes at me and blow kisses across the table.

"VICK-EEE!" She throws her arms out but Minty pushes past me and squeezes in beside her. Not that I want to sit hugging Joolz right now because her voice is becoming really shrill and annoying – in fact it's borderline embarrassing being here with her in this state, especially since a group of middle-aged, flannel-shirt dykes that I recognise from the lesbian mothers' posse are throwing her dirty looks.

"VICK-EEEEEE!"

"Naw, fuck off," says Minty. "I'm not watching you two paw each other all night. Yous are staying separated."

I run my hand across my face – I'm starting to wish I went straight home.

For the next half-hour Joolz and Liane get stuck into a tray of two-for-one cocktails, while I decline their offers of more alcohol and Minty sends me up to the bar for beer because she's worried Joolz and I might try to sit together.

"Is it the West End you stay, Julie?" Minty asks.

"Why do you want to know?"

"Just asking."

"Well, it's not like I'm going to invite you over or anything."

"I was just asking."

"Well, I can tell you this much," says Joolz, "it's not the West End."

"I suspected that," replies Minty, grinning. "I've Bunburied all over the West End."

There's an awkward silence that looms for several seconds. Liane rescues the conversation by asking how Joolz and I met.

Minty pulls a face. "Aw here we go... Did you have to ask that?"

I start to tell the story of the night I found Joolz's lipstick in Sandy's.

"There I was– "

"Hang on, let me tell it..."

"Ok." I sit back in my chair, fold my arms and grin.

"I was sitting in Sandra Dee's totally bored out of my tits, in fact I was just about to leave when I dropped my lipstick..." Joolz pauses. Takes a deep drag of her cigarette. I smile at her as I wait for her to tell the tale of how I came to the rescue.

"So I bend over to pick up my lipstick– "

"As you do," says Liane, giggling as she mixes the rest of an orange cocktail with a red one, shaking it around until it turns a cloudy pink.

"When this girl who I actually thought was a boy at first– "

"Eh?"

"Marches over and nearly tramples on my fingers." Everyone laughs except me. Hmmph.

"Anyway, I say thanks to her and I am about to walk away when she offers to buy me a drink," says Joolz. "I could tell she definitely fancied me." She sticks her tongue out at me and they all erupt into hiccupping hilarity. "But I didn't think she was my type... But then I was bored and Paris had fucked off to the toilets to sniff poppers with JJ and some tranny guy..."

"Awww, that Paris was a minger," says Liane. "I always hated the way she said 'me and ma buuurd'"

"Buuuurd," Joolz repeats, and the two of them crack up again.

"Any-way," Liane continues, "so then what happened?"

"Then some clown stole my purse."

"And I found it," Minty pipes up.

"And I walked her home," I volunteer.

"Awww, how romantic." Liane tilts her head and gives me a sickening, simpering smile.

"Romantic? I had no money, my mobile phone battery had run out," says Joolz. "She fucking FOLLOWED me home."

"I DID NOT follow you."

"Ok, she INSISTED on walking all the way from Merchant City to King's Park at three o'clock in the morning."

"Awww, but that's really sweet," says Liane.

"She lives in Merchant City."

"Ok she was trying to get into your pants."

"Hey, I was being kind and considerate."

"When we got to my house, she tried to get off with me on my doorstep. Then when I told her nothing was going to happen between us, she told me that she didn't know how to get home so I had to call her a taxi."

"Ah, you dinnae tell me that, Romeo," says Minty. She nudges me with her elbow to get my attention.

I tell her to fuck off.

☞ ♥ ☜

Minty finally gets up off her ass. "I need to go to the bog. Come wi us, Vick?"

I tell her to go by herself.

"Aw c'mon," she says, "I've got something important to tell you."

"That's what you said the last time."

"Aye, but this time it's like mega important."

"Ok."

I follow like a dog.

She asks if everything is alright with me and Joolz.

"We're both fine."

"Just saying. Plus, it seems to me like your girlfriend's being a bit of a bitch towards you."

I'm about to tell her to shut her fat mouth when Joolz roars at us: "DO YOU WANT HER TO HOLD YOUR HAND AND WIPE YOUR ARSE AS WELL?"

The lesbian mothers look over again, murmuring and shaking their heads in disapproval.

"Ok. So what now?"

It's the same old shit again. Do I really need to go home at twelve? Can't I just stay out clubbing?

"You know I can't," I tell her, trying not to slide on wet toilet paper that someone's thrown all around. "I got work to go to."

"Aw, come on," she begs. "It'll no kill ye tae have one late night, will it?"

Actually it just might.

"Plus that lassie that I've been talking tae off gay dot com – the one that's just moved up here fae Brighton – she said her and her pals will be in Bennet's the night.

"This could be ma big chance wi her."

"So take your chance."

"Aw c'mon..."

I am furious at Min right now. Not just for dragging me in here, but for all the other tiny bits of bullshit that have been building up between us recently. But I've also got a stupid, stinking headache and I'm way too exhausted for an argument.

I fish out a rolled-up five-pound note out of my back pocket, slide it into her palm and say: "Buy her a drink on me."

Joolz doesn't go back to her house like she planned. Instead, she comes back to mine and we end up having a massive row. During the row, which could technically be classed as two rows – because Joolz is so drunk that we have to have an interlude so that she can run to the bathroom to throw up – she tells me that she thinks I'm wasting my talents hanging out in gay bars all the time with Minty 'and all those other idiots'.

"What do you mean I'm wasting my talents? I'm not the one who's so pissed she tried to sit down in the middle of the road tonight and I'm not the one who's talking about jacking in her college course and, in case you've forgotten, I'm working my ass off doing this play and one day soon I *will* be making a living out of acting, you just watch..."

"Some-whey-ere o-ver a rain-bow," sings Joolz, "pigs will fly-yyyy..."

The argument grinds to a halt after that and Joolz strips off and gets into my bed naked. I try not to even look at her or say another word cause talking to someone in her condition is pointless, pretty soon we're both lying in silence with our backs to each other.

She hums a couple more notes from 'Somewhere Over a Rainbow' followed by 'We Could Have Been Anything' from *Bugsy Malone*. I pull the pillow up around my ears.

☞ ♥ ☜

When Joolz finally wakes up she's really hung-over. Her hair is an explosion and her eyes have black panda smears from where she's forgotten to take off last night's make-up. In short, she looks like shit. I've been awake for hours and I'm no longer pissed at her, I nod good morning to let her know this. She doesn't say anything at first, just makes a noise like a balloon deflating and then disappears deep under the covers. I sit up on the bed next to her and ask if she wants an aspirin or something. She doesn't answer.

I make her a cup of strong black coffee and leave it steaming by the bed along with a glass of water while I organise some toast for us both. From inside the kitchen, I can't help over-hearing the loud groans and the sound of squeaking bedsprings coming from Minty's room. I grin to myself and leave the last two slices of bread in the bag.

Eventually Joolz comes out of her cave and she gives me a hangdog look.

"I am sooo sooo sorry about last night, baby," she mumbles, reaching out for a hug. "I was well out of order... I'm so stupid sometimes." She seems genuinely embarrassed by her drunkenness and I'm pleased about this because I never want to experience a night like that again.

"Forget about it," I say and wrap my arms around her neck and kiss her on the forehead. "How you feeling?"

"Absolutely crap."

I nod.

I offer the plate of toast to her, knowing she probably won't wanna eat anything. She doesn't, but she drinks the coffee and the water and she asks if she can smoke. Normally I would remind her at this point that she'd promised to quit, but I don't because I have more important things I want to talk to her about and I don't want to get bogged down with petty details.

"What time is it?"

"Almost noon."

I tell her I've already been for a jog and back, had a shower, washed my hair and put the finishing touches to a short story I'd been writing.

"But I thought you were working at eight this morning?"

"I called in sick."

"I'm sorry," she says and hugs me from behind. "That's my fault again, isn't it?"

"No."

"Well... You would have been at work if it hadn't been for me."

"Probably."

I pick up the green and white pen that's lying on the desk beside my journal and hold it out to her. "This is yours by the way, you dropped it here the other night."

"Thanks," she says. "I think I had about ten of these pens at one point and I seem to be leaving a trail wherever I go."

She takes it and drops it into her handbag, and I eat my breakfast and watch quietly as she brushes out her hair.

"Joolz?"

"Mmhmm?"

"Did you really mean what you said about me wasting my talents?"

"I shouldn't have said that," she says, quietly.

"But you did," I reply, as I scrape a burnt bit off the toast with the edge of my knife. "And I think you're probably right in some respects."

"What do you mean?"

"I have a really shit job, baby. And I spend most of my time complaining about how shit it is instead of actually doing the things I wanna do."

"So you're going to quit?"

"Ha. I would love to. But I need the dough or my rent doesn't get paid."

I finish eating and put the empty plate down on the floor. Everything is quiet for a few minutes. "But I have been thinking about going to drama college... Will you help me make an audition tape?"

Nineteen

*T*he *lesbian pen's name was Radclyffe Orlando Sackville-West. And she was a member of the ballpoint family.*

Born on a tiny assembly line in a factory in Elephant and Castle sometime around late July of 1987, Radclyffe was the offspring of a charity called The London Lesbian Line. She spent most of her earlier years together with a cluster group of her unemployed sister pens, inside a brown and white spotted Tupperware mug, behind a potted cactus, on the window sill of the fourth floor of the Women's Archive Trust for Scotland. This, of course, was until she was obscurely plucked by one Christine Elizabeth Platt, a wart-fingered student of English literature and queer theory, who recognised Radclyffe's obvious talent for essay writing despite a lack of previous experience in either autography or manuscription.

And although Radclyffe did not possess the fluidity of an ink gel or fountain pen, nor could she claim kinship to the Watermans or prestigious Parkers, the partnership she had with Christine Platt was found to be a most amicable one. For she loved nothing more than putting words on paper, especially long meandering sentences that praised the literary merits of her favourites Woolf and Shelly and Carter. And she spent many snug nights thereafter tucked between the thumb and forefinger of the thirty-year-old scholar.

At least, that was, until the dreaded day when Christine 'lent' Radclyffe to a dyslexic client who had come to the archive to participate in an adult literacy programme. (It was a most uncomfortable experience and Radclyffe never even so much as learned the person's name, for the handwriting on the official form was completely illegible – and having no eyes or ears or other sensory abilities she had no way of gleaning pieces of information that weren't written down). And so this is the sad story of how Radclyffe Orlando Sackville-West fell from grace after falling from the anonymous person's coat pocket (having never been returned to Christine Platt), and how she was subsequently kicked along a pavement and through two sets of revolving doors before being picked up once again.

And it was in the sweaty palm of a square-handed nose-picker named Frank Unwin that she next found herself. Ham-fisted, he thrice dragged the unimpressed Radclyffe across a torn off piece of a beer-ringed drinks flier that was advertising a 'cocks in frocks' night at Bennet's nightclub. Radclyffe was appalled by the penmanship of Frank, which was sloppy, slumping and backwards sloping, unlike the upright, neatly printed font of her former mistress. Oh how she longed to be back in Christine's loving grip! She might have cried then if only she'd had the ability. But so refined was Radclyffe Orlando Sackville-West that she didn't leave so much as an inkblot. Frank wiggled her round plastic bottom against the septum of his nose, and then in each of his ear holes alternately, before discarding her on the wet wooden table.

'Oh woe is me,' thought Radclyffe. 'I am rooted yet I flow.' And she began worrying at once that she might never again have the opportunity to quote from another precious poem or novel. 'Each has his past shut in him like the leaves of a book known to him by heart,' she told herself, silently, 'and his friends can only read the title.' And then, after a moment's hesitation, she began to question her very existence. Why was she here? Why was she even on this earth if not to write great sweeping sentences that mimicked the very essence of Brontë's feelings as she walked across the moors? She had been thrown aside like a Latin proverb, and she was thoroughly suspicious that this was because of her gender and overt sexuality.

'Why, if I was a man...' she began, but did not get to finish her stream of thought as she became distracted when she was once again lifted up into another set of hands.

These hands were small, cool and calloused, and yet gentle, and Radclyffe correctly guessed that they belonged to a female. (This was a relief, for her recent and, indeed, only experience of being fingered by a man was so horrible a one that she hoped never to repeat it.) She also noticed, in settling into the woman's tender grasp, that she was left-handed and had a tiny paper cut on the edge of her thumb. And as Radclyffe was guided to press the words 'Tracy' and 'The Importance of Being Earnest' onto another (drier) drinks flier, she hoped to wonder that this person was also a scholar like Christine. 'Perhaps they know each other,' she mused. 'Perhaps they are on the same university course?' And 'Perhaps,' she thought, with a wave of excitement, 'we shall be reunited!'

But Radclyffe's burst of hope was short-lived, and she was once again dispensed against her wishes to another personage who, she noted, was almost certainly female and another left-hander. The *woman's name was Julie and she didn't care one jot about the well-being of the poor lesbian pen; after she'd finished scribbling she unzipped her handbag and carelessly tossed Radclyffe into its black abyss. And Radclyffe, now too exhausted to continue feeling outraged, began to think of her literary heroines and how many of them had been persecuted before finding greatness. And with this thought she comforted herself as she disappeared amongst the loose change and the paper hankies and the other miscellaneous pieces of clutter that she could not readily recognise.*

"I really like it," says Sam.

"Thanks."

She takes another slug of Coke then slides the printout of my story back across the table.

"So what happens next?"

Umm. "What do you mean?"

"What happens to the pen after it disappears into the woman's handbag?"

I shrug.

The fact that she doesn't realise that this is the end of the story is making me wonder if it's actually really shit.

"I hadn't really thought about it," I tell her, dropping my eyes. "I guess I could try to write another instalment."

"No," says Sam. "You shouldn't force it. I think it's great as it is."

"Hmm. Ok."

I scan the new food options: vegan sloppy joes, spicy piquant chickpea burgers (also vegan and gluten-free), tortilla veggie-dogs (with or without the chillies and cheese, contains egg)... Sandy's have totally revolutionised their menu recently, which is down to yours truly, which was the whole point of inviting my parents here today – only we are still waiting for Mamma who texted Sam almost an hour ago to say she was gonna be late.

"So..." says Sam, "what else have you been up to?"

"Just... stuff, I guess."

She nods and waits for me to expand on this, but after about ten seconds, when it becomes obvious that I'm not gonna, she puts on her reading glasses and picks up the menu.

This is awkward. So far I've given Sam the lowdown on the play, my love life, my work life and the new suit I saw in the window of Fraser's that I'd really like to buy for the Butch/Femme party, which is this weekend and the day after Joolz's twenty-first birthday. I practically opened up a vein when I let her look at my writing. Even though what I'd really like to talk about are the new additions and the subtraction from my family quota. There are so many things I want to tell her but I need to wait till Mamma gets here (cause it wouldn't be right), and even then I dunno how I'm gonna spill the beans. It's not like I can just announce 'Hey, by the way, I just found out my old man's popped his clogs' and 'Did you know he had two secret love children?'

"Is everything alright?" asks Psychic Sam.

She tilts her head to the side, which is a thing I do often but never realised till now that I probably inherited the gesture from her. I may have fished my hair and eyes out of the George Mann gene pool, but it was at the Sam Haggarty school of physical and emotional expression that I earned my diploma.

Sam never met my father. "Thank god for that," she'd probably say. Ma says she thinks Sam woulda liked him though, because he was a charmer and he could talk a queen bee into giving up her hive. I'm not so sure about that actually, Sam's pretty intuitive when it comes to people, which is probably one of the few traits she never passed onto me. I never really learned how to read people, which is why I always lose when we play poker. Mamma's kind of the opposite of both of us – she trusts everyone, which is how she winds up being a doormat.

I think Mamma will probably be ok with Dad dying. But then you never can tell. For instance I thought I was ok with it, because I never cried when I found out or felt like I missed him, or had any instant feelings of shock/horror. But then the past couple of nights I've been having trouble dropping off, and when I do I have this re-occurring dream that I'm in a cemetery and I'm violently smashing a bottle of Buckfast off his gravestone. Joolz says I must have suppressed a lotta rage towards him over the years and now it's finally coming out. But I know it's more than that. Aside from the anger, there's a kind of sadness that comes and goes. I can't stop feeling guilty that I never opened those letters. George Junior said Dad's dying wish was to be reunited with me, and I could have given him that but I didn't.

"Yeah," I smile. "Everything's great." I pause. "But I think I might be coming down with something, because I got no appetite today."

"You're not pregnant are you?" she grins.

"Very funny."

Sam's phone rings and she snatches it up and out of her pocket.

"Hey... No, we haven't eaten yet... Oh you're joking." Pause. "Well, I think she might be going somewhere after this but I'll check..." Sam turns to me and says that Mamma has only just got home and do I want to go over there for dinner instead.

I roll my eyes and shake my head. I don't even wanna try to disguise how pissed off this makes me. And why should I? Here I am making all the effort and she can't even be bothered getting on a frigging bus. Worse, she can't be bothered calling *me* or sending *me* a message to explain why she can't be bothered.

Apart from a couple of stroppy text replies telling me she's busy, I haven't actually seen or heard from Mamma since the night I dubbed the 'pasta disaster'. I think she's still pissed at me because I never called her on her birthday. It's not like I never tried though. I got the busy signal and then forgot to redial later. Besides, I did take flowers around to the house that time she wasn't home.

Sam puts down the phone.

"I told her you were busy tonight."

"Well, I am." Pause. I drain the last few dregs of my strawberry milkshake then clunk it back down on the table.

"So..." she continues, "I suppose we might as well just go ahead and order food then."

Sigh.

"Your mother really wanted to come today, Vicky."

"Yeah, it sure looks like it."

Sigh again.

"She sounded really tired on the phone."

Oh boo fucking hoo. Ain't we all tired. Come to think of it, Sam isn't looking too hot these days. They must be whipping her like an omelette in that new gym of hers.

"She's just this minute back from an important business meeting."

Ha. I fold my arms across my chest.

"Business meeting? What kind of important business does *she* have to meet about?" I'm tempted to ask if Ma's minding her own or someone else's.

"She's looking for premises for her new café."

"Her what?"

Sam frowns.

"Your mother applied to Business Gateway and they gave her a mentor and a start-up grant to help open a vegan wholefoods café."

"Oh... Well... She could have said." I specifically arranged to have dinner with them today because they were both meant to be off work. I might as well have just posted a note about Dad's death in the blue-rinse rooms online.

"I'm surprised she hasn't told you. She handed in her notice last Friday and she's not stopped talking about it."

"Well," I say, "I knew she wasn't happy in there... And I guess she did say something about opening a café... But then Mamma says a lot of things and never actually does them..."

"What do you mean?"

"Well, it's like that time she was gonna open a homeless soup kitchen and then there was her idea about wanting to foster kids..."

Sam is quiet for a moment. Then her face gets really serious and she says: "Vicky, one of the things that first drew me to your mother was how incredibly passionate she was– "

"Aww that's disgusting," I tell her. "I really don't wanna hear about what you two get up to in the sack..."

Her face darkens.

"I'm not talking about sex," she says.

Thank god.

"When I first met Maria, I thought she was the most incredible and inspiring woman I had ever come across. She was vivacious and warm-hearted and generous... And she wanted to help everyone all the time, even if it meant putting herself out."

"Yeah, and just look at what she turned into."

She ignores me and keeps talking.

"Your mum is the best chef I know," says Sam. "She's talented and resourceful and what's more – she really loves to cook."

"That's true," I concede.

"She really, really deserves a chance at running her own place."

Maybe.

"And even if it doesn't work out, I'll still be proud of her for giving it a shot."

Sigh.

"Yeah, well, I've been telling her for years that she's too good to be working in that crummy kitchen. Peeling potatoes for minimum wage is ok as a stop gap when you're twenty-five or under, but you don't wannabe someone else's bitch your entire life."

I take a deep breath and look over my shoulder to see what's keeping the table service. My stomach is heaving and all this talk of food and cafés isn't helping. I already skipped two meals today so I have to get something down my neck.

"Well, sometimes folk don't have a lot of self-confidence," Sam replies. "And it doesn't help when other people put them down." She sighs. "This is why it's important for you to support your mother in what she's doing right now."

Hmmph. It's not like I'm not proud of her for stepping up and trying something new. It's just that Ma's never there for me whenever I need her to listen. Now, suddenly, I'm expected to gush praise all over *her* because she's in some kind of spotlight. Yeah, right.

"Mamma should just get over it already and deal with herself. If she wants to open a café she should just get on and do it. She shouldn't need anyone to hold her hand."

Sam slams her fist down so hard on her placemat that it makes the pepper cellar, at the other end of the table, jump and two sissy boys over by the bar turn around and stare.

"That is *exactly* the kind of attitude that gets my goat."

Eh?

"Sometimes, Vicky," she says, through clenched teeth, "I think you're the most selfish and immature individual I've ever come across. And that's saying something, considering how long I've been out on the gay scene." She takes a deep breath. "Now I didn't come here to sit and listen to you mouthing off about your mother. I get enough of it at home when she starts moaning about you with your music and your writing and stuff. I wish the two of yous would just sit down and sort it out because I'm fed up hearing about it."

"Oh."

"I've had a shit morning and an even shitter week, and I was looking forward to coming here and seeing you and just chilling out. So if you want to talk to me about your short stories or about how well you're doing in your play, how much you love your girlfriend or about what's really eating in at you – because I'm not stupid, I know there's something you're not telling me – then fire away. If not, well, I might as well go up the road because I can't be doing with all this petty crap." She stops. Takes another deep breath. "Do you understand?"

I nod. I don't know how else to respond. Sam has never spoken to me like this. She has always been the passive parent, the good cop to Mamma's Gestapo.

I open my mouth to say something but no words come out.

"What can I get yous?" intervenes an incredibly wobbly Scarface on roller skates. She is wearing a black and white apron and a shiny new Betty Boop hairdo.

I order another strawberry milkshake and a veggie dog with everything on it. Sam gets a coke and a chickpea burger and some rainbow fries, whatever they are.

"I wouldn't like to have her job," Sam comments as the weirdo-on-wheels skids kamikaze-style back towards the bar, almost knocking over two lesbian pedestrians in the process.

"I thought you were a good skater?" I say, remembering a story she once told me about how, when she was a kid, she pretended to be a boy for a season because they wouldn't let girls play in the ice hockey team.

"Yeah, but I don't think I'd suit the frilly get-up."

"You could be right," I tell her.

Sam smiles at me, and I grin back even though my jaw feels like it's made of glass.

Eventually I tell Sam about Dad and the twins, about how I'm thinking of having George (and Georgia too, if she wants) come live with me. "Anything to get them away from their loser of a mother," I say. "It ain't fair that they've got to come home from school some days and find her lying in a pile of her own shit and piss. And who knows what's next – she could choke on her own puke and then those kids would have to deal with a dead body." Sam nods sympathetically.

"And it doesn't sound like there's anyone offering them any help. Somebody oughta be talking to them – a bereavement counsellor or social services or something. So that's why I gotta step up and take care of things, because George is a nice kid and he could really go places if he just had somebody he could lean on. Kat says he does well in all his classes and none of the teachers have any problems with him. I know you probably think this is all really sudden and I'm not up to it... But I really believe I could help these kids. And one thing you and Mamma taught me is you don't walk away from the people you care about. And OK, I might hardly know them, but they are my brother and sister. Do you know what I mean?"

Sam makes a temple of her hands.

"Go on, say it," I tell her, "say I'm talking all foolish and I can't hardly take care of myself never mind two teenagers."

She shakes her head.

"What? You don't think I'm crazy? Or you just got nothing to add?"

"You're so like your mother sometimes," she says and smiles, pushing her glasses up onto the crown of her head.

We both sit silent for a few moments, watching Scarface trying to keep our dinners on the plates at the same time as trying to stay vertical *and* navigate the tea-time crowd. She manages it apart from a rogue mushroom that bounces onto the floor then hits my right sneaker.

"Sorr-ee," she grins, and then she gives us our orders the wrong way round.

"Mamma would probably tell me I was being stupid," I say finally.

Sam puts down her knife and fork and looks me square in the eye.

"Actually, I don't think she would."

Ha! Wanna bet?

"You should talk to her about it," she adds.

"Yeah, right."

I can just imagine it, Mamma crunching up her face and telling me I'm a nobody who has nothing, and how I would be a right shitty example to a pair of growing kids.

"I don't really know much about these things," she continues, "I think there's a lot of red tape to go through and– "

"Hey, I would do whatever it takes, sign whatever it takes, go to court– "

"Let me finish, please, Vicky."

Sigh.

"I think that maybe having someone in your life, someone who looks up to you and trusts you could really be the makings of you. I think you making contact with George is one of the best things I've heard in ages."

"Are you for real?"

"Absolutely! I think you're going to be an absolutely fantastic big sister, because you've got so much to offer. You're smart, you're sensitive, you're a good listener... When you want to be..."

She grins and I make a face.

"But... I also think that because of your age, and because of the twins' age, it wouldn't really work out with your being their guardian." She pauses. "Plus you've not really given their mother's feelings any consideration in all this. Ok she's an alcoholic and she has problems, but she's just gone through a bereavement and now you're going to steam in there and try to take away her children?'

I shift around in my seat. "Well, when you put it like that..."

I never thought about any of those things. I wouldn't want to make someone's situation worse – especially when I've met so many women who've had their kids ripped away from them because their ex-husbands (and society in general) didn't approve of their lifestyle. And maybe two teenagers would be a bit of a handful.

I half-finish my meal and throw my napkin down on the plate, "I just want to get to know them, and I want to help them."

"I know that, pal," says Sam, softly. "The best person to talk to now is your mother. You and her should sit down on your own and have a coffee or something."

I nod.

She tilts her head, "So will you do that for me?"

I tell her I'll think about it.

☞ ♥ ☜

It's six twenty-five and Joolz has her laptop back and I'm in Easy Wet talking to her while I wait for the twins to arrive.

```
Private_Chat
Romeo+Juliet


Juliet> I read the story you sent me
Romeo> u did?
Juliet> its really good
Romeo> thanx
Juliet> have you ever sent any of your stuff off to
a publisher?
Romeo> no
Juliet> I think you should
Romeo> I duno
Romeo> they might think its no good
Juliet> well you never know unless you try
Romeo> wel see
```

I hear my name being called and two blonde heads pop up from around the side of the monitor.

```
Romeo> I have 2 go now
Juliet> will you send me the next chapter?
```

```
Romeo> what nex chapter
Juliet> the lesbian pen one of course!
```

I don't get a chance to tell her that there is no next chapter because there's a mighty crackling noise and a flash and all the lights and the computer screens go out.

Twenty

There comes a point in a lot of good gangster movies where the wise guy narrator decides it's time to get outta the game. Maybe it's because he's taken one too many bullets, or maybe it's because he don't trust his friends no more, or maybe it's simply because he's made his millions and he wants to get fat and settle down someplace peaceful and sunny with his wife and his legitimate children and a business that's on the up and up.

Personally, I've been feeling a little bit of all those things lately, but the cherry on top of the icing on top of the cake was when my newfound, tiny, trick of a kid sister asked if me or any of my clubbing cohorts could hook her up with some ecstasy.

Now maybe I shoulda seen it coming. What with her drinking and her expulsion she was hardly a paragon of saintly behaviour. And maybe I shoulda drop-kicked her no good skinny ass right back out on the sidewalk the minute she came strolling up to me with a mouth full of attitude and a head full of hairspray, but I decided to humour her instead.

So I take Georgia and her brother to McDonald's for a milkshake and a portion of hot apple pie. And after a short talk on the criminal implications of selling drugs to a minor, I tell her exactly the kinda merchandise she can expect to get from me.

"So is that a naw then?" she says, eyes flashing, jaws chomping on hot pastry. "You cannae get us any sweeties?"

Pause.

I could probably get hold of any drug I wanted. Dealers are operating from toilet cubicles all over the gay scene and they're not choosy about their customers.

"Sure," I say, picking my words carefully, "I can easily get you some sweets..."

Georgia's smile widens as do her brother's eyes.

"Would you prefer Jelly Beans or Swizzels?" I say.

"Eh?"

"My girlfriend loves Parma Violets although I can't stand them, and there's a shop over by the train station that..."

George sniggers so hard that he accidently spits some milkshake on the table.

"Very funny," scowls Georgia. Then she turns to George and tells him that he's gross.

"Wassamatta, kid? You said you wanted some sweets – maybe you'd prefer Haribo or Skittles?"

She ignores me and takes a cheap zippo and a packet of cigarettes out of the pocket of her black tracksuit top. "I'd rather you didn't smoke," I tell her, just as she goes to light one up. She stops, looks at me, then curls her lip, and I wait for the 'screw you, creep-o' or equivalent piece of abuse. It doesn't come though.

I watch George who's lowered his eyes and is mopping up the watery pink ice cream with a white napkin.

Georgia sighs. Then she stabs a finger into the apple pie. Yellow goo spills out.

"This cake's mingin by the way," she says.

☞ ♥ ☜

When I turn on my phone I have a missed call from Mamma, an 'I love you' teddy bear picture message from Joolz and three identical text messages from Zest asking whether I think she should dress butch or femme for the party on Saturday.

I'm so tired now. It's only ten o'clock but it's been one long day. And even though I don't feel like having a thumb correspondence with anyone, I know if I don't reply then Joolz will worry, Ma will think I'm ignoring her and Zest will keep the messages coming until her phone implodes.

I fire off a happy face and a love heart for Joolz, followed by a happy geek face and a 'why don't you come as a bit of both?' at Zest.

I don't know what to say to Mamma. My hand hovers over the redial button but it's like I just don't have the energy to push it.

Eleven PM. Exhausted yet I still can't sleep. Every time I start to close my eyes I remember the cemetery dream and they spring open again.

Five past midnight. I get up to drink a glass of water and to piss. When I come back I turn on the light, take out my notebook and begin to write down all the good, bad and ugly things that are in my head.

☞ ♥ ☜

Two AM. I've just put down my pen and laid back on the bed when my phone buzzes and an epic text from Mamma comes through. She says she's really sorry that she missed the dinner, and am I OK? She then goes on to say how shocked and sorry she was to hear about my Dad <sad face>, and if I'm free anytime soon maybe we can meet up and have a chat about it <happy face times three>.

I text back:

Sure, how about Sunday after work?

She replies:

Sunday's fine.

☞ ♥ ☜

It's after three when I finally get to sleep and then I'm up again four hours later. In the shower and out and no time to stop and have breakfast, I just grab my bag and apron and a piece of toast and I'm out the door.

I'm so late I have to run all the way to Buchanan Street. It's raining and I forgot my coat. There are messages on my phone too but I've not had time to read them. Not had time to rehearse my lines for tonight. Not had time to do anything.

I'm so focussed on trying to not be late that I don't see that my lace is loose until I –

Crash. "I'm sorry." I've knocked some random homeless person off their pitch, scattered the coppers from their grubby polystyrene cup all around George Square.

I stop. Breathe. Dig a fiver out of my pocket and give it to them. Tie my shoelace and take off again.

Shit. I'm half-way through the escalator that leads up to our café when I spy Maggie from behind – that's when I remember I'm not even working this morning.

I took a day's holiday (much to Maggie's horror) so that I could shop for Joolz's birthday present, but after two hours of tramping around inside Buchanan Galleries all I have are sore feet and a monster headache.

Usually I'm good at picking gifts. I've always had kind of a knack for getting right inside people's heads – especially women's – and finding out exactly what they want. Sure, I've seen things that I think Joolz might like: sexy underwear, perfume, a She-Ra 'Princess of Power' t-shirt, a singing dancing hamster in a ballet skirt... But none of them feel special enough. And most of the store windows are filled up with fake snowflakes and Christmas-themed gifts, as well as the half-price crap they've got left over from Halloween – somehow, I don't think she'll be all too impressed if I get her a Santa hat or a zombie gangster's moll outfit.

I would, of course, definitely be impressed with seeing her wear the gangster's moll outfit. But I'd have her leave off the deadly make-up and fake bullet hole in the head.

I head outside into the rain again and down Sauchiehall Street where I spy a charity shop that is showcasing a giant Care Bear with a love heart on its belly. I ain't seen Care Bears for sale since the eighties, I was never much of a fan but curiosity snares me.

The shelves inside are full of retro soft toys: He-Man and Thundercats dolls, Cabbage Patch Kids and a shitload more Care Bears – there are blue bears with rain clouds, green ones with shamrocks and pink ones with rainbows. I lift a gay bear up to see if it has the original trademark love heart on its ass. It does. A few of the other bears look a bit worse for wear, their faces are saggy and the colour in their plastic eyes has faded.

I only remember them because Dad gave me one just like this when I was small, and because Shazia used to have a collection. In fact, I actually gave her *my* Care Bear about a month after we started going out.

Thinking about this makes me sad – it's funny how I've not

seen either of them in years and yet they can still get to me after all this time. I'm standing there curling the pink lock of hair on the bear's head around my finger and hugging it to my chest when a sales assistant creeps up from behind and clears her throat.

The afternoon is a bit of a washout. I order lunch in Sandy's but only eat a quarter of a sandwich, then I start writing episode two of the lesbian pen story but only manage half a paragraph. After that, I try to go over my lines for the last act of Earnest but I can't concentrate and the words all just blend together.

Ma texts me once and Joolz texts me twice and Zest texts me at least a dozen times – I reply selectively. Eventually I send George a message asking which cemetery they buried Dad in, and he tells me, and I go all the way out there, but that's a wasted journey because I have no idea where his headstone is.

It's just after six in the evening and I'm in Sandy's again having a drink with Joolz, she's helping me run through my lines:

ALGERNON> Have you told Gwendolen yet that you have an excessively pretty ward who is only just eighteen?

JACK> Oh! One doesn't blurt these things out to people. Cecily and Gwendolen are perfectly certain to be extremely great friends.

"I'll bet you anything," says Joolz, gently.

JACK> I'll bet you anything you like that half an hour after they have met, they will be calling each other sister…

"Good," nods Joolz. "Do you want to stop there?"

I do but I don't. This is the best part of my day, the only good part so far, and I want to stay huddled in our corner of the bar, but I know I can't because I agreed to meet Zest here and I can already see her coming through the front door towards our table now.

"Yeah," I say, quietly, "I guess I should."

Zest grins at us and I give her a wave.

"I'll bet you anything," says Joolz, "give her half an hour alone with you and good old Gwendolen will try and get your clothes off."

"Shut up," I say, "she's just a kid."

I try laughing it off but really it bothers me. It's not just the puppy dog eyes she gives me or the morning to midnight text messages, it's the fact that I've allowed it to continue, when really I should have nipped this thing in the bud months ago.

Zest walks over to our table and puts her schoolbag down on a chair. "Hi Romeo, hi Juliet," she says. "What's so funny?"

☞ ♥ ☜

As we walk to rehearsal I tell Zest about the present I got for Joolz's birthday.

"That is sooo cool."

"You really think so?"

"Yeah, defo." She adds, "I would love someone to buy me something as cool as that."

Now I'm really not sure I did the right thing, cause Zest is a bit of a fruit and nut bar after all. I change the subject and tell her that Joolz and I are now officially girlfriend and girlfriend.

"She asked me last night if I'd go steady with her and I said 'yes', and then we changed the status on our gay dot com profiles to 'in a monogamous relationship'."

Silence.

The kid is looking straight ahead with her eyes fixed against the horizon.

I knew this was gonna be a difficult conversation, but then I also knew that I had to let Zest down firmly but gently, once and for all.

"That's brilliant," she says finally. "I'm really really happy for you, Vicky." She don't look happy though.

"You're a good friend, Kirsten," I say. "One of the best."

She doesn't reply.

"That's why I need *you* to watch my back."

"What do you mean?"

"Well," I say, looking shiftily around as we begin walking up the front steps of the GLC. "There are a lot of people who don't like me..."

Zest sighs.

"Everybody likes you, Vicky."

"If you say so." I press the buzzer. "Well, there are a lot of people who would love to fuck things up for me and Joolz..."

"It's Kirsten and Vicky," I shout into the intercom. The door farts open.

I half expect Scarface to be lying in wait for me, but the room is empty save for Broadbent who is eating a pre-packed Marks and Spencer's meal and reading a copy of The Stage.

"Anyway, all I'm saying is I need you to tell me if anyone says anything or– "

"I got your back."

"Thanks."

"I just wish someone would fancy me," she pouts.

"They will, kid. One day soon they'll be lining up at your door."

Tonight's rehearsal is the most suckiest rehearsal we've had yet. And the problem is it's me who sucks! First of all, I manage to fluff my lines during act one after Lady Bracknell asks how I carelessly managed to lose both parents. Then, in the second act, when it comes to the part where I'm supposed to explain to Prism and Chasuble about the untimely death of my imaginary younger brother, I get some kind of weird stage fright and just stop talking altogether.

"Is everything ok, Vicky?" asks Broadbent.

"Yeah... Sorry... I just forgot where we were."

"Should I start this bit over?" asks Minty.

"We don't have time," says Broadbent waving her script, "just go from Dear Mr Worthing."

CHASUBLE> *Dear Mr Worthing, I trust this garb of woe does not betoken some terrible calamity?*

JACK> *My father… Sorry, I mean brother.*

Broadbent frowns.

MISS PRISM> *More shameful debts and extrava-gance?*

JACK *(shaking his head)* > *Dead.*

CHASUBLE> *Your brother Ernest dead?*

I'm doing it again. Everyone is looking at me and I'm just standing here like a dummy. What makes it worse is that everyone else has seriously got their shit together – even Robbie and Minty have got their lines down par and they've only had five days to practise.

Minty repeats the last bit again. Silence.

"Quite dead," interjects Broadbent.

"I'm sorry," I tell her, "I'll get it eventually."

"Yes, well," she retorts, "I'll be drawing my old age pension *eventually*."

I decline all offers of going to the pub and walk home on my own in silence. I just can't handle listening to another night of who's fucking whose ex-girlfriend and all that trivial crap.

I take the stairs two at a time, and once I get inside my room I thump the door behind me and hurl myself down onto the bed.

Sinatra mews loudly and darts out from behind a pillow.

"Sorry, old girl," I say, and she purrs, cocks her head at me and then slowly pads towards me as I lean my back against the headboard and hug my knees up to my chest.

"Why is it that every frigging time something goes good for me, something else happens that turns it all to shit?" Sinatra leans into me, rubbing her head angrily against my hand and the back of my thigh. "Eh? Why does that always happen to me?"

She mews in response, excited that I'm finally paying her the time of day.

"Yeah, that's what I think too."

She climbs up onto my lap and I sit hugging her for about ten minutes solid. I feel bad because not only am I never home, but today I noticed a random brand of cat food in our cupboard that I don't buy. Eventually I hear a key turning and Minty's heavy footfalls. She knocks on my door and when I don't answer she comes in anyway.

"I heard about your da," she says, standing by the foot of the bed.

I shrug.

"Well, if you want to talk about it or that..."

"Thanks," I say, "but I'm fine."

She turns to walk away. Then, "I was just about to put on a film," she says. "D'ye fancy watching *Gangster No. 1*?"

The clock on my wall says it's just after eleven. I'm on an early shift tomorrow, I haven't slept in days and I hate the guts of that worthless movie. Minty hovers in the doorway with an awkward look on her face, arms across her chest.

"Yeah," I say, forcing a smile. "I would really like that."

Twenty-one

I meet the twins in town during my break and we take the bus towards Mosspark Boulevard and the cemetery where Dad is buried. Maggie's plan to make everyone work split shifts this week has actually paid off for me, because I can go pay my respects and be back and still have time for a leisurely lunch – not that I'll have the stomach for it.

"So have you ever been in a cemetery before?" says Georgia the ghoul, tapping her long black nails on the metal handle of the bus seat. She has dyed her hair black since I last saw her on Wednesday and has transformed herself from a tracksuit-wearing gum-chewer to a pseudo-goth in dark jeans and Dr Martens.

"Yeah," I replied, "once." Shazia's aunt died whilst we were dating and I was invited to the funeral because I was her 'best friend'.

"I have too," she says, "millions of times. I love going up to the Necropolis where they've got the big Celtic gravestones, it's one of my favourite places."

As the bus lurches towards a pile-up of traffic, I brace myself for the stories of underage drinking and the sex and drug taking that goes with it. It doesn't come though.

"Georgia wants to be an archaeologist when she's older," says George proudly.

"Oh right," I say.

"Yeah, and before you say anything I know I fucked up by getting expelled."

"Uh-huh."

"Mum went up to the school yesterday," says George, "and she seen Mr Fisher the history teacher who's also Georgia's guidance teacher..."

"Aye, and him and Miss Astrof put in a good word to the heidie and because of everything that's happened recently and wi Dad dying they're giving us another chance."

The bus is moving again and it's our stop next. Two sets of teenage eyes are staring at me, obviously waiting on my reply.

"That's great," I say. "I hope you don't blow it."

"No chance," she replies, standing up. "This is us here." Pause. "And there's Mum and her pal waiting on us."

☞ ♥ ☜

Ma never told me that she'd been in touch with Deirdre Mann. And she never told me that she was gonna be here today. Much later, when we sit down to hash out all the mother–daughter crap, she will swear that she never knew my father was dying or that I had a brother and sister, and certainly not what was in those letters. "Honestly, Vicky, if I knew any of that, I would not have kept it from you."

☞ ♥ ☜

Cemeteries are supposed to be dark at all hours of the day and night. They're supposed to be cold and creepy and deadly silent, but I can hear bird song and children's laughter in the distance, and there's more than a hint of sunshine beating down on my back.

Deirdre Mann bends down and replaces the rotting flowers on Dad's grave with a new bouquet. Her hands tremble and when she goes to stand up straight again she rocks backwards on her heels and Ma puts a hand on her shoulder. Georgia's next, she kneels down and whispers something; then George steps forward, dry-eyed yet solemn; and then Mamma, who I'm surprised to see has her handkerchief out and is dabbing at her face. Finally, it's my turn, I crouch down beside his headstone and open up my rucksack, I take out the rainbow Care Bear and lay it down beside the flowers.

☞ ♥ ☜

I fly through the rest of the day on automatic pilot: I go to work, I go home, I have dinner, I go to rehearsal and then I go back home. Maggie doesn't give me any hassle or at least I don't notice it, and even Broadbent is semi nice to me. If I didn't know any better, I'd say I was a machine that was masquerading as me because suddenly the tasks that normally tie me up in knots are done without complication.

"Look," says Kat, as I am tying a ribbon around Joolz's present. She's pointing at a cheeky cerise badge that is pinned to the front of a fuchsia pink birthday card.

"Sweet," I reply.

"Do you think she'll like it? I got all the L.I.P.S. girls to sign it." The card is blank inside but Zest, Kat and several of our friends have added their own personal messages in sparkly silver and gold ink. "I tried to make a cake earlier," she adds. "But it collapsed in the middle."

☞ ♥ ☜

Joolz's birthday night out is in a straight bar called Bonkers. Not that she particularly wanted to go to a straight bar (she admitted that she'd much rather go to Sandy's), but because she hasn't told some people yet that she's gay, and because some of the people she has told are not entirely comfortable with her being gay, she thought it would be a more 'appropriate' venue.

"Personally, I think I must be bonkers for setting foot in here," I tell Kat out of the side of my mouth as a burly bouncer stops me, frisks me, looks at my ID for the second time and finally lets us both pass. "I mean, I'd quite like to get through the weekend without a stab wound."

"Relax, Vicky," she grins, "you make this place gay just by turning up."

"Very funny," I reply, forcing a smile.

I'm glad that Joolz's family have declined the invitation to her party. Not just for my sake, but for Kat and any of the other L.I.P.S. girls who're thinking of joining us this evening. It's not that I'm embarrassed by my friends – more the opposite – they're all fragile in their own way and I can't stand the idea of someone being cruel or judgemental towards them.

"Any idea who's going to be here tonight?" Kat asks.

"People from her college course, some friends from school..." People who'll want to quiz me about how I know Joolz and where I met Joolz, and what exactly am I to her...

"Good," she replies, "so if she's not out to the world already, she will be by the end of the night."

☞ ♥ ☜

In some ways meeting your girlfriend's friends for the first time is even scarier than meeting her parents: you need to be especially careful about how you tread with friends because they're the ones she talks to about her love life, because if they think you're no good they can convince her to dump you in a heartbeat. Of course I'm not speaking from personal experience (only what I've witnessed), cause I only got close enough to one other girl for that, and she always had an excuse as to why she couldn't introduce me to people.

Just like Joolz has friends splattered around the country from her various clubs and extracurricular dancing activities, most of Shazia's close friends went to a different high school. This made keeping me a secret from them extremely easy, and she even had a 'pretend' boyfriend with whom she would make out on the alternate weekends that she didn't spend with me. Not that it means much now, but I'm pretty sure that if I had ever met Shazia's friends they'd have taken one look at me and fancied me too... And then, when they'd have taken a second look – they'd have come after me with their brothers' baseball bats.

☞ ♥ ☜

Inside the club it's swarming with teenage girls in high heels and boys with over gelled hair and cigarettes tucked behind their ears. They're linking arms and lips and hips on the dance floor, and it reminds me of the old school discos where kids dressed up like mini adults, drank cheap cider and then spent all night chucking up in the toilets or sucking face with a kid from another registration class. Joolz told me once that discos were the things she missed most about high school, and that at least ten boys would come up to her every time and tap her on the shoulder to tell her that their friend over there had a crush on her. They made me miserable though, partly because I can't dance and partly because I never did the whole teenage binge-drinking thing, but mostly because nobody ever came up and tapped my shoulder. Frankly, the only difference I can see here tonight is that there's no obligatory row of plastic seats against the gym hall wall for the saddos who don't manage to cop off.

"So much for eighteen to thirty," I say, squeezing past a boy-girl octopus who have obviously bribed their babysitters to allow them out of the house.

"Tell me about it," says Kat, "I just saw a bunch of my fourth year pupils."

I join a snaking queue for the bar and Kat goes off to the cloakroom so that she can redeploy her handbag.

Minutes later, a fight breaks out between two teenage idiots with buzz cuts. A girl in a spectacularly short skirt is weeping and wailing and shouting at them to stop, and I recognise her as being one half of the octopus couple. This happens only a few feet away from me, and the stewards are quick to intervene, but not before idiot number one bites octopus boy's earlobe off and spits it out at his feet.

I grimace then turn away, thankful it isn't a dyke drama at least. Of course, the chances of meeting a lesbian in here tonight who isn't part of our party would be like finding a long-serving male member of Her Majesty's Pleasure who hasn't taken it up the ass.

I hug Joolz's present to my chest as I'm jostled once, twice, three times by queue jumpers. I hope she likes this gift. I really really hope so. What if she doesn't though? What if it just isn't her thing? And what if all her friends know this and they laugh at her because it's so sucky?

Kat is back. Somehow she has managed to get served before me and is holding two bottles of something luminous yellow in one hand and grabbing my hand and pulling me out of the queue with the other, dragging me towards the dance floor.

"SAY CHEESE!"

Someone comes up behind me and puts their arm around my neck, a camera flashes and a crowd of blonde posers rush towards us to get into the picture.

"This is my sister's friend, Vicky," says the voice belonging to the arm. There is no hint of sarcasm, no giggling from Siobhan, and for my own part I'm too dazzled with the strobe lights and the camera flash to say anything that might contradict her statement. I just smile and nod and say hi to whomever I'm being introduced to, and I'm glad to be able to agree with them that 'it's too noisy in here' because it means they don't try to make conversation and –

"LOOK THERE SHE IS!"

Joolz is sitting amidst a huddle of friends, a parasol-filled cocktail in each hand; she's leaning over the table, laughing, and having such a great time that she hasn't even seen me yet. Probably she wouldn't even miss me if I weren't here.

She's getting up to dance now, pushing back her chair whilst I stay rooted where I stand, watching her. I love the way her hips glide, the way she always tosses back her hair when she does that sexy little pout – it doesn't matter that I know she stole those moves from a Britney Spears video. Joolz looks so slick in her skinny-fit jeans and her tight white top with ice cream cones on each breast, and I want to go over there and kiss her right now on the dance floor.

And I almost do.

Except

I see a picture behind her on the wall, of Elvis Presley and some random hetty chick, and it reminds me that I can't even hold her hand tonight.

And then

I look around me at all the necking boy-girl couples encircling me like adders and something inside me freezes.

Right from the beginning, I knew it was a bad idea coming to this place. Some broad sits down next to me, says her name and then begins asking me the kind of questions I've been dreading. I spin her a line about a bar in Merchant City and I throw in Liane's name and she seems happy with that. I'm not happy though. It's like a déjà vu, like I've been transported back in time three years and I'm dating Shazia Queen of Closetland all over again.

☞ ♥ ☜

We'd been going out for almost a year when I finally convinced Shazia to take me to a party at her house. I'd never met any of her family before and she claimed that it was because I would find their Filipino humour boring.

"Mamma has a habit of meeting all these random Filipino women in the grocery section of Safeway and then inviting their whole family for dinner," she said. "I don't even know why you would want to come, it's not like a big deal or anything."

It was a big deal to me and of course I wanted to go. I'd never had a girlfriend before so, obviously, I'd never been grilled by any girl's parents. It sounds stupid but I wanted it all. I wanted the whole Romeo and Juliet love affair (without the dying part of course). I wanted to throw stones at Shazia's window at midnight, climb up her drainpipe and through the bedroom window. I wanted to woo her all the time but then I also wanted to experience all the shitty parts of being in love, like having to prove I was good enough for someone's daughter.

I really enjoyed the party at the start. I got to taste pancit bihon (rice noodles) and suman (sweet rice wrapped in banana leaves) and play Takip-Silim (Blind Man's Buff) with the little kids. But what I especially liked was listening to the Filipino women talking. Their conversations were a strange mix of English, Scottish slang, Chinese and different dialects of Tagalog. It was fun trying to work out what they were saying before Shazia jumped in with her translations.

"Dahlia, how you say 'puki' in English?"

"Oh my god, did you just hear that?" said Shazia. The wives cackled with laughter and the husbands just shook their heads. "Daisy just asked how to say 'vagina'."

In fact, the only part of the evening that really did stink was that I had to lie about who I was. Every time someone new spoke to me, they'd start off by saying: "Oh, so you must be Shazia's friend!" and "How long have you two known each other?" Then Shazia would burn bright red and interrupt the conversation.

☞ ♥ ☜

"Vicky!" shouts Joolz as she comes charging across the room and throws her arms around my waist. "I thought you lot weren't coming till about eleven?"

"Broadbent cut us loose early." I grin at her and then I blush and stumble backwards, smiling at her from behind my fringe.

"Your hair looks nice tonight," she says, and I grow even redder.

She's still got her arms around me and she's nuzzling into my neck and I'm thinking 'what the fuck?' because she was so specific about who could and couldn't know about us and where I could put my hands when we were around other people, and I can just imagine all the homophobes that are here tonight, gaping at us.

"Careful, someone might see," I tell her.

"I couldn't give a flying fuck anymore," then she grins and leans in and I can smell the alcohol on her breath but I don't care either. She gives me the world's sexiest kiss and there's a round of applause and someone – it turns out to be one of the blonde posers – screams: "I knew it! I knew you were a gay!" and then she's straight into her handbag, pulling out her mobile phone.

"I'm really glad you came," Joolz tells me.

I'm beginning to relax. She takes my hand as we walk over to the bar and she buys me another yellow alcopop; we go to a table that's away from the sound system and sit talking while she begins opening her present from me.

Several people gather around as she picks at the edges of the Sellotape.

"Umm, maybe you should wait and open it in private," I say, suddenly aware that there are about twenty people watching us.

"Why? What is it?" She looks at me, slyly. "Kinky underwear?"

"Umm no."

"Hurry up and open it!" shouts Siobhan, waving a Bacardi Breezer bottle.

"Is it a sex toy?" Joolz probes again. The back of my neck feels hot and prickly and my ears are beginning to burn. I get up, take hold of my girlfriend's elbow and pull her towards the upstairs toilets.

"Oh, so masterful," she giggles as we close the door behind us, shutting out the heat and the music.

"Careful," I say, as her nail extensions burrow under the gaps, "it's kinda breakable." She umms and ahhs until I finally take the present from her and cut through the paper with the tiny penknife that's attached to my house keyring.

"Oooh," says Joolz, and her eyelashes flutter and her lips tremble, and I know right away as she cradles it in her hand that she really likes it, that I didn't fuck up.

Twenty-two carat gold-lavished porcelain music box – the card in the jeweller's said. *This is an ideal gift for anyone who is fond of ballet.*

"It's beautiful, Vicky." She runs her index finger over the picture of the two young lovers neatly embossed on the lid. "How did you..."

"Now that would be telling," I say, knowingly. "It's a recreation of the original painting. If you open it, it plays a Russian ballet." I hop from foot to foot, watching Joolz's facial expression as she slowly unfastens the latch on the music box.

"Prokofiev," she whispers, as she holds it up against her ear. "Romeo and Juliet's melody."

Joolz zips the box inside her handbag, and then pushes me backwards into an empty toilet. The floor is wet and I lose my balance, landing on my ass, legs akimbo and knocking my head on the sanitary bin.

"Oops," she giggles. "Are you ok?"

"Uh, yeah."

My ass is slightly wet as I pull myself up onto my feet and pick soggy white tissue paper off the back of my leg. Joolz pushes the door closed behind us, locks it, and turns around to face me with a cheeky smile. She reaches towards me then smoothes down my shirt, and my hair, and then begins kissing me without a word.

"I'm glad you came out," she mumbles, still kissing me, her hands pressing into the flesh of my back.

"Uh-huh. You said that already." She's trying to get her hands down my pants, her long white fingers straining, but I keep guiding them back to my waist. My feet are slipping on a wet

240

spot and so I press Joolz's back up against the toilet door. My hands are on either side of her head for balance, spread out like I'm under arrest, as I continue to kiss her lips, her ears and then her neck. Joolz lifts up her t-shirt then pulls my face down towards her breasts. My mouth is around her right nipple and my hands are working on the zip of her pants, when suddenly a toilet flushes.

"Shit," says Joolz. She pushes me away from her and we stand for the next two minutes trying not to giggle or even breathe as the outside door opens, allowing music and voices to filter in.

"Dirty bitch," says Joolz, once the door is safely closed again and outside noise is but a muffled background hum. "Didn't even wash her hands." I fall into a fit of silent laughter, clutching my belly. She signals for me to be quiet and we listen as the outside door opens and closes again and someone else comes in, footsteps clipping across the tiles. Someone coughs. The footsteps are replaced by running water. Joolz holds one finger up to her lip and I nod, hand over my mouth.

This is turning out to be a really great night after all. Who'd have thought it? I am so fucking glad to be here.

I stand biting my lip, grinning to myself and thinking about how much I love this girl, how I never want anything to happen to change the way I feel about her, how everything – even the shit with her brother wanting to knock my block off – is worth it just to be with her.

"Ok I'll go first," mouths Joolz. She unlocks the door and slides it open a quarter of the way. "Fuck, it's only Mylene." She laughs and lets the door bounce open.

Someone sighs.

"Stop calling me fucking Mylene."

Zzzippppp. Record scratch. Mylene's voice has jarred me.

I know that voice. How could I ever forget that voice?

I look to where Mylene, my girlfriend's best friend all the way through high school, is standing over at the sink with her back to me. I can see her reflection clearly in the mirror. Her hair that was once in midnight black curls is now a sleek milk-chocolate brown, her lips and breasts are fuller, and I notice, as she dries her hands on a piece of tissue paper, that she is wearing a white gold ring on her engagement finger. She takes a brown lip pencil from her purse and when she looks up again, she sees me in the mirror. Her face is like a dead goldfish, lips frozen in a solid 'O'. She looks away again, flicks her hair over her shoulder and then puts the pencil back in her purse. I bend my head and put one hand over my mouth like I'm gonna be sick. My head feels like I've got a lump of ice packed between my ears. Joolz says something that I can't hear, my name is mentioned, and she laughs.

"Hey Vicky," Joolz shouts, "come here a minute." I go to her. She squeezes my hand and I flush red. "Now, be honest," she says, "d'ye not think Shaz is the double of Mylene Klass from Hear'Say?"

Twenty-two

Joolz reaches into her handbag. "What do yous want to drink?"

"I'll get them," I intervene. Shazia breathes an audible sigh of relief.

For once I'm not trying to be showy by flashing my cash around. I'm just anxious not to be left alone with Miss Not-so-distant-blast-from-the-past.

"A Malibu and Diet Coke for me, please," says Joolz.

"Shaz?"

It had been on the tip of my tongue to call her Mylene, but I changed my mind at the last moment. I'd always hated the name 'Shaz' because I thought it made her sound like a showgirl. She agreed with me once upon a time, but obviously her hair colour and her sexual orientation are not the only things she's altered.

Shazia's eyelashes flutter, and it irritates me how fucking sexy I still find her. The bitch is poker-faced though, allowing me no clue as to what she's thinking behind those dark eyes and taut lips.

"Jack Daniels with coke, please."

But of course, how could I forget?

The night of Julian's party was (as far as I'm aware) the first and last time that Shazia Sarwar had ever set foot in the pink triangle. I arrived early, all spruced up like I was going to my big gay prom, and I waited, patiently, in the wind and rain outside the hotel for her. Shazia, of course, was half an hour late and blamed it on a hair appointment. This was to be our ritual for the next two years: we'd make an arrangement and she would break it, turning up to meet me (or not) whenever it suited her. I didn't care, though. The way I felt about her back then, I woulda waited till hell froze over.

I remember thinking that she looked especially stunning that evening. She was wearing a slinky, black wrap-over V-neck dress with narrow shoulder straps, it had the cutest little diamante starburst detail sewn on. Her hair was perfect: ironed into tight, neat braids that fell just below her shoulders, they were like a stream of black velvet ribbons rippling in the breeze. I also remember how her cheeks turned pink when I told her how amazing she looked.

"So do you," she replied. And then she changed the subject by asking if we could get a taxi because she didn't want her mascara to run.

The driver smiled at me through his mirror as I told him to keep the change.

"Thanks son," he said, as he dropped us off on the corner of Virginia Street. We fell out of the taxi, laughing at his mistake, and Shazia linked arms with me as I practically skipped the rest of the way to the bar.

We spent the next couple of hours in Sandy's where we were greeted by a medley of twenty-something gay men who were all, it seemed, trying to get into the birthday boy's pants. They were very nice to us, and Julian bought us a peach schnapps each, but none of them were remotely interested in hanging around with a pair of kids, especially not ones with vaginas. This was fine by me, and I didn't care one iota that nobody else from work showed up (although I did feel a tiny bit bad for Julian) because I got to be alone with Shazia.

Queuing outside Bennet's later that night I was probably the most excited I'd ever been in my life up until that point. I had this ridiculous idea in my head that it would be like the queer take on Rick's bar in *Casablanca*, and there'd be tuxedoed butches and svelte femmes in cocktail dresses and maybe an old black stud with a baby grand piano just sitting there ready to back me up on my debut serenade. Not so. I learnt that soon enough. But for those ten grand minutes when I stood outside freezing my ass off on the sidewalk, I felt like I was about to be crowned king of someplace suitably sweet.

And then we almost got thrown out before we even got in.

It was a guy that I, now, know as Bruno who was the bouncer on the door. He was the only one wearing a bowtie (I never trust a dude in a bowtie) but then he was also topless and wearing tight blue Levi's. Shazia whispered to me that she thought he looked like Richard Fairbrass and we giggled so much that he stopped us and asked for ID. Of course, being fifteen and sixteen we didn't have any and we would've been sent home right then and there, if not for the swift intervention of the one and only Rachel Hunt.

"Alright Vicky?" she said. "Yer looking well. Is this you out celebrating the big eighteen?"

She gave me a wink. This was back when she worked as a nightclub gorilla herself, way before she owned Sandy's and became a stickler for licensing laws.

"Umm... Yeah..."

"You know these kids, Rachel?"

"Of course I do!" she replied. "That's Sam Haggarty's stepdaughter. I can't believe you don't know Vicky."

"Oh right." He paused, beginning to mull it over. Then he looked at me again and grinned. "I recognise you now." He shook his head and laughed to himself. "I can't believe you're eighteen already."

"Believe it!" I told him, summoning up all the bravado that was in me and pushing out my chest.

"Let them through," said Rachel. "No charge tonight, girls, since it's your first time."

"Wow thanks!"

"But Rach, what about this other yin, she's not got any– "

"Now Bruno," began Rachel, putting an arm around him, "do you value your balls? Because I wouldn't want to be the person who turned away Sam Haggarty's daughter's..."

"Ah, well, I wouldn't want to mess with big Sam, right enough..." Then he let us pass, and just as we were about to walk into the great gay abyss, he shouted: "Must run in the family, eh?" And a huge broad grin broke out over his face, displaying a gold-capped tooth. Shazia must've been wondering what the fuck was going on. I hadn't told her anything about Ma and Sam. But whatever she thought she never mentioned it to me. "Have a good night," he said. "And tell big Sam, Bruno Johnson says hi."

The air inside hung thick with the smell of body odour and cigarette smoke, and instead of the anticipated jazz music and cocktails, all I could see and hear were more topless musclemen sweating to the sound of dance music and butch women in plaid swigging bottles of beer. I soon got over my disappointment though and grabbed us a table in a discreet corner.

Shazia thought she could smell someone smoking weed. I didn't know what weed smelt or even looked like. I'd only ever smoked normal cigarettes once before and I couldn't get the hang of it. I changed the subject then and asked if she would like a drink.

"I'll get them," she said.

"No, allow me," I insisted. "What would you like?"

Watching her from the side of the bar as she asked for a light from a faggy guy in a pink t-shirt was agony. I was so desperate for her to love me, to pay me attention, that I was scared to leave her by herself in case someone stole her away.

And when she proceeded to arch her back and throw back her head as she inhaled from a long white cigarette, frankly, I was hooked.

"What can I get you, sweetheart?" It was Sam's ex-girlfriend, Lisa, who broke the spell. She didn't recognise me with my new haircut though, and I couldn't be bothered making small talk, so I simply paid up and scurried back to our table with the drinks. Jack Daniels with coke for both of us.

The pink t-shirt guy beckoned me closer as I passed, leaned in and said: "Take it from me, honey, you're definitely in there." *I wish*, I thought and smiled back.

As I slid back into my seat, Shazia was lighting up another cigarette. "That's not... umm... weed, is it?" I asked.

"No," she replied, rolling her eyes. "Menthol."

Suddenly I felt naïve and immature sitting next to her. Like a little kid who is tagging along beside their big sister or the annoying first year who is crushing on the sixth-year prefect.

"But," she added, "I'm still certain I could smell hash."

She watched me over the edge of her glass as she sipped, fingering the rim with her nail. It was hard to believe she was only fifteen. To me, she looked and sounded much older and her knowledge of spirits, and the way she drank them down, showed that she was no stranger to alcohol.

My fingers and palms were clammy with sweat and left a row of sticky prints on my glass. I had never tasted Jack Daniels before. Ma had never let me drink spirits. "You're too young," she'd said. "Stick to shandy or beer." I think she was worried that I'd end up like my Dad, who once told me that his own father allowed him to have his first pint when he was just eight years old.

I gulped a mouthful of whiskey, coughing as the warm liquid burned all the way down my throat.

"Take your time," she scolded.

I blushed, pushing my drink to the side. "Ugh, that stuff's heinous!"

Shazia cackled.

"You've got a really dirty laugh, you know that?"

She cackled even louder.

I casually asked about the guy who gave her the light when I was up at the bar. I was quietly confident that he was batting for the boys' team, but it would have been my kinda luck to have my love interest chatted up by someone of the opposite sex.

"Don't know who he was," she giggled. "But he asked if I was your girlfriend!"

I smiled, uneasily.

"And what did you say to that?"

No reply.

Shazia pointed over my shoulder. "Oh. My. God."

"What?"

"Did you see them?"

"See who?"

"Those two women holding hands... Do you think they might be..." a dramatic pause "Lesbians?"

I shrugged. "You never know."

She looked at me mischievously. This was my chance to tell her. Tell her everything. There would never be a more suitable time. This *is* a gay bar and they *are* lesbians and I'm a... I'm a...

☞ ♥ ☜

I'm gay.

"Vicky, I've got a confession to make..."

"Listen, umm, there's something I should tell you..."

We both giggled.

"You first," she said. I watched her as she set her glass down and sat up attentively.

"No, you." I winked at her, "Ladies first."

"Well," she began.

But her story was lost behind the caterwauling of Gina G and her trashy, repetitive dance anthem.

She tried again, and I leaned in closer.

"When I saw you at first, tonight," she continued, cautiously, "I thought you were a boy."

"Yeah, I know." I grinned. "I knew you didn't recognise me."

"I even thought you were quite..." She paused, then blushed and put her hand over her face. "I can't even say it."

"Just say it."

Gay. She thinks I look gay. She already knows. She thinks it's funny.

"Umm, quite attractive."

My insides were turning over, turning inside out; all around me the club was spinning and my heart was smashing against my rib cage. I leant in further and said: "Have you ever kissed a girl?"

Shazia put out her cigarette and looked at me all cute and wide-eyed, and shook her head, slowly. We were sitting side by side and one of her hands was rested on the table in front of us. I edged my hand closer until our fingertips were almost touching.

"Have you ever wanted to?"

I chewed my bottom lip. We locked eyes. Then gently, I tilted my head and brushed my lips against hers.

☞ ♥ ☜

Shazia and I stayed together for nearly two years, but that was the last time before my eighteenth birthday that I ever went to Bennet's. We never went out on the scene. It wasn't like that with us. We weren't like that. She had convinced me that I didn't need other gay people in my life and, for a while, I believed her. I thought that we were the same; I thought that we wanted the same things, even though she kept telling me over and over that she didn't identify as a lesbian. She said that I was the only girl she would ever love. The only one she could ever love.

When you love someone, you gotta be able to trust them with your life. Otherwise there's no point. For a while, that's the kind of love I thought I had.

☞ ♥ ☜

Three years is a long time, but I can remember our last conversation vividly.

"I CAN'T just dump Danny."

This was the boyfriend she swore she hadn't slept with, the guy who was supposed to be the patsy, the cover-up.

"Why the fuck not?"

"Cause then my friends would start asking questions."

"So?"

"And they might find out about us."

Sigh.

In the beginning I didn't mind being her secret lover. It even seemed kinda sexy, a bit James Bond-ish. But the longer we were together, the further away it felt like she was pushing me. It hurt even more that she could lie so easily. If she could lie to them, she could lie to me.

"So, what, I'm not good enough, is that it?"

"You know that's not true."

"Is it?"

"You don't understand."

She always said that.

"I'm trying to understand."

"I wish I could share you with other people... I really love you but..."

But. There was always a *but* with Shazia.

I knew exactly what was coming next.

"Don't you dare pussy out on me, girl."

"It's over, Vicky," she whispered to me down the phone.

"What, you can't tell me to my face?"

"No," she said, firmly. "I know you, Vick, you'll try and talk me out of it."

"You saying you don't love me anymore, is that it?"

"I do still love you but..."

"I think I deserve to know the reason."

She paused. I could hear her trying not to cry into the receiver.

"Vick, you know why."

"No, I don't. Not unless you tell me."

"I have told you."

"Then tell me again."

"What we're doing," she sobbed. "It's wrong."

"I don't know what you mean."

I knew exactly what she meant.

"I told my parents about us the other day."

"And?"

This was news to me.

"My mum said I couldn't be– I couldn't be– g-gay because I wasn't brought up like that."

"Brought up like what?"

"She said there was nothing in my childhood that would make me– make me– turn out to be..."

Silence.

I begged her to talk to me.

"Goodbye, Vicky."

The receiver clicked and a droning filled my ear. I stood cradling the phone to my cheek as tears rolled down my nose, spilling into my mouth and down my chin. Finally, the receiver slipped from my hand and fell with a dull thud on the carpet. She wouldn't answer my calls. She wouldn't answer my letters and, pretty soon after that, she stopped coming into work.

And here she is. Just like that.

I watch Shazia and Joolz from the safe distance provided by the rising cigarette smoke and the writhing, dipping, diving bodies that separate us. Easy to see why anyone would fall for either of them. Shazia is dark-skinned, slim yet well-proportioned with firm, toned sexy curves. Joolz, on the other hand, has a wasp-sting waist, piercing blue eyes and sharp, striking features. Both are wily, charming and wise, and have it going on in the bedroom department. And both have, at some point or another, lured me into situations that could well have ended up dangerously.

"She's quite a hotty that Mylene girl," says Kat, sneaking up behind me and curling her hand around a cocktail glass.

I tell her that I wouldn't know, that I haven't really noticed and then I take my change and stomp over to where they're all sitting. Then I realise I've forgotten to pick up the drinks and I stomp back.

☞ ♥ ☜

We stay in the same seats at the same table for the next portion of the night. Joolz's feet are killing her she tells us, or she would have had me up dancing by now and Shazia claims to be doing the 'best friend looking out for her bit', although I know that the reason she's really not getting up is because she's scared I might blow her cover. Kat tries to do her Sherlock Holmes impression by periodically asking what's bothering me, but I don't tell her nothing and she soon becomes bored of that and starts asking Shazia questions about where she's from and how she knows Joolz and that's fine by me.

Of course Joolz gets up to dance eventually, with Siobhan and some other randoms, and Kat disappears off to the toilet, leaving me in isolation with old whiskey breath.

"I see you've grown a taste for it?" Shazia says, pointing at my drink.

"What?" I spit the word out. Make it known that I am not pleased to see her.

"You used to hate whiskey."

This is too much. It's bad enough that she didn't burn herself at the stake after we broke up, but to actually try to have a conversation with me...

"I used to hate a lot of things," I tell her. "And I used to be in love with you."

She sighs. "Vicky, I– "

"Don't." I say, holding my hand up. "Just don't."

She closes her mouth and drops her hands into her lap.

"It doesn't matter anyway," I say, "because I'm in love with Joolz now." There is a stark pause, followed by the thump thump thump of that horrible Destiny's Child song where they start rapping about how gorgeous they all think they are:

...*Michelle, can you handle this... Beyoncé, can you handle this... I don't think I can handle this...*

"Good," she says, finally. "I'm happy for you." But I can tell that she's no more excited about me being Joolz's girlfriend than I am about her being Joolz's best friend.

"So I take it that Joolz doesn't know about you and me then?" I ask.

Shazia shrugs and her hand hovers nervously over her fag packet. "This isn't a conversation I want to get into right now," she says. "I had a bad feeling about tonight. Right before I left the house I phoned Joolz and told her I felt sick."

"Joolz coming out must have been a bit of a shock," I say, ignoring her sob story.

"Understatement," she replies, lighting another cigarette and taking a deep drag. "She kept asking me to meet you..."

"And you kept making excuses."

"Yes. But I never thought in a million years– "

"What? That the girl your lesbian best friend was dating could be me?"

She shakes her head.

"So you weren't in the least suspicious when Joolz told you she was seeing someone called Vicky who went on gay dot com under the name 'Romeo'?"

"She didn't tell me your real name."

"You might have asked."

"I could have..."

"But then you didn't want to know I suppose."

"No," she replies. "I put all that in the past. I wouldn't have come tonight if I'd known."

"I wish you hadn't," I snap, push back my chair, stand up and walk off towards the exit, away from the music, away from her.

I need space, time to think. Do I tell Joolz? What do I tell her? Of all the damn broads in all of Glasgow, why did Joolz have to pick *her* as a best friend?

If I were in Sandy's right now and it was karaoke night I would stand up and sing a jazz song that describes the way I'm feeling.

Someone touches my arm and spins me round as they pass, it's Joolz, she beckons me to follow her back to the table. She sits down in the booth, tilts her head and smiles at me, then she turns to say something to Shazia. I wonder what they're talking about. Me? I hope not. I shudder to think of them comparing notes on my bedtime habits.

I don't think you ready for this jelly... I don't think you ready for this jelly...

I'm looking at Joolz but she's not watching, she's leaning in and laughing at something her sister is saying. Shazia is looking though, she's staring right at me and she's moving her lips. If I had a microphone I might wrap the cord around her neck right now. I might break my guitar over her head. Why did she have to come back? Why now? After everything I've done to try and get myself as far away from her as possible... Why does she still make me feel like this?

... cause my body too bootylicious for ya baby...

Joolz looks up as I walk over, slip my arm around her neck, lean in and kiss her. Shazia's eyes are all over me like sticky willies in summertime, she gives us a tight smile and then stands up, fumbling to put on her jacket. "I'll call you when I get in," she says and plants a quick kiss on Joolz's cheek then jerks back.

"No! No! No!" begs Joolz. "You've got to stay till the end."

"I really don't feel well."

"Vicky, tell her she should stay longer."

I glance at Shazia then down at my feet. "Yeah, you should stay longer." Kat tells her too that she should stay.

"No, honestly..."

"Come up and dance with me one last dance before you go." Joolz is up and is taking her shoes off and putting them up on top of the table.

"Honestly, I REALLY REALLY don't feel well. I'm just going to phone a taxi."

"Well, then we'll all go. And me and Vick will walk you down."

I bolt upright at the sound of my abbreviated name. 'Vick' – that's what Shazia always called me but Joolz never has.

I look at Shazia but she looks away. "No, you two stay," she says, firmly. Then she adds, stiffly, without making eye contact, "It was really nice to meet you, Vicky."

☞ ♥ ☜

"What's the matter, grumpy bear?" Joolz asks me a little later. "You're in a right grouchy mood."

"I'm fine," I say, and then I ask if she wants another drink even though she's had plenty.

"What do you think of Mylene then?"

What can I say?

"I hope she's alright actually," she adds, "maybe we should walk down and get her?"

"I'll go," I decide. "You can hardly walk." Joolz giggles. "I hope you are having a good birthday."

"You're cute," she tells me. Then she smiles and hiccups and hiccups again, and I know this means that she is.

☞ ♥ ☜

She's walking towards the taxi rank with her hands tucked in her coat pockets and I'm having to run to catch up with her.

"Shaz-i-a!"

I scuttle across the road, narrowly avoiding cars. It's raining heavy now and I've left my coat inside. She looks around and continues walking. I'm not sure if she saw me and chose to ignore me but I follow her anyway.

"Wait up," I call. Her feet scuff to a halt on the wet, black pavement. "I thought you were phoning a taxi?"

"I did," she replies. "They said it would be at least an hour. Thought I'd have more chance walking to Central." We both pause and look at each other, awkwardly. I can't think of what to say. "Look, I'm sorry if I ruined your night..." she begins.

"Forget about it."

"I shouldn't have come."

I sigh.

She looks so beautiful and yet so vulnerable, so fucking different from the vixen back in that club who was giving me attitude; so different from the girl I thought was a goddess who terrorised me into thinking I would never fall in love again.

A dark wet strand of Shazia's hair flickers in the wind. She blinks away the rain and pushes it behind her ear. The rain is slapping against the sides of our faces as we stand, frozen. I watch that same strand of hair roll free, slide diagonally across her face and catch itself to the side of her nose. I reach up and brush it aside with my fingertips. Her skin is smooth and moist and surprisingly warm despite the weather. My heart hammers in my chest as our eyes lock and she takes hold of my hand, softly squeezing.

Then I open my mouth to tell her how sorry I am, how I want to be able to work it out with her, maybe try and be friends with her, salvage something from this mess. I'm about to tell her how even though I think she should come clean to Joolz, that I won't blab, that her secret's safe with me if that's the way she wants it

And then she kisses me.

No warning, she just launches herself right at me and plants her lips on mine. And just for a brief second I let it happen. I allow myself to feel her hand on my waist and her tongue brushing against my teeth–

"No!"

I break away and see how the sudden rush of guilt and embarrassment has flooded her face. Then I look around to see if anyone else has witnessed us, but it's too dark to tell and there's nobody in the street but random drunks and cab drivers.

"I've got to go," she gasps.

"Shaz, wait– "

It's too late though, for she is already gone. And I am standing, watching her run away from me for the second time, unsure whether or not I'm supposed to go after her. I stand there for god knows how long, long after I see her flag down a black hackney at the corner of the road. And as that cab rides out of my line of vision, I feel a faint yet familiar stab in the pit of my stomach.

☞ ♥ ☜

I arrive back at the club dripping wet. Joolz has started a debate about the lyrics to Pink's new 'Get the Party Started' single, and is trying to convince everyone and anyone who will listen that Alecia Moore is a closet lesbian.

"IIIIIIII'm coming out... So you better get the party started."

"It's 'I'm coming UP'," argues Siobhan.

"No way."

"It is," says Liane. "You just want it to be 'coming out'."

"Well, it sounds better," says Joolz. "Doesn't it, Vicky?"

"Mmmhmm."

She asks if something is the matter and I tell her that I'm just tired and that it's time I was going.

"Awwww..."

I tell her that I'll call her in the morning and then we can hook up for our shopping trip. That's all I can say. I can't even proper kiss her goodbye or hardly look her in the eye after what just happened.

I go to the bathroom on my way out and Kat is standing by the sink washing her hands.

"Where in the hell have you been?" I say. (I'd actually forgotten about her but don't want to admit this.)

"Awww see that chicken korma I had..." she puts her hands on her belly and makes a pained face.

"Spare me the details."

"Everything ok?" she asks.

"Not really."

I kick the toilet door nearest to me and watch it fly back and forth. My ankle smarts and I think I may have broken a toe.

"Come on," she says, grasping me by the shoulders. "Calm down. That's not going to help."

I take a deep breath, turn on the cold water tap and spray my face. Kat pulls herself up onto the worktop and sits there, silently, flicking her ash into the sink as I launch into my Mylene/Shazia story.

"And that's the goddamn truth," I say, taking a deep breath. "That's the first time I seen her in all these years..."

Kat clicks her jaw back and forth and a smoke ring forms in front of my face. "You have to tell Joolz before someone else does."

"How can I tell her?"

"How can you not?"

"If she finds out I fucked her best friend..."

"It was before you two even met. And it's not as if anything's happened between you two while you were going out with Joolz." I reach over and take what's left of Kat's cigarette and take a drag as I watch myself inhaling through the mirror. "Look at me," she says, pulling my chin around to face her. "Has something happened?" I don't wanna answer. I can feel the smoke clogging in the back of my throat. I turn the side of my head so that she can't catch my eye. "That's great, that's just great, Vicky."

I accidentally exhale through my nose. I cough then stub the cigarette out in the wet sink. "It wasn't like that... It was a mistake... *she* kissed me..."

My cellphone rings. It's Joolz and I can hardly hear a word she is saying.

"You'd better go talk to her," says Kat.

"Shut up – no, not you, honey – I think she's OK now."

I end the call and slip my phone back into my pocket. "She just wanted to ask I'd found you ok, and if you still had... umm... diarrhoea."

Kat shakes her head. "She's going to find out sooner or later, you know."

"Not unless someone tells her."

Twenty-three

It's Saturday afternoon, one hour before L.I.P.S, and Zest, Kat, Mikki and I are in the archive rehearsing our lines for the second act of Earnest. We've just got to the part where the two Ernests finally get their comeuppance when Joolz arrives and stands, quietly, by the door.

GWENDOLEN> *Is your name really John?*

JACK> *I could deny it if I liked. I could deny anything if I liked. But my name certainly is John. It has been John for years.*

CECILY> *A gross reception has come... No, shit, that's not right...*

"A gross deception," quotes Joolz, "has been practiced on both of us."

"Exactly," smiles Kat, "that's what I meant."

"Sorry, did I put you off?" she says. "I can go away and come back."

She winks at me and turns to go back downstairs, and I go red – not because I feel shy or anything – but because I haven't told her everything about last night. And she did ask me on the phone this morning what happened when I went to accompany Shazia to the taxi rank. Because she wanted to make sure I hadn't said anything 'too gay'. I told her I had not and that we didn't really talk much. And that's not a lie exactly. But it's not like I could have told her the whole entire truth because then I'd be dumped, and Shazia, well, she'd have had some explaining to do.

Frankly, I still can't get my head around the whole Shazia/Mylene thing. One minute she's straight and then she's my girlfriend, and the next she's breaking up with me because her mother thinks lesbians are the Devil's spawn; and then, just when I think she's relocated under a rock for good, she's back with a pseudonym and a sexy new hairdo and she's trying to stick her tongue down my throat.

I sat for half the morning trying to write a story about it: I put down how we met and fell in love, how I took up singing anti-love songs for about six months after she dumped me, then I did a couple of paragraphs on how I used to feel about her compared with how I feel now – but really it solved nothing. After that, I wrote a version from Shazia's point of view, and that sort of helped a little.

Only problem now is – Joolz has been harping on about going with Shazia and her boyfriend for a drink sometime and I don't know what to say to her.

"No, it's ok," says Kat, calling her back. "I think a fag break is in order."

We call it a day and put our scripts away. Others are starting to arrive: Mikki The Hat, Rosie, a couple of baby goths I've never met, and bizarrely enough, Mel and Cherie, whom I've not seen or spoken to since they quit the show.

Today's L.I.P.S. workshop, it turns out, is salsa dancing tutored by Mel (and heavily chaperoned, I'll bet, by Cherie). Thankfully, we're not staying because Joolz and I are going to get our outfits for the guys and dolls party tonight, plus I'll also have to look for costume props for the show.

"I really wish we could have stayed," says Joolz.

"Well, *you* can if you want," I tell her.

I actually don't know what's worse, a super-femme shopping trip to Buchanan Galleries or an afternoon of sensible shoe wearers trampling on each other's toes.

"What?" she says, raising an eyebrow, "And miss the chance of seeing you try on a dress?"

"Very funny."

We say goodbye to everyone and Joolz grabs my ass as we're walking down the stairs.

"Hey!"

"I think you'd look really hot in a dress."

"No chance!"

"And why not?"

"Because you know why not."

I open the door. Let her go first.

Joolz sighs. "You're such a spoilsport sometimes."

"Am not."

"Are too."

"Look," I tell her, "we've been through this. I'm butch and you're femme and that's that."

"Well," she replies, "maybe it's time we mixed things up a little."

☞ ♥ ☜

Somehow I don't think this shopping trip is turning out the way Joolz had expected it would. I think she thought it was gonna be like in the movies, where you've got two girly girls who both own walk-in wardrobes and fifty plus pairs of shoes going out shopping and taking pictures of each other trying on big hats. So far she has found six dresses and a pencil skirt that she really wants, and all I've got are a pair of braces and a straw boater to wear on stage.

"What about this then?" she says, holding up a black crepe blazer with a corseted waist.

"No."

She sighs. This is about the fifty-millionth item she has pointed out to me, and I have given the royal thumbs down to all of them.

"What size are you, anyway?" she asks, taking a pair of super skinny pants off the rail.

"Small, I guess."

What I mean is 'small man' or 'extra small man' if they have that dimension, or else 'extra large boy' – which is what I am in Ma's catalogue.

Joolz holds them up against me looking pleased. They are black with a very subtle grey pinstripe and would probably look ok if they weren't a) lycra and b) made for someone who wants to seductively straddle a chair and pretend their name is Louise Redknapp.

"I'd say you were probably an eight... a ten at the most."

Mmm.

She puts the pants over her arm and then picks out a striped bustier to match.

"This would look so sexy..." she begins.

"I don't think so."

"Why not? You said you wanted something butch? Trousers are butch."

My feet are sore, I am beginning to sweat, and I don't have the energy to argue.

"I think I might just wear something I've already got," I say, quietly.

Her face falls. She sniffs then turns her head away.

"Fine," she says, "I give up. I tried my best but– " She lets the sentence hang there in the air whilst she picks a speck of lint from one of her dresses. Then she sighs and dumps the lot, including her own jacket that she took off because she was hot, over the top of another pile of clothes without even using the hangers and stomps off across the store.

I grab the clothes and sprint after her. What else can I do? She is almost through the exit doors when I shout: "OK I'll try the trousers on, damn it!" I didn't mean to say it so loud. The heads of several shoppers have turned in our direction, and a few bored workers have also abandoned their floor sweeping and garment folding duties to see what's going on. The security guard, a brawny middle-aged butch with a flat top, is looking me up and down, and I can't decide if it's because she fancies me, or because she's decided that I'm a traitor to masculine womankind, or maybe she just suspects me of being a really crap shoplifter.

Joolz spins around and smiles. She grabs me by the elbow and practically skips along to the fitting rooms, chattering all the way about how good she thinks my ass will look in this outfit and how she's really pleased that I'm finally trying out new styles.

We're approaching the female fitting assistant who's handing out number-of-items tags, and my hands are tingling and I feel short of breath. It's not so much the trying on of femme clothing or going into a women-only area that bothers me, more the idea of being verbally abused and humiliated because I don't fit into the average person's perception of what a woman is meant to look like.

"I'm sorry," begins the girl who is the epitome of Dita Von Teese and Marilyn Monroe and all those beautiful, busty, big ass, hourglass figured, lacy lingerie-wearing broads rolled into one, "but you're only allowed three items per person at a time."

"Oh."

"That's ok," cuts in Joolz. "We're together." She smiles at the girl and the girl smiles back, and then she takes all the clothes from me and separates them into two piles and gives one to me and keeps one for herself and asks if she can leave the skirt and one dress at the desk and come back for them.

"That's fine," replies Dita Von Roe. "I'll look after these for you."

"Thanks."

"Cool," I add.

I do the death march towards the first open cubicle, hands shaking, legs buckling, my bladder giving me gyp. Joolz tries to follow me in but I close the door and zip the curtain over, and tell her in no uncertain terms that if she wants me to do this then she better leave me alone.

"Boo!" she says.

I ignore her.

She giggles.

She is next door to me now giving me a running commentary on which outfit is too tight, too loose and too minging, and I am still looking at myself topless in the mirror when she raps on the wall and asks me to pass her the other dress.

In my reflection I can see the curves of my biceps, and those dips between my shoulders and elbows I'm so proud of. My belly is smooth, solid, not quite a six pack – but hardly a belly at all – and just the way I like it. My breasts are small, which is fine by me, I don't really think about them much except when I'm choosing a new sports bra. I work hard to look this toned and this good. And I like the way I look... At least I usually like it, but these pants are so clingy and so far up my ass...

"Are you ready yet?" calls Joolz. "How are you getting on?"

"Ok." I reply, grabbing a piece of lycra from around my hip and stretching it with my thumb and forefinger.

"Let me see."

I pull the bustier over my head in a hurry. Open the door.

Joolz's face is deadpan. Her eyes are roaming all over my body, drinking in every detail of me. Because there's a built-in bra and padding inside the bustier it gives the impression that I'm more endowed than I actually am, which makes me feel like I've been vacuum packed.

My face burns. And I need to piss badly. And I really just want to get out of this get-up and get out of the store altogether.

"Wow," says Joolz, finally. "Just wow."

Next, it's back to her place to get ready – because despite the fact that her family properly want to kill me, Joolz persuades me that it'll be ok because no one else'll be home and, also, she will make it worth my while, nudge, nudge.

I am seriously duped when she pushes me down onto her bed, straddles me, and then proceeds to wax my eyebrows and my underarm hair.

Two hours later, we're walking through Glasgow City Centre hand-in-hand, Joolz in her little cute pinstripe skirt, fishnets and a plastic tommy gun; me all gussied up like a prize turkey: make-up, high heels, the works. She's not talking much, and I think she's in a bit of a mood, which could be because her period came right before we left, but it's more likely because I wouldn't put out. Pretty stupid, really, if it is the second reason. Well, not really stupid. It's just that *she* wanted to fuck *me* ('for a change') and she wasn't too happy when I tried to explain that that isn't how I roll.

Cold sweat slides down my back as we fight our way through the biting wind. I have a blister starting on my little toe and my balance is a bit awry and, at this moment, I am holding onto Joolz for balance rather than romantic reasons but I don't think she's cottoned on.

I tell myself that I can do this, that it's no different from being on stage and wearing face paint or some stupid costume that is essential to the show. "I am an actor," I say over and over again under my breath.

"What was that, honey?"

"Nothing."

She squeezes my fingers. "You'll be fine," she says. "You look gorgeous."

Maybe she's not in a mood after all. Maybe I'm just being paranoid.

I nod, grit my teeth, and look straight ahead. About a hundred yards in front of us there is a group of male teenagers queuing outside a straight club and techno music is blasting from the open door.

"Oh my god! LESBIANS!" shouts one guy who is wearing a metallic-patterned shirt and a pair of aviator sunglasses pushed back on his shaved head.

We cross the road to avoid them and I brace myself for the usual barrage of abuse. Instead, all I hear is the same guy saying, "And they're fucking gorgeous, both of them."

I smile despite my discomfort. The only other times I've been the object of male attention is when I've been cruised by gay men who thought I was one of them. If Sam or Harry or any of the older butches were here, they'd say something about women not being put on this earth to cater to the carnal tastes of the typically sexist, straight, white man – and I know they're right – I should probably feel all indignant right now, but fuck it, it feels good to have someone tell you that they think you're hot.

"Hey, yous are pure lovely," says his friend in the pink Ben Sherman shirt.

"Do yous fancy coming home wi us?"

"Stu, ya fucking prick, man," the guy with the cool glasses says, "gonnae shut up." He waves at us as we go past and nods. "Have a nice evening, ladies."

"Wow, Vicky Romeo," Rachel whistles, as I step through the doors of Sandra Dee's. "Check you out!"

I pause for a minute, blushing furiously as she trails her eyes down from my head to my toes in a not so chaste or god-parental way.

Now, I *know* that I look good tonight. I'd have to be an idiot to think otherwise. Joolz spent a lot of time styling my hair, making it straight and smooth and sleek, and she's recreated my face to give me smoky bedroom eyes and a glossy, midnight rose coloured pucker. In fact, I look so hot that if I saw myself in a bar I'd probably try to get into my own pants. But still my heart is beating fast and my perspiration problem is spiralling.

"You got your tickets?"

I nod, hand them over and somehow resurrect a smile. I can see a wave of nudges making its way around the room – ending at Joolz and me.

"IS THAT VICKY?"

Kat and Zest and Minty are at a table near the door and they're collectively gaping. Joolz squeezes my arm. "Remember, you look gorgeous," she whispers, raises a hand and runs her fingers through my gel-free hair.

My friends are on their feet now and they're rushing towards me. Kat is the first to speak and she begins by telling me that she would never have recognized me if it wasn't for Joolz. "I mean," she bumbles, "you look so... so..."

"So very fuckin heterosexual." Minty has a look of disgust on her face. (I didn't even know she was coming tonight.) She is dressed up as the corpse of Clyde Barrow in a blood-covered suit and a bullet-through-the-brain mask, her arms folded tight across her tits.

My hands twitch and I rake my fingers through my hair, tuck a stray lock behind my ear.

"Well, I think you look beautiful," says Joolz loudly, so that everyone around us can hear. She gives me a hug. This is the first time anyone's ever used that word to describe me. Cute? Maybe. Sexy? Definitely. But, beautiful?

I tell her thanks and begin to study my watch. It's five past nine. That's another two hours and fifty-five minutes before I can escape.

"It's well seen this is a costume party," snorts Minty. "I thought you were dressing up as a gangster not a skankster?"

Joolz puts her arm around my waist and begins steering me towards a table near the door. "Just ignore her," she says, softly. "She's just jealous."

"Aye, well," Min says to the back of my head, "I'm only saying what every other cunt else is thinking."

"I think she looks really pretty," pipes up Zest, who has obviously spent a lot of time and effort sewing half of an evening gown onto half a suit jacket and one trouser leg. I mouth 'thanks' to her and then split my attention between listening to what else Minty's got to say and who's coming through the door."And what would you know, Wigfield?" Minty sneers, rearranging her bullet-through-the-brain mask so that none of her hair is poking up from under the latex. "Are you supposed to be a hermaphrodite or something?"

Zest's bottom lip trembles. She looks at Minty then at me then back at Minty. More L.I.P.S. girls are starting to arrive and some of them are tipping their heads at me and saying I look good; others are murmuring that I'm very brave to dress up femme, and braver yet to wear these heels. And then, just as I'm about to praise Zest for being the best dressed, she pushes past me and past the crowd of onlookers and runs through the door out into the night. There is silence, followed by laughter, and then Kat runs out after her.

Minty just stands there guzzling her pint and pretending that nothing has happened.

"I can't believe you," I say to her. "That was really shit what you just did."

"Who? Me?"

I shake my head. I am sick to death of her bullshit. Sick to death of the bitching and the whining and the making other people feel like crap just because she's the one who's not happy.

I open my mouth to tell her this but I'm low on saliva and the words stick in my gullet. From across the room I can see Paris and Scarface and Mel and Cherie pointing at me, and they are all fucking laughing. Then Minty says something about being a team player, which I don't quite catch, and the whole room begins to spin.

"Come on, Vicky," says Joolz, pulling on my arm. "People like her aren't worth it."

My head is hot and light and it's as if someone's pulling me upwards by my hair. I know that the best thing I can do now is take her advice, just walk away and say nothing, just fucking walk. And that's exactly what I'm trying to do when Minty, swaying and smirking, shouts from behind: "Aye, well, it's easy to see who wears the strap-on in that relationship."

Her words shudder through me like a punch in the guts. I baulk. All I can see now is a kaleidoscope of faces: Min's grinning one, Joolz's pained expression, Mel, Cherie, Scarface... They are all blurring together now like three-eyed Siamese hyenas. I am cold all over and yet my entire body, even my butt crack, is soaking.

"Fuck this," I say, finally, gulping air like a fish on the shore. Then softer, because my chest and my lungs and all my insides ache, "I'm outta here too."

I walk as fast as I can out into the street, no plan as to where I'm actually going. I just wanna get away from everyone, but everywhere I turn there are drunks and other night-time revellers meandering in my way.

'If you're part of a crew,' says the voice of hasbeen wise guy Henry Hill, *'nobody ever tells you that they're going to kill you...'*

"Vicky, wait!"

'See, your murderers come with smiles, they come as your friends...'

"Vicky, can you please just wait?"

'And they always seem to come at a time that you're at your weakest and most in need of their help.'

I stop in the middle of the sidewalk but I don't turn around. Joolz's breathing is laboured and I let her catch right up before moving on in silence.

"Where are you going?"

Shrug.

"Is that it? Are you not even going to talk to me?"

She pulls on my arm and I swing around to face her. Her eyes are filling up with tears and I'm fighting to stop mine from doing the same.

"Don't cry," I say, swallowing hard. "You'll ruin your make-up."

She sniffs. "Shall we go home?"

Back at my place, I go to the bathroom straight away and rip off the offensive fancy-dress outfit and roll it into a ball. I then scrub my face with soapy water till it's red and puffy and face paint free. Joolz watches me but says nothing. No need to explain why I left the party, no need to tell her that I'll never let her pick my clothes again. I put on my flannel pyjamas and give her one of my baggy t-shirts to wear, and we sit for the longest time on top of my bed, just hugging and saying nothing. She has her arms tight around me and her face is leaning on my shoulder, and it feels so good.

A little later we go under the covers and begin to kiss and kiss and, slowly, our hands begin to work their way up under each other's shirts and then her hands snake down over my hips and inside my–

I squeal. I didn't mean to. It just came out suddenly because I wasn't expecting it.

"Fucksake Vicky! You act like I'm molesting you or something." She punches the mattress and lies back down with her cheek against my shoulder.

Silence.

It really was quite an embarrassing, over-the-top, high-pitched noise and I can't believe it came from inside me.

"I'm sorry," I tell her.

She sighs. "No, I'm sorry." Then whispers. "What is it? What am I doing wrong? Why won't you let me..." She's holding my hand to her chest and staring at me, waiting for the answer that I don't know how to give, and in my own chest there is an invisible weight pressing down heavily.

Shazia would never have tried to get me to talk about this. We never really talked about the sex we had. It just existed. Like a ghost or some unexplained phenomenon. Shazia told me where she liked to be touched, and I obliged. One time I did pick up the courage to ask her to make love to me, but she just burst into tears and said that she couldn't. She thought it was wrong. I never asked her again. I never asked anyone again. I just took it into my head that this was another part of being butch. Nobody ever tried to correct me on it.

"Might as well go to sleep," says Joolz, "if you're not going to talk to me." She rolls away and over onto her side.

"No."

"No what?"

"No, don't go to sleep."

I take a deep breath and guide her hand down towards my pussy. Every inch of me is shaking as I let her stroke me with the palm of her hand.

"Tell me what you want me to do," she whispers.

I take three short gasps, run the tip of my tongue over my suddenly dry lips and say: "I don't know... I... anything..."

She kisses me again and I weave my arms around her back. Goosebumps rise on my skin, my nipples become rigid and my arms quiver as she spreads my legs with a slight nudge of her knee. As Joolz touches me, I think about that first time I ever met her. How amazing she looked beneath the dim lights of Sandy's with all those swirls of blue cigarette smoke rising from her lips. I remember how I tried to come across all cool and suave, like I'd gotten my leg over a thousand times before. I remember the way she looked at me like she didn't know whether or not I was for real. And I remember how her laughter rose above the music as I blew the whole act with that one corny chat-up line. And somewhere in amongst all that I tell her I love her and she says it back.

I don't even notice that I'm crying until she raises her head and, leaning over, kisses my tears away.

"No one's ever... done that to me... touched me... like that before," I stutter.

Joolz blinks. Her hand becomes still again; my head is leaning on her other arm and with it she gently strokes my hair.

"Why not?"

When I don't respond, she asks again, this time more hesitant.

"Did I hurt you?"

I shake my head.

"Did you like it?"

I pull the covers up around us and grin. And grin.

Twenty-four

I'm dreaming. And in the dream, I'm on a Broadway stage all done up in a tux and tie with a red carnation in my buttonhole and a pair of black patent brogues. Joolz is there too, wearing a fascinator and a red, off the shoulder dress, and we're singing the words to 'Something Stupid'. The whole thing is very contrived and very jazz hands, and I know it's not real, especially when the song ends and one of the audience members gets up out of his seat and walks towards us, and it turns out to be Dean Martin, and he holds out his hand for me to shake and–

"Get up!"

Joolz is shaking my shoulder violently, shaking me right out of my gorgeous technicolour fantasy. Her fingers are cold and I'm getting a draft, and the duvet that I've been cocooned in begins to slip away, just like the images of Dean and the spotlights and my Moulin Rouge-ified girlfriend.

"Get up!" she repeats, with force.

I stretch, rub my face, fart, sniff, do all the things folk normally do when they've just been hauled out of a deep sleep and they're not totally with it. I had been hoping to get a glimpse of Frank and Sammy Davis Junior before I got going, but clearly it was not meant to be.

Finally, I open my eyes and grin.

"Hey, sexy lady."

Joolz is wearing my house robe and I can see the curve of her breast below the sinking neckline. I reach out to touch her but she slaps my hand away and shrinks back. I had only wanted to feel the smoothness of her skin, to prove to myself that she's not some kind of mirage, but she has obviously misinterpreted it as a grope.

"I love you, you know that...?" I tell her. I feel lightheaded and ridiculously happy. I have never felt as happy as this. I have never felt as secure or as loved as I have with her. I would totally marry her right here right now if it were possible, if it were legal... I start to tell her all of this because I want to reassure her that what I feel for her is the real deal, and not just about sex, or having some sort of eye candy on my arm, but she holds a hand up and stops me half-way through my speech.

Only when I stop talking do I suddenly notice that her eyes are ringed red and that her mouth is twisting and trembling at the corners.

"Joolz," I say, tentatively tilting my head, "is everything– "

"Who is she?"

"Eh?"

"Don't play games with me, Vicky. Just fucking tell me."

I sit, brow furrowed, running a hand through my hair.

"I'm sorry but I really dunno what you're– "

Joolz picks up a scrap of lined paper that is lying on the bed and begins reading aloud from it: "The Continuing Adventures of Radclyffe the Lesbian Pen." She takes a deep breath and I try to intervene, try to explain, try to take the paper from her but she twists her body out of reach and continues in a tight, high voice: "Radclyffe Orlando Sackville-West (aka the lesbi-an ball-point pen from Elephant and Castle) did not know who the mystery woman writer was, nor had she ever heard of Vicky Romeo, the handsome ex-lover whom the woman had kissed suddenly, and with wild abandonment, in a surprise encounter outside a nightclub after three years of estrangement."

There is a writhing in my stomach, as if my innards have sud-denly become a pile of jiggling, squirming maggots.

"Shall I continue?" says Joolz, her eyes blazing.

I shake my head and lower it.

That story was never meant to be read by anyone else. I was supposed to burn it or rip it up, get rid of it along with any trace feelings I might still have for Shazia.

Joolz sighs. "So it's not just a work of complete fiction then," she says, dryly.

I don't answer. I don't see the point in digging myself into a bigger hole.

"I didn't think so."

I can hear my heart bumping against my chest.

She sighs again, deeper this time. Then she lets the paper fall down onto the bed.

"I'm really sorry..." I tell her. "I swear to god, baby, it was her who kissed me."

She won't let me near her to give her a hug; she won't look me in the eye, even when I keep saying over and over that she's the one I love, the only one, and that I would never cheat on her or do anything to–

"I'm only going to ask you one last time," she says, in a small, choked voice. "Who is she?"

☞ ♥ ☜

Long after Joolz has left, long after I tell her that I can't break a confidence and she tells me that there's no future for us as a couple because the trust is gone, there is a sharp knock on my bedroom door.

At first I think she's come back, that she's changed her mind, but then Kat's voice is asking if I am awake and still available to help her get her things into the removal van. I had forgotten that she was leaving today, forgotten that I was supposed to go over to see Mamma after I'd seen her off.

And despite the fact that I don't feel like going anywhere or helping anyone right now, I keep to my promise. I wipe my eyes with the back of my hand then drag myself out of bed and into a pair of grey jogging bottoms and a t-shirt that quite fittingly says 'shit happens'.

☞ ♥ ☜

Kat already knows about Joolz, and so do Minty and Robbie who are in the living room eating a fry up and dragging furniture, respectively, when I come out of my room.

She gives my arm a squeeze and tells me to give it time.

"Yeah, yous'll work it out," says Robbie, with an encouraging smile.

I nod and tell him thanks, lift a box of miscellaneous paper-backs and start towards the stairs. I don't know how much Kat's been told, and how much of that information she's passed on to Robbie, but I can tell by the way she keeps avoiding eye contact that she doesn't fancy my chances of a reunion.

Minty prods a fried egg with a knife, soaks the watery yolk up with a slice of buttered bread. "Well, you know what they say,

Romeo..."

I ignore her. I've just remembered that I'm still pissed off with her for last night.

"The only way to treat a woman," she says, "is to make love to her if she's pretty and to someone else if she is plain." She laughs out loud. "What's that supposed to mean?" I say, hackles rising. I am one step removed from punching her stupid mouth.

"Nothing," she sniffs. "Just that there's plenty more fish in the aquarium."

"Are you coming, Vicky?" asks Kat, frowning.

I tell her I am. And on that note, I tramp downstairs, disgusted, hoping that Robbie is right and Kat's hunch is wrong, and that Minty will choke on her breakfast.

An hour or so later, Minty drops a chest of drawers on my fingers and Kat almost runs me over with the rental van as she backs out of the driveway; then my train to Paisley breaks down, making me even later for my visit to Mamma's house – putting the cherry on top of the icing on top of what has already been an exceptionally shit day.

I cross my arms in my lap and stare outta the carriage window, down at the empty tracks, wondering how I can fix things with Joolz. Wondering if I can ever fix things. I come to the sorry conclusion that, even if I could go back in time to stop her reading that stupid story (or even further back, so that I could avoid the set of circumstances that led to the writing of the story), what happened on Friday night would still have happened eventually, and I would still have kept Shazia's secret. So Joolz and I would still have broken up.

And, truth be told, I had known the instant Shazia reappeared that everything was about to go wrong. I didn't know how or when exactly, but straight away I had this tightness in my chest and a lightness in my feet, and it decided me in my own head that my relationship with Joolz was surviving on borrowed time. And the thing is – I don't feel a bit angry towards Shazia, not about any of this. Perhaps I should. Funny thing is, it actually helped seeing her again, helped to cauterize the pain she'd caused me in the past.

Sigh. *So that's it*, I think to myself as the carriage begins to rock and rumble. It's over. No point in calling Joolz up and begging her to stay. I used to think that if you loved someone, and they loved you back, then that was enough. I understand now, all too clearly, that nothing that involves matters of the heart is ever so black and white.

☞ ♥ ☜

When I finally arrive at Ma's house, I know instinctively that something isn't right. Because a) she isn't watching the Sunday EastEnder's Omnibus, b) there is a pile of untouched ironing on the settee, and c) she doesn't moan or say a word to me about the fact that I am two hours late. In fact, she doesn't say anything at all when she opens the door, just simply nods and about turns and goes off into the kitchen to make a pot of coffee.

☞ ♥ ☜

Mamma and Sam have broken up, and Sam has moved out. I learn this over the course of the next few hours, over several espressos and an Indian takeaway (because neither one of us feels like cooking).

At first I sit awkwardly in my chair, drinking it all in, not sure what to say. We have never been the type of family to share our innermost feelings and, aside from an obligatory New Year's exchange, Mamma has not hugged or kissed or comforted me since I was a child.

"So..." I begin, doubtfully, "was there someone else involved?"

Sam never struck me as a deserter or a cheat, and she was always so bloody dependable, but people can surprise you.

Ma shakes her head.

"No," she says, definitely. "There was no one." Then a few moments later she smiles with what looks like an air of apology and adds: "No, we simply fell out of love."

She looks away after that. My jaw clenches. I think for a moment that I might burst into tears. But I don't.

She asks if I want another drink and I agree.

"Same again?"

"Yeah, thanks."

She doesn't say any more about Sam when she comes back, she simply changes the subject to what is happening in my life with work, the play, and my brother and sister. And, likewise, I don't mention anything about Joolz or our split because we don't talk about things like that. It seems in bad taste to whine about an ex-girlfriend that I have known for such a short time when here she is picking up the pieces of a spent decade.

She gives me a jug of egg-free eggnog and a box of tiny, home-made vegan tiramisu cakes to take away with me. I eventually edge my way towards the front door, not really wanting to leave her on her own but scared to stay because the idea of Mamma crying on my shoulder is all a bit overwhelming. We stand there on the doorstep, half-in half-out for a good part of twenty minutes, her eyes glittering, her bottom lip quivering and just as I'm saying goodbye and am about to turn around, she grabs me with both arms and crushes me against her large bosom.

A half-hour later, I see Sam as I'm leaving Central station on my return journey. She's coming out of the twenty-four hour newsagents next to the station taxi rank and she doesn't notice me. I think she might be drunk actually. I consider calling out to her, but a sudden hoarseness in my throat takes over and I just stand there open-mouthed, staring, as she makes her way down the road.

Twenty-five

It's Friday night and we are three-quarters of the way through act three, the part of the play where Dr Chasuble comes back and accidentally exposes Miss Prism's identity to Lady Bracknell, thereby almost completing the puzzle of the handbag and the three-volume novel. For the first time since we started rehearsing we actually have a full cast, and Broadbent warned us all when we arrived that we would not be going home until we'd finished an entire dry run of the script. And it's going pretty well, all things considered: Minty and I are barely speaking; communications between Salsa and Mikki are strained (it turns out they had a one-night stand); whilst Kat and Robbie having, surprisingly, reverted to being 'just friends' again, seem to be getting on better than anyone else. And between work and rehearsing and going to see Mamma most days, I haven't had time to mope around or think about Joolz.

I mime the presentation of the battered handbag. Robbie does his 'aghast' face and we fly through the last part of the scene with gusto and no mistakes whatsoever. And Broadbent, for the first time since I met her, smiles and actually applauds us.

There are nine hours and forty-five minutes left until the show and fifteen minutes till the technical rehearsals start. Everyone is here this morning and ready with all their props and costumes, apart from Scarface – who, despite the fact that she has limited acting ability, has some seriously good skills when it comes to camaraderie and smoothing over arguments between cast members.

I am really excited now. The twins are coming and so is their mother, and Mamma texted me first thing in the morning to say that she has sold all ten of the tickets I had given her and that she was looking forward to tonight. Chocolate Frappuccino Boy and Caramel Macchiato Girl (who are dating now, thanks to yours truly) and Laptop Bob will be here too, and I was half-tempted to invite old Maggie moan-pants, but decided against it.

Robbie and Minty are setting up, lifting all the big antique-looking furniture for Algernon's flat when Broadbent stalks in with a grim face and commands us all to stop what we are doing.

"I'm sorry to disappoint you all," she says, drably, "but Penelope Mess has pulled out of the performance."

Silence.

"Without a replacement," she continues, "the show can't possibly go ahead."

There is a loud clatter, followed by a 'watchmafuckintoesyacunt'. I might have laughed at the sight of Minty hopping around the room under a different set of circumstances, but not today.

Mikki Blue slams down her coffee cup and shouts: "That is pish! She is fucking getting it by the way."

There are a few grunts of agreement, and I'm included in them. Broadbent sighs and says: "Yes, well, I feel a bit like that myself right now, but I don't think that's going to help anyone."

She sinks down into a plastic chair and rubs her temple with the palm of her hand.

As I watch her, I feel a surprising and unexpected rush of sympathy.

Now, I've never liked the woman and I've made no secret of that. And if this had happened a month ago, I would've blamed everything on Broadbent for her dire choice of leading lady. I never expected Scarface to take the play seriously, but as the weeks went on and things began to take shape, I started to understand that this 'project', as Broadbent had called it, was more than just about putting on a good show. Zest, for example, has gained confidence and became quite the comedian both on and offstage and Kat is toying with the idea of writing her own script. I don't really know what Scarface personally got out of it because I never asked, but she was undoubtedly the glue that held the cast together, if only because we were teaming up to bitch about her.

I realise too that Broadbent must be gutted. Despite everything I think about her, she did put in a lot of hours and she kept whipping us whenever it seemed like we might toss in the towel.

I ask her if Scarface gave any reason for pulling out.

"Apparently she fell and broke her ankle."

"Ouch," I reply.

"Fucking idiot," says Mikki.

"Well, that's what happens when you put a dyke in roller skates," says Minty. No one laughs.

"Is there nothing we can do?" I ask.

I am on tenterhooks, waiting for Broadbent to say that she is gonna save the day by stepping into the breach herself – only she doesn't.

"I'm really sorry guys..." she begins.

Zest has started to cry.

"Hey, it's OK." I tell her as I move over and put my arm around her and rub her back. Turning to Broadbent, I say: "Surely, you could play Lady Bracknell?"

She doesn't answer, just blinks back at me, strokes her chin and mumbles, "If only we'd thought of an understudy..."

Kat, who's said nothing throughout all of this, stands up and takes out her cellphone (a new one I haven't seen before, it's purple with a fliptop). "There is one person I think might be able to help us..." she says, brightly. "My new flatmate is a pretty good actress..."

Everyone is frozen in silence and anticipation.

I give her a quizzical look but she ignores me and quickly dials a number on the keypad. A few moments later. "Hello, Julie?"

My heart lurches into my throat.

"You know that favour you owe me? Well, how are you fixed for the next twelve hours?"

I stare at Joolz as she delivers her lines. She arrived here, with her impeccable make-up, looking sexy as ever, less than half an hour after Kat made the call, and she just got on with things no questions asked. And the weirdest thing of all is that she's been perfectly pleasant to me.

I didn't know that she'd moved out of her parents' house and I didn't know that she'd gotten a job as a roller-skating waitress (although it stands to reason that Sandy's would need more workers since half their staff are in the play). And whilst

I know that I should be concentrating on my own dialogue, I find myself wondering what other important life changes she's made, and if her feelings for me are still the same.

LADY BRACKNELL> My nephew...

I notice she's had a couple of inches taken off her hair and had some strawberry blonde highlights put in.

LADY BRACKNELL> ...you seem to be displaying signs of triviality.

Perhaps she's seeing someone else now. Kat would know. But would she tell me if I asked? I don't know if I'd want to know. A horrible thought strikes me: what if it's Kat that she's seeing? What if that's why her and Robbie have broken up? The two of them have been getting pretty chummy recently. What if they're more than just 'flatmates'?

"Jack," she says, "it's you."

I blush.

"Sorry."

An hour left till the big performance. Salsa is fixing the fountain for the Manor House garden. I ask her if she's all prepared for tonight, and she just shrugs and says: "Ready as I'll ever be."

I'm beginning to act frantic, pacing up and down backstage, worrying that I'll somehow manage to make an ass of myself and that Mamma will then give me the 'I told you so' speech. I tell Salsa that I don't think I can go onstage, that I can't remember my lines, that I'm feeling sick all of a sudden. She says I'll be just fine and palms me off on Zest and Mikki who are running through their dialogue for act two.

Broadbent is smoking a cigarette and talking to the guy who's come to help us with the lights. Minty is eating. Robbie is fixing his make-up. Kat and Joolz are nowhere to be seen.

Fifteen minutes to go. I need to pee. No, I don't. Kat is on her cellphone giving someone directions to the theatre. Zest is turning her wig inside out and doing William Shakespeare impersonations. Mikki has got the hiccups from laughing at Zest. Robbie is still doing his make-up and Salsa is still adjusting the props. Minty is reading a rock music magazine and periodically eating the props. Broadbent is smoking her fifty-thousandth fag of the evening. And Joolz – Joolz is frigging meditating.

Broadbent shushes us. "OK, first of all," she says, "I'd just like to say thanks to all of you for taking part. It's been brilliant working with you– "

"Hooray!" Zest cheers.

Broadbent smiles at her. "Kirsten, fix your hair," she says, then turns her attention back to everyone, "I just want you to go out there and give it your best shot and..."

Broadbent's boyfriend (cause we've now established that he is, in fact, her boyfriend who used to be her girlfriend), Al, rushes into the dressing room. "Oh my god, Tracy, we have sold ALL the tickets."

"Hooray!" Zest cheers, again.

"We're going to have to put out extra seats."

"Can we do that?" asks Broadbent

"Well," says Al, "we've promised the L.I.P.S. girls free entry and there are fourteen of them out there so far."

I'm standing behind the curtain, waiting for my cue. I feel weird dressed up as a man, kinda like that night I dressed up femme, and yet different somehow. Broadbent has given me a five o'clock shadow and a moustache using crepe hair and something called spirit gum to make it stick to my skin. It makes my top lip itch, and I worry that I might be allergic and that I'll get a rash.

The safety pins that Broadbent used to strap down my breasts are cold against my armpit. I always thought I had this tiny bosom – not so when you're trying to hide it. Tonight she made me strip to the waist in front of her and then she wound a six-inch wide medical bandage around me. I told her I could do it myself, but she insisted because she said it can be dangerous and you can cause yourself serious injuries – like fractured ribs or a punctured lung – if you're not careful.

"Break a leg," whispers Zest. "Break a leg, everyone."

Joolz is standing right behind me. I turn around and she gives me a tight smile. "Break a leg," she says, quietly, and then she holds out her hand for me to shake. I stand staring at it for a moment, as if it's an adder waiting to bite me. There is a tightening in my chest and I'm about to lean in and grab her fingers when she lets her arm drop.

An alphabet soup of cheesy phrases bounces about noiselessly in my voice box. I want to say 'I'm sorry' and 'good luck' and a whole load of other things. But she simply turns away and I realise with a jolt of excitement that the show is starting.

Mikki is onstage pretending to play the piano. Salsa walks on with the cucumber sandwiches, which are actually gherkin because there were no cucumbers left in the whole of Tesco Metro.

I am counting down the seconds till it is my turn – till I have to become John Worthing, a thirty-something, heterosexual, upper-class gentleman of Victorian values, a man who pretends to have an imaginary reprobate younger brother so that he can leave his stately countryside home to go slumming it in London under an assumed name and do all the things that he pretends to disapprove of in his fictional sibling.

It's almost time. I try to take a deep breath but find it's impossible with all the damn bandages.

LANE> Mr Ernest Worthing

I cross myself and walk onstage.

The audience roar and clap at the end of act one, and not one person seems to have noticed the huge faux pas I made when I said I was coming up to town to expose myself to Gwendolen (instead of 'expressively propose').

The curtain comes down and we all breathe a sigh of relief. "Well done," says Broadbent. "That was brilliant."

Al arrives with the half-time orange juice, bottled water and chocolate biscuits. "That was so funny!" he says, patting me on the back.

"Thanks."

"I thought you and Gwendolen really bounced off one another."

"She's great isn't she? She cracks me up."

"Oh yeah," he nudges me, "something we should know about?" I just laugh. He's actually not a bad guy, and an actor himself apparently, and now I know that he's a he I don't feel so awkward around him.

"What is it thingmy says again?" he grins. "The way you and Gwen flirt is...'"

"PERFECTLY DIS-GRACEFUL!" shouts Mikki, as she marches towards us. I blush a bit as I notice that Joolz is standing over in the corner, smoking a cigarette, and probably listening to the entire conversation. "I thought you were brilliant, old bean."

"Very kind of you to say so, my dear chap."

"But I must say, I felt you were somewhat rather lacking in the scene with dear Aunt Augusta."

"What do you mean lacking?" I ask, quickly, falling out of old chap mode.

"Steady on, I just mean that you looked rather a bit too happy for someone who's supposed to hate the dear old bat."

"Yes, I felt that as well," says Broadbent, crossing over to where we are standing. "I think you need to act a bit more desperate, Vicky."

"Desperate?"

"Think Michael Redgrave."

"OK."

"You're totally in love with Gwendolen. You'll do anything for her."

"Yeah."

"But Lady Bracknell doesn't want you to marry her daughter..." says Broadbent.

I look over at Joolz again. She is stubbing her cigarette out against the wall. I want to go over and talk to her but Broadbent has me trapped.

"...so I think there has to be a lot more tension between the two of you," she concludes and adds, smiling, "but apart from that I thought you were excellent."

I look over my shoulder again but Joolz is gone. "Scuse me," I say, "I have to go to the bathroom."

I hear a toilet flush as I go through the door. I turn around and switch the cold tap on and pretend to be washing my face. But then I stop because I remember that I have a fake moustache on.

"Hey," I say to Joolz as she comes out. I've decided to play it cool.

"Hi," she says, stiffly.

"Do I look ok? I think this thing is coming off."

She cups my chin and lifts my face up towards the light. I get tingles through my entire body.

"You've just got one wee stray hair..." she runs her finger along the edge of my mouth until she catches it. "There," she says and holds it up for me to see.

My heart is racing now and I can feel the underarms of my shirt becoming patchy and wet. She turns away from me and switches the tap on to rinse her hands.

"Listen Joolz," I begin, "I've been wanting to talk to you about something... I mean... about us... I..."

She sighs but says nothing.

I swore to myself I wouldn't do this but... to hell with it...

"I really really miss you," I tell her.

Silence.

"Do you still love me?"

No answer.

"Do you?"

Sigh.

"Tell me you don't love me and I swear I'll walk away and never bother you again."

"Tell *me* who the girl is," she finally replies, haughtily.

I feel a little breathless now, a little bit shaky, but I'm also giddy with relief.

"So you DO still love me!" I have this surge of renewed energy now and I want to sing and shout and dance around the room.

"Well, maybe... I don't know..." her face is gradually turning red now. "I mean that's not really the issue here... Maybe when we've finished the play then things will be different."

"I hope so."

I really really hope so.

"Maybe," she says, dropping her eyes, "we can try and be friends."

Friends.

I swallow hard.

"I don't want to be friends," I say, and it comes out sounding ten times more spiteful than I mean it.

She curls her lip. "Fine then," she says and flicks the water from her hands and dries them on her dress. She turns her back and marches out of the toilet. I stand there with my mouth slightly agape and whisper: "I want to be your girlfriend."

I'm not sure what I was expecting from her, but this wasn't it. I want to rewind, to start the conversation all over again–

"Vicky?" The door is thrown open again and Joolz sticks her head around it.

"You better move because we are on in about thirty seconds."

Act two flies by. The audience is in eruptions over Cecily's diary. Kat bought this huge furry cerise note pad with sparkly silver hearts from Girl Heaven in the Braehead shopping centre. Robbie and Minty are hysterical as Prism and Chasuble, and backstage everyone is laughing and Broadbent is telling us all to shush because the audience will hear us. Mikki is flawless as Algernon, the way she delivers her lines is making me struggle to keep a straight face. But Zest really steals the show: just before the curtain comes down her wig gets caught in her parasol.

We have a short toilet break before act three. I follow Joolz into the ladies to try to talk to her again but she pulls Kat into a cubicle with her and the two of them stay there giggling until after I leave.

Act three drags on a bit at the beginning. This is partly because Mikki and I are having trouble saying our lines while pretending to enjoy the horrible prune and banana muffins that Broadbent got as props.

Joolz enters as Lady Bracknell. I am standing with my arm around Gwendolen and Joolz has a look of disgust on her face, when she stares in my direction I turn quite pink. It's clear that whatever her and Kat were talking about in the toilets was something to do with me. She probably told Kat the entire conversation we just had. Probably added a few bits to it as well. Well, fuck her. Fuck both of them.

The tension between us is sky high. It's like a game of ping-pong. Every time Lady Bracknell opens her mouth, I cut her down with one of my lines and she is just as quick to retaliate.

LADY BRACKNELL> You must be quite aware that
what you propose is out of the question.

JACK> Then a passionate celibacy is all that
any of us can look forward to.

The audience is silent all the way through my interaction with Joolz, right up until the part where I produce the notorious handbag.

Sweat beads are pouring down the back of my neck and adrenalin is coursing through me as the last few lines of the play are delivered. And even though I am mad as hell at Joolz and Kat and Minty right now, I'm also incredibly grateful to them for turning up tonight to do this show, because – boy-oh-boy – we are all fucking nailing it!

LADY BRACKNELL> My nephew, you seem to be displaying signs of triviality.

JACK> On the contrary, Aunt Augusta, I have now
realised the vital importance of being earnest.

☞ ♥ ☜

All the cast and crew plus their family and followers have been invited to Sandy's for an after show party, and Rachel has dutifully supplied a finger buffet plus one free drink each. I'm really not up to it, and woulda preferred to leave straight away with Mamma, but she convinces me to stay and 'celebrate'. She tells me that she's proud of me and that she was wrong to discourage me from an acting career. I know I should be happy to hear that but, well, I'm just not.

I must be the only person from our cast who isn't on a post-show high. Most of the actors are pissed already because we haven't eaten anything since lunchtime, except for the random bites of the notorious banana muffins, and we are constantly having congratulatory drinks thrust at us – which is fine in itself, except that there's also all the rigmarole of posing for photographs and signing programmes. A couple of feisty femmes I've never met before ask if I will sign their chests but I decline. There are so many people here tonight that I know: girls from L.I.P.S., staff from the archive, even some of the old mob from my Vagina Monologues days whom I haven't seen in years. I don't see any of Joolz's family though, or Sam.

I am so busy wallowing and throwing back the Jack Daniel's that I don't notice Pippa Black till she's standing next to me and pumping my hand up and down. I finally come to life and take in my surroundings. "Oh my god, it's so brilliant you came!" I tell her, and I genuinely mean it. I had heard through the grape-vine that she had cancer, and I remember this on spying the flo-ral bandana wrapped around her head and the absence of her crazy hair.

"How are you?" I ask, gravely.

She dismisses my question with a smile and a flick of her wrist and moves on to tell me how good it is to see me too, and what a fantastic John Worthing I made!

"I'm so glad Tracy invited me. Not that she could have kept me away. Her and Allen have been staying with me since she moved to Glasgow, and she's always talking about you and how talent-ed you are..." She insists on buying me another drink and then slips a card with her phone number into my hand before telling me she is heading home because she's 'getting too old for all this clubbing palaver.'

"Mmm," I say, "me too."

And then she is gone. And I am sitting at an empty table, in amongst all the madness, on my own.

☞ ♥ ☜

"So... What exactly happened wi you and your burd, anyway?" Minty asks, pulling up a chair beside me and dumping a plate of sausage rolls and pickled onions on the table.

"Dunno," I shrug. She is the last person I wanna speak to right now.

"I thought you two were pure together forever an aw that?"

Her voice is an irritant in my ear and I'm so close to yelling at her to just damn well shut her noise. Instead, I throw more booze down my neck.

"And who's that wee black burd she's wi? She's a stunner. Zat who she's shagging now?" She points a thumb over to a table by the door, over towards where Joolz is sitting with, horror of hor-rors, Shazia.

I can't help but stare. There's an empty cocktail jug on the table and two half-filled glasses, my two favourite femme fatales are having an argument when Joolz gets up and starts putting on her coat. I watch her walk out just as Kat is coming through the door. Shazia runs after her. Kat pulls on her arm to stop her walking past. Joolz whips around and screams at both of them to 'fuck off' and stamps out into the foyer.

"Women," says Minty, rolling her eyes. "I'll tell you something, Romeo... yer fucking well shot of her."

My head is spinning and I can hardly see straight, and yet somehow I've pushed myself to a standing position and I'm hell-bent on pursuing Joolz to make sure she's ok.

"You've went out wi some mad cows," continues Minty, oblivious, "but that yin's got to be the fucking prize heifer."

I pause. Then I pivot. Then I swing at Minty, landing a cracker of a left hook square across her jaw. She falls backwards, crashing from her seat and into the buffet table, toppling sandwiches and breadstick dips around her ears.

She gets up. Grabs me. "What the fuck was that for?"

"YOU FUCK!" I scream at her. "DON'T YOU FUCKING TALK ABOUT HER LIKE THAT, YOU LOUSY FUCK." I'm hitting her and kicking her. And she's warding off the blows with slaps and scratches and a dirty great bite to my forearm. Finally she goes for my hair and she yanks on it hard.

"Ah leggo my fucking hair!"

"You let go of ma hair first, ya tube."

Rachel is behind me now, pulling me away from Minty, leading us towards the exit and telling us to calm the fuck down. "Tell *her* to fuckin calm down, man," says Minty. "She's fuckin mad she just fuckin went for us." I tell her I won't calm down and that I'm gonna kill her. "I havenae fuckin done anything," she says.

"YOU LIAR," I shout as Rach drags me outside. "YOU LOUSY, FAT LIAR."

"Heh, who you calling fat ya skinny fuckin anorexic lookin..."

"Will the pair of you just shut up and tell me what's going on," says Rachel. "I thought yous were supposed to be best pals?"

I'm sitting outside now, on the front steps, with my head in my hands.

"It was just a joke," says Minty, breathing hard. "Look... I'm sorry, ok? I never meant tae..."

I hold up a hand to make her stop.

"Forget about it." My voice is thick with alcohol and tears.

"That's the spirit," grins Rachel, who has been looming over us the whole time, seemingly content with our resolution she slaps me on the back before disappearing back inside the pub.

I feel like an idiot *and* a jerk, truth be told. And I'm not even angry with Minty. Not really. I tell her this and I apologise for socking her one, and for calling her fat, and she calls me a fucked-up fuckwit or something equally abusive.

Someone shouts me from behind. It's Kat and she's out of breath.

"Julie knows about you and Shazia," she says. "They had a bit of a bust-up as you could probably tell."

I nod, remembering the reason I had got into the fight in the first place. The outline of Kat's face begins to blur as more tears come, and I can't do anything to stop them. "She's not back at the flat, and I tried calling her mobile," she adds, "but it went straight onto voice mail and I don't know where she's gone."

From the very first moment I ever laid eyes on her, I knew she was special. Julie Turner was the woman I wanted to spend the rest of my life with.

Twenty-Six

I wake up feeling like shit. Turns out I slept in my suit. I even forgot to take off my tie for God's sake. I grab at the knot and pull it away from me, eventually loosening it and tossing it to the floor. The place looks like shit, anyway. It looks like it's been torn apart: CDs kicked across the carpet, a hi-fi speaker overturned and a trail of bread crumbs that I follow all the way back to the kitchen.

I shuffle towards the cooker and stick the last two slices of bread under the grill. My shades are there, poking out from under the top left ring, and one of the legs is broken. I sigh, wedge them on anyway and pull down the blinds.

After that I open the fridge door and – THUNK! – my body and brain are so out of sync that I manage to, somehow, whack the damn thing off my leg. A ceramic magnet bounces off and shatters as it hits the floor. I bend over to pick up the pieces: a fragmented rainbow that previously said 'PRIDE' is now missing its 'P' and 'E'. Minty brought that magnet back from Brighton.

Minty.

Fuck.

I press my palms into my face.

Suddenly all the fragments of last night are gluing themselves back together.

I rearrange the broken pieces of the magnet on top of the kitchen table. I got some superglue somewhere that could probably fix this, but first I need to get myself and the rest of the house sorted.

I begin by stripping my duvet and scooping up what's on the floor. I push the bed right over towards the window, so that I can get to all the junk underneath.

There's a sharp crack.

Kneeling with my head pressed sideways against the floor, I begin running my fingers into the places I can't see, until they come into contact with a small plastic tube.

It's a lipstick. Joolz's lipstick.

I'm lying face down on my pillow, weeping into the palms of my hands. I dunno how long I've been lying here. The tears just keep coming.

Something is seriously rotten in this picture. This isn't the way it's supposed to happen. This is the part where the babe is supposed to return and throw herself into my arms and tell me she loves me and she'll never leave me again.

I roll onto my back and close my eyes. Wish I could go to sleep and never wake up. Wish I never met that girl.

There's a knock on the bedroom door. I ignore it. The knock comes again.

"Come on, open up! It's opportunity knocking!" I sigh and tell Minty I don't wanna see anyone. "Vicky," she says, "you better not be trying to commit hari-kari in there."

I tell her to fuck off.

She says she thinks I should open the door.

I don't wanna open the door. I don't want anyone seeing me like this.

"Vicky, open the fucking door or I'll fucking kick it open." I open the door.

Minty's gone and Joolz is standing there in her place.

"What da fuck?"

I wanna throw my arms around Joolz. I wanna squeeze her until she pops. I wanna kiss her and hold her and... Something catches my eye. The door behind her – Minty's door – is half-way open and there's a hanger on the knob that says:

DO NOT DISTURB: WOMEN AT WORK

Underneath there's a picture of two women doing it.

Why that dirty rat...

I can't believe it. I can't believe that my best friend in all the world has fucked the girl I love and now she's throwing it all up in my face like it's a joke. I never in a million years woulda imagined her capable of such heinousness. And for what reason? Because we had a confrontation? Because I went berserk and slugged her one? This whole situation is sick and horrible and it feels like acid burning away at my gut. This is the ultimate

betrayal. I will never fucking forgive her for this. I'll never forgive either of them. Not ever.

"It's not what you think," says Joolz, somehow reading my
mind.

I ask her if she's a psychic now.

She says she knows it looks bad but she promises there's been
no one else since me.

"I don't just give my heart to anyone," she says. "Not like
some people."

That smarts.

She says she doesn't even know what she's doing here. She
says she woke up with all her clothes on and she thinks someone must've slipped her a mickey finn or something last night.

A likely story.

"You're nothing but a non-guild actress," I tell her.

She asks me what I mean by this but I don't reply because I
don't really know what I mean. I just heard that line in a movie
one time and always wanted to use it.

"Where's that snake in the grass, Minty?" I ask her, "You better
tell her she's to come claim her one-way ticket to the morgue."
I start to walk away from her and she follows me. She starts to
weep and pull at my arm. "Come on, baby," I say to her, "what
do you think you're doin?"

BZZT!   **BZZT!**

I reach into the pocket of my pants and pick out my cellphone.
A text message. I read it and shake my head.

"It's Minty," I say, holding out the phone.

"What are you telling me for?" says Joolz, "I don't want to
read her message."

"I think you should read it," I say.

"What does she say?"

"Read it."

The corners of my mouth are twitching. Slowly, apprehen-
sively, Joolz is moving to take the cellphone from my hand. I'm
watching her, my eyes locked on hers. I pause as our skin meets,
our fingertips touching around the sides of the handset.

"I'm not sure I want to know what the Mud Monster's got to say."

"Oh, believe me you do."

I let my hand linger for a moment longer than my brain thinks it should. And all the time I can't take my eyes off Julie Turner's face: those eyes, those lips, that smile.

"You go to... sorry... got... two hours... to get your love life sorted," reads Joolz.

"Stop acting like a cup of pussies... I think that's meant to say couple... yous are pissing everyone off. PS. You'd better not shag in the living room."

I have to cover my mouth with my hand to hide my grin.

"So..." says Joolz, folding her arms across her chest and shifting her weight from foot to foot. She's been standing at a really weird angle up until now, and I only just noticed it's because one of her shoes is missing a heel. "So..." she repeats, smiling, "that's what the stupid cow was up to then? Trying to play cupid? For a minute, when I got up, I thought she'd slipped a fucking roofie in my drink."

My own smile vanishes. I'm teasing her. I want to see how far I can push her before she breaks down and begs me to take her back.

"Obviously Min's wasted her time. I'll see you around, Julie. Good luck with the acting and all that."

"Hang on!" she squeals. "I was only joking. Fucksake. VICKY!"

She moves towards me just as I am about to open the door – I'm only pretending that I'm gonna walk out on her – she grabs my shoulder making me spin around, and as she does this she falls forward on her dodgy high-heel shoes and we both go tumbling to the floor.

I'm on my back and she's on top of me in a very sexually suggestive position, and I really can't stop myself from laughing.

"What was it you wanted to tell me, babe?" She's got one knee grazing my crotch and her cleavage is practically in my face.

She takes a deep breath. Her cheeks are burning and her throat sounds all choked up. "Vicky, I love you," she says. Her voice sounds high and squeaky and the tears are starting to dribble down her nose. "I'm– I'm s-sorry I've been such a cow. Don't go.

P-please don't go."

"I love you, too," I whisper. Then I lean forward and cup her face in both hands and I kiss her. I can taste her tears and my mind is racing and I'm still half-way through kissing her when she says the words:

"M-marry me."

"What?" I pull away but I still have my hands around her face. "What did you just say?"

"Marry me."

"Are you serious?"

"I love you," she sniffs. "And-and-and I want to spend the rest of my life with you and..."

"But you know that gays can't actually get married right?"

"Oh I don't care about a stupid bit of paper. We can move in and be wives and adopt a fuckload of cats without all that!'

"Then yes. A million times yes. I can't think of anyone I'd rather marry." We both sniff in unison and then burst into giggles. "There's only one thing you have to promise me, though..." I say, and I struggle to generate my most sombre of expressions.

"Anything," she whispers as I reach up to squeeze her hand in mine.

"You have to go on top more often!"

The EE-EE-EE of the smoke alarm jolts me back to reality. Joolz is not here. She's never coming here again. It's over. I roll out of bed and throw her lipstick into the wastepaper bin and then I go through to the kitchen and throw out the remains of the last two slices of bread.

There is Slipknot music coming from Minty's bedroom and the tell-tale signs of a pancakes and eggs breakfast. I shiver and pull my shirt collar up around my chin. Breakfast is now a choice of cold cereal or a microwaved Pop Tart. No milk either. I drink two black coffees then pour orange juice over my Weetabix.

Rocking back and forth in the armchair, whilst flicking through yesterday's newspapers, I count three good luck cards belonging to Robbie pinned up along the wall. A pink envelope with

Robbie's name has been ripped open and discarded on the coffee table. There is a brown ring left by my second cuppa.

I wonder how many cards Joolz received. How many programmes did she sign last night? How many offers of dates and one-night-stands did she get from fans? Did she take any of them up on it? And how much does she know about Shazia and me? Who was it that told her? And, finally, remembering the worried look on Kat's face at the end of the night, and how we looked everywhere in the Merchant City for her without success, I wonder where Joolz is and what she's doing now. I continue flicking through The Herald till I get to the obituary pages. My exercise for this week's creative writing class is to write about my own death. I search the coffee table for a pen and, not seeing any notepads to write in, settle with a discarded pink envelope from one of Robbie's cards. I test the pen by drawing patterns around the coffee stain and, finding that it still works, I draft the following headline:

LESBIAN DIES CHOKING ON PUBIC HAIR

That's just the sort of thing that would happen to me. Joolz's would be something like breaking her neck whilst trying to do a backflip in her sleep. I continue writing:

VICKY ROMEO PLUS JOOLZ R.I.P.

The relationship between Italian-born lesbian actor, Vicky Romeo, and aspiring prima ballerina, Julie Turner, has died.

Ms Romeo and Ms Turner met in Sandra Dee's on September 21st 2001 and in the months that followed, they toured Glasgow's pink triangle as offstage lovers. Their acting careers began a decade before they made their historic debut, performing side by side in 'The Importance of Being Earnest' as part of an all-lesbian cast.

In one of her earliest interviews with the Women's Archive Trust for Scotland Newsletter, Ms Romeo recalled how she was declined the role of Danny Zuko during her high-school production of 'Grease' because 'they said two girls playing opposite each other as the lovers was inappropriate.'

During their relationship they combated issues such as butch-phobia, femme-phobia and inverted homophobia.

A pioneer of the femme movement in Glasgow, Ms Turner came out to her mother just weeks before her last performance, her mother's reaction was said to be 'critical'.

Speaking of the couple's relationship, religious education teacher, Kat Astrof said: 'It was so sad to hear about them. The way they were when they were together, it gave everyone hope that butch and femme couples really could work out in modern society.'

Their relationship is survived by a used lipstick.

☞ ♥ ☜

It's a quarter past nine and I'm sitting in Sandra Dee's diner with a can of Pepsi Max and a copy of Raymond Chandler's *Farewell, My Lovely*. I'm just at the part where Philip Marlowe works out that Mrs Grayle, the millionaire, is really the nightclub singer, Little Velma, when Minty interrupts me.

Minty puts a slim pink lily with a long green stem on my table.

"It's no fae me," she says. "It's fae the burd up at the bar."

I shrug and continue reading. Moose Malloy has just discovered that the love of his life, Little Velma, was the one who ratted him out to the cops.

"Do ye no want tae know who?"

I shrug again. Minty and I have kinda made our peace now, and no more's been said about our brawl, even though she's still got a real nice bruise on her cheek to remind us of it.

Little Velma shoots Moose Malloy. I saw that coming.

Minty knocks three times on the side of my head with her bare knuckles.

"Hey!"

"That's opportunity knocking," she says, and she points over towards the bar, towards the redhead in the grey, pin-stripe trouser suit who has her hair tied back underneath a black glittery trilby.

When I catch her eye, the redhead tips her hat at me.

"Joolz?"

"Personally, I think she should stick to wearing short skirts," says Minty, and then she walks off.

Joolz crushes her cigarette into the ashtray with one finger and then strides over towards me. "Hi," she says.

"Hi."

"You're looking good."

"Thanks. I like the hat."

"You can try it on for size if you like." She takes off the trilby and sits it on my head. She's made me lose my place in the book now.

"Shaz told me everything."

"Uh-huh." The words are dancing in front of my eyes.

"And I don't blame you for keeping it a secret."

"Oh."

"So..." she says.

I look up and let the pages of my book fall shut.

"I just wondered..." Dramatic pause. "Seeing as I didn't get to tell you in person how fantastic you were in the show the other night..."

I stare at her with my mouth open, unable to speak.

"Vicky..."

"U-huh?"

"Could I buy you... I mean... give you... a kiss?"

☞ ♥ ☜

I'm sitting in Sandra Dee's filling in an application form for the Royal Scottish Academy of Music and Drama. It's quiz night and Mamma's getting the drinks while Kat and Robbie are arguing over question number three: 'Where does the gay slang language polari originate from?'

"Oi," calls Minty from behind the bar, "vadda the Gorgeous T.B.H. just over there by the door."

"What's a T.B.H. when it's at home?" says Kat.

"To be had," I translate. "Look at the gorgeous– "

"I get it."

Julie Turner walks over to our table and she's got her arm linked with the arm of a foxy, forty-something redhead. "Hey everyone," she says.

She turns to me. "Vicky, you remember my mum don't you?"

I smile at Joolz and then I smile at her Ma. "It's good to see you both." I wink. "I'm really glad that you came out."

Acknowledgements

In no particular order, I would like to say a very special thank you to:

Tom Leonard, Liz Lochhead and everyone else at Glasgow University who read, listened to and critiqued the awful early drafts of this novel.

Antonia Layzell for listening (multiple times) to increasingly better drafts and for being an all-round goody and superhero.

Giles Gordon for his early encouragement and support.

Zoë Strachan for consistently championing my work over the past eighteen years and for always having something nice to say about me.

Fiona Mackellar for her continued friendship and advice, and for always having something sarcastic to say.

The Scottish Book Trust for awarding me a writing mentorship, and to Lindsey Fraser for being a brilliant mentor.

Elaine Warden for two decades of writerly solidarity.

Nathaniel Kunitsky for persisting.

About Ely Percy

Ely Percy is a Scottish fiction writer based in Glasgow, a memoirist and an epistolarian. Their first work *Cracked: Recovering From Traumatic Brain Injury* (JKP, 2002) took the form of both a creative and an academic text. They graduated with distinction from Glasgow University's Mphil in Creative Writing in 2004 and since then their work has appeared in many reputable literary journals (e.g. The Edinburgh Review, The Scotsman Orange, New Writing Scotland, Causeway). Over the last sixteen years, Percy has facilitated countless writing workshops for various groups, they've been writer in residence in a prison, edited a lesbian publication and worked as a community librarian in a LGBT centre. *Vicky Romeo Plus Joolz* is their first full-length published work of fiction.

www.elypercy.com

Fabulous human beings who helped make this book happen

This book was made possible thanks to each and every one of our 130 Kickstarter backers. Thank you, we did it again! A particular few people showed extra generosity and we would like to extend a special thank you to them here (with their permission). We couldn't have done this without you all!

Anne Hamilton
Nikki
Vaneet Mehta
Siobhan Walsh
Jane Alexander
Liz Richardson
Lizzie Huxley-Jones
Lola Keeley
Michael Lee Richardson
Sophie Norman
AR Crow
Heather Pearson
Siobhan Dunlop
Emma Vandore
Claire Heuchan
Abigail Williams
Kirstie English
Elaine Lithgow
CJ Jessup
Eve Morris
Melanie

Tasha Turner
Margot Atwell
Stephanie NicAllan
Shona Bruce
Paul Kaefer, Quatrefoil Library
Sue John
Nyla Ahmad
Lidia Molina Whyte
Brenton & Jackie
Niki Harbron
Fiona Mackellar
fragglechick
Nicola Burkhill
Michiko & Becky
Novice Wye Dangle of Order of Perpetual Indulgence, Glasgow Mission
James McDonald
Robert W Archambault
Tess Brooks
Kerry Rush
Ellen Desmond
Del LaGrace Volcano
Amelia Conroy
Rachel Aitken
Siobhān Carroll
Lenka
Brendon and Nichola
Antonia Layzell
mammabear
Ciara Conway
Eris Young

Kit de Waal
Kerry Mullan
Shelagh
Iain Maloney
Steven Fraser
Heather Valentine
Ruth Sundberg
Heather Palmer
Mary Johnston
Morgane Bellon
Kirsty Hunter
Rosie Prince
Tifa Robles
Richard Flynn
Garry Mac
Jo Campbell

About Knight Errant Press

We are a small, queer, Scottish press dedicated to promoting and amplifying fierce and relevant voices and stories. We publish intersectional, genre blending and unapologetically queer work.

Our recent publications:

F, M or Other: Quarrels with the Gender Binary, Volume 1 – an anthology of stories, poetry, essays and comics exploring the quarrelsome nature of gender.

Queering the Map of Glasgow – a small collection of stories and poems with queerness and Glasgow at their heart.

KnightErrantPub

 KnightErrantPress

 knighterrantpress

www.knighterrantpress.com